£1

Victor Tapner took his first reporting job in South Wales after leaving school. He worked on a number of specialist journals and travelled in Europe, the United States and Pakistan as a reporter before joining the *Financial Times* as Night News Editor. In this position he has had direct involvement in the coverage of many recent international events, including the US-Soviet arms talks and the 1987 Stock Market crash. His poetry has won commendations in national and regional awards. He is also a blues music fan. He lives in Essex.

GW00392127

VICTOR TAPNER

Cold Rain

GRAFTON BOOKS

A Division of the Collins Publishing Group

LONDON GLASGOW
TORONTO SYDNEY AUCKLAND

Grafton Books
A Division of the Collins Publishing Group
8 Grafton Street, London W1X 3LA

Published in paperback by
Grafton Books 1989

First published in Great Britain by
Grafton Books 1988

Copyright © Victor Tapner 1988

ISBN 0-586-20392-3

Printed and bound in Great Britain by
Collins, Glasgow

Set in Plantin

For Rosalind, Alex and
Hannah, with love

1

Scannell pushed his hands deeper into his anorak pockets and leaned against the wall of the warehouse. The contact was late, and Scannell would give him only another fifteen minutes. It wouldn't be the first time that someone had promised information for a story and then failed to turn up. No doubt the man had lost his nerve.

Watchful and impatient, Scannell eased himself away from the wall, brushing a smear of crumbling mortar from his sleeve. He lit a cigarette and took a few aimless paces up the cobbled street. In the distance, he could hear music from a rock-café and the reassuring sounds of traffic up by Nassauplein. He'd have preferred one of those more public thoroughfares for the meeting – even an open park – but the man had insisted on excessive cover. He had probably taken his cues from spy cases in the popular press.

Scannell drew up his collar. During the journey in from the airport, it had started to drizzle, and the dampness was now penetrating his clothing. But while the discomfort was an irritation, his annoyance was reserved for the contact's apparent assumption that he alone was at personal risk: a delusion menacing in its innocence.

Sauntering back to the doorway, Scannell's eyes focused on the windows of the warehouse opposite. In only one – a third-storey casement – was there a light: probably in a part of the building designated as a cheap 'sleep-in' for the backpack brigade. Fleetingly, he was aware of a figure passing behind the panes' illumined layer of grime – a woman, he thought, who disappeared almost immediately from view.

He finished his cigarette and trod it underfoot. Then, as

he brought his head up, he heard a trundling noise. An amalgam of disparate images had begun to fuse together in his mind. Like the warehouse opposite, the one by which he was standing had a hoisting-beam fitted with a wheel and tackle that jutted out from a roof-level recess. He'd noticed the beam on the path from the canal, but he'd thought it was disused – a touch of the city's trading history preserved for the tourists.

As his brain communicated the message that the hoist was, indeed, operable, the movement dissolved into a bewildering numbness followed by a flood of pain down the right-hand side of his body. He thought he'd heard the clatter of the wheel, but perhaps not. . .

The casualty officer that Monday evening of 8 November 1982 at the Queen Juliana Hospital by Vondelpark had been a young French-Canadian named Louis Fillion. Just after nine o'clock, he had been called away from his hasty supper in the staff canteen to examine a patient who had been brought in by ambulance following an emergency call.

By the time Fillion arrived on the ward, the patient had started to regain consciousness and was speaking in incoherent snatches. His clothes were encrusted with blood and dirt and, as Fillion told the police later that evening, he'd at first expected to find serious injuries. However, on closer examination he'd decided there was no need to admit him to intensive care. Apart from the concussion, the patient was badly cut and bruised, and two of his ribs were cracked, but there was no evidence of internal haemorrhaging.

The man's identity had been determined by the police officers from the *hoofdbureau* who had accompanied the ambulance. The source of their information was a UK National Union of Journalists membership card in his wallet. Issued by the union's City of London branch, the card established that Thomas Scannell, membership number 13565, was a bona fide representative of the British press,

8

and was recognized as such by the police and the armed services.

When Scannell regained consciousness some time after midnight, his first sensation was one of pain. It ran the length of his body, as though he had been rolled across rocks, and it hurt him to breathe. Through the dim lights of the ward, he tried to take in his surroundings, but his vision registered only a blur. Somewhere close by, he could hear a soft moaning, and only became aware with the passing of time that he was making the sounds himself.

A nurse leaned over the bed and loosened the sheet that lay across his chest.

'Lie still,' she said. 'Rest.'

The next morning the pain had eased, to be replaced by a feeling of fear and disorientation. Apart from waking to find himself in hospital, with only a vague memory of the nurse talking to him the night before, he had no knowledge of anything that had happened since he'd last left his office. It was as though a curtain of darkness had been drawn across his memory.

Seeing that he was awake, one of the nurses brought him a cup of tea.

'What happened?' he asked her. He wondered whether she'd be able to understand him. He'd noted that everyone on the ward seemed to be speaking a foreign language. He knew it wasn't German, so presumed it must be Dutch.

The nurse spoke broken English and seemed a little surprised at his question.

'You don't know?'

He frowned. 'I can't remember.' After a pause, he added: 'Am I in Holland?'

The nurse nodded, and studied him with concern. 'Amsterdam.' She put the tea on the bedside locker. 'I help you to sit up. I fetch the sister.'

The nurse was scarcely more than a girl, but she handled him with skill and confidence. Even so, as she eased him forward, he felt a stabbing pain in his chest, and his head swam. The nurse quickly leaned him back and let him breathe. After a minute or two the nausea passed and he soon sank into a deep sleep.

The next thing he was aware of was a scratching of metal above his head. He opened his eyes and saw that another nurse was drawing a screen round the bed. When she had finished, she leaned over him.

'You have visitors, Mr Scannell – the police. The doctor said they can see you.'

Two officers in navy-blue uniforms were standing at the bottom of the bed. Scannell felt a momentary return of the anxiety he'd experienced earlier, and wondered whether they were ordinary officers or ones from some special division – in contact with London, perhaps.

As the nurse helped to raise him in the bed, he again felt sick.

'Do you want some water?' she asked him.

Scannell nodded as he fought against a rising dryness in his throat. After filling a glass from a jug on his locker, the nurse held it to his lips. Turning to the police officers, she spoke quietly to them in Dutch.

She took Scannell's glass. 'I told them they mustn't let you talk for long.'

One of the officers, a young man with a trimmed beard, stepped round the bed. 'Five or ten minutes, Mr Scannell – that's all we need.'

Scannell closed his eyes and lay back. The darkness gave him a refuge from the questioning that was about to come as well as from his own agitation. After a moment or two he heard a chair scrape on the floor.

'What exactly were you doing here, do you know?'

Scannell opened his eyes, and turned his head. The officer was sitting almost level with the pillow.

'You were found near the Brouwersgracht . . . the canal. Did you know that?'

Scannell tried to think back. 'Was I in an accident?'

'A hoist. Something fell.'

Scannell said nothing, just stared emptily.

'Is there anyone you know who lives here?' the officer asked. 'Perhaps you have friends in Amsterdam.'

'No . . . no one.'

'Could you have been on your way to see someone? A business contact possibly?'

'Maybe. I can't remember.'

'You're a journalist, I understand. What about any of your recent articles? Have they offended anyone?'

Scannell turned on the pillow. 'Should they've done?'

The officer shrugged. 'It was just a thought. You don't know of any information you might have come here to pick up?'

'I'd have said if I did.'

Scannell lifted his head as he spoke, but the nausea quickly returned.

'Don't you normally let your news editor know where you're going? Isn't that what most reporters do?'

'Sometimes. If we're good, they let us out on our own.'

Glancing out of the window to the car park, Scannell saw that visitors were arriving. He gazed absently at an area of shrubbery. Much of the foliage had been stripped bare; his mind felt the same.

'You realize that your injuries could have been much worse?' the officer said. 'Hitting your head like that . . . you could've been killed.'

'What was it? . . . What hit me?'

A flash of light, like the light from a window, was scorched on Scannell's memory, but beyond it was only darkness.

'We don't know,' said the officer. 'There was nothing on the hoist . . . nothing attached.'

'I may've seen something . . . Something black. That's all.'

The officers kept their promise and left as soon as the sister instructed. Scannell relaxed with the belief that they were preparing a standard report.

11

2

That same morning a meeting had been hurriedly convened in the anonymous office building in Curzon Street, Mayfair, which serves as the headquarters of DI5, the British security and counter-espionage service, often mistakenly referred to by its former name of MI5.

The meeting was held in the conference room at fourth-floor central, the larger of three offices in a suite previously occupied by the Press and Broadcasting Monitoring Section. The section had been decentralized in early 1980 following, ironically, the threatened disclosure of its existence by a Sunday newspaper. Although the editor concerned had complied with a Home Office request not to publish the report, the press had won an important victory, forcing the government to dismantle the core of what had become simply a vehicle for news distortion. But there was a sting in the tail, because another section, known by the facelessly bureaucratic title of Unit Nine, had been set up in its place, and its responsibilities were, if anything, even more hostile to the spirit of news media independence.

Before the start of the meeting, Rodway, the unit director, had summoned three of his field staff. The last to arrive was Arran, the deputy night controller, who, since going off duty at 6 A.M., had been waiting at home for the call.

'It was stupid beyond belief,' Rodway said, when the meeting began. 'The man's lucky to be alive.'

'Sir, it was intended to . . .'

The field agent who had interrupted broke off when he saw Rodway's expression. Rodway turned to Arran.

'I want a full explanation.'

Around the table the tension bristled. As well as Arran's

two assistants, a man from the personnel vetting section was present.

Arran decided to try to give the best account of his actions that he could in circumstances which were about the worst imaginable. Somehow he had to convey the fact that he had simply sought to carry out a routine security manoeuvre which had gone hideously wrong.

'The reporter was on his way to meet a contact, sir,' he began. 'Someone called Hermann. He's a prime activist in the European Anti-Nuclear Organization. We had reason to believe he had some names.'

'Names?'

'Feeders. At least five of our agents in the peace movement.'

'Informants or personnel?'

Arran swallowed. Throughout the night he'd had growing doubts about the quality of the unit's information.

'At least three personnel . . . Mr Elizabeth, Mr Bertha and Mrs Harry.'

Rodway stared. 'What reason did you have to believe that?'

Arran noticed that the vetting section representative had looked up from his notepad.

'Field information, sir. It seems that Hermann's suspected for a while now that we're deploying personnel – not just relying on feedback.'

'I see . . . And where did the information come from?'

'Mr Elizabeth. He's been fairly reliable so far.'

Rodway gave a deep frown. 'Fairly?'

'*Mostly*, sir. According to the same source, Hermann hasn't got much support in the organization's hierarchy. The feeling is that he's treating his work like some personal mission. He's even given up his job.'

Rodway looked over his half-rim spectacles. 'So I understand.'

Arran paused, sensing that the explanation was a wasted

exercise. Even so, he felt compelled to go on. Although he held himself to blame for what had happened the night before, Rodway had to be made to see that the demands to protect the network had placed him in an impossible position.

'At first we didn't think he was anything to worry about. Lately he's been getting closer though . . . Working on it full time.'

'How did you know he'd contacted the reporter?'

Arran hesitated. He'd realized from the start that this was a key weakness in his defence. 'As far as I know, it was all through Mr Elizabeth.' He turned for confirmation to one of the assistants who dealt with network traffic. The man nodded.

'So it was just guesswork then, that Hermann was going to hand over the names?'

Arran shrugged. 'I suppose it was . . . ultimately.'

'And yet you decided to have the reporter cut down!'

This time, Arran was silent. Put in such a way, the action sounded absurd. At last, he replied emptily: 'He was supposed to have been warned off, that's all.'

'Being hit by a crate . . . You call that warning someone off?'

'It wasn't meant to happen like that. Someone miscalculated.'

Rodway's mouth tightened. 'Perhaps you thought you were operating in New York or Moscow?'

There was a short silence.

'No, sir.'

'You understand you could be charged with attempted murder?'

Arran experienced a watery sensation in his digestive tract. Next to him, he could sense his assistants sitting rigidly.

'We had to stop him, sir. His news agency would've made a meal of it. Names in all the national papers.'

'Why was there no authorization request?'

'Communications only learned about it yesterday evening. We couldn't do anything about Hermann . . . not arrest him. The police there didn't have anything to hold him for.'

Rodway glared. 'Then no action should've been taken. All those personnel have been given thorough credentials. No editor would accept a story that relied solely on the claims of one informant.'

'We spoke to Operations. They were worried that the personnel involved could have been put at risk.'

'It was no business of Operations! You were Night Control. The decision was yours.'

Arran wasn't going to argue any more. He said simply: 'Yes, sir.'

One of the assistants, apparently anxious to give Arran support, added cautiously: 'We weren't sure how much evidence Hermann had against them, sir.'

Rodway turned. 'I'm sure you weren't.' He cast his eyes round the table. 'The fact is, the whole of Unit Nine deployment has been put at risk. I've instructed the vetting section to hold an internal inquiry. In the meantime, all of you will be suspended from duty.'

3

Hermann lay on a low wooden bed bolted to the wall of the cell. He'd been without sleep for so long that his mind was bordering on delirium. Set in the ceiling was a bare lightbulb covered by a wire cage. He guessed that behind the cage was a closed-circuit television camera so that the guards could watch him. Every time he tried to drift off, one of them would hammer a baton on the steel door, or yell through the grille for him to stand up. Sometimes he refused, and they would slam open the door and pull him to his feet. Their last little joke had been to douse him with a bowl of ice-cold water. His clothes had only just begun to dry.

The police officers had arrested him at his home, four of them, the night before last, on his return from Amsterdam. Later that night they'd driven him to what appeared to be an operational outpost in the Hertfordshire countryside. The Residence one of them had called it. It was at the end of a long gravelled driveway behind high gates, and inside was a warren of offices. Even at the time of night that he'd arrived, lights were on in several of the rooms, and people were still working.

The cell, in the basement of the building, measured about four metres square and smelled strongly of disinfectant. Its walls were painted brown, and there was a slop-bucket in a corner under a wash-basin. Soon after his arrival, the guards had taken away his belt, shoes and watch. There was no window, so he was unable to tell whether it was night or day. He knew that as soon as he fell asleep, he would lose track of time altogether.

As he lay on the hard bed, he heard bolts being drawn back on the outside of the door. Two guards stepped into the cell. Their faces were new to him, and he presumed the

16

shift must have changed. Already, he'd been put through long sessions of questioning over his role in the movement, but so far he'd avoided saying anything significant – only that he was engaged in research work. He had asked for a lawyer, but the interrogators had refused.

During the last, and most intensive, session, which had gone on for about an hour, one of the interrogators had hit him. That had been a turning point. He'd vowed that he would tell them nothing more, no matter what physical or mental torment they inflicted. Rightly or wrongly, he'd committed himself to a cause, and there was no going back.

'Get up,' one of the guards said.

Hermann looked up, but didn't move. He was shivering because of his damp clothes. One of the guards bent down and, gripping the shoulders of his shirt, dragged him off the bed. His shirt had already been torn: now it was ripped from the neck to the sleeve. Down the front was a spattering of blood from the previous session.

The other guard helped pull him up from the floor, and between them they half carried him through to the interrogation room across the passageway. He was pushed roughly into a chair in front of the table, behind which sat a thin-faced man in a suit, his maroon tie held with a gold pin. The interrogators, it seemed, had changed shift as well. From the moment Hermann had been brought into the room, the man's eyes had followed him, dark, like studs.

'Tell me,' the man said at last, 'who do you think you're helping by all this?'

Hermann didn't speak.

'I'm interested to know what you people hope to achieve. Is it some sort of crusade?'

Hermann fought to stop himself being drawn into answering. The interrogator sat back in his chair and intertwined his fingers.

'Let's go back a bit, shall we? You were a teacher, weren't you?'

17

The interrogator's tone had softened after the underlying scorn of his opening remarks. Now it was encouraging, almost sincere. Hermann preferred the more aggressive stance of the previous interrogators. They'd given him something firm to fight against.

'Where was your last post?'

Hermann gave the name of the school in south London where he'd been employed until the previous February.

'I understand you have no family – no one to worry about where you are.'

In his half-conscious state, Hermann couldn't make out whether a sinister meaning was buried in the statement.

'I asked for a lawyer,' he said.

The interrogator nodded. 'All in good time. I thought it might be useful to get one or two things sorted out first. Obviously, different people see things in different ways. In your position, you can afford to ignore the national security implications. Unfortunately, it's a luxury that has its price.'

Hermann sensed the man was finding it a strain to keep up the conversational tone.

Hermann looked across the table. 'What're you charging me with?'

The man's face was open. 'I wasn't aware we were charging you with anything.'

'You can't just keep me here.'

The interrogator gestured loosely. 'Well . . . we'll see.'

He took a thin cardboard file from a drawer. Opening it on the table, he extracted a sheet of paper and studied it.

'You contacted a reporter . . . someone by the name of Scannell. Can you tell me why?'

Hermann had become alert. He recognized the document; it was a list of names that could only have come from among the papers at his home. To find it, the police must have turned the house upside down.

'How did you get that?' he demanded.

The interrogator ran a finger thoughtfully along the hollow

of his cheek. 'You've been a busy boy, haven't you?' After a pause, he added: 'How did you get the names?'

Again, Hermann refused to answer.

'Who was your prime source for all these? Presumably you talked to someone?'

Hermann tried not to think. He wanted to blot the name from his mind. That way there would be less chance of him disclosing it under pressure.

'I take it you didn't put the list together from a telephone directory?'

That was true enough. It had taken the best part of eighteen months to collate it; eighteen months after Hans-Heinrich Kepler had given him the original information.

Suddenly, Hermann's tiredness got the better of him, and he became angry.

'I said I wanted a lawyer.'

'You're a regional treasurer, is that correct? For north London, isn't it?'

'I don't have to answer your questions.'

'A job like that must be quite a responsibility. I imagine a considerable amount of money passes through your hands.'

Hermann was sure he detected a threat.

'What do you mean by that?'

The interrogator frowned. 'Mean?'

'You won't find anything there. I've kept all the books in proper order.'

'I'm glad to hear it.'

'You can check with the bank.'

The interrogator paused. 'Thank you . . . We have.'

He looked at Hermann for a long, hard moment.

'That will be all for now,' he said, and nodded to the guards.

Hermann was taken back to his cell. He was left alone for long enough to fall into a light sleep, then one of the guards came in and cracked his baton down on the bedframe. It missed Hermann's head by the width of a finger.

4

Scannell lifted his eyes from the newspaper that he was re-reading and looked around the television-room. Only two other patients were in there with him. One was asleep in an armchair. It was mid-afternoon; Scannell felt restless and bored.

It was nearly a week now since he'd discharged himself from the hospital in Amsterdam and returned to London. He'd hoped to be back at work by now, but his plans had been thwarted when he'd collapsed in the lift at his apartment block in the Barbican complex. One of the security men had found him. The consultant who'd examined him had said he'd have to remain in hospital until the checks were completed.

He focused again on the newspaper's main stories and tried to see how many of their details he could remember. About a quarter of an hour later, a woman appeared at the door. She was carrying a bundle of paperback books. As she came into the room, she greeted him with a brisk smile.

'Hello – Mr Scannell?'

Scannell looked up. He thought he'd seen her before, but he didn't know where.

'Yes . . . ?' he answered slowly.

The woman extended her hand. 'Celia Forde . . . Residents Association. You may remember me – I deliver the newsletter.'

'Oh . . . yes.'

For a moment he'd been puzzled, thinking she was talking about an organization for patients. Then he realized she meant the Barbican.

'Actually, I live on the floor below you,' she said. 'You've probably heard the wild parties!'

Scannell gave a half-smile and started to lift himself from the chair.

'No . . . don't get up. I won't stay for long.' She put the books on a coffee-table and unbuttoned her coat. As she took off her scarf, she shook her hair. 'God, it's windy out there.'

Scannell watched as she tidied herself unfussily. She was a few years older than him, he guessed. Not unattractive. The dress and shoes she was wearing were probably more expensive than she could afford.

'I hope you don't mind me barging in like this.' She didn't wait for an answer. Reaching for the books, she began untying the string that held them. 'Compliments of the association. No men's mags, I'm afraid.'

Scannell watched her with curiosity. 'Tell me, how did you know I was in hospital?'

She smiled. 'Oh, someone on the committee mentioned it. We thought well, poor soul, we ought to do something . . .'

Scannell nodded. 'Thanks.'

'I know what it's like being cooped up in these places. I was in last year for a scrape . . . Ghastly! I tell you, I started to think they'd be carting me out between planks.' She pushed the books across the table. 'Hopefully there's something here you'll like. We didn't know what sort of things you read.'

'Anything's fine.'

Later, when she'd gone, he wondered why the association should have taken an interest in him. He'd never contributed to their fund-raising campaigns. Maybe some people just liked being good neighbours.

Towards the end of the afternoon, Rodway was called upstairs at Curzon Street. The office, in contrast to his own, was spacious and modern, designed to impress.

21

'Whisky?'

Rodway declined.

'They're after someone's skin,' he was told. 'Just a warning.'

The man behind the desk was Fairweather. He was a good fifteen years younger than Rodway, who had only a partial knowledge of his superior's area of control. It was typical of F Branch's secretive management system; typical of the service, in fact.

Rodway mentioned the inquiry.

'It can't do any harm,' said Fairweather. 'I take it you've found out how the fiasco happened?'

'Yes.'

'So you're trying to keep the bureaucrats happy then?'

'I suppose so.'

Rodway was surprised that Fairweather didn't want to know more. He guessed that the representative from the personnel vetting section had already given him a written account of the meeting with his field staff.

'There's something I want you to see,' Fairweather said.

From a drawer in his desk, he produced a file of newspaper cuttings and started to glance through it. Rodway noticed an expression of contempt as he flipped the pages: the contempt of someone producing incontrovertible evidence.

With increasing disgust, Fairweather read out headlines at random: '*Engineering union seeks CND affiliation* . . . *Nuclear protesters threaten US bases* . . . *Tories deny smear campaign* . . .'

Placing the file on his desk, Fairweather left it open: a deliberate gesture, presumably, to heighten the discomfort.

'That's just for the third quarter of the year. Every one of those stories is a boost for the anti-nuclear movement.'

Rodway scanned the file, knowing too well the truth of Fairweather's words. For months now, things had been going badly: leaked stories, reports of organized smear campaigns against the peace protesters, the exposure of Conservative Party links with hysterically anti-Soviet groups. The government's image had been bruised, and there were no signs of an end to the assault.

'Not all the reports are accurate,' Rodway said.

Immediately, he sensed the ineffectiveness of his response, and wasn't surprised when Fairweather exploited it.

'No, but most of them are. In any case, it doesn't matter much, does it? By the time we can hit back, the damage has been done.'

Fairweather glanced again at the random selection of headlines in the file. Rodway followed his eyes. God knows, he was as disturbed by the movement's successes as Fairweather was.

Fairweather looked up. 'What are the main sources for all these, do we know?'

'Diverse.'

'I'm sure they are. There must be one or two correspondents who're making the running though. What about the reporter – the one your highly-trained operatives have put in hospital? Who does he work for?'

'The Aldwych News Agency. It syndicates stories to the Fleet Street papers. He was commended in last year's National Press Awards.'

'Well, there's part of our problem for a kick-off.'

'But by no means all of it.'

Picking two or three dried leaves from a plant on the windowsill beside him, Fairweather crumbled them as though they were the elements of the movement he so patently despised.

'Let's be clear, shall we? Unit Nine was established for two simple reasons . . . To discredit the peace campaign and to minimize anti-nuclear coverage. So far, you've failed on both counts.'

Rodway bore the censure in silence. He felt an intense dislike for the man brought in from the policy section to oversee the unit's work. It was a dislike born of a prejudice Rodway tried to suppress, but which nevertheless kept surfacing: Fairweather was an upstart, the product of some Home Counties grammar-school whose academic achievements may have secured him a senior position in the service, but not the manners that should have gone with it. The attitude: demanding and aggressive. The shirt-collar: too crisp. The accent: demonstrably acquired.

'I accept some of your points, but they're not all justified,' Rodway countered. 'There have been other stories. Some of them have undoubtedly brought the campaign a measure of disrepute.'

Fairweather's eyebrows shot up in surprise. 'A measure? . . . then it's a bloody small one! You've only got to look at what's happened to CND. Not long ago they were just a bunch of vegetarians standing outside power stations. Now there's one in every household. Whatever it is, it's not a movement whose reputation's falling to bits.'

'Our task is to minimize coverage,' argued Rodway defensively. 'We can't hold back the tide of public opinion.'

Anger flared in Fairweather's eyes. 'That's exactly what we *have* got to do.' As he spoke, he brought the edge of his hand down sharply on the desk. 'The movement's got to be cut off at the knees! Like it or not –,' he pointed at Rodway, 'you're a dirty tricks department, and I want to see your job done properly!'

Rodway saw the position was impossible. No amount of explanation or rational argument would convince Fairweather of the lengths to which the unit had gone to try to win ground from the mounting campaign. The man's only interest was in results, but these were difficult to obtain and impossible to measure, against such an intangible force. The movement was, after all, a national emotion.

'Are we under political pressure?' he put to Fairweather.

'What do *you* think?'

'I presumed it was the case.'

'It's hardly surprising, is it? The government can't afford this rain of propaganda.'

There was a short silence, then Rodway said: 'We don't have much room to manoeuvre.'

'No excuses. The position's simple: we've got to sew things up before any more damage can be done. We're playing for high stakes. If the Americans are made to pull their missiles out, the country's main line of defence goes down the tube.'

'Some would argue that a strengthening of the conventional forces would help to maintain the balance.'

'That's crap! If it was left to them to fight the Russians, we'd hold out till about teatime. The nuclear threshold was crossed years ago. There's no going back.'

Rodway had some sympathy with Fairweather's view, but the approach was untenable. If the government's policy was sound, it would be endorsed through the ballot-box. That had always been the maxim, even in the service.

'Our ministerial masters might've forgotten,' Rodway responded, 'but this country still retains a vestige of democracy – and a free press.'

'That doesn't stop it being redirected.'

'Meaning what, exactly?'

'Meaning I want to see some solid stories appearing. Pro-government . . . pro-nuclear. Get at the correspondents who've got a bit more than half a brain.'

'Surely that's Secretariat N-160's responsibility?'

'Since when? Their job is positive: to inform. Straightforward nuclear salesmanship for the Defence Ministry. Our job is to *dis*inform. We've got to get some shit-stories going out.'

'The European group is fully infiltrated. We've got all our feeders in place.'

'Fine, but that's not much good if they're not feeding anything through, is it? I want to see them getting their hands on some first-rate dung! An outfit like that must have its share of queers and commies, for Christ's sake.'

'We're doing what we can . . . given the budget constraints.'

'No excuses, damn it! I want those personnel to be *used*. They've got to take every chance they get to undermine the organization. Let's see them taking some initiatives for once. I'm telling you, Rodway, I want *blood*.'

Rodway's patience was exhausted. The man was talking about an operation requiring months of subtle shaping before results could begin to be assessed, not one that could be started and finished before the election speeches began.

'I've just put three of my field staff under suspension for doing exactly what you've outlined,' Rodway said. 'Do I call off the inquiry?'

Fairweather smiled, acknowledging the irony.

'Your agents were too impetuous. Let the buggers sweat for a bit. I'll make sure the Dutch police don't try to bring any charges. This has got to be done softly. It's not a battle of brawn – it's a war of words.'

Scannell was discharged from hospital the following Monday, although the doctor had suggested he stay longer for observation. It crossed his mind that the request had originated elsewhere.

'I'll come to outpatients if I have any problems,' he said.

The ward sister had booked a taxi to take him home. It dropped him at the entrance to the Barbican complex. After paying the driver, he climbed the stairway, keeping a steadying hand on the metal balustrade. Although his ribs were bandaged beneath his shirt, every step he took sent an arrow through his abdomen. The sister had advised him to rest for a fortnight. He felt he could rest for a month.

The gloom of the stairway did nothing to alleviate his growing sense of dislocation. At the hospital, the busy atmosphere of routine and efficiency, and the chatter of the nurses on the ward, had helped to relieve it. But it had now risen again inside him, and all he wanted was the seclusion of his flat. There he would be able to work, even if it was only background reading. He recalled the exercises he'd been given those years ago on the self-treatment of depression: keep working, keep the mind and body active. His instructors had taken every precaution.

Scannell had chosen to live at the complex precisely for its anonymity. Raised walkways and open ramps jutted with a brutal geometry above rectangular pools of water, their hanging shrubs forming errant patches of vegetation in an inorganic environment. There was no danger here of interfering neighbours; he doubted whether he'd seen the couple who lived in the next-door apartment more than half-a-dozen times since he'd moved in two years before. At least, that sort of privacy had been the case until the visit to the hospital by the woman from the Residents Association.

His flat was in a block on the complex's Aldersgate side. On letting himself in, he shut the door and stood in the hallway, listening.

There was no sound.

Since his first morning in hospital in Amsterdam, he'd wondered whether anyone would be taking the opportunity to search his home. Although he'd been confident that they would find nothing, he still harboured anxieties about how deeply his affairs were being investigated.

Walking through the three main rooms, he quickly noted details.

The kitchen: a few items of crockery stacked to dry. He remembered them from his last evening meal. The cupboards were tidy and, apart from a slightly obnoxious smell coming from an unemptied rubbish bin, everything was as he'd left it. He emptied the contents of the bin down the waste-disposal unit before continuing.

The living-room: his conclusions were the same. The television was switched to its usual channel. A book was still open on the coffee-table.

The study was a more exacting task. Here, in this

converted bedroom, he kept all his papers and private files – those of little use to him at work, but still a valuable store of information. After making a coffee, he eased himself into the chair at the desk and spent more than an hour processing the material, looking out in particular for missing documents. As far as he could tell, all the files were intact. In the desk drawer was an envelope of Swiss francs he'd neglected to exchange after a trip the previous month to Geneva. The money was untouched. His passport and birth certificate were still in the box of personal documents he kept under the bed.

It was early evening when he finished the exercise. The concentrated effort had helped to relax his mind, but something still nagged. He couldn't settle until every corner of the flat had been inspected. It wasn't a phobia, he told himself; just necessary caution.

It brought results, too.

As he was watering the rather wilted collection of plants in the study, his attention was drawn to the cassette-recorder on the windowsill. He'd been using it the day before the accident to transcribe an interview. Although the cassette was still in the recorder at a point corresponding to his notes, he was concerned to find the machine still plugged into the wall socket. He always unplugged appliances when he'd finished using them, and this small discrepancy was enough to convince him there had been a visit during his absence.

The intruders had otherwise been thorough. He could find no signs of another slip-up. To satisfy himself that he'd left no confidential papers in his study, he spent the evening sorting through them again. They contained nothing, he concluded, that wouldn't belong in the files of any professional journalist.

The only thing still troubling him was a telephone number scribbled on his desk pad. The writing was his own, but he couldn't recall making the note. He dialled the number. No one answered. Replacing the receiver, he lit a cigarette and tried to remember what had happened that night.

A blaze of light, and then nothing.

Had he, as the police officers in Amsterdam had suggested, been meeting a contact? His mind was a grey, empty screen: missing hours in a memory that had been trained, for the sake of his survival, to catalogue every word and event of significance.

Before going to bed, he poured a glass of whisky and, as he sat on a stool in the breakfast area beside the kitchen, he noticed that his hand was shaking. Downing the whisky in two short swallows, he admitted to himself that, for the first time in his career, he was frightened.

5

When the guards came for Hermann, he was curled on the bed. At some stage, maybe the day before, they had turned off the heating to his cell. They'd stopped bringing him food, too, and the icy dousings were coming every three or four hours. His clothes were sticking to his body like softened skin.

Since his arrest, five days at least had passed. He'd long given up trying to keep track of time. There was little spirit left in his body now. In a way, it was like being drugged; he felt incapable of either mental or physical resistance.

'On your feet,' one of the guards said.

A baton was thrust hard into his stomach, and he absorbed the pain.

'I said, on your feet.'

Wearily, Hermann eased over on to his back and raised himself. It occurred to him that the guards' callousness was artificial; they couldn't possibly enjoy administering such treatment. After all, they had nothing to hate him for; nothing personal. He was simply a prisoner in their charge.

As he started to stand, a knee was brought up into his throat and he gagged. His head was pulled back by the hair. The other guard was bending down close to his face.

'Don't fuck us about, Hermann. D'you hear?'

Hermann heard. He heard the sound of the interrogator's mellifluous voice in the past sessions, the promises of lenience, the threats of violence if he continued to refuse to talk.

Between them, the guards hoisted him to his feet.

'You're coming out again,' said the guard who'd jabbed him with the baton. 'More games.'

They supported him as he shuffled out of the door and into the passageway. The cream tiles on the walls reflected a stronger light than the brown paint of the cell, and he could see the guards' faces in starker detail. Neither of them looked inherently brutal; it must have been their uniforms that made them able to act the way they did. Somewhere outside, he guessed, they had wives, mothers, children. He wondered whether they talked about their work.

Even now, he was resolved not to divulge any information. So far, he had managed to limit his answers to his knowledge of the Unit Nine's infiltration network. That much he'd been prepared to talk about: he wasn't telling them anything they didn't already know.

When they came to the door of the interrogation room, he automatically turned to go in, but the guards pulled him past. This was a new departure, and he looked at them in bewilderment. He'd become used to a routine, and was inwardly alarmed by the change.

At the end of the passageway were two opposing doors, one wooden, the other steel with an inset grille, like the door to his cell. The shorter guard pushed open the wooden door with his shoulder, and Hermann found himself in a large washroom. The facilities were basic: two long ceramic washing-troughs, a gutter along the floor that served as a urinal, and three lavatory pans in a row along one wall. This was all still preferable, though, to the slop-bucket and basin in the cell. There was also an open-fronted shower cubicle with a concrete surround stained brown by water trickling from a leaking pipe-joint.

What surprised Hermann was that the interrogator – the smart one with the tie-pin – was in the room. Today he was wearing a double-breasted blazer. He was standing with one of his feet perched on the ridge of a pan. Bond Street shoes. The smoke from his cigarette was strong in the air.

'I hope they've been treating you well,' he said.

Hermann didn't reply.

31

'When we spoke last time, you told me some names – remember?'

Hermann stood looking at him.

'We've done some research . . . Nobody in the organization knows anything about what you were doing.'

Hermann remained expressionless. 'I talked to lots of people,' he said.

The interrogator considered his answer. Then he dropped his cigarette in the pan where it gave a light sizzle. He turned to the guards.

'Okay, let's get started. We've wasted too much time.'

As he spoke, he came across towards Hermann. His shoes were almost silent on the concrete floor.

The interrogator stood an arm's length away, looking at him critically. He stretched out his hand and ran a finger lightly under Hermann's left eye where there was a bluish swelling. Hermann's face remained impassive. He was too tired to flinch, his reflexes too dulled.

'Surface damage,' the interrogator remarked, casting a reproving look at the guards. 'Bad workmanship.'

The fingers were soft; the touch menacing. Hermann wondered what rank the man held, and in what part of the service he was employed. Special Branch? Military security?

'Your shirt,' the interrogator said. 'Take it off.'

Hermann stared. The instruction was unexpected and failed to register.

'Take it off,' the man repeated. There was a sharp inflection in his voice.

Mechanically, Hermann's fingers fumbled for the buttons. The interrogator looked at one of the guards.

'Help the fucker, will you!'

The shorter guard stepped round in front of Hermann and undid the shirt. He slipped it over his shoulders. Stripped to the waist, Hermann began to shake visibly. He was uncertain of the interrogator's intentions.

'Now the trousers.'

As the interrogator spoke, he took a step back and seemed, to Hermann, to be waiting for a reaction. All the time, he sustained a look of affected boredom, as though this were some mandatory ritual he had to go through before he could fulfil his aim. He lit another cigarette.

Ever since his arrest, Hermann had nursed deep doubts about how he would respond if he were subjected to real pain or, perhaps worse, physical degradation. Those anxieties now rose to the centre of his mind, moulding his thoughts into a singular core of terror. Only now did he become aware that he was being supported on either side by the guards. Jointly, they worked to loosen his waistband, then pushed his trousers and underpants down to the floor. At a nod from the interrogator, one of the guards pulled them over his feet and tossed them in a bundle by the wall.

Apart from his socks, Hermann was naked. He tried to cover his genitals with his hands, but the guards locked his arms at his sides. The interrogator walked slowly round him, as though inspecting an animal shorn for the slaughterhouse. Coming round to face him again, he said: 'I want to know three things. First, your original source of information. Second, how many copies you made of your report. And third . . . where they are.'

As he had done many times during the periods of questioning, Hermann found himself trying to eclipse Kepler's name from his consciousness. Whatever his mental preparations for this moment, he still found it unbelievable that this was happening to him; happening here in his own country, a bedrock of liberalism.

Hesitating, he said lamely: 'I've got a right . . .'

The interrogator turned. 'You're a turd! You've got *no* rights!' Lifting his cigarette to his lips, he drew on it slowly and let the smoke filter from his nostrils. All the time, he kept his eyes fixed firmly on Hermann. 'The source,' he said. 'Who was it?'

For perhaps a quarter of an hour, Hermann deflected the

33

questions. Not once did the interrogator raise his voice, not once did he lose his poise. Finally, he simply stopped asking questions.

'Put him in the trough,' he told the guards.

Hermann was taken over to the washing area. One of the guards stood by him, holding his arms almost casually, while the other guard dropped a cylindrical metal plug into the drainage hole of one of the troughs. Then he fetched a wooden board that had been propped against the side of the shower cubicle. From a cupboard in the corner, he took a coil of thin rope.

Hermann watched the activity with nervous fascination. As he considered what speciality of discomfort was being prepared for him, a combination of stubbornness and fear clouded his thinking. To some extent, he saw himself as an amateur caught up in a world where others could call on resources of will beyond his capability.

He focused on the guard, then cast his eyes towards the interrogator. There was a limit, presumably, to what they could do to him. They had to be accountable to some sort of authority.

Suddenly, behind him, the other guard snatched his ankles, sending him heavily to the floor. They stood over him, watching as he shambled to his feet using the metal supports of the washing-trough. As soon as he was up, the guards grabbed him by his arms and legs and dumped him on his back in the trough. He tried to tip himself out, striking weakly at one of the guards, but they pinned him down. The board was placed over the trough so it formed a makeshift lid, then it was tied firmly in place.

When Hermann tried to raise his arms, they were trapped. If he lifted his head, he could just see over the trough's rim. The guards were standing on either side of him, but he couldn't see the interrogator. Soon the muscular strain of keeping his head raised proved too much, and he was forced to rest it on the bottom of the trough. At the same time, he heard a tap being turned and felt the cold trickle of water against his back.

'Make things easy for yourself, Hermann.'

As the interrogator was speaking, Hermann experienced a new kind of fear, one that spread to his body's spinal system, de-activating his nerve junctions. Each fibre, each sinew contracted as though he were psychological prey for a creature that could draw out his thoughts like plasma.

Neither the interrogator nor the guards spoke as the trough began to fill. Hermann started to struggle fiercely, pushing his arms and knees upwards against the restraining board. As more water came in, so his panic mounted, until he was thrashing wildly. Sight, sound, memory, touch: all fused as a concentration of senses.

'It'll take about three minutes for the water to reach the top,' he heard the interrogator saying. 'A minute for each answer.'

Hermann stopped moving for a moment, his energy temporarily spent. A slow pulsation in his eardrums blotted out all coherent thought. He tried turning, first left, then right, but the water was feeling its way like invisible fingers up his face. He took in mouthfuls of water.

At once, an unwieldy violence took hold. The capillaries behind his eyes began to swell as blood was squeezed upwards to feed his fury. Against his neck, he could feel the water rising. He was yelling at the guards to set him free, but they gave no response.

Briefly, he experienced a detached calm, like he imagined a condemned prisoner might feel when all procedures for a reprieve have been exhausted. He tried to maintain this equilibrium as he felt the wetness crawl over his cheeks but, as he sucked in a mixture of water and air, he coughed and retched. The interrogator was talking to him again, looking down on him, repeating his questions, but his words seemed to melt into a silent mimicry. Lips moved; eyes stared;

but no sound penetrated Hermann's private, hallucinatory world.

In a last vigorous reaction, he braced his knees and fists against the board and drove upwards. All the strength that had been lost during the sleepless hours in the cell was instantly summoned. For a second, as he strained, his face was submerged, and water gushed into the passages of his nose and throat. Muscular spasms made him vomit, clouding the water round him.

A frenzied lurch brought his head above the surface, but before he could draw breath, a hand came down. With the effort that it might take to drown a baby, it pushed him back under the water.

As he fought to conserve the last of his air, hot filaments seemed to be drawn under his skin. Patterns of light, searing and fragmented, burst against the wall of his sight. Then the air was expelled and his body heaved, forcing him to vomit again. This time he swallowed some of the sour mixture as it was thrown out, his body's reflexes turning against him as they worked to the last.

In the end, there came a further wave of intense heat and then one of cold as the blood emptied from his brain. He opened his eyes, and saw rings of blackness rippling on the surface of the water. Slowly, the rings merged, and all sources of sound and light shut down . . .

When he came to, he was being carried back to his cell. Still naked, still wet, he was dumped on the bed. The guards left without a word.

Now, lying in the silence to which he had become accustomed, he felt a deep, inner revulsion. He almost wished they had let him drown. The reason for his self-castigation was that in those last few micro-seconds of conscious thought, he had uttered Kepler's name. There was nothing he could do to make amends for the breach of confidentiality; nothing to compensate for his weakness under the ultimate threat. Whether they would have killed him, he seriously doubted, and the awareness that they had only needed to make him think they would, added to his humiliation. He had tried to fight them, and they had won. Deep inside, he had always known it would be the case.

6

From the window beside his desk, Scannell could look out over the Aldwych, the sweeping crescent at the southern end of Kingsway from which the agency took its name. As with all such media-based organizations, the hub of its activities was the main newsroom, and it was there that Scannell went, three days after his return to work, to deliver a story.

'It's the piece you asked for,' he told Estabrook, the news editor.

Estabrook looked up from his seat. 'What, early copy?'

'It'll give you time to rewrite it,' Scannell replied with a measure of sarcasm as he walked away from the desk.

He found Estabrook arrogant, not least because of his habit of overhauling reporters' stories, often without discussion, until they bore little resemblance to the originals. The antipathy was, Scannell suspected, mutual.

'I'll be in my office if anyone wants to maul it,' he said.

He went out to a corridor and narrowly avoided bumping into a library assistant who was hurrying from another of the correspondents' offices clutching two bundles of files. With a look of harassment, she stopped Scannell and showed him the folders.

'I've been searching for these since yesterday morning. Perhaps you could tell some of these people to send the files back when they've finished with them. Half these offices are pig-pens!'

The girl stalked off to the lift. Having seen the clutter that some of his colleagues amassed around them – press releases long since out of date, discarded invitations to publicity events, government reports which had once made lead-story news but were now just one more layer of garbage – he had to agree with her. In contrast, his own office was organized for efficiency. Behind his desk were two filing cabinets, fully indexed. On top of the desk was a stack of trays for documents in use as source material. It was the only way he could work, and it dated back to his first few months of training at one of the world's most extraordinary educational establishments.

He found it strange that, at a time when he was striving to focus on the missing images in his memory, Gaczyna should have remained so firmly in his mind. It was almost twenty years ago that a fresh-faced Leningrad languages graduate had embarked on the first stage of a career that was to erase his identity so completely. If he'd known then the price that he would later have to pay, he might have had second thoughts about accepting the selection committee's invitation to enrol. At that time, though, the name Scannell would have seemed as foreign as Sergei Petrovich Lyudin sounded now. To even think of himself in his original guise would be to underestimate the school's indoctrination process.

Gaczyna. It was conceivable that the CIA had somewhere like it, but certainly no West European intelligence service possessed the financial resources to set up a counterpart. He remembered how impressed he'd been when he'd arrived there, just as though he were living and working in a Western town. And the school's newspaper too, *The International Herald*, on which he'd sharpened his journalistic claws. It could have been any quality English-language newspaper on any news-stand between San Francisco and Inverness.

All those years after attending his induction classes, he could still hear the words of Krolikov, his course tutor, ringing through the lecture room: '*Self-discipline plus self-control equals self-survival.*' From that day, the maxim had been branded in his mind. During the twelve years since his first posting in Australia, it had enabled him to carry out his work with machine-like efficiency. Until, that is, the night of his accident.

Following his return to work, he had started to pull himself together, but the lingering fears as to what he might have said, and to whom during the blank period when the accident had occurred, prevented him from making a full recovery. The unusual hesitation he'd just felt in handing his story to Estabrook illustrated the point. It was a state of mind that had to be overcome.

Later that morning, following the daily features conference, the editor stopped at his door.

'Is everything all right?'

Scannell had been about to make a telephone call but, on seeing Household, he replaced the receiver. Household came into the room and shut the door. Scannell guessed what was coming.

'No problems? I mean, after the accident?'

Scannell sat back to appear relaxed. 'No. Why?'

Household went to a chair on the other side of the desk. 'I just wondered. You can get stale when you've been away, that's all.'

Scannell felt his skin prickle. He hadn't realized his condition was so obvious.

'I was a bit rough at first, I know. I'm all right now, though.'

'Glad to hear it.' Household paused for a moment, then added: 'You still don't remember what happened?'

Scannell shook his head. For the past few days he'd been recalling random snippets of a telephone conversation, but he didn't know who had been on the other end of the line, nor what had been discussed. In the recesses of his mind, it was a man's voice he could hear, like the remnant of a dream.

'I see something for a second, then it goes,' he said reflectively. 'Just a light.'

He still had no notion whether it was the security service that had set up the accident. From the time he'd regained consciousness, he'd presumed it was, because the only way to remain a step ahead of them was to think the worst.

'How're the ribs?'

Scannell broke from his reflections. 'Okay . . . I only get the pains while I'm awake.'

Household smiled. 'Incidentally, how are you finding things with Estabrook?'

So that was it. Estabrook had already started making his complaints.

'Why? Has he said anything?'

'No. Did you think he might have?'

Scannell shrugged. 'Who knows? These are shark-infested waters.'

'We can always arrange for some more time off. There's plenty of reporters on the desk who can help out – if you're having any difficulties.'

'Difficulties?'

'You've got a large specialist area. We can't afford to let our coverage slip.'

Scannell recognized the implied criticism. He knew his reporting had been erratic since he'd been back. It was the missing hours. He found concentration difficult.

'Are you complaining about my work?'

Household gave a mild shake of his head and eased back in his chair. 'I'd let you know if I was.'

'So why the concern?'

Household pondered for a moment. There was a courteous, prevaricating air about him, almost like that of an academic, which set him aside from more bluff Fleet Street executives. He carried his self-effacement through to his manner of dress, favouring the type of worsted suit that a country solicitor might wear.

With slight awkwardness, he said: 'All these anti-nuclear stories you've been doing . . . I don't want them to be at the expense of other things.'

'I thought they were part of my brief.'

'Certainly, they are. But we've got to make sure the proportion's right.' He made a balancing movement with his hand.

Scannell noticed how Household avoided making any further suggestions until he came to leave. Then, as he went out of the door, he turned back briefly.

'Don't forget, the time's there, if you want it.'

When he had gone, Scannell lit a cigarette and stared at his typewriter. He loosened his tie. A blurred image of a light in a window came into his mind. Then, as always, it faded . . .

At lunchtime, a call came through to Scannell's office from a trade union contact, who worked as a volunteer at the London offices of the European Anti-Nuclear Organization. One of the organization's officials had been arrested, the contact disclosed. Scannell had a vague recollection of the detained official's name, but he couldn't put a face to it. Apparently, the man had been charged under the Official Secrets Act for receiving unauthorized information from a civil servant.

Hermann . . . The name clawed at Scannell's memory throughout the afternoon. On checking back through the cuttings of his past stories, he remembered having met him once before when he'd provided information on the cost of the government's 'Chevaline' programme for modernizing the Polaris submarine fleet. The information had been used as the basis for an exclusive news story in advance of an announcement in the House of Commons. But that was in the past. Since then, as far as Scannell could recall, there had been no further word from him.

And yet, in the background, there was something more . . .

It was obvious, when he came to it. Before leaving the office, he checked Hermann's address in the telephone directory. It was Point Hill, Greenwich. The telephone number corresponded with the one scribbled on his pad at home.

That weekend he caught a flight to Amsterdam. He walked along the canal to the street where the police had told him he'd been found. Now he knew where the recurring image of the lighted window originated from. Hermann had promised information, damaging information, that could gravely embarrass the government.

Scannell looked up at the hoisting beam at the top of the warehouse. In his mind he could hear the rush of a heavy load falling, the clatter of the wheel overhead as he'd slumped to the wet, cobbled street. It had been no accident.

On his return to London, he stopped by Hermann's house. It was locked and silent, the curtains closed.

7

The dacha stood in modest gardens outside a village on the road to Klin. It was a brick-built, nineteenth-century cottage and had, before the revolution, served as a lodge on a country estate. Now it was on the books of the First Chief Directorate of the KGB, offering a retreat from the departmental cut and thrust for those select personnel in Active Measures who were powerful enough, or pushy enough, to get their names on to its occupancy rota.

On the second weekend in December, it was Alya Tiverzin's turn to sample its comforts. As always on such occasions, she took the opportunity to play hostess to several of her colleagues. Thus it was that her field operations controller, Oleg Merkulov, and two other officials found themselves being marched off on a brisk tour of the garden, with its leafless birch trees and apple orchard, which ran down to a small, ice-covered lake.

Coming out of the birch woods by the lakeside, Merkulov lingered behind the others for a moment, reflecting on the bleak landscape. At the same time, his hand felt instinctively in his overcoat pocket for a leather-covered flask. He was about to bring it out and risk a shot, then admonished himself. No, now was not the time. The Mistress would not approve.

As Tiverzin led them up a narrow incline by the lake, she turned and, in her familiar guidebook manner, said: 'We get geese here in the summer.'

'In that respect, comrade captain, you must find it little different to being at the office.'

Merkulov had been unable to resist making the joke although, as he might have foreseen, Tiverzin ignored it.

44

'We'll go in for drinks,' she said. 'The others should be arriving soon.'

Merkulov was relieved at the prospect of getting out of the cold. An hour and a half in the back of the chief technician's cramped Zaporozhets had been no way to spend what remained of his weekend. Still, at least it seemed that Tiverzin was going to have the decency to look after her guests, even though she would probably make a mental note of every drop that passed their lips.

As they walked across the rough lawns to the cottage, Merkulov switched himself off from Tiverzin's running commentary on the delights of the dacha. It was almost as if she had exclusive use of the place, rather than the one weekend every two months she'd been allocated on taking up her appointment. In the end, he could only smile. Everything the woman did, even hosting these weekend gatherings, was geared to her advancement in the directorate. Among her colleagues, there wasn't anyone she would genuinely call a friend. It was impossible to guess what motivated her. Whatever the reasons, Merkulov had no doubt that if he were in Kochev's shoes as divisional head he would be wearing padding between his shoulderblades. The woman's knife was being sharpened for the plunge.

Indoors, she served lemon tea and cognac. To give her her due, the cognac was French; none of the cheap Armenian liquor from the service's general stores. Presumably it had been bought on a special 'entertainments' voucher: another indication that she was being granted concessions normally reserved for staff a rank or two higher.

During the next half-hour, the group was joined by two representatives from Directorate S. This was a surprise for Merkulov. Although he'd expected the meeting to be high-powered, he'd had no idea that officials from the sister directorate would be invited. Knowing that their department controlled 'illegal' agents stationed abroad, their presence told him one important fact: word about the Amsterdam incident had spread wider than Tiverzin might have liked.

A desk official from the International Department also joined them, confirming Merkulov's observations. Now he understood why Tiverzin had invited them along, rather than waiting for the monthly inter-departmental conference. If she acted now, there was a better chance of limiting the damage. Even so, it appeared she was in for a tough session, and Merkulov found it difficult to be sympathetic.

When the gathering was complete, Tiverzin offered more drinks, then ushered everyone through to a large room at the front of the cottage. Blotters had been arranged round a long mahogany table. In its centre was a tray of glasses and a water-jug.

Merkulov turned to Panchenko, the chief technician, and said quietly: 'She doesn't do things by halves, eh? You'd think she was chairing a Central Committee meeting!'

The remark, masked by the general conversation, brought an embarrassed smile to his colleague's face. The two men waited until the more senior officials had taken their seats, then found places at the table. Tiverzin, at the far end, raised her hand.

'To begin, gentlemen . . . I know there have been some recent developments in our operations, but I thought we'd restrict our discussion to short-term policy details. That way we'll keep to some sort of timetable. I appreciate that you've all got to get back this evening.'

After she had given a brief summary of the division's affairs, the officials from the other sections asked questions about Lyosha's general strategy and its training schedules. At first, Merkulov, who'd seen the Line N report, thought she was going to get off lightly. Then one of the Directorate S officials picked up on her opening statement.

'You gave the impression that you might've had problems, comrade captain.'

Merkulov smiled to himself. This was Sofinsky, divisional chief of operational funds and, as such, the highest ranking

KGB official at the table. Merkulov had been expecting him to get his barb in before too long, but the thrust of his attack showed the concern over what had happened. Tiverzin was going to have to stay on her toes. Although the UK division didn't come under Sofinsky's direct control, he had a powerful influence over its financial affairs. An unflattering report from him to the budget director could cut the operation off at the flourish of a pen.

'We haven't got any cause for alarm, comrade major,' said Tiverzin. 'It's important to step up the protective surveillance budget though. We're on the verge of success.'

Merkulov watched as Sofinsky sat forward. It was impossible to predict how he would react to the call for more funds.

'With respect, captain, I understand that your so-called recent developments have been described as a severe operational blunder.'

Tiverzin looked coldly across the table. The woman had the ability to meet accusations with instant aggression; she never yielded.

'You do realize there are more than a dozen journalists in the network. Until this thing happened, not one of them had attracted any attention from British security.'

At this point, Sofinsky's Directorate S colleague joined the offensive.

'They're all under 10-10's control, is that right?'

'At ground level, yes.'

'Doesn't that mean you're risking wider exposure? If Novost is in any way connected with him, then the whole operation could come under threat.'

Tiverzin looked as though she found the suggestion impertinent. 'There's no question of that! None of the agents know they're part of a network. They all function independently. That's how it's been all along.'

Sofinsky, who had been making notes, looked up. 'Is 10-10 under suspicion?'

Tiverzin poured a glass of water. Merkulov had to admire

her spirit. Kochev would almost certainly have buckled under Sofinsky's criticism. As Merkulov waited for her answer, he felt an inner tension. As far as he knew, 10-10 was Lyosha's master agent. Sofinsky, it appeared, was probing to the operation's core.

'Our only concern is Novost,' Tiverzin said after some thought. 'We've alerted London.'

'Concern?'

'I've told you, he had an accident. I don't think there's any need for me to go over the details.'

'On the contrary, I'd be most interested to learn how it happened.'

Merkulov could sense that Tiverzin was being drawn into a corner.

'He was in Amsterdam. Something fell on him . . . outside a warehouse. It's as simple as that.'

Sofinsky's eyes showed a flicker of surprise. 'Just that? I'd heard he was on his way to pick up information . . . high-grade.'

There was a short silence. Farther down the table, Zaytsev, the Line N administrator who had driven out from Moscow with Merkulov and Panchenko, offered Tiverzin his support. Addressing Sofinsky, he said: 'He's a peace movement feeder. He . . .'

Tiverzin cast a cutting glance down the table and Zaytsev stopped.

'Novost has been highly effective in disseminating anti-nuclear propaganda,' Tiverzin told Sofinsky. 'The peace movement has gained a lot of support because of his stories. His news agency can get blanket coverage in the national press. He's a crucial placement.'

'Is it possible that the accident was a coincidence?' asked the official from the International Department. 'Or was it set up?'

'This is ridiculous!' Tiverzin protested. 'Just one agent, and everyone goes into a blind panic.'

Sofinsky looked up again from his notepad. 'Apparently his apartment was spot-searched by British security staff.'

'That was while he was in hospital. You *are* aware, of course, that he's a defence correspondent. It would have been surprising if they hadn't taken the opportunity to go over it.'

Sofinsky put down his pen and lit a thin cigar. He waved the smoke away from his face.

'You must appreciate, captain, that we can't expand budgets just because some careless agent has an accident. If you're worried about him, pull him out.'

On hearing this suggestion, Merkulov felt his muscles contract again. He knew how it would go down with Tiverzin. If Novost had to be withdrawn now, the operation could be set back by months. Her chances of getting Kochev's job could go out of the window.

Tiverzin's eyes fixed on Sofinsky. 'That, major, would be a disaster. Don't you understand? . . . We've got public opinion in Nato shifting towards the peace movement. The last thing we want to do is start pulling out key agents. All the statistics show . . .'

'I'm not disputing the statistics,' Sofinsky interrupted. 'I'm presenting the practical view of the budget department.'

'Then the department should change its view!'

There was a silence at the table as Tiverzin's cutting response appeared to bring the discussion to an end. Sofinsky, who made a final note in his pad, gave no indication as to whether he was impressed by her demand.

'I'll talk to the director,' he told her. 'You'll have an answer in due course.'

Tiverzin faced him formally across the table. They were like courtroom adversaries, each seeking to dominate the other by a combination of intellect, showmanship and will. Somehow, though, Merkulov couldn't help seeing it all as a sophisticated game.

'Thank you, comrade major,' Tiverzin concluded. 'I don't have to tell you what's at stake. There's only got to be one country that sends its missiles back, that's all. It'll be an open invitation for the others to follow.'

8

Once or twice after coming out of hospital, Scannell had run into the woman from the Residents Association. On one occasion she'd called at his apartment with a man she introduced as the association's treasurer. They were canvassing for new members.

'I'm sorry, I don't have the time to be involved,' he told them.

To take the edge off his rebuff, he wrote out a cheque for twenty pounds for the association's fund. Slipping it among her papers, the woman smiled.

'Thanks. If we can't get the bodies, cash is the next best thing!'

The next time he met her was one morning when he happened to be passing through the complex's underground car park on his way out to work. She was peering under the bonnet of her car, an ageing Renault, which clearly wouldn't start. When she saw Scannell, she looked up.

'Oh, hello.' She gestured despairingly towards the vehicle. 'Fantastic, eh? Witness – modern technology at its finest.'

Bearing the hospital visit in mind, Scannell felt obliged to stop. 'What's the problem?'

'I've got a damn delivery to make, and now the damn car's died on me!'

Scannell glanced at his watch. Any delay would make him late for the early editorial conference.

'Can't you call a garage?' he suggested.

The woman laughed bitterly.

'What, with their bills? You must be joking. It's a week's wages just to get them to wipe the oil off the dipstick. No,

50

I'll get my son to look at it. He might be able to do something – like destroy it!'

Scannell was about to walk on when the woman reached into the car and grabbed a package from the back seat.

'You wouldn't do me a favour, would you? Do you go anywhere near Charing Cross Road? It's some freelance typing. I was supposed to have dropped it off half an hour ago.'

Scannell hesitated. 'I normally take a taxi . . .'

'Tell you what – I'll fetch my son. If you could just give him a lift . . .'

It was impossible to refuse. Scannell waited for a cab at the car park entrance. A few minutes later, the woman came back with a boy of about fourteen. He was tall – taller than her – and rather outlandishly dressed in a studded canvas jacket. On the journey through the traffic Scannell tried to strike up a conversation with him.

'Why aren't you at school?' he asked.

The boy turned away from the window. 'I'm off sick.'

Seeing that the boy didn't want to be drawn further, Scannell opened a newspaper. The boy resumed staring out of the window, his mother's package beside him on the seat.

For the rest of the day, Scannell was vaguely disturbed. There was nothing about the woman to suggest that she was anything more than what she appeared to be – presumably a divorcee who was struggling to keep up appearances. But it was odd that he should have met her on three separate occasions in so short a time.

To add to his general uneasiness, a series of enquiries he'd been making into Hermann's arrest had been going badly. All attempts to gain access to the prisoner had been blocked. Indeed, it was impossible even to find out where he was being held on remand. Even Hermann's own lawyers had been obstructive, simply giving the information that an application for bail had been rejected and that no date had been set for a trial. Further contacts with the anti-nuclear groups and the National Council for Civil Liberties had revealed only that Hermann had been working on a special project, the details of which he'd kept to himself.

A final discouragement had come during the afternoon from Household, who had refused to relieve Scannell of news reporting duties to concentrate on the Hermann story. Estabrook had undoubtedly been behind the rejection which, in a way, was justifiable. Why, after all, release a correspondent to work exclusively on an investigative feature when it was already difficult to maintain full coverage on general news?

So here it was, potentially the last big story he would get to handle before his recall to Moscow – and it was heading for failure. There would be no chance of extending the posting; just the prospect of an instructor's position which had no doubt been set aside for him at Gaczyna, or one of the lesser outposts. Twelve years of survival behind enemy lines, then a desk and a lecture-room and a handful of graduates masquerading as spies. Most of them would go straight into offices at the directorate – tomorrow's technicians and paper-shifters. One, or perhaps two, out of the batch would get a prized foreign posting. Then, like him, they would serve their time until some young high-flier who still didn't know the meaning of isolation would be sent out as a replacement. There would be no praise at the end; no gratitude. Just the desk, empty and bare.

It was in this dispirited mood that Scannell, during the evening, had telephoned an escort agency. He'd tried to tell himself that he wasn't falling back into his old ways, but the delusion was slender. What added to his frustrations, if he was honest with himself, was the knowledge that the woman from the Residents Association was making herself available – he could sense it. It wasn't often that happened, and it took all his reserves of self-denial not to let himself be tempted into taking a step he might later regret.

The woman from the agency came at about 8.30. She was

the one they'd sent the time before last. Scannell was pleased about that, because he remembered that she hadn't made him feel she was in a hurry. Also, he appreciated the unelaborate way she dressed. In her green pressed suit, she could have been a secretary or company receptionist. At least the agency could be relied on for discretion. It was an important consideration, if women like that were coming to your home.

In the living-room, he offered her a seat. Flicking her hair back, she undid the tiny cloth buttons on her jacket and sat down on the sofa, crossing her legs. On her calves, Scannell could make out brownish hairs like faint brush-strokes. A mild lust stirred inside him.

'Drink?' he offered.

'What is there?'

'Wine?'

She nodded. 'All right. White, if you've got it.'

Scannell fetched a bottle from the fridge and poured two glasses. When he handed one to her, he noticed the slight tremor in his hand. He hadn't been able to shake it off.

'We thought you'd forgotten us,' she said as she reached for a cigarette in her handbag.

Scannell looked dismissive. 'I've been busy.'

They talked uneasily for a few minutes, until the woman stood up and went to the lavatory. When she came back, instead of resuming her seat on the sofa, she picked up her glass from the table and moved closer to Scannell, who was standing by the window. Through the night mist, he could see the illuminated dome of St Paul's, a large moon in the City's galaxy of lights. The woman ran her hand down his shirtsleeve.

'Shall we go through to the other room?'

Scannell nodded. He'd been wanting to make the move himself, but hadn't known how to, not without sounding impossibly clumsy.

The woman went out to the hallway and Scannell followed.

Under her blouse, he noticed, there was a slight spreading around the waistline. It was something he didn't find unpleasant, but it made him wonder how long the agency kept the girls on its books.

Approaching the door of the spare bedroom, the woman said: 'It's in here, isn't it?'

Scannell nodded. 'Straight through.' He never liked to use his own bed at such times.

He took a towelling gown from the wardrobe. Sitting on the bed, he loosened his tie and looked on as the woman started to unhitch her skirt.

As he followed her movements, a familiar guilt rose inside him. Although he tried to rationalize his actions as a necessary release, that didn't prevent him feeling squalid. It wasn't the first time he'd experienced such a problem.

'Leave it a minute,' he said.

The woman turned and looked at him questioningly. 'How d'you mean?'

'It's all right,' he said vaguely. 'Just leave it for a bit. Have another drink.'

The woman did up the clasp on her skirt, and reached for her wine on the dressing-table.

'Is anything wrong?'

Scannell shook his head. 'No. I just wondered . . . how have things been? I mean, since you were last here?'

The woman sat down on a cane chair. She took the cigarettes from her handbag.

'All right. Why?'

Scannell shrugged. 'No reason.' He saw that she looked a little irritated. 'You've got kids, haven't you?' he asked.

'Yes . . . one.'

He thought of his sister's children. They would be almost grown up now, although he always remembered them in their school shoes and coats, going off in the morning to the school on the Izmailovo housing complex.

'You're not married, though?' he said.

The woman eyed him with deepening suspicion. 'Look, what is this?'

Scannell frowned. He guessed that she would be finding his stalling odd.

'It's okay,' he assured her. 'I just like to talk sometimes. I haven't got people . . . family.'

'Oh?'

The woman sipped her wine; she clearly felt uncomfortable.

'Do you have boyfriends?' he asked her.

'One or two.'

'Do they mind . . . this?' He gestured loosely.

The woman smiled and reached for an ashtray on a bookcase. 'Sorry, love. That's my business.'

Scannell fell silent. He wondered whether to ask her to leave. Then, as he was considering what to say, she came and sat next to him on the bed. She started to run her hand across his shoulders.

'Are you sure you're all right?' she asked him.

He put his glass on a bedside table. 'Perhaps we'd better give this one a miss.'

As he started to get up, the woman took hold of his arm.

'You're not worried, are you? You weren't last time.'

Scannell looked down at her for a few moments, then let her ease him back on to the bed. He studied her eyes to see if she was laughing at him, but there was no obvious cynicism.

'Relax,' she said, and let her hand brush over the front of his trousers.

With a sharp reflex, the muscle of his sphincter tightened. Slowly, she lowered the zip on his fly.

'That's better.'

She undid the buttons on her blouse. Scannell knew he was going to give in. It had been nearly a year. He'd promised himself there would be no more.

The woman stood up and took off her skirt, folding it over the back of the chair. Scannell also undressed and put on the bathrobe. He went across the hallway to the bathroom and ran a basin of warm water. While the tap was still running, the woman came in. She was wearing only a bra and blue cotton pants.

'I'm glad I didn't have to ask,' she said. 'Some men don't like being told to wash.'

Opening his bathrobe, she lathered her hands and soaped his genitals.

'It's getting big,' she said. 'You've been saving it for me.'

After she had dried him, they went back to the bedroom. For the first time, he moved to touch her body, fumbling at her breasts and rear.

'Steady,' she said, and steered him towards the bed. 'Don't get over-eager.'

The young woman in denims waited until the two other full-time campaign officials with whom she shared an office had gone home. Like her, they had been working late, making early preparations for a series of Easter protests which needed to be co-ordinated months in advance. On the floor below, two or three people in the subscriptions department were still working, but they would soon be leaving. Now was the time to act, and quickly.

She went up to the cluttered attic office which served as a reference library and cleared a space on a desk. If she had been disturbed, she was prepared to say she was undertaking research for an article in the organization's magazine. It would have been a plausible explanation, but one far from the truth.

Today, as on other days, Hazel Goddard concentrated on the membership files. After a skilful search, she located a blue cardboard folder. She worked with haste to compile notes and put together a package of photocopied documents. The file was the twelfth on members of the international executive that she had analysed in the past five weeks, although this one, on someone called Hans-Heinrich Kepler, had been a special request from Central Office.

The task was nerve-racking. At one point, as she scribbled notes, she heard footsteps on the floor below. She immediately froze. It sounded as though they were coming from the stairs, and she guessed it was one of the administrators returning to his office after a late appointment. With the papers laid out in front of her, she would have no way of disguising her activities. Sweat prickled on her neck. Resisting the temptation to shovel the papers into a waste-basket, she calmed herself and rehearsed the explanation.

But the questions didn't come.

She listened as the footsteps stopped by a noticeboard in the corridor; then they passed through to the records office. Shaken, she continued with the file analysis.

Forty-five minutes was as much time as she dared give herself. If she worked too late, people would start to ask questions.

When the time was up, she gathered the papers and placed them back in the filing cabinet. Among the items she had discovered was information on the executive member's political affiliations: he had once belonged to the West German Communist Party and had recently been a member of an educational delegation to Budapest. This was all further evidence of the left-wing affiliations she'd been instructed to unearth.

Someone back at Unit Nine was getting explosive ammunition; Goddard only hoped it didn't go to waste.

The woman from the escort agency was sitting on the bed putting on her stockings.

Scannell had gone out to the living-room to fetch the rest of the wine when there was a knock at the front door. Still in his bathrobe, he hurried out to the hall, glancing at the bedroom door to make sure it was shut.

The caller was the woman from the Residents Association. She was holding a bunch of flowers.

'Something to brighten your life. Just to say thanks for this morning . . . helping me out with the package.'

Scannell took the flowers without a word. He was at a loss to know what to say. The woman seemed to be waiting for him to invite her in. He was preparing his excuses when the bedroom door opened and the woman from the escort agency came out, zipping up her skirt.

'Have you got . . . Oops! Sorry, I didn't realize.'

She immediately disappeared back into the bedroom and shut the door. Scannell shifted awkwardly.

'Busy, I see,' said the woman at the door. She looked faintly amused. 'One of your journalistic contacts?'

Scannell shrugged. 'An old school friend.'

The woman lingered briefly then, with a parting smile, said: 'Oh well, some other time perhaps.'

When she'd gone, Scannell went into the bedroom.

'My bloody zip's broken,' the woman said. 'Sorry if I've screwed things up for you. I didn't hear her knock. I just wanted to know if you had a safety-pin or something.'

Scannell shook his head. He held out the flowers. 'Do you want these?'

The woman smiled. 'No. Put them in water. Champagne and chocolates are more my style.'

Scannell admitted a slight disappointment that the woman from the Residents Association had called at such an inopportune moment. There was something about her that had fixed in his mind: an underlying sexuality perhaps, a refreshing directness. Having written off the possibility of getting to know her better, he was surprised to receive another visit the following Saturday morning. He was at the desk in his study preparing his monthly accounts when the doorbell rang.

'Sorry about the intrusion the other evening,' she said. 'I must do something about my timing.'

Recalling his embarrassment, Scannell scratched his head.

'Can I come in for a moment? I just wanted a quick word with you about our newsletter.'

Almost involuntarily, Scannell looked at his watch.

'It won't take long,' she said. 'I was chatting to the editor of it the other day. He wondered if you could tell us what you thought . . . The professional eye.'

Scannell shrugged non-committally, but stood aside to let her in. Following him through to the living-room, she took a copy of the newsletter from her handbag. She spread it on the coffee-table.

'What do you think? A little masterpiece, isn't it?'

Scannell gave a faint smile and tilted his head uncertainly. 'Fine. The layout could be a bit more . . . dynamic. Apart from that . . .'

The woman laughed. 'Damning with faint praise, if ever I heard it. Or perhaps I didn't detect *any* praise!'

Scannell gestured as though ready to excuse. 'When you're doing it on a shoestring . . .'

He cast his eye over the newsletter to appear interested and made some general comments about its presentation. Handing it back to her, he considered offering her a coffee, then decided against it. Things could get complicated.

'It looks okay to me,' he said.

'But no Pulitzer prizes . . .'

Scannell smiled.

The woman adopted an unusually hesitant expression. 'You wouldn't be interested, I suppose, in contributing? You know . . . just now and again. To give it a *soupçon* of class.'

This was the question that Scannell had been expecting from the start. He had already prepared his answer.

'Fleet Street rates?'

The woman laughed again. 'You could buy us out after one article! You wouldn't consider doing something on a more . . . well, let's say, *friendly* basis?'

Scannell was slow in responding. 'Sometime, perhaps. If I feel I've got something to say.'

The woman stood up. 'Well, let us know when the Muse strikes!'

As she picked up her bag, Scannell noticed her glance round the room with interest, observing its blend of antique and modern furnishings. He'd spent a lot of money on the flat; people expected it.

'What type of journalism do you do?' she inquired.

'I'm a defence correspondent.'

She turned to leave. 'Exciting.'

'So is lion taming . . . I wouldn't recommend it for a living though.'

He showed her to the door.

'By the way,' she said, 'come down for a drink one evening. I still owe you a favour.'

It seemed there was something in her tone that suggested she was offering more than a drink. Scannell hesitated.

'I'm up to my eyes at the moment. I . . .'

She started walking towards the lift. 'Monday at nine. Don't worry if you can't make it. We can always fix another time.'

One of the guards was the first to sound the alarm. The monitor that had been trained on Hermann's cell for the weeks of his internment had suddenly gone black. Swinging round in his chair in front of the console, the guard pulled his colleague to his feet.

'Something's wrong. I'll go and check. Call central control.'

Hermann's cell was at the other end of the corridor. The guard ran its length, pulling from his trouser pocket the chain that held his keys. From the moment he'd noticed that the monitor had malfunctioned to the moment he opened the cell door, no more than thirty seconds had elapsed.

As he entered, his eyes focused with bewilderment on the

object swinging from the wire cage over the light. It was the prisoner's grim determination that stunned him. The shirt, torn into strips and plaited to make the noose. The trousers, ripped in half and stuffed inside the cage to blot out the camera's lens. The slop bucket, overturned and kicked away. The man must have been planning it for days.

The guard shouted for assistance, and his colleague came running. One wrapped his arms round Hermann's thighs, while the other stood on the slop bucket to cut him down. Laying him on the floor, they tilted his head back and administered the kiss of life. Both of them had practised the drill at innumerable training sessions, but then, somehow, it had always worked. Here they could see from the prisoner's chalky eyes and his flaccid hands that they were wasting their time.

9

On the last Monday of January, the section heads of the Defence Ministry's Secretariat N-160 had been due to hold a strategic planning conference as they do at the end of each month throughout the year. The secretariat, known more familiarly in Whitehall as the 'holocaust desk', is responsible for overseeing Britain's nuclear weapons policy. Its discussions are minuted and summarized for the ministerial box, although the main purpose of the exercise is to co-ordinate departmental work programmes. The meetings take place after normal working hours in the unadorned office of the assistant secretary who directs its affairs, and it was to this office that Geoffrey Whymark, head of the section responsible for opinion poll analysis, was summoned shortly before such a routine conference was due to begin. But as he was about to discover, this preparatory discussion was not minuted, and it was far from routine.

The moment he stepped into the office he sensed an air of displeasure, although Sherrington, the director, offered him the customary drink.

'We'll discuss your report before the others come up,' Sherrington said, handing him a glass of scotch. 'On the whole, it was fine . . . nice presentation.'

Whymark sat stiffly in his chair. He noted an element of doubt in Sherrington's words.

'There's just one thing,' Sherrington added, taking a seat behind his desk, 'I'm a little concerned about the actual . . . results.'

'I was asked for a full assessment,' Whymark said.

Sherrington nodded. 'Yes, quite. It's just that . . . Perhaps we're not focusing precisely on the point at issue.'

Whymark didn't have to have Sherrington's misgivings spelled out. He'd deliberately left it until the end of the previous week before letting him see the analysis in the hope that Sherrington wouldn't have time to read it before the meeting. Clearly, Sherrington had studied it over the weekend.

'We did a complete breakdown of all the available results,' Whymark explained. 'The report shows the conclusions that emerged.'

'True, but I think it's a question of . . . emphasis.' As he was talking, Sherrington picked up a copy of the report and flipped its pages. 'I do have to say, I feel it's really little more than an apology for the anti-nuclear movement.'

Whymark could see Sherrington's emerging dissatisfaction, and felt resentment. Sherrington's staff had commissioned it, after all. What did he expect?

'It's an objective analysis. We feed the data in, then extrapolate our findings.'

'Yes, I'm aware of the methods you use,' said Sherrington. Now there was noticeable irritation in his voice. 'But look –' he held out the open pages, 'we've got here widespread hostility towards US arms policies . . . growing fears of a nuclear conflict . . . disillusionment with government defence strategy . . .'

Running his eyes over the neatly numbered paragraphs in the section of conclusions, Whymark couldn't apprehend how such a professionally correct document could be criticized.

'It's an accurate reflection of public opinion,' he argued.

Sherrington looked up. 'Is it though? Is this *really* what people think?'

Whymark hesitated. If he stopped to ask himself, he wondered whether he ever considered the source material he used as people's actual views. To him, they were statistical samples to be balanced and weighed, ingredients in a laboratory experiment.

After some moments, he replied: 'We can only work from the information we have to hand.'

Whymark watched as Sherrington, once or twice shaking his head gently, studied the remaining conclusions. He was an authoritative-looking man, broad-shouldered, with greying hair. This air of distinction made things worse – almost as though he saw the report as disrespectful.

'What are your own – your *personal* feelings about all this?' Sherrington asked. 'For instance, d'you think it would be fair to make this sort of information public?'

Whymark shrugged vaguely. 'I don't know. It's not my job to make those sorts of decisions. We're a process department.'

'Yes, *exactly*.'

Whymark noted a hint of scorn, and his bitterness deepened. His staff had done a thorough job. It had taken weeks to sift the morass of detail.

Sherrington took off his reading glasses and placed the report on his desk. 'You understand, we're talking about material that will shortly be required for inclusion in a major policy speech by the Secretary of State.'

This was a surprise for Whymark. He'd had the impression that the report was a background document for the secretariat's files.

'No one told us that,' he said.

Sherrington leaned forward. 'Did you think you were working in a vacuum?'

There was a long silence.

'I don't see what we can do,' Whymark said at last. 'We've incorporated the results from all the mainstream polls.'

'Then I suggest you cast your net wider. Whatever happens, we've got to be able to show that the peace movement's claims are a sham.'

Whymark said nothing. He couldn't see why the burden had to fall on him. It wasn't the section's fault that the figures didn't fit the government's image-building campaign. Several times in the past, he'd been forced to give way under pressure from above. This time he was determined to stand his ground.

'I thought we were civil servants, not political propagandists.' As he spoke, it almost seemed as if the words were coming from someone else. Somehow, they sounded too articulate, too refractory.

Typically, Sherrington ignored the response. 'I've decided not to present the report at today's meeting. In the next four weeks I want you to gather additional material so that we can amend the results.' He picked up the report and, slipping on his glasses, cast his eyes again over the conclusions. Then, placing the document back on the desk, he added: 'I'd recommend a complete re-draft.'

Whymark was stunned. It was the biggest blow yet to his professional integrity. What he was being asked to do was little short of fictionalization. He couldn't understand the need. Surely, if the department wanted to increase the acceptability of a nuclear-based policy, then it had to find some sounder justification. There were other sections, other means. For a start, television interviews could be secured for ministers; there was a campaign to distribute leaflets to universities and colleges. Didn't these areas provide enough scope for scoring publicity points?

'Of course, it depends on whether additional information exists,' he said.

Sherrington shifted the report to one side of his desk, as though he wanted to remove it from his thoughts.

'How many research assistants have you got on your staff?'

'Seven.'

'That would seem to be sufficient to find an appropriate result.'

Whymark considered the instruction, and mustered what resistance he could.

'What if a wider analysis indicates a similar pattern?'

Sherrington clasped his hands on the desk and smiled with forced politeness.

'I trust it won't.'

10

Several times in the weeks after Christmas, Scannell went to supper at Celia Forde's. On each occasion he listened avidly to everything she said, mentally dissecting the most innocuous statements, all the time waiting for the giveaway remark that would tell him she was a DI5 plant. But it hadn't come.

She'd mentioned on the first evening that she was a civil servant – a clerical officer in the cashier's section at the Department of the Environment – and his suspicions had immediately been aroused. In the following days, though, he'd taken the precaution of making inquiries, and she'd checked out. Besides, no security service liked to use agents encumbered with children, especially intrusive teenagers. She was hardly DI5 material.

One evening they went to a concert at the nearby arts centre. It had been Celia's suggestion; Scannell had little interest in music or the theatre, but he had agreed to go, mainly to try and gauge what she wanted from him. During the interval, they ordered drinks at the bar.

'I've been given promotion,' she told him, when they had found seats. 'They've put me in the salaries section.'

Scannell studied her eyes. At once his mistrust had returned. Had he been wrong? Was this the first move against him?

'Is that better than the cashiers?' he asked her.

'It's more money. That's where *my* interest stops.'

'I thought they paid you well. The Barbican's hardly a cheap place to live, is it?'

Celia laughed. 'The flat? The sum total of seven years of marriage, that is. My husband gave it to me as a going-away present!'

Scannell said nothing. The explanation was plausible.

'Anyway, I don't know what ideas you've got about the Civil Service,' Celia added. 'They don't pay a bean. Why do you think I have to do all that freelance work?'

'Why stay there, if it's that bad?'

'Show me something else at a couple of thousand more and I'll take it.' Her eyes suddenly lit up. 'You don't want a secretary, by any chance, do you?'

Scannell smiled and shook his head. 'No. We don't go in for such luxuries.'

Celia offered him a cigarette. 'You know, that's the first time you've smiled this evening. You should try it more often. It suits you.'

Scannell dropped more questions into the conversation. In the end, he decided he had no grounds for doubting what she was saying. As she reached for her glass, he looked at her face, for the first time taking in her rather ordinary features. He realized that it was the sparingly-applied make-up and the short, auburn hair, swept back, which saved her from looking plain. Tonight there was something about her relaxed mood that compelled him to ask the question that had been on his mind every time they'd met.

'I know this might sound presumptuous,' he said, 'but why do you want to keep on seeing me?'

Celia, who was sipping her drink, gave a slight gawp. 'Give a girl a break! You make it sound like I'm trying to *thrust* myself on you.'

Scannell averted his eyes. 'Sorry, I didn't mean it like that. It's just not something women often do.'

'What generally, or with you?'

'With me.'

Celia flicked her hair back and grinned. 'Don't sell yourself so short.' She followed this up with a look of mock concern. 'You're not a bit the other way, or anything, are you?'

Scannell raised an eyebrow, but said nothing.

Celia sustained the frown, then sat back, her expression

showing relief. 'Of course not.' She held up a finger and knowingly tapped the side of her nose. 'The old school friend . . . I was forgetting.'

After the performance, they went back to her flat. Her son, who had gone out earlier in the evening, still wasn't home. Celia immediately became anxious. In a way, her reaction surprised Scannell. He hadn't seen her as the type to be troubled by small domestic matters. After all, the boy was old enough to look after himself. It was around eleven o'clock when he came in.

'Where do you think *you've* been?' she demanded.

He dropped his coat over the back of an armchair. 'Out.'

'Out where? Who with?'

'Just out.'

As the boy went through to his bedroom, Celia glanced at Scannell and gave a tired shrug. She prepared a light supper which was marred by a tense atmosphere at the table.

Half-way through the meal, the boy turned to Scannell and said: 'Why do you come down here so much anyway?'

Scannell glanced at Celia, who gave her son a furious glare.

'Richard! Don't be so rude! How d'you think that makes Tom feel?'

As soon as the meal was cleared, the boy went back to his room. Scannell and Celia sat at the table finishing a bottle of wine. Scannell had noticed when he'd been to the flat before how the boy seemed to resent his presence.

'Don't worry,' Celia said. 'He's a pain in the neck. He's like it when you're not around as well. Most of the time he's worse!'

She fetched a bowl of fruit from a shelf. Scannell took an apple and started to peel it. He wondered whether he was wrong in keeping up the visits; whether the risk was too great. Memories of his instructors filled his mind: how they'd toughened him for his solitary assignment. At the school there'd been Yelena, but they'd soon put paid to that. Don't ever become involved, they'd warned him. Remember, it wasn't only his own life he could be endangering. So it was that, over the years, he'd learnt to control his relationships, to keep them in check. For one thing, you never knew who might be watching. Now he was alarmed that something might have begun to crack.

A short time later, he went up to his flat. He was about to go to bed when there was a knock at the door. It could only be Celia.

'I wanted to apologize,' she said. 'I'm sorry if Richard upset you.'

Scannell shrugged. 'He's just a kid. He's okay.'

He invited her in and fetched a bottle of whisky from a cupboard. Pouring two glasses, he topped them up with water from the tap.

'Sorry, no ice.'

Despite the time, he wasn't annoyed that she'd come up. After her company during the evening, his flat had seemed oddly silent and unwelcoming. It was apparent, too, that Celia was in no mood to sleep. She began to talk, mainly about her work, but the conversation came round to the subject of her marriage. Her former husband, an oil engineer, was on a contract in Mexico, she said. Consequently, Richard saw little of him, although there was a drawer full of postcards in his bedroom.

'What about you?' Celia ventured. 'I mean, apart from the lady visitor, you live up here like some sort of hermit. Have *you* ever been married?'

Scannell put his whisky down. 'No. They tell me it's bad for the health.'

'Who's "they"?'

'My bank manager.'

Celia smiled. 'Girlfriends then? Is there anyone permanent?'

He wondered why she was fishing, and what for. He ran his teeth over his lower lip; it was slightly numb. What with the wine earlier, he'd drunk more than was wise. Suddenly, all his suspicions flooded back and he felt embittered. Whatever move he made, he was trapped. He directed his resentment towards her.

'I asked you when we were out why you wanted to keep seeing me. You didn't answer my question.'

Celia seemed a little shocked by his bluntness.

'Do I?' she said. 'I mean, keep wanting to see you?'

Scannell fastened his eyes on hers, seeking a sign, any sign, that would tell him she was faltering. If only he knew . . . if only he could be sure.

'You tell me,' he answered cryptically.

Celia fell quiet. Her usual vivacity had faded.

'You keep looking at me like . . . I don't know, like you're accusing me of something,' she said at length.

Scannell's forehead creased in puzzlement. 'Really? Why should I do that?'

There was another silence. Slowly, she lifted her eyes.

'Tom, why are you being like this?'

'Like what?'

'Like you are. Is it because of Richard . . . what he said?'

Scannell wouldn't be drawn. Better to let her make her own assumptions.

Eventually, refilling the glasses, he said: 'If you want me to sleep with you, why don't you say so? Why the charades?'

Celia picked up her cigarettes. She lit one and lifted it away from her mouth. Scannell looked at her without expression. Even now, he couldn't tell whether his words had made contact with that part of her which she always managed to shield. Although he'd needed to force her into a corner, he'd sounded more brutal than he'd intended.

After some moments, she said: 'Is that what you think of me?'

He didn't answer.

'Like I told you, I've been divorced for nearly seven years. Do you know how many men I've been to bed with in that

70

time? I'll tell you . . . two. How's that for a love life?' She broke off. Then, seemingly regaining her buoyant composure, she added: 'You might not see the problem, darling, but it's not too easy getting laid when your son's in the next room.'

'You seem the sort who could cope.'

Celia settled back in her chair. 'We've all got our fronts, haven't we?'

Scannell frowned. At once he felt a flush of shame. In the end, he uttered simply: 'We make choices.'

Later, he went out to the kitchen to rinse the glasses. Celia sat on a stool in the breakfast area. After a time, she said: 'So maybe I wouldn't mind sleeping with you. Is there anything wrong in that? It's different for men. They can pay for it when they want it.' She paused. 'Still, you seem to know all about that, don't you?'

Scannell dried the glasses and put them in a cupboard. He looked at his watch. Something inside him wanted to ask her to leave, but he knew he'd gone beyond that point.

'Well?' she said, almost irritably. 'Do you want me to stay?'

'It's nearly two o'clock. What about Richard?'

Celia cast her eyes down, then looked up with mild embarrassment.

'I'll go down in the morning, if you like, before he's awake.'

That night Scannell broke a prime operational rule: for the first time since Gaczyna he made love to a woman for whom he felt something more than a basic sexual need. Somehow she seemed to be opening his life, but he daren't contemplate what his feelings meant, or where they would lead him to.

11

At 11.40 A.M. London time the TWA Boeing 747 lumbered across the tarmac at Heathrow Airport and began taxiing for take-off. On board were 286 passengers, and among those in the first class section was Peter Quigley, MP, who, in a recent government reshuffle, had been appointed Parliamentary Under-Secretary of State for Defence Procurement.

Quigley adjusted his seatbelt and looked out of the window at the service vehicles gathering round a Lufthansa Airbus, whose passengers had just disembarked. His new job had forced him to become conscious of aircraft technicalities and, as he studied the Pratt & Whitney turbofan engines, he made a mental note to strengthen his contacts with the aerospace company if he had time at the end of his visit to the United States.

This was only one of several impromptu business meetings he hoped the trip would yield. For these opportunities alone, he had been more than willing to accept the invitation from Kalatronic Systems Incorporated to attend the opening of a $57 million guidance systems production plant at Syracuse, NY. There were, however, two additional reasons for his satisfaction at receiving the complimentary ticket, which had come through the London merchant bankers Corston Grant, representing Kalatronic's UK interests.

First, it would allow him to renew an association with Max Goldberg, Kalatronic's chief executive. The two men had first met when Goldberg was on a twelve-month post-graduate course at the London School of Economics in the early 1960s. At the time, Quigley had been an undergraduate and treasurer of the Students Union.

Second, he hoped to visit his sister who was married to a Manhattan lawyer. Kalatronic had offered to make available an executive aircraft to fly any of the VIPs to New York's La Guardia Airport on the day after the opening of the plant. Although his time was limited, this would at least allow a brief family reunion.

As the aircraft moved slowly to the start of the runway for take-off, Quigley didn't question Kalatronic's motivation in inviting him to the ceremony. Politicians and dignitaries the world over received similar invitations every week to attend such functions. Some they accepted, and some they didn't. On this occasion, Kalatronic had hooked their big fish, and Quigley was happy to be hooked.

Tossing a cigarette end out of the car window, Merkulov took a side turning off Neglinnaya Street to a car park behind Moscow's Central Department Store.

Even after two months, he still felt an undisguised pleasure driving the Moskvich. It was the first new car he'd owned and, although he'd put his job on the line to acquire it, he judged the risk to have been worth taking. Tiverzin had admired it briefly in the directorate car park, but she hadn't thought to challenge his ability to pay for it. In any case, since the accident in London, she'd had other things on her mind. The car was plausibly within the reach of a well-paid bachelor who was prepared to save hard, and neither Tiverzin nor any other senior staff official would know he'd never held on to a kopek in his working life.

The ultimate proof of legitimate ownership was the plastic wallet of papers and certificate of purchase in the glove-box. The fact that he'd bought the car through an unofficial dealer at hardly more than half its stipulated retail price was not recorded on the documentation.

Locking the car, he crossed the road and walked along Petrovka Street to a big tourist hotel, the Prague. It was mainly used by customers of Sovincentr, the state-run travel organization for foreign businessmen. Most of the current guests were with Dutch and Finnish delegations. Merkulov went into the foyer and mingled with them as they gazed indifferently at the ranges of luxury goods in the windows of the hard currency shop; goods scarcely even available to officials like himself, let alone the ordinary Muscovite.

Taking his mind away from these symbols of Western consumerism, he wondered when the moneychanger would arrive. It annoyed him that he should be kept waiting, but there was nothing he could do about it. The monthly payment on the car had to be made, or the man could cause trouble.

As the minutes ticked by, Merkulov's irritation increased. A KGB officer only had to be observed away from his office or usual social environment for the investigators of the Second Directorate to start asking questions. Finally, he became too restless in the foyer and went to the bar for a beer and vodka. Through a dividing window he could keep his eye on the main entrance.

He was half-way through his second beer when at last he caught sight of the moneychanger coming through the revolving door. Merkulov left the bar and went to the men's toilets on the opposite side of the foyer. The moneychanger followed him, and the two of them went into a cubicle. They had barely started a conversation when the main door to the toilets opened and the moneychanger froze. They listened to the stranger urinating, and Merkulov fought off a stupid impulse to laugh. He looked at the moneychanger, noting the taut facial muscles and the darting eyes: he was only a young man, but the stress of conducting his illegal business had already taken its toll.

As soon as the stranger had gone, the moneychanger said to Merkulov: 'Hurry. This place is too busy.'

Merkulov took out his wallet and handed over a wad of ten-rouble notes.

'On time again,' said the young man. 'That's what I like.'

'I'll need an extra few weeks for the next payment. I've had problems.'

'What – not enough bribes?'

The moneychanger spoke without smiling. Merkulov wondered if he knew the truth of his statement, but guessed it was a common enough assumption about KGB officers. In any case, there was no evidence to support a testimony.

'It's just temporary.'

After some thought, the moneychanger replied: 'You know me. I don't operate for nothing.'

'What do you want?'

'A favour. Some of the places where I do business are getting too risky. Your friends in the special division are on my back all the time. Get them off.'

'You should change your patch.'

The young man eyed Merkulov maliciously. 'I had to wait long enough to be able to work the one I've got. You're in a position to make sure I keep it.'

'Those police work from the security directorate. They're nothing to do with my department.'

'It's all the same. You can pull strings.'

'It's impossible.'

The young man stared at Merkulov who, after a short time, suddenly felt a searing pain in his genitals. He hadn't been watching the young man's left hand, which was now squeezing him tightly. Merkulov endured the pain in silence, knowing that a scream would bring the hotel security staff running.

'You'd better be on time with your next payment then, my friend,' the young man warned through clenched teeth, 'or I'll pull a string of my own – and you'll be on the end of it. Just remember, I know where that car came from, but no one in your department does – yet!'

After a long sleep to shake off jet-lag, Quigley went downstairs to a pre-arranged breakfast meeting with Kalatronic's senior directors in the dining-room of the secluded hotel. Goldberg, who had arrived late the previous evening from the company's San Francisco office, was seated among the group at the table.

He stood up eagerly as Quigley came in, and the two men exchanged greetings. The brown hair was now grey, Quigley observed, and the waistline thicker, but Goldberg's broad smile and aggressive handshake were still the same.

'Glad you could make it, Peter,' Goldberg said. 'Hopefully we'll have a chance to talk later. Is everything okay? The room? . . . The hotel?'

Quigley smiled. 'First class.'

Discussion at the table centred on the company's sales targets and its plans to expand its markets among the European Nato countries. One director from the north-eastern operation, who was sitting next to Quigley, talked at length about an anti-surface-to-air missile system, known as Polecat, which was apparently under development. Quigley could barely understand a word of the technical sales pitch, and was thankful when Goldberg stepped in to damp the man's enthusiasm.

'Mr Quigley's a guest,' he said. 'He doesn't want to be sold systems over the breakfast table.'

The day's schedule was tightly planned. VIPs were given demonstrations of computer systems and taken on tours of the plant. Quigley was accompanied by the research and development director to explain the technicalities, and was beginning to wonder if he shouldn't have delegated the invitation to the equipment expert who controlled the day-to-day running of the arms purchasing agency.

In the evening, however, he was on firmer territory when he was called on to give a short opening speech at a country club reception. He was seated next to Goldberg at the top table and at last the two men had the chance to renew their old friendship.

'Sorry time's been so tight,' said Goldberg when Quigley

had given his address. 'That's quite a title you've got yourself.'

'I've been able to take advantage of one or two openings.'

Goldberg nodded. 'I thought you had your eye on a Treasury post.'

Quigley smiled, impressed by Goldberg's up-to-date knowledge of the British political scene. 'Defence was a good second best.'

Later in the meal, Goldberg broached the subject of the British anti-nuclear movement.

'Are those bastards crazy?' he said. 'If any European country unilaterally disarms, it might as well open its frontiers and let Moscow wheel in the SS-20s.'

'I don't disagree,' said Quigley. 'The peace movement's membership has increased, and we're doing all we can to contain it.'

'There are some people here, you know, who reckon it's getting out of hand.'

Goldberg's observation seemed to contain an element of warning, and suddenly it dawned on Quigley that his old friend's awareness of British affairs was perhaps a little too comprehensive. He wondered if he'd been primed by the State Department.

'Is that an official notification, or a personal observation?' he asked.

Goldberg gave one of his broad smiles. 'A general assessment.'

For Quigley it was answer enough. He decided to argue on generalities.

'Some of your television coverage over here is unrepresentative. Many of those in the movement are just weekend protesters. The campaign could still fizzle out.'

Goldberg nodded, but appeared disinclined to take the point. 'What about our advisers? Is there a role for them, do you think?'

Now the truth was coming out.

'You mean the CIA?'

Goldberg shrugged. 'Or whatever. They've done a good job on the peace movement here.'

Quigley gave the only response he could. 'It's an internal matter.'

Goldberg lit a cigar. 'Sure. That's your prerogative.'

The tone of condescension irritated Quigley, and he felt a rising desire to put Goldberg in his place.

'Remember, it was the plan to deploy US missiles in Europe that reinvigorated the peace movement. That's not to say the policy was wrong – on the contrary – but it's only realistic to expect a backlash.'

'They could louse it up for us,' Goldberg warned.

Quigley picked up a brandy which had been poured for him, and revolved the glass gently in his palm. It was clear now why he had been invited.

'I'm intrigued to know about the acquaintances you've been speaking for,' he said. 'Are they in Washington or Langley?'

Again, Goldberg smiled. The reference to the CIA's headquarters hadn't been lost on him.

'Let's just say I'm an interested observer, and one or two people have made their views known to me,' he said. 'Whatever the situation, we've got to maintain a first-strike capability that can blow Moscow up its ass!'

12

Celia got the call just as she was about to leave work for the evening. It was from the personnel director's secretary.

'He'd like you to come up,' the woman said.

Celia had only met Greengross once before. That was on her first day on the staff after an induction course. Like all the other directors in the building, he was a grey figure in a grey suit she sometimes passed in the corridor or stood silently beside in the lift.

Knocking at the door of his secretary's office, she was shown in by one of the typists.

'You're to go straight in.'

Celia adopted an air of confidence and went through to the director's suite. He wasn't alone. She recognized the man sitting beside the desk as Larsen, who most people believed was in Protective Security. He'd interviewed her briefly when she'd joined the department.

Greengross smiled as Celia walked in. He was a middle-aged man; slightly effeminate, she thought. He offered her a chair.

'It's nothing to worry about,' he said, as if sensing her uneasiness. 'You spoke to Accounts D a few weeks ago.'

Celia nodded brusquely. 'That's right.'

'And you agreed to undertake a small assignment, I believe, regarding one of your neighbours.'

'Yes.'

She smoothed her skirt: a nervous gesture. The director on his own would have been all right, but the presence of Larsen made it seem as though she was facing an examination board.

'How are you getting on?' Greengross asked.

'Fine.' She nodded brightly. 'I was told to get to know him.'

'Quite. And I gather that has now been accomplished.'

'Yes.'

Celia felt uncertain about how much they knew. She wondered whether his remark contained any hidden reference. Greengross gave another of his caring smiles. It was impossible to tell whether they were genuine.

'Perhaps you could be a little more specific,' he said.

Celia hesitated. They couldn't possibly know . . . not all that had happened.

'He's come for dinner a couple of times,' she told him. 'That's about it, really.'

'Would it be possible to give us some idea of the things you've talked about? . . . Just generally.'

Celia was thrown for a moment. She couldn't remember a word she and Scannell had spoken. Nobody had suggested she keep a record.

'Just ordinary things,' she replied guardedly. 'I wasn't told to ask him anything special.'

Greengross held his hands flat and studied the nails. Looking up, he said: 'Has he spoken about his work, for instance?'

'He's a journalist.'

'Yes.' His voice held a note of irritation, then he pulled himself up. 'Yes, we know that. Has he said anything about the nature of his stories?'

Celia frowned. 'No . . . I don't think so. He's a defence correspondent. I don't know that much about journalism. I didn't think to ask.'

Greengross nodded sympathetically. He looked at Larsen who, throughout the conversation, had been making notes on a clipboard.

'What about his family?' Greengross continued. 'He's not married, we know that, but has he spoken about his parents at all – or any brothers and sisters?'

Celia shook her head. It was difficult to see what he was leading up to.

'He hasn't mentioned anything.'

At this point, as though deciding Greengross had been allowed to question her for long enough, Larsen sat forward. He set the clipboard down on the edge of Greengross's desk.

'Has he spoken about his political beliefs?'

He was a slight man – mousy, sort of – but his tone was tougher than Greengross's; more demanding. Celia found it hard to think back, and felt it unfair not to have been more fully briefed.

'No,' she said firmly. 'I tried to get him going, but it wasn't any good.'

'Would you say he was on the left?'

'I don't know. He doesn't seem to care.'

'Wise not to push it,' Greengross said.

Larsen ignored the interjection. 'What would you say if you were asked to broaden the scope of your brief?'

'In what way?' Celia's reply was cautious.

'We require more information.'

'It depends what you want me to do.'

'What we've discussed. Find out about his family background, his political views, journalistic contacts . . . Any possibility of links with radical groups.'

'I don't know . . .'

Celia's voice tailed off. Radical groups? It confounded her why they should be so interested in Scannell. She could understand the need to undertake surveillance on people involved in sensitive work but, even though Scannell wrote about defence matters, he didn't fit into that category. She was no departmental lawyer, but the action seemed to skirt dangerously close to the limits of operational guidelines. Ever since Scannell had first come to supper she'd experienced feelings of guilt; these were now increasing by the day. It was as though she was plotting behind his back.

Again, Greengross seemed almost to be able to read her concerns.

'We would have preferred to have assigned an experienced field agent, of course, but you happen to live nearby. It's a natural cover, you understand.'

'I'm just a desk officer. I haven't had the training.'

Greengross paused. 'I'm sure that can be taken care of.' He sat forward and neatened some papers on his desk. 'You've done a good job so far, Mrs Forde,' he added reassuringly. 'You've laid the ground for a friendship. He can't be an easy man to get to know.'

Celia was comforted by his words. 'It's uphill all the way. I deserve a medal every time I get him to open his mouth.'

Larsen picked up his clipboard. 'You'll take it in stages, obviously.'

Celia looked questioningly at both men. 'How am I supposed to acquire this information? I can't keep going round with Residents Association papers.'

'Perhaps you could form a closer liaison,' suggested Larsen.

Celia felt a moment of alarm. 'What?'

There was a short silence. If she had interpreted his meaning correctly . . .

'An attachment,' said Larsen, looking up from his notes. 'Closer contact.'

'You mean . . . sleep with him?'

Larsen fastened his eyes on her, his fleshless face devoid of expression.

'The relationship should take a natural course.'

Celia stiffened. She knew enough of the department's workings not to feel outraged that they should expect her to agree to such a proposition: in their terms it was an expedient. Even so, it would be unwise to tell them what had gone on between her and Scannell. She decided to make excuses.

'He's got a girlfriend. I saw her when I called at his flat.'

She noticed Greengross glance at Larsen, who replied

matter-of-factly: 'We've had him under temporary surveillance. She's not important.'

Celia noted the point and seized on it. 'If he has casual women, that's even worse. What if I contracted something embarrassing?'

'Should the relationship become intimate, you would of course receive regular medical attention.'

'How generous.'

Celia watched as Greengross turned to Larsen and took an envelope file from his drawer.

'Would you like me to . . .'

Larsen nodded. Greengross opened the file and picked up the top sheet of paper. Celia waited as he scanned the typewritten details. After a few moments he looked up.

'You were recently promoted – to grade seven, I believe.'

'Yes.'

'It has been suggested you should be promoted to grade five. You'll also be realigned from desk officer to field officer status.'

Celia tried to quell a wave of panic. She'd only agreed to carry out the assignment because they'd said it wouldn't involve her in extra work. Now they were suggesting something much deeper. She wasn't ready for it. She wouldn't be able to carry it through, not without Scannell knowing.

'I can't be a field officer,' she told them. 'I've got my son to look after. I need the routine.'

'Your routine needn't change drastically,' said Larsen. 'You would be expected to maintain your daily pattern.'

'Do you mean I can keep the job I've got?'

'For a period we'd like you to transfer to the main office at Marsham Street . . . to reinforce your cover. Your workload will, in fact, be reduced.'

Celia was thinking fast. Perhaps she was over-reacting. If she didn't have to actually do anything, there was nothing to lose. Her feelings for Scannell didn't come into it; she could tell Larsen and Greengross what she liked.

'When would my pay rise take effect?' she asked.

Larsen, it seemed, had it all worked out. 'It would be backdated to the point when the assignment began. We don't see it lasting more than a few weeks. After that, you can transfer back to your present job. You'll be entitled to keep the higher grading and salary.'

Greengross looked enquiringly at his colleague. 'Did I understand that a clothing allowance would be granted during the period of the assignment?'

'That's correct . . . Within defined limits.'

'Judging by what you want me to do, I'll only need underwear,' Celia observed drily.

Larsen remained unruffled. 'You'll be entitled to a monthly subvention.'

Celia was surprised at what they were prepared to give her, and wondered how far they could be pushed.

'What about a car allowance?' she asked. 'Don't field agents get that?'

Larsen's mouth was compacted. Making a note on his clipboard, he circled it for prominence. He was showing impatience.

'Arrangements could be made,' he said.

Celia turned to Greengross. 'Would my salary be on grade five medium band, or top?'

Greengross hesitated. 'We envisaged medium. Given the inexperience factor . . .'

'I might be prepared to do it, if it was top.'

Larsen's eyes became calculating slits. 'Do we understand that you have agreed to undertake the assignment?'

'Possibly.'

'I'll arrange for your coding to be changed,' said Greengross. 'There'll be some minor form-filling, but that can be done in due course.'

'You can carry on working here for the time being,' Larsen concluded. 'Meanwhile, we'll organize some special instruction in surveillance.'

13

As soon as Scannell stepped out of the customs gate at Frankfurt Airport he was aware that he was being followed. It wasn't that his 'watcher' was inherently gauche or unpractised; just that, over the years, Scannell's eyes and brain had become finely tuned sensors, and the man in the green corduroy car-jacket waiting at the counter of the currency exchange bureau had held his gaze for half a second too long.

This initial alert was backed up by the fact that, as Scannell went through the airport's main entrance to the taxi rank, he saw the man get into a red Mercedes that had drawn up at the kerb by a bus-point some distance away. He glimpsed the car once more on the short run along the autobahn into the city centre, then lost sight of it amid the dispersing traffic. All the same, he had taken a mental snapshot of the man in readiness for the next time he saw him. As Scannell was planning to stay in the city until Friday, and it was now only Monday evening, he was sure there would be a next time.

The following morning he made a telephone call from his hotel room, and found that the man he wanted to contact was due home in the early afternoon.

'I'll come then, if that's okay,' he told the man's wife. He spoke in faltering German, which had been his third language at university.

'Are you English?' the woman asked, switching the conversation into Scannell's ostensible mother tongue.

'Yes. I flew over from London last night.'

Scannell gave her his name and that of the news agency.

'You're a reporter?' the woman said. 'You know he never gives comments to the press.'

'This is for general research. I'll explain when I see him.'

Scannell rang off and spent some time at the tourist office gathering maps of the city and information on public transport services. It was the first thing he did whenever he arrived in a foreign country. Although he had visited West Germany frequently, and Frankfurt more than once, he wasn't so familiar with its tram and underground systems that he could afford to be careless. One could never tell when a quick departure might have to be made.

After lunching at a modest restaurant off the Theaterplatz, he set off on a lengthy walk across the Eiserner Steg. The address he was going to had been given to him by one of Hermann's associates in the European Anti-Nuclear Organization. The name of the contact had been one of several on a list. Now he would find out how much Hermann had really known.

The house, across the River Main from the city centre, was built on four storeys – not a cheap property. It was set back from the road. An ageing Peugeot was parked outside, next to an even older Volkswagen Beetle. Scannell climbed the steps to the front door. An attractive woman in her mid-forties answered it.

'Frau Kepler?'

'Yes.'

'I phoned this morning. My name's . . .'

The woman nodded with slight impatience. 'My husband's expecting you. You *are* the reporter?'

'That's right.'

She showed him into a spacious hall. The house was even more substantial inside than it appeared from the street.

'Please, wait here a moment.'

The woman went through to a back room. She fetched her husband, whose tall frame caused him to stoop as he came through the doorway. He was dressed in an old jumper and ill-fitting jeans. His wife made a hurried excuse and left the two men together. Kepler extended his hand.

'You wanted to see me.'

'Yes . . . it's about some research I'm doing. Some people in London gave me your name.'

Kepler's forehead creased. 'People? . . . In London?'

'Friends of someone called Jack Hermann.'

'Hermann?' Kepler eyed Scannell warily.

'You know what happened to him?'

'Yes . . . I heard.'

'That's part of the reason I want to talk to you.'

Kepler, it turned out, was a man of some caution. Despite his casual appearance, his attention to detail was far from sloppy. Before agreeing to discuss anything with Scannell, he wanted to see his official identification. A National Union of Journalists press card wasn't sufficient on its own; Kepler only accepted its authenticity when it was backed up by credit cards in the same name.

He showed Scannell through to a large study. The room was untidy, but in a busy, rather than disorganized, way. The clutter was mainly papers and books, presumably related to Kepler's work as a lecturer in history at a Hochschule. What struck Scannell most of all about the room was that one wall was lined with filing cabinets, each one with its drawers clearly categorized. This appealed to his own sense of orderliness, and he found himself warming to Kepler after the unpromising reception. Kepler, now that he had satisfied himself over Scannell's identity, also seemed to be more responsive. He picked up two dirty mugs from among the papers on a table.

'I'll just get these washed up. Coffee?'

'Thanks.'

A minute or two later he returned, and plugged in a battered electric kettle on top of a filing cabinet. 'I keep this in here . . . the kitchen's on the next flight up. And so,' he said, smiling, 'the last vestige of exercise disappears.' While he waited for the kettle to boil, he went on: 'You mentioned Hermann. Did you speak to him after his arrest?'

87

'No. He was held incommunicado. They charged him under the Official Secrets Act.'

'Meaning what?'

'No one could get to him. In those cases, the courts do what they like . . . they just cite national security.'

'I thought Britain was supposed to be a democracy.'

'It is, when it suits the people who run it.'

Kepler poured the coffees and pulled up a second chair to the desk. The two men sat down.

'Still,' Kepler said, 'I'm sure you haven't come all this way to discuss the finer points of the British judicial system.'

'No. Actually, I'm after your help.' Scannell hesitated, wondering how much he ought to say. In the end, he decided that he might as well be as open as possible. It was often the best way of achieving results. 'Do you know what Hermann was working on at the time of his arrest?'

'No. Should I?'

'He was collating information. I was supposed to have met him the day before he was arrested . . . I met with an accident instead.'

'An accident?' Kepler looked concerned. 'Were you hurt?'

'No, not badly.' Scannell paused. 'Hermann is thought to have got names together . . . evidence that the anti-nuclear movement has been penetrated by DI5.'

'Our organization?'

'The British section, certainly. It may have gone further . . . I don't know.'

Kepler frowned. 'How do you suppose I can help on that?'

Scannell eyed Kepler directly. Now was the testing moment.

'I've been told it was you who gave him the names in the first place.'

There was a long silence.

'Who told you that?'

'Hermann's friends. They said you'd provided him with his source material.'

Kepler scrutinized Scannell intently. 'And if I did?'

'I was hoping you might be able to help me in the same way.'

After some thought, Kepler said: 'Tell me, Mr Scannell, do you believe in nuclear disarmament, or is it something you just happen to write about for a living?'

Scannell waited before answering. 'I suppose you could say both.'

'You have to understand that I'm not prepared to do anything that would simply give you a cheap story.'

Scannell considered how best he could tackle the man's obdurate stance. It would be no good lying to him; he would see through that at once.

'Obviously, if I get a story, then my agency will syndicate it to the newspapers. That's what they're in business for. A lot can be exposed, though. It won't do the organization any harm.'

'No? Telling the world it's riddled with infiltrators?'

Scannell weighed up the reply. Kepler had a point.

'It's better than letting things go on as they are. At the moment you're hamstrung. No one's co-operating. Everyone I've spoken to in the organization is paranoid.'

Kepler thought. 'First and foremost, you have to understand I'm a multilateralist. That's to say, I'm opposed to the nuclear policies both of Nato and the Warsaw Pact. Ideally, I'd like to see a full international treaty . . . the elimination of strategic and theatre weapons on both sides.'

'Isn't that a lot to hope for?'

'It is . . . which is why I'm prepared to work for a unilateral move – even if it's only a gesture.'

For half an hour or more, Scannell and Kepler talked. While the German seemed to have a depth of intellectual integrity, he was still reluctant to help. The trip was turning out to be a waste of time.

'Look,' said Scannell, becoming irritated by Kepler's stalling. 'Over in England a man was arrested because he tried to bring things out in the open. Now he's dead. He worked for more than a year to get the substantiation he needed – for information that you gave him. If nothing's done, then all of that work will have been worthless. Give it another six months – I guarantee, your organization will be broken.'

When Scannell had finished, Kepler contemplated what he'd said. Then he mentioned, rather oddly, that he'd grown up in the days of the Third Reich.

'A schoolfriend of mine once told me a secret,' he said. 'He had a grandfather living at the family home. The old man was half-Jewish. God knows how the boy had found out – it's possible, I suppose, that he'd heard his parents talking. I don't know why he told me, either. To be honest, I didn't know much about Jews. I suppose I thought they were sort of – I don't know – thieves, I guess. When my father came home on leave, I told him what the boy had said. Then, a couple of weeks later, he suddenly stopped coming to school.'

Kepler reached for a cigarette.

'It wasn't until I was much older . . . fifteen or sixteen . . . then I started to wonder about what had happened. You see, what I didn't realize at the time was the significance of the unit my father served with. He just happened to wear a black uniform with a silver badge.'

Kepler held the tips of his fingers together and looked almost challengingly at Scannell.

'He was an officer in the SS.'

Scannell's mouth was dry. The tissue at the sides of his throat seemed to have welded itself into a closed conduit. He said nothing.

'You can appreciate, Mr Scannell, why I do not readily dispense information.'

Scannell remained silent.

'If I were to let you have access to my files,' Kepler concluded, 'I would require an assurance that the material would be used for the sole purpose of uncovering the infil-tration network.'

Scannell nodded. 'I'll get the editor to put it in writing.'

Kepler sat thoughtfully, then stood up. 'Very well. It's a little late to start anything now. I suggest you come back in the morning. I'll make some time to go through the files with you.'

One of the men closed the door of the kitchen cupboard and looked slowly round the room. He had found nothing. Walking through to the living-room, he watched as his colleague ran his hands under the cushions of the arm-chairs.

'Anything?'

'No. You?'

'No. He's very good. Even if he is clean, you'd have thought there'd be something. The place is just too bloody clinical.'

'I know. There's no confidential stuff, for a start. All reporters get things leaked to them. Everything in his files is from an official release.'

When they had finished searching Scannell's kitchen and living-room, they went back to the study, which they had already inspected once. This time they concentrated on the furniture and cupboards rather than the files. When this task had been carried out, one of the men went through to the main bedroom and pulled the cardboard box from under the bed. He started to sift its contents.

'That's been done once. I saw it in the first report.'

'Then we'll do it again. It may be the only opportunity we'll get. He's expected back at the weekend.'

The two men itemized the contents of the box.

'Everything's here . . . birth certificate, driving-licence, expired passport . . . the lot.'

'All sound?'

'I reckon.'

The senior of the two men took a hand-radio from his pocket. He spoke to someone outside the flat.

'We shouldn't be much longer. Twenty minutes . . . half an hour.'

Finishing the cataloguing of the items in the box, the other man took out a handful of badges and school certificates. He read the citation on one of the certificates and looked up.

'Issued by Somerset County Council.'

'That's where he went to school before his family emigrated. Special Branch have made inquiries.'

'And . . . ?'

'Nothing. The names are on record. Otherwise everything's blank. No relatives . . . no old friends. One of his teachers was traced, but she couldn't remember him. She's pretty ancient . . . well into retirement.'

The junior of the two men pushed the box back under the bed and let the quilt fall. His colleague, in the meantime, took a small canvas envelope of tools from an attaché case and inspected a joint on one of the legs of the pine bed. He shone a pen-light into the joint, then held a microphone detector close to it. He listened to the series of clicks which speeded up the closer he held the instrument to the joint.

'It's still there . . . Still live.'

'What about the other one that was mentioned in the report?'

The men went out to the living-room. Against the inner wall was an antique cabinet with glass-fronted doors. Together, they eased it away from the wall.

'Steady,' said the senior man. 'There's porcelain in here. Some of it could be worth a bit.'

He took out the largest of three screwdrivers in the toolkit and gently prised back a small area of skirting-board behind the cabinet. When he shone the light in the gap, a silver disc glinted. Holding the detector close to the skirting-board, he again obtained a live reading. He put the tools away while his colleague stood looking at the gap behind the woodwork.

'Don't we know who installed them yet?'

'No. They're simple FM transmitters . . . Standard availability. All we know is that it wasn't us.'

'What's the range?'

'About a mile or so, I should think. A mobile receiver could pick up the transmissions – or someone in another flat.'

'What about one of the embassies? The East Europeans?'

'Could be. He's vulnerable to recruitment.'

The senior man bent down to push back the skirtingboard. When he stood up, his colleague shook his head in slight annoyance.

'I don't see why we were told to come back. There's nothing here that Fairweather doesn't already know about. It's a waste of time.'

'It's confirmation, if nothing else. Come on, let's get this cabinet back.'

As a final exercise, the men went through to the bathroom. They looked through a pile of laundered towels and also inspected the contents of a shaving-cabinet.

'What about the bath?'

The junior man removed the side panel. He knelt down and ran the beam of the pen-light across the floor and behind the water pipes.

'Just dust and cobwebs.'

He replaced the panel. Then, as he was standing up, one of the floor tiles close to the wall shifted under the pressure of his hand. For a moment, he thought nothing of it. The tile was properly grouted. None the less, being professionally inquisitive, he gave it a gentle push at one end. It rose a millimetre or two, and the grouting came up with it.

'Just a minute.' The man pressed his thumbnail into the grouting. 'This is putty.' He reached for one of the screwdrivers. Carefully, he scraped the putty from around the tile, which he then prised up. Underneath it was a small, folded sheet of notepaper. The man opened it and saw a list of names. He looked baffled, and handed it to his colleague.

'What do you think? Do they mean anything to you?'

The senior man studied the list perfunctorily, then took a closer look.

'Shit,' he said softly. 'At least two of these are Unit Nine personnel!'

Scannell switched off the videofilm on the television and sat for a moment in silence. He couldn't make up his mind what action to take. The man he'd first seen at the airport had been shadowing him all week. Whoever his controllers were, they had to be second-guessed. They either expected their man to be challenged or ignored. But which?

Finding his question impossible to answer, he directed his thoughts elsewhere. From the bar and restaurant downstairs, the sound of muffled laughter and conversation permeated the upper floors of the hotel. He considered phoning Celia, but replaced the receiver before dialling. There were things he had to tell her, but they could wait.

He poured a glass of schnapps from a bottle in the refrigerated drinks cabinet. On the coffee-table in front of him were the results of three days' arduous research. Two positive lines to follow up when he got back to London. Kepler's cuttings library had been good.

Kepler: presumably it was a common enough German name, but the man had turned out to be anything but ordinary. In the past three years, he had written and produced upwards of a dozen anti-nuclear pamphlets. For someone with a heavy lecturing schedule, it was an impressive output. His cuttings files had turned out to be more comprehensive than any Scannell had seen on an individual subject. They covered details of almost all aspects of the anti-nuclear movement since its early growth.

The strongest line to come up had been on a Dutchman named de Puydt. All the information was there in cuttings spanning a six-year period: his ties with West German environmentalist groups; a suspect move to Britain; questions asked about his role in the European Anti-Nuclear Organization. Although he was based in Amsterdam, there was material to suggest that he was working for the British and German intelligence networks as an *agent provocateur*. Among the key elements of this circumstantial evidence was the fact that he had avoided being charged on two separate occasions after being arrested for inciting violence at demonstrations in London and Bonn.

Then there were the cuttings on the case of a woman protester at the Molesworth missile base in the UK. Verification might prove difficult, but the pointers were clear: a child ordered into care after accusations of neglect; a conflicting paediatrician's report. It seemed to have been a clear attempt by the British government to score a propaganda point.

Scannell flicked through the photocopies of the cuttings with the intention of making further notes, but he was too exhausted to concentrate. He would be able to put the pieces together when he got back to London.

Reaching over to the dressing-table drawer, he took out his travel documents. He always checked them in advance of a flight. With West German emigration officials, it paid to be cautious.

Before he left Frankfurt, though, there was still the problem of the 'watcher' to be resolved. Twice he had spotted the man since the time at the airport: first in a restaurant on Berliner Strasse, and again at the Palmengarten. It was impossible to tell which service he worked for. He had spoken in flawless German to the waitress in the restaurant, which indicated that he might be a member of the country's BND. It wouldn't be the first time that Bonn had helped DI5 out. The man could, though, just as easily have been from the CIA's Central European division.

Scannell finished his schnapps and phoned room service for a meal. While he was waiting for it to arrive, he reached a decision. There was only one thing to do: flush the man out. It was always possible that he'd been planted as bait – that his controllers would be expecting a challenge.

As he checked through his passport and air ticket, he began to formulate a plan.

Celia's mind drifted through sleep to a wakefulness aggravated by petty fears. As always, the curtains of her bedroom were not quite closed, allowing an insipid orange light from the walkway below to delineate the objects in the room around her.

Somewhere in the distance she heard a car accelerate through traffic lights. Ever since her interview with Larsen and Greengross she had been sleeping badly and she was learning, at some half-aware level, to identify the sounds of the night.

She wondered what had woken her. Perhaps it was the dull ache in her bladder. Slipping on her dressing-gown, she pushed the bedroom door open. Something had caused her to feel alarmed, and she listened in the darkness.

The flat was silent.

She switched on the hall light and went through to the main room. Supper dishes on the table; a basket of washing waiting to be ironed. Again she had fallen prey to her own imagination.

She went to the bathroom, then back to bed. Now she was wide awake. It added to her discomfort that, with half the night to go, she might not be able to sleep any more. The worst thing was, in the morning she was supposed to concentrate. They'd already started her on the field surveillance course and she felt she'd hardly learnt anything. In fact, the instructions she'd been given had only added to her difficulties. The methods of orthodoxy had made her see how poorly she'd handled the assignment so far. She was convinced Scannell knew her true role.

She wondered what he made of her. Even now, it was

difficult to think of him by his first name, although she had started to use it in conversation. Familiarity somehow didn't suit him; he was strange and solitary. The problem that Larsen and Greengross failed to see was that he didn't *need* a woman.

She pulled the duvet round her shoulders and tried to close her mind, but she was soon staring at the digital green minutes on her bedside radio. Three-thirty, and the alarm was set for six-fifteen so that she could tidy the flat before going to work. Once again, Richard would have to put up with the mess.

The image recurred of Larsen and Greengross sitting across the desk. She didn't know them, obviously, not as people. Presumably, though, they went home to their families in the depths of the suburbs and didn't think about their grubby plan after they left the office each evening. It was left to her to live with the guilt and fear, the anxiety of betrayal.

She considered whether what she was doing did, in fact, amount to betrayal. Certainly, when she'd first met Scannell, she'd had no more feelings towards him than she had towards any man in the street. The problems had only arisen since she'd started to see him as she saw herself: a human being trying to come to terms with an isolated existence.

Switching on the bedside lamp, she picked up a magazine. She'd read a page before she realized she hadn't taken in a word.

What did Larsen and Greengross want her to do, for God's sake? Put bluntly, of course, they were suggesting she become a prostitute. Just because she'd already slept with Scannell, it didn't make their suggestion any the more acceptable. Her moral standards weren't any higher than the next person's, but she couldn't bring herself to approve of Larsen's and Greengross's attitude. Instead, she now had barriers of her own to cross, and the enforced complications had made her angry and perplexed. Would she be doing it for her own pleasure, or because it was a part of the job? At the moment, she had no answer.

She switched off the lamp and tried to salvage what was left of the night, but her brain was too active. What, after all, was Scannell supposed to have done? Why the department's concern? They hadn't told her yet, and she doubted they would.

On lying back down, she had subconsciously placed her hand between her legs, softly squeezing. As the skin began to moisten, she let her fingers drift inwards and circle slowly. The warm, familiar waves began, and she was at last able to relax. She had slept alone for so long now that the actions were habitual; she scarcely realized what she was doing.

By 9.30 in the morning, the flower-sellers in the subway below the Hauptwache had set up their stalls and the street musicians were establishing their territories for the day.

Scannell went to a travel agency in the underground shopping complex and changed the time of his flight, moving it forward by twenty-four hours to six o'clock that same evening. After that, he went to the nearby Kaufhof department store and bought a suitcase and a selection of cheap clothes from an oddments counter. Finally, when he got back to his hotel, he paid his bill and made a call from the reception desk to book a room for two nights in the nearby town of Bad Homburg. He knew his incongruous actions would raise the interest of any surveillance agent.

At 3 P.M. he telephoned from his room for a taxi, with the instruction that it should come to the hotel's rear entrance. He sent a porter down with the new suitcase, packed with his own clothes, and gave him money to cover the cost of delivering it to the hotel in Bad Homburg.

Scannell then packed the oddments of clothing into the suitcase he had brought with him from London and took a taxi to the main station.

As he paid off the driver, he looked at his watch. The

time was just gone four. Still an hour before his flight check-in. He was in no hurry; the S-bahn trains ran regularly to the airport.

He had a beer in the station bar, all the while keeping a lookout for his tail. So far, it seemed, he'd failed to show up.

It wasn't until Scannell was at the airport, in the queue at the Lufthansa desk, that the man finally appeared. This time he was wearing an open navy blue coat over a suit, and was carrying a brown leather briefcase. He could have been any travelling businessman.

Scannell handed in his suitcase for weighing and collected a boarding card. There was still almost half an hour before he needed to go to the passport desk. He picked up his shoulderbag and went for a coffee, leaving the man concentrating on the flight departures board.

When Scannell walked back through the hall on his way to the departures gate, the man had moved. Now he was at a magazine counter. It was still impossible to tell who he worked for. None of the services had particular trademarks for surveillance techniques at field operative level. Whoever his employers were though, the man looked as though he could handle himself.

Involuntarily, Scannell's body-frame tightened under the flow of adrenalin. At such times, a few moments of preparation could mean the difference between life and death. Unzipping a side pocket of his shoulderbag, his fingers felt for a penknife that he'd bought along with the clothes at the Kaufhof. With a minimum of sharpening, its short blade had been turned into a lethal instrument. Improvisation was a key to his profession. It was surprising how many different types of weapon could be carried, even at such high-security establishments as an international airport, although he knew, had he wanted to try, that he would never have been able to get it past the checkpoint.

Several people were in the queue to show their passports,

and Scannell used the time for re-focusing on the details of his plan. The man had moved again and was now sitting in a distant rest area. He was reading a book, the briefcase at his feet. The element of surprise would give Scannell an edge of a second or two, that was all. His palms were sweating and there was a hollow feeling in his stomach. He didn't know whether the man was carrying a gun, although he supposed that, if he was, he would be under instructions not to use it; not in such a public place. Still, you could never tell how people would react if they panicked, and the man would not be expecting the tables to turn so suddenly.

The queue moved forward. Scannell took his passport from the shoulderbag and held it open for the controller to inspect. He glimpsed the lean-faced photograph of himself which had been taken six years earlier, soon after he had joined the agency. The dark hair, then longish over the ears, showed no traces of the grey that was now creeping up from the temples. Definitely, in the intervening years there had been a perceptible ageing, although, even then, his eyes had harboured a certain worried look. It had probably been with him since the day he was recruited.

'*Pass, bitte.*'

The controller's hand was held out. Scannell pushed his passport across the desktop. As always, when travelling, this was his moment of greatest anxiety. Although the document was perfect, and he had used it scores of times, the thought was never far away that some abnormality would be spotted and he would be called into a back room where interrogation would begin.

After a glance at the photograph and a cursory flip through the pages, the controller handed the passport back. With inner relief, Scannell took it and moved along with the queue. Only a few steps to go and he would be into the security zone, virtually committed to going on the flight.

But that wasn't part of his plan.

By turning his head a fraction, he was able to steal a glance at the man still supposedly engrossed in his book. Scannell slipped his passport back into his shoulderbag. Then, as though suddenly realizing he had lost something, he moved to one side of the queue and began to rummage through the bag. Seconds later he left the queue and walked hastily away across the hall. Behind him he sensed that the man would be getting to his feet, but it was no time to turn and see.

Scannell sharpened his step, ignoring the porters who crossed his path with trolleys. On the far side of the hall was an exit leading to a car park. He headed towards it, his pace increasing all the time. The doors opened automatically as he reached them. If the man had followed him, he would be able to see clearly where he had gone.

As soon as Scannell was outside, he started running. He looked round now. Sure enough, through the doors, he could see the man hurrying across the hall after him. Going up a ramp, Scannell ran into a parking area, but instead of continuing up to the next floor as might have been expected, he ducked behind the nearest car.

He listened, breathless, his heart beating unpleasantly fast. He clicked open the penknife and put it in his jacket pocket, familiarizing himself with the position of the handle. Soon he heard the sound of footsteps coming up the ramp. The man was running too. Scannell edged forward, flexing his hands. He was squatting on his haunches, ready to spring.

The man caught sight of him a second before he drew level with the car. At once, he veered away, but Scannell was already on his feet. As the man turned, Scannell's arms snapped round his neck and waist. A moment later, Scannell lifted his right foot and hooked it round the man's ankles, bringing him to the ground. Locked together in their own momentum, they sprawled across the concrete, each grappling for a hand-hold on the other.

Scannell felt fingers gouging at his face, but there was

little strength in them. The man had been caught off-guard, and his reactions lacked co-ordination. In a single movement, Scannell twisted the man's neck upwards and forced his arm behind his back. It was a simple but effective unarmed combat tactic which had surfaced from somewhere in the text-book implanted in his mind. As the limb was levered back, the man cried out. Scannell paid no attention, but dragged him between two cars, out of view from anyone walking or driving past.

Laying him against a concrete wall, he jammed his knee into his throat.

'Who are you with? Who sent you?'

The man struggled to free himself, but Scannell's knee was secure. As soon as the man moved, the knee pressed harder.

'Are you with the BND?'

The man's face was deepening in colour; his eyes glazing. He shook his head.

'*Kein Englisch . . . Kein Englisch!*'

Scannell reached into his pocket.

'Then I'll give you a quick lesson in linguistics.' He pulled out the knife and held the blade close to the man's face. 'I want to know who you're working for and why you've been following me.'

There was a lull as Scannell waited for the man to answer. He pressed the point of the knife upwards into the soft flesh under the left eye.

'Come on . . . *who?*'

It would only have taken a second or two before the man was forced to provide answers but, at that moment, the sound of a car mounting the ramp caused Scannell impulsively to look up. It was a crucial lapse of concentration. Even as Scannell's head turned, the man brought his right hand up in an arc, the blow cutting across Scannell's neck, stunning him briefly. The knife went spinning across the floor. A second, conclusive blow to the stomach made

Scannell lurch forward and, before he could recover, the man was on his feet and running.

Scannell was soon after him, but there was a gap between them of twenty or thirty metres. The man ran out of the garage and round the front of the airport building, then through an entrance which took him into a waiting-hall. By the time Scannell came through the doors, the man was already on his way to an adjoining hall which led down to the S-bahn. People barely gave him a second glance; most of them probably thought he was rushing to catch a train.

As Scannell came through to the second waiting-hall, he glimpsed the man on an escalator leading down to the S-bahn, but when he reached the lower level, his quarry had disappeared.

Scannell looked around. The platforms were brightly lit and spacious. People were waiting for the train into the city, and Scannell passed among them, all the time glancing back at the escalators to make sure the man didn't try to elude him from behind.

Then a wave of cool air passed along the platform: a train was approaching through the tunnel. As it pulled up and its doors opened, Scannell stood and waited, looking up and down the platform, but he saw nothing. It wasn't until the train's doors were about to close that a figure emerged from behind a stairway. The man sprinted across the platform and into one of the last carriages. Scannell whipped round and also made a dash for the train. The doors were already closing, but he managed to hold them open so he could squeeze through. He almost fell into the carriage, and apologized to a woman whose baggage he had scattered. After he had helped her pick up the cases, he leaned against a seat, catching his breath.

At least he had time to think. It occurred to him that, being at the front of the train, he had one supreme advantage. When it pulled into Frankfurt's main station, the man would have to walk past him. Although the train was scheduled to stop at intermediate stations, these presented no problem. All Scannell had to do was look out of the open doors and make sure the man didn't try to get off.

When, a quarter of an hour later, the train drew in at the terminus, Scannell lingered on board, waiting for the man to come past. He kept a lookout for the navy blue coat, his eyes focusing intently on the dozens of passengers as they milled up the platform.

It was the fixed image of the man which nearly cost Scannell his efforts. Among the crowds, the man almost passed unnoticed. He had taken off his coat, and his suit was undistinguishable from all the others. It was only a clumsy movement he made in attempting to mingle with a group of teachers in a school party that gave him away.

Scannell immediately jumped off the train and started to push his way through the crowds. The man had seen him and had broken into a run. He was soon close to the exit point and now had the advantage over Scannell. Because of the automatic ticket system, there were no barriers, and he raced through to the main concourse of the station with Scannell bobbing and weaving as he strove to keep him in sight. The man headed down the bank of escalators which led to an underground precinct.

Scannell chased the man past delicatessens and magazine stands. Still he showed no signs of flagging. At the far end of the precinct there were a number of exits. The man took the one which led up to Baseler Strasse where the main tramlines interconnected. Scannell followed him up. The pavement was wet after a downpour, reflecting the glow of the street lamps.

Glancing round at Scannell, the man hesitated, as though wondering whether he could brazen out a confrontation. Instantly, he seemed to change his mind and looked at the road, weighing up his prospects of cutting across. As Scannell approached him, he made his decision and rushed out into the traffic.

The street was wide and, in the illuminated darkness, the man dodged the cars as though he were performing stunts in some maniacal circus. For a time, it looked to Scannell as though he might make it to the far side. A car seemed to brush him, but it swerved into an inner lane and he continued his erratic course. The trams, though, set in their rails, had no way of changing direction. The one which came round the corner from Münchener Strasse could do nothing more than give a peremptory clang of its bell as the driver applied the brakes. The wheels screeched on the wet metal and the overhead cables, suddenly tightening, sang like a whiplash. Twisting round, the man was caught for a second in the narrow beam of the tram's headlights before he was folded under its chassis.

Scannell waited as a crowd gathered round the body, then he disappeared down into the brash glare of the precinct.

14

From the far side of the bar on Amsterdam's Leidseplein, the man from the surveillance agency watched as de Puydt bought drinks for himself and his contact. They were too far away for him to catch their conversation – or to tell whether they were speaking in Dutch or English – but their seriousness indicated they were discussing business.

Ordering a drink for himself, the man from the agency placed a packet of cigarettes and a box of matches on the bar. For some minutes he continued watching the two men, who remained unaware of his interest.

De Puydt, who looked to be in his early thirties, was carrying a leather holdall. During the course of the conversation, he reached into it and handed a document to his contact. The action was swift and discreet. To the surveillance agent's professional eye, it showed a rehearsed coolness. As the document changed hands, the agent reached for the cigarette packet. He toyed with it as if he were about to take out a cigarette, then, as though changing his mind, put it in his pocket. The operation was so well executed that even the barman, who was standing only a few steps away, could have had no idea that a series of photographs had been taken.

In the normal way, the agent had little use for sophisticated gadgetry beyond a pocket cassette recorder. The camera concealed in the cigarette box – a 35mm Tessina subminiature – was his only other concession. He had adapted it so it could be used without being removed from the box.

About five minutes later, de Puydt left the bar, but the agent didn't follow him. He guessed from the man's pattern of movements over the last week that he would be heading for the Jordaan district in the north-west of the city where he had a houseboat out beyond the Prinsengracht. There was little point in repeating the surveillance trip; the other man had now become the focus of interest.

After another drink, the contact left the bar. The agent followed him out by a side door. As tailing operations went, it was routine. There were plenty of people on the street up to the flower market, and numerous shop doorways to provide cover. The problem came when the man decided to flag a taxi that was heading back to the rank at the Central Station. As the vehicle pulled into the kerb, the agent quickly walked towards it, making a mental note of its licence number. The contact climbed in and, as the taxi pulled away, the agent entered its number in a notebook.

From his experience of cab drivers, he didn't think it would cost him too much to find out where the passenger had been dropped off. In any case, with the news agency in London paying the bill, there was always room for a little creative balancing of expenses.

15

Scannell had seen a good deal of Celia since his return from Frankfurt. The enforced absence had given him time to think; to map out how far he was prepared to let the relationship go. When he'd got back, he'd told her there could be nothing permanent. She'd understood that.

One thing that had kept them becoming too close was Richard. The boy's moods were difficult to tolerate. There had been no more blatant displays of hostility, but the underlying resentment was still evident. Most of the time, Scannell only went to the apartment when he knew the boy was likely not to be there. Celia also seemed to prefer it that way.

The change occurred unexpectedly. On arriving home from work one evening, Scannell had gone down to Celia's thinking that Richard would be out. It was a Friday, when the boy normally went to a sports club. This time, however, he had returned late from school after taking part in a chess tournament. When Scannell came down, he had shut himself in his room.

'His team lost,' Celia said. 'I'll talk to him when he's stopped stewing.'

Richard emerged when supper had been prepared. For some minutes he ate in silence, then said: 'I played like a kid.'

Neither Celia nor Scannell spoke. Scannell knew how much the game meant to him. It was the only intellectual activity for which he showed any inclination. Towards the end of the meal, Scannell asked him what the problem had been.

The boy looked up. 'It's not worth discussing.'

Scannell had expected a churlish answer. This time though, instead of letting it ride, he found himself irritated by the childish petulance.

'What's the point of playing if you're not prepared to lose?'

Surprised at the response, the boy was silent for a moment, then replied: 'What do you know about it?'

'A little. I used to play – at university.'

'Congratulations.'

At this, Celia turned. 'Whatever you might feel like, you can at least be civil. Tom was only taking an interest . . .'

Scannell lifted his hand slightly from the table. 'Don't worry. Leave it.'

After the meal, Richard returned to his room. Some time later, he came out carrying a chess-board on which pieces were arranged. Without a word, he put it down on the coffee-table by the chair in which Scannell was sitting.

A minute or two later, after standing and watching the television, he said to Scannell: 'If you want to know – that's where he got me.'

Scannell studied the pattern of the game. 'Who had the last move?'

'Me . . . black.'

With Richard's guidance, Scannell worked back five or six moves.

'That one was weak,' he said, tapping a black bishop.

Richard sat in the chair opposite, and they replayed the game as far as the boy could remember it. Afterwards, they set up the board afresh. By that time, Celia had gone to her room to catch up on her typing work.

'Do you play a lot then?' Richard asked.

Scannell looked up. 'I used to . . . when I had more time.'

They constructed and analysed games for the rest of the evening, with Richard keeping notes of moves and formations. Scannell pointed out the worst of the boy's faults, demonstrating stronger variations.

'Look for a gain in tempo,' he advised. 'Force your opponent to waste moves.'

Towards the end of the evening, Celia sat with them.

'Where did you go to university?' she asked.

Scannell, his eyes still on the pieces, remained quiet, as though contemplating a tactical advance.

'What?' he said abstractedly. 'Oh – Brisbane.'

Celia showed surprise. 'Australia? I thought you must've gone to somewhere like Oxford or Cambridge.'

'I grew up in Australia. My parents emigrated.'

'Really? . . . When did you come back?'

'A few years ago.'

Scannell tried to be vague, but he didn't want to appear reluctant to answer. Her curiosity was natural enough.

'Did your parents come back as well?'

Scannell raised his head. 'My parents are dead.'

The conversation ended abruptly.

'I'm sorry. I didn't mean to pry.'

Scannell shrugged. 'It doesn't matter. It was a long time ago.'

16

It was 1.15; the contact was late. Scannell sat at a corner table in the City Pipe restaurant near St Paul's, waiting impatiently. The time had been clearly stipulated: one o'clock.

Folded on the table was a copy of the *Guardian*; Scannell was reading *The Times*. Both newspapers were there to identify him, and no one else at the surrounding tables was reading. At least the contact wouldn't be able to make a mistake.

Scannell was following instructions given in an anonymous letter which had been left the previous day at the news agency's reception desk. He had no idea who the contact could be.

As he sat at the table, his restlessness increased. The more he thought about it, the more concerned he became over the conspiratorial manner in which the meeting had been set up. Was it a trap – an elaborate plan by the authorities to compromise him? Would he be offered information, then arraigned under the Official Secrets Act? It had happened to Hermann. Perhaps they were trying to do the same to him.

Lighting a cigarette, he inhaled deeply. The length of time it was taking to build up his dossier was imposing an unbearable strain on him. Household, who had eventually granted his request for more time to produce an investigative feature, was becoming impatient, while Estabrook was growing openly hostile at only having part of Scannell's services. The flow of material was erratic and often difficult to substantiate. During the past few days he had received word that a representative of the National Council for Civil Liberties had managed to communicate in prison with a former DI5 officer who had been represented at a secrets trial by the same law firm as had acted for Hermann. There had been a suggestion that both men might have been legally manipulated but, now that Hermann was dead, that would be impossible to prove.

The most promising developments were still those that had arisen from the visit to Frankfurt. Apart from evidence he'd elicited from a social worker in Cambridge over the decision to take one of the Molesworth protester's babies into care, he was also making headway with another lead. The private surveillance agency that he'd hired in The Hague to keep a watch on de Puydt had come up with some promising results, although further corroboration was needed.

A waitress came up to the table and asked him if he wanted to order.

'In five minutes,' he said. 'I'm expecting somebody.'

He asked for an orange juice.

A short while later, he looked up from his newspaper as a man carrying a briefcase came down the basement steps. There was a wariness about him, an alert look. Scannell continued reading as the man entered the restaurant and hung up his coat. Then, out of the corner of his eye, he watched as the man approached the table. It had to be him.

'Mr Scannell?'

Scannell looked up and closed the paper. He nodded, not knowing what to expect.

'Do you mind if I sit down?'

'Go ahead.'

The politeness, the bearing: the man had to be in a position of authority.

Whymark put his briefcase under the table. When the waitress came, he asked for a large whisky.

'I apologize for these absurd arrangements,' he said to Scannell. 'It had to be done.'

Scannell nodded. His mind was working fast to try to categorize the man. Was he in business? A partner in a professional firm? A DI5 plant? Any of the options was possible.

The waitress came with Whymark's whisky and took their orders for the meal.

'What did you want to see me about?' said Scannell.

Whymark was slow to answer. 'It's a little . . . difficult.'

Scannell studied the face across the table: mild-mannered, but showing deep disquiet. There was a hint of deviousness in the eyes, or it may have been caution. In any case, Scannell was careful not to drop his guard.

'Do you have information?'

Whymark hesitated. 'In a manner of speaking.'

'Are you from the NCCL?'

It was a spontaneous guess on Scannell's part. The man looked puzzled.

'I'm sorry?'

'The National Council for Civil Liberties. Are you a representative?'

'Oh,' said Whymark. 'No. Nothing like that.'

He drank his whisky quickly. Scannell presumed he was trying to settle his nerves.

'Where do you work?' Scannell asked.

'I'm an official.'

'An official what?'

'Just an official.'

Scannell's alarm bells rang, and he decided to let the man do the running. Throughout the first course, they spoke barely a word.

'What made you contact me?' Scannell asked eventually.

'I have some confidential information. It's paramount that I shouldn't be identified as the source.'

Scannell bristled. The request was all too familiar. It made him wonder again if he was being set up. Several times in the last few minutes he had glanced around to see if they were being watched from any of the other tables. His instinct said no, but you could never tell.

'Can you give me an idea what it's about?'

Again, the man retreated behind a curtain of banal conversation until Scannell's tolerance became stretched. The Cambridge woman had been tricky enough, but here was something else entirely.

Scannell put down his knife and fork. 'This is pointless. You ask to see me and then refuse to say anything.'

An uncomfortable silence followed, then Whymark said: 'This is all extremely difficult for me.'

'If you like, we can talk some other time.'

Whymark shook his head. 'No. You have to realize that I'm not doing this out of self-interest. I don't want any payment.'

'For what?'

'Talking.'

'You haven't talked.'

There was a rough edge to Scannell's remark, fully intentional. This time he wasn't going to be messed about.

After giving the observation some thought, Whymark said: 'I've been asked to do certain things . . . Things that I consider to be professionally and morally unsupportable.'

So that was it: a vengeance motive. Gradually, the mist was beginning to clear.

'Are you a civil servant?'

Whymark hesitated again, then nodded. 'Yes, I am.'

'You're taking a big risk.'

'I don't need to have that explained to me.'

Scannell wiped his mouth with his napkin, which he then folded in his lap. The guessing game, coupled with the man's slightly pompous manner, was becoming tiresome. Scannell rested an elbow on the table.

'Listen, I'm taking a risk as well. Before you go any further, if you want to leave now, we'll forget we've had this conversation.'

Whymark helped himself to more wine. 'I made my decision before I came.'

'In that case, you'll have to give me your name and position. I want some sort of verification about this information you say you're going to give me. I want to know it's authentic.'

Whymark shook his head. 'I'd prefer not to give you my name.'

'What's the information?'

'It's something I was involved in . . . a report.'

'Have you got it with you?'

Whymark gave him a challenging look. 'Would you guarantee not to publish any of it?'

'Why show it to me?'

'Journalists sometimes use things for . . . well, background purposes.'

Scannell considered the proposition. 'If we take this any further, you have to know how I work. I don't expose my sources, I don't publish sensitive information for the sake of sensationalism and I don't take unnecessary risks – particularly where other people are involved. But I don't give guarantees or undertakings that I might have to break . . . not if I think publication's in the public interest. Above all, I don't accept information unless I know it's genuine.'

The conversation continued over coffee, but Whymark refused to show Scannell the report, or to expand on why he had asked to see him. In the end, Scannell stood up and laid his napkin on the table.

'You'll have to excuse me. I've got work to do.'

Whymark got to his feet. 'No, I . . .'

'Contact me when you've decided what you want to tell me.'

Whymark motioned uneasily. 'I'm sorry . . . I've wasted your time.' Then he added: 'Please, sit down.'

There was something in his tone that made Scannell

believe he was at last breaking through. None the less, he decided to appear reluctant to be persuaded.

'I must see the report.'

The man nodded. 'I understand.'

Eventually, Scannell sat down. When he had caught the waitress's eye, he ordered more coffees. Whymark took a document from his briefcase.

'This is a detailed analysis . . . opinion poll research,' he began hesitantly. 'It was conducted over the second half of last year.' Opening the report, he turned to the back. 'The summary of the main points is here . . . the last two pages.'

Scannell quickly read the summary. 'You're in the Ministry of Defence?'

'Yes.' Whymark told Scannell his name. 'I'm a chief statistician. Until recently I was head of the opinion poll analysis unit in Secretariat N-160.'

Scannell was unable to mask his surprise. 'The holocaust desk?'

'Yes. It's acting as the central control section. All the smaller units have been wound up.'

This was a fact generally known to defence correspondents, but Scannell recognized the importance of letting someone talk when they were on home ground. Hopefully, Whymark would soon get on to more important details. It was a basic journalistic skill: applied psychology.

'Why were they wound up?'

'Cosmetic changes. The government wants a less visible propaganda profile. One presumes they don't want to seem hysterical . . . not in the run-up to an election.'

Now the man was starting to go beneath the surface.

'Did you write this report?'

'I directed the research and analysis.'

'Is it scheduled for publication?'

'No. It's been superseded.'

While they were speaking, Scannell leafed through the document. It was typical Whitehall format.

'Because of its damaging conclusions?' he said.

Before replying, Whymark studied Scannell with suspicion, as though trying to gauge the effect of what was being said.

'I was told to doctor the results. I did, in fact . . . at least, to an extent. It wasn't enough for them. I refused to go any further, and that was that. End of career.'

As he was speaking, the man showed signs of distress. He had clearly been hit hard.

'You were sacked?'

'It's a question of semantics. They prefer to call it re-deployed.'

Whymark brought out a second report from his briefcase, along with a file of newspaper cuttings. 'This is what I was instructed to produce.' He pushed the report across the table. 'The recommendations are on the last page.'

'The cuttings . . . What are they for?'

'Articles the newspapers produced, based on the report. It was re-drafted in days. The statistical base is completely spurious.'

Scannell picked up the report and looked at it with interest. 'I wrote it up last week for our newswire service. It got wide press coverage.'

'You'll see it's completely different to the original draft. It's outrageous. No professional analyst could be a party to that.'

Scannell sat back and stirred his coffee. 'Is that why you decided to seek contact with the press?'

'It's one reason.'

'What are the others?'

Scannell could see that Whymark was again becoming edgy.

'I can't tell you that,' he replied.

'So what do you expect me to do?'

'I don't know. Publish a story showing . . .'

Scannell sat forward.

117

'. . . Showing what? That a Defence Ministry official was told to doctor an analysis as a political expedient? It happens every week.'

'It's symptomatic of the manipulation of the Civil Service,' argued Whymark. 'I haven't spent the best part of my life working up to become a political puppet!'

'So you're pushing a story because you've got a grievance.'

'Of course I've got a grievance! I was removed from my job because I refused to compromise my integrity.'

The conversation died as the waitress approached with the bill. Scannell wrote a cheque.

'What's the rest of the story?' he asked when she had gone.

Whymark shook his head. 'It's too sensitive.'

Scannell chewed his lip. He knew he'd gained control. It was time to drive the stake home.

'You've given me some nice material here. What if I decide to use it? You'll be instantly pinpointed as the leak.'

Even as he said it, Scannell wondered if he'd pushed him too far. He saw Whymark's jaw tighten.

'Is that a threat?'

'It's a statement of fact. You've already put yourself on the line by coming to see me. If you want me to do anything worth while, then let's start talking sensibly.'

There was further procrastination, further evidence of doubt. Scannell held on for some minutes, then made his irritation obvious by quickly draining his coffee cup. It was a bluff; crude and artless. None the less, it worked. Just as Scannell was about to get to his feet once again, Whymark said: 'I was the secretariat's liaison officer with DI5.'

For a moment, the flow of blood through Scannell's body stopped. Whymark was staring at him across the table.

'Now do you understand when I say things are sensitive?'

Scannell nodded. Easing himself back into his seat, he said: 'Tell me what you can.'

'The Defence Secretary made a speech last week. He

issued a report as well. It gave details of the political affiliations of members of the national executive of the European
Anti-Nuclear Organization. I was in charge of the analytical
research for that speech. I don't have to tell you where the
source material came from.'

Scannell reached for his cigarettes. 'They've got someone
inside the organization?'

'A prime source, in the main London office . . . and
others.'

'You refused to handle the information?'

'No. I argued that it was misguided propaganda. All the
connections were with legitimate organizations. It wasn't as
though there was a Kremlin plant.'

Scannell tried not to let himself be distracted by the irony
of the man's last remark. 'You said you weren't motivated
by self-interest.' He paused. 'Politics is as much self-interest
as anything.'

Whymark's frown deepened. 'I'm concerned about abuse
of power and manipulation of facts to defraud the electorate.
The organization's got its moderates . . . the department
knows that. That didn't matter, though. They were totally
ignored.'

Scannell tried to use Whymark's animated state to prise
loose more information. He took a long shot.

'This plant they've got inside the organization's headquarters . . . Do you know who it is? Can you give me a
name?'

Whymark said nothing. He looked at his watch, then put
the reports back in his briefcase.

'I can't say any more. I'll have to go.'

He stood up and thanked Scannell for the lunch.

'What about copies of the reports?' Scannell asked. 'Can
I have them?'

Whymark put on his coat. He looked worried and confused.

'I don't know. I need time . . . to think.'

17

Rodway faced Blom, the director of personnel vetting, across the long, polished table in the conference room at fourth-floor central. With its high ceiling and elegant olive-green drapes, the room gave an air of importance to any discussions conducted behind its doors. On the end wall, above the fireplace, hung a portrait of Sir David Petrie who was reputed to have used the room when, as director-general of the service during the Second World War, he had held weekly debriefing sessions for ministers. The early grey light from the window caught his face, stern and forbidding.

It wasn't difficult for Rodway to see how much the balance had tipped against him since he'd sat with Blom's staff representative in the same room on the morning the field agents had been suspended. If Rodway had ever regretted a decision, it was having allowed the vetting section access to the unit's operating schedules and documentation; all its innermost machinery. The move had opened the way for an alliance between Blom and Fairweather, and Rodway recognized that he had put himself under investigation that day along with his agents. Now that the inquiry had come full circle, the result would be as crucial to his own professional future as to theirs.

'I thought it would be advisable for us to talk before we sent for them,' said Blom.

Rodway nodded, and in businesslike fashion, said: 'There are a number of issues we need to discuss.'

Blom looked up from the report on the table. 'Indeed.'

This time Rodway kept his silence. He just wanted Blom to announce his recommendations, to get the meeting over with. It was peculiar, the mixture of regard and distrust he felt for the man. He was certainly professional, particularly in the way he'd managed to keep the outcome of the inquiry under wraps. There hadn't been a single leak, not even in B Branch, where internal gossip seeped through to the drains. But he had a reputation for being 'difficult', and it was a fact that staff turnover in the section was among the highest in the non-operational divisions. Strictly speaking, Blom was a grade lower than himself in the departmental hierarchy, but given the section's wide powers, there was little to be gained in trying to exert authority over him.

Apart from a copy of the inquiry's findings, Blom also had in front of him a sheet of paper which he was studying carefully. At last, passing it across the table, he said: 'This was found in Scannell's flat.'

Rodway looked at the list of names. He found it difficult to believe what he was seeing.

'Who by?'

'Two of our staff attached to Special Branch.'

'Is it the original?'

'No, a copy. It was passed on to my liaison officer.'

'I take it the original was left in place?'

'Yes, for obvious reasons. Protective Security are stepping up their surveillance.'

Rodway looked at the list again and placed it on the table. Two Unit Nine personnel. If Scannell was getting that close, Fairweather had every right to be concerned.

'What do you suggest we do?'

'They'll have to be withdrawn. Even if Scannell's got no substantiation, it would be reckless to keep them active.'

Rodway's mouth creased. 'I didn't realize he knew as much as this. Which contact did he get the names from?'

'We don't know. He's got a whole range. It might have been any one of them.' Blom's eyes locked on Rodway. 'He's a threat, John.'

'We're doing all we can.'

'The Americans had someone watching him in Frankfurt. They wanted to test his response.'

Rodway nodded. Blom's sources of information were even better than he had thought.

'It was a pity,' Rodway remarked. 'They lost a good man.'

'There have been too many mistakes. First the accident, then Hermann . . . now this. The West German police have been instructed not to ask questions.'

Rodway's troubled look stayed with him. Blom was toying with a pencil, an irritating habit.

'Hermann was suicide,' Rodway said. 'No one could have foreseen that.'

'He was pushed too hard.'

'Tell that to Fairweather. He was responsible for the interrogation.'

Blom sorted silently through the papers. Eventually he came to a point of reference.

'Special Branch have been conducting preliminary inquiries into Scannell's background. You were aware of that, of course?'

'I was.'

Rodway declined to add that he had only found out about the investigations by chance at a meeting with a Special Branch commander.

'It seems he spent part of his childhood in Somerset,' said Blom.

'Yes, I understand his parents emigrated to Australia.'

Rodway had felt obliged to offer his own information to counter Blom's one-upmanship. However, Blom chose to ignore it.

'The officers managed to track down one or two people who remembered the family. The parents hadn't kept in touch with anyone. There are no known relatives in this country.'

'I believe there are no contact addresses in Australia either.'

Blom raised his eyes. 'No. It looks as though Special Branch will be putting in a request to extend the inquiries there.'

This intention disturbed Rodway. While such an investigation could prove useful, it would be expensive, and the funds would have to come from the Unit Nine budget. He voiced his doubts, and Blom changed the subject.

'I've read your report on the intelligence coming through from the European Anti-Nuclear Organization. I think you ought to apply for phone taps. It would be possible to make a case to the Home Office on grounds of national security.'

Rodway nodded his agreement. 'A request has been made from this office.'

He noticed Blom's eyes narrow. There was a short silence, then Blom reached for the report.

'I presented this to Fairweather earlier in the week. He's endorsed the recommendations. I'm afraid the news might not be what you wanted.'

Rodway sensed a stillness in the room. Blom seemed to be deliberately prolonging the suspense.

'The agents will have to face full disciplinary proceedings.'

Rodway sat unmoved. It took a moment for the blow to make its full impact. Even now, he could hear Fairweather promising that no such action would be taken. Given the agents' own admissions, it would be impossible for them to ride it out.

'Has a date for the hearing been set?'

'Fairweather wants it out of the way as quickly as possible. They'll remain under suspension.'

There was little to be achieved by discussing the recommendations. Rodway now had only one course of action open to him: if Unit Nine was to be rehabilitated in the eyes of the branch controllers, he had to show that it could act fast and effectively. Scannell was the unit's prime target, and he had to be hit. What Rodway had in mind for the reporter was, in professional terms, the equivalent of a sentence of death.

18

The elegant offices on the Herengracht, once the private residences of Amsterdam's wealthiest merchants, were closing for the evening when Scannell met the freelance surveillance agent in a canalside café. The agent, Van Noort, had sought the meeting three days earlier in a phone call to Scannell's office.

'I traced the owner of the taxi,' he told him.

He had mentioned nothing in the call about de Puydt's exchange of material in the bar on Leidseplein. This was because Scannell, on hiring the agency, had given explicit instructions that the case should not be discussed over the phone – only face to face. It was an expensive arrangement for passing on information, so Scannell hoped that what Van Noort had to tell him was worth the cost of the trip, both in time and money.

'Did he tell you where he dropped the contact?' Scannell asked.

The agent nodded. 'It cost me a thousand guilders.' Raising his hand rather obtrusively, he beckoned a waiter. 'Here in Amsterdam, I'm afraid, nothing comes cheap.'

Scannell did some rapid mental arithmetic. The currency conversion, at the rate he'd been quoted on his arrival that afternoon at Schiphol Airport, worked out at nearly two hundred and fifty pounds. If it had been half that, he would have thought it outrageous.

Van Noort, however, gestured lightly, as though the amount was of no consequence. 'He asked for two thousand at first. I brought him down . . . fifty per cent.'

Scannell wondered what the response would be when he submitted the bill to the news agency's cashiers – always supposing, of course, that Household would sign it. While the editor had supported the request to engage the surveillance firm's services, the expenses wouldn't be limitless, particularly if they were coming out of Estabrook's newsdesk budget. Scannell reached for the glass of *jenever* that Van Noort had insisted on ordering.

'A thousand? They won't wear that.'

Van Noort gave a confident smile. He tapped a cigarette from a packet that he'd taken from his shirt pocket.

'Perhaps you need to think a little more imaginatively, Mr Scannell.'

He offered a cigarette across the table, but Scannell brought out his own. Van Noort's attitude had begun to rankle.

'I'm imagining,' said Scannell, 'and I don't like what I see.'

Not to be put off balance, Van Noort gave a throaty laugh as he lit his cigarette and exhaled the smoke through a wave of his hand. 'What did you want me to do – let him go? He knew I needed the information. He's in business . . . like you –' he motioned towards Scannell, then back towards himself, 'like me.'

Scannell glanced at him deprecatingly. 'Is that the sort of observation my company's paying for?'

Van Noort reached for his glass. He downed the gin in a single, well-practised swallow, then picked up a jug of beer that he had ordered with it.

'Before you criticize my methods, perhaps you'd care to know what he told me.'

Scannell nodded. 'We've paid enough for the privilege.'

If Van Noort saw the sarcasm in the remark, he let it ride.

'I got the address of the contact,' he told Scannell. 'He was staying at a hotel near the Westerkerk. A smart place . . . no expenses problems there.' Pausing for his barb to sink home, he took out a notebook and flipped one or two pages. 'Here –' he pointed to a name and spoke it slowly,

'Malc . . . olm Yardley. I'm sorry, my pronunciation . . .'

Scannell made a note of the name. 'And . . . ?'

Van Noort took another drink of beer, turning the glass slowly in his hand, as though it contained mysterious secrets.

'And what, Mr Scannell?'

'Did you find out anything more about him?'

Van Noort put down the glass and rested his cigarette in the corner of his mouth. The posture added to the slightly raffish image he seemed to like to project.

'I carried out a little additional research, yes.' He stopped and gazed across the table. His eyes held a trace of a smile, as though he were enjoying an elaborate game. 'This Yardley . . . he works at your Ministry of Defence in London, it seems.'

Scannell's attention increased. He made a further note. Despite his personal feelings about Van Noort, his estimation of the man's professional abilities had suddenly begun to rise. Perhaps he had been worth the money after all.

'That's very good.'

Van Noort nodded obligingly. 'Thank you, Mr Scannell.'

There was a short silence as Scannell compressed the spine of his notebook so it would lie flat on the table.

'You'd better tell me all you've found out. It could be useful.'

'Do you know –' Van Noort turned another page, 'something called Secretariat N-160?'

Scannell nodded. 'Yes, I've heard of it.'

'Yardley was transferred there – last year.'

'Where from, do you know?'

Van Noort turned back to the previous page of his notes. 'I have it here. Ah . . . research and development . . . administrative section.'

Scannell nodded his appreciation.

'Would you like me to follow it further?' Van Noort asked.

Scannell considered this. After some moments, he shook his head and put his notebook away.

'No. What you've got's fine. I think it's the company's intention to make a profit this year.'

Van Noort shrugged indifferently. 'Perhaps it's just as well. It could take time.'

Scannell was thinking fast, trying to recall the secretariat's line-up of personnel. The name of the contact wasn't known to him, but it would be a simple procedure to check him out. As for de Puydt, a more thorough search through Kepler's files could prove useful, but there was certainly enough material on him already to satisfy a libel lawyer that his role could be detailed in a story.

He was about to finish his drink and leave when Van Noort said: 'Would it interest you to know I've got pictures?'

'Pictures?'

'I had a camera.'

Now Scannell really was impressed. 'Are both men identifiable?'

Van Noort took from his jacket pocket an envelope containing three photographs. At first, Scannell's new-found regard began to evaporate. Two of the photographs were blurred because of camera-shake and were, on their own, useless. However, the third was much clearer. The lens had been held at an awkward tilt, so the picture sliced diagonally through the Defence Ministry official. His face, though, was clearly discernible and, what's more, de Puydt was fully in the frame. The camera had caught the two of them as the document was being handed over.

'They'll be added on to the bill,' Van Noort said blithely. 'An extra five hundred.'

'Guilders?'

Van Noort smiled. 'Yes, Mr Scannell . . . guilders.'

'I think we should be able to stretch to that,' Scannell agreed. He would have readily paid double – out of his own pocket. 'Where are the negatives?'

Van Noort held out the envelope. 'In here.'

Scannell checked. They were all there.

'Send the invoice to my agency. I'll make sure it goes through.'

Before leaving the café, they arranged a further meeting. Scannell asked for the surveillance level on de Puydt to be lowered, but for occasional checks to be made.

He chose to walk back along the canal to his hotel, enjoying the invigorating March air. Suddenly his feelings of personal failure over the progress of the story were beginning to lift. He liked cold evenings. Somewhere, he supposed, people still took troika rides through the snow.

When he got back to his hotel, he ordered a glass of beer from room service and spread the photographs on the dressing-table. Studying them closely, he let de Puydt's features stencil themselves on his memory. This was a man he would need to know more about. Slim and bearded, cheeks slightly wasted. Eyes alight with nervous energy . . . or perhaps that was reading too much into an instant image. As for the other man, Yardley, he had a pale, puffy face. If he hadn't been attached to the security service, he would probably have been at the Foreign Office.

Scannell pushed the photographs to one side. It had taken a long time to get this far. Now, suddenly, with one small square of paper in his possession, his efforts looked as though they might be rewarded. It was the first hard evidence he'd received connecting the Ministry of Defence with a supposedly official representative of the anti-nuclear movement. It was what he'd been waiting for since his work on the story began.

19

The family-run restaurant was behind Arbat Square, an area of crooked streets in central Moscow. It was only moderately expensive, and drew most of its customers from among the managers of the offices on nearby Kalinin Avenue. Apart from its prices, it had, in Merkulov's eyes, one added attraction: in all the times that he'd been there, he'd never seen anybody from the directorate. When your discussions were private, that was an important consideration.

As Merkulov had expected, when he told Tiverzin why he'd requested the meeting, her face showed only a trace of alarm, but he recognized the expression as one of controlled fury. He'd witnessed it before, and flinched from the unpleasant duty ahead of him. He sank a glass of pepper-vodka to steel his nerves. Tiverzin had only heard the beginning.

'It's been corroborated from computer records,' he told her. 'It's not good. She's been activated. Her name showed up on a DI5 induction course list.'

Tiverzin received the information passively, reaching for a glass of mineral water which the waiter had brought along with a 100-gram spirit flask for Merkulov.

Finally, she said: 'Why didn't we know before now?'

Merkulov was at a loss. For days he'd avoided reporting back to her, not because he necessarily had anything to conceal, but he'd anticipated her reaction to the Line N message. The report, encoded by the London embassy's illegal support staff, had provided a terrible confirmation of his fears.

'The lists have only recently been fed on to the embassy's computer. No one had checked. They hadn't thought. That's why it's taken so long to come through.'

Tiverzin didn't respond at once. Her thoughts seemed to have been caught in a time-trap. At last, she looked up.

'What grade is she?'

'Clerical officer. We don't know how she was recruited.'

'Aren't there any records? . . . An introductory contact?'

'No. Just her code and classification on the list. That's how we found out.'

'What do you mean? *Who* found out?'

'The course was monitored by our Active Intelligence Unit. The surveillance cell that's watching Novost just traced back.'

'And it's taken them till *now*?'

Merkulov cast his eyes down fleetingly. 'It was too obvious . . . I said, no one thought of it.'

Tiverzin took another sip of water. As she put down her glass, Merkulov noticed the calculation, the resourcefulness in her eyes. He remembered now where he'd seen the look before; it was at the dacha when she'd been arguing with Sofinsky. It was a look that could command obeisance from the toughest Lubianka interrogator.

'Is she a permanent field agent?' she asked.

'The surveillance cell think she's been given a cosmetic promotion, just for this assignment.'

'I don't want to know what *they* think, I want to know what *you* think.'

It was worse than Merkulov had thought. If he wasn't careful, she'd blow a valve. It was going to be difficult to calm her down.

'I think they're probably right. She was living at the apartment complex long before Novost. Our people would have used her in the same way.'

'In which case, we're assuming she was activated as an expedient.'

'Yes.'

'So who's controlling her?'

Before answering, Merkulov summoned a waiter and

ordered food. While Tiverzin studied the short menu, Merkulov tried to formulate in his mind what he was going to say. By the time the waiter went back to the kitchen, he had prepared his answers.

'As far as we can tell, she's taking instructions from an offshoot of the Protective Security division.'

'Protective Security? Why them?'

'They've got a liaison unit at the building where she used to work. She's been moved to another office since this thing started.'

Merkulov had no trouble providing Tiverzin with a full brief. Since the arrival of the Line N report, he'd analysed its contents down to the last character on the directorate's electronic decoder. Time and again he'd run the original message through. There had been no mistake. As an agent, Novost's time was fast running out.

'Could he use the woman as an information source?' Tiverzin suggested.

Merkulov shook his head. As he saw it, it would be trying to salvage the unsalvageable.

'She's only got access to low-grade material. There's no way we can use her . . . not for that.' Merkulov re-filled his tumbler and let the spirit sink slowly to his stomach. 'Do we alert Novost?'

Tiverzin reacted sharply; more sharply than he'd expected. 'No!' She glared across the table. 'No . . . Not till I give the instruction. He's got to continue to believe he's working alone. Keep the surveillance cell on a short rope.'

'We can't step up the Line N traffic. They'll know something's up.'

'I didn't say that,' Tiverzin snapped. 'Just let them know we'll be taking all the major decisions at this end. As well as that, I want the embassy to open an escape route for 10-10.'

It was Merkulov's turn to look perturbed. If she was going

that far, things must be serious. To pull out the lead agent would cripple Lyosha for months.

'10-10? Are you sure?'

'A precaution. If anything happens to Novost, we've got to be able to get the others out.'

Although Tiverzin wasn't spelling it out, Merkulov knew the focus of her concern. It was the threat which the exposure of Novost could pose to the larger Operation Aleksei. If that was undermined, the repercussions would be devastating. The Service A controllers would stage a clean-out of the UK division, and that would hit everyone, from Kochev down. Tiverzin, with ultimate responsibility for all the Lyosha agents, would be held directly to blame.

'Do we upgrade his risk status?'

Merkulov realized the absurdity of the question even as he asked it. The look he received from Tiverzin was scathing.

'Obviously he'll have to become Category A. I want service reports from you every three days.'

'What about the woman?'

'Do we know what her brief is?'

'The surveillance cell have got listening devices in both apartments. So far she hasn't let anything slip.'

'And Novost?'

'We're watching . . . in case he loses his grip.'

'Does he suspect her?'

'We don't know. The cell say he's playing it by the book.'

Tiverzin's anger had begun to cool, and she became thoughtful. From the look of fatigue on her face though, it was clear she could see no easy solution. She pushed her plate to one side. She'd hardly eaten a thing.

'Their relationship? It is . . . sexual?'

Merkulov's food stuck in his throat. The question, coming from her, sounded peculiarly sterile; she might have been asking about his office routine.

'Normal. Middle-aged stuff . . . No third parties!'

132

'All right, all right.' Tiverzin shook her hand abruptly. 'You can spare me the details.'

Merkulov helped himself to some herrings from a plate. The lighter intrusion had broken the tension.

'It's possible he's waiting for the thing to play itself out,' he said. 'There's a chance he's already feeding a line to her controllers . . . to screw them up.'

After Tiverzin's plate had been taken away, she said: 'It's fortunate he's got a good *confrère*.'

Merkulov was aware of the reference, although Tiverzin had never spoken about it to him before. It was the directorate's practice to maintain in each area of operation a circle of key agents whose job was to act as protectors of field agents in difficulty. These *confrères*, as they were known, were the elite of the 'illegal' agent force, carrying the rank of KGB colonel. Merkulov had, in his early days, hoped for such a post himself, but was now thankful for a quieter desk life at home. Such agents were destined to spend their entire lives in their host countries, for which reason only married couples were selected for the job. Merkulov had no idea who Novost's *confrère* was, and doubted if Tiverzin knew more than a code name.

'How much longer do we keep Novost in place?' he asked.

'I don't know. Hopefully only another month or two. Then we'll close his line.'

'What's the score with Sofinsky? Will we get the budget go-ahead?'

Tiverzin showed more than a hint of animosity. 'Sofinsky's always a problem. Novost completed his overseas tour of duty more than a year ago. That doesn't help matters.'

'Has Kochev got anything in mind . . . for when Novost gets back?'

'The practical training section have allocated a place for him as a field instructor.'

'Where?'

'The Kuchino centre.'

Merkulov shrugged, and poured another drink. 'Poor bastard. They call that a reward?'

'He'll do a good job.'

'Maybe, but it's hardly something for him to look forward to, is it?' Merkulov reached for some black bread. 'Anyway, if they've got a place for him, is it that important to keep him in London?'

Tiverzin's brow drew tight.

Seeing the sign, Merkulov added simply: 'I mean, it *is* only one story.'

At this, thin wires of passion burned deep in Tiverzin's eyes. 'You'd better understand, comrade, we're close to success. Three months, four at the most – that's our time window before an election. It's nothing. There isn't another agent with a chance of getting a story like that.'

Merkulov looked up. 'And the woman? What do we do with her?'

'Is there a direct threat to the network?'

'Not immediate.'

Tiverzin nodded. 'Sofinsky mustn't be told about her. This is solely an Active Measures campaign.'

Merkulov's face crinkled in a frown. 'It could be difficult. The financial division is monitoring us closely.'

'They don't have any contact with Line N. No code access.'

Merkulov registered his willingness to heed the instruction, but said: 'Is Sofinsky that much of a danger?'

'He wants the operation shut down. If he finds out about the Novost woman, that'll give him an absolute excuse. We won't be able to stop him. He'll walk all over Kochev.'

'Is that why he wants to shut it down, because of Kochev . . . the job?'

The waiter brought coffee for Tiverzin and she sugared it heavily.

'He knows Kochev is on his way out. For someone like Sofinsky, that's enough.'

Merkulov raised his hand in a throwaway gesture. 'Sofinsky's not in line . . . He's financial, not operational. Everybody knows the job's yours.'

'If Lyosha succeeds, maybe,' Tiverzin reflected. 'But that would put me in the running for the deputy directorship of the international division . . .'

'That's what Sofinsky's after.'

'Certainly it is. He's assessed the situation. That's why we need to make sure we've got an escape route for 10-10. We'll also have to make contingency plans for an emergency shutdown.'

Merkulov hesitated. 'Of Lyosha?'

'What else?'

Tiverzin's instruction added to Merkulov's surprise. Such a consideration meant the operation was even more vulnerable than he'd suspected.

'It would take us weeks to close it invisibly. There's no way we could keep all the agents posted. We'd have to find non-active jobs . . .'

Tiverzin said nothing for some moments. Merkulov watched as she lifted a spoon and stirred her coffee. Despite her general demands on him and the other desk staff, he had to give her credit: she had steered the operation through rough waters. He knew she wouldn't let go of Lyosha until the position was irretrievable.

'Whatever the outcome,' she told Merkulov, 'they'll find out sometime that we had early information on the woman. If Lyosha succeeds, that won't be a problem. I'll just say I knew that Sofinsky would have tried to close it down.'

She sipped her coffee and, by her grimace, Merkulov knew it tasted strongly of chicory root. The restaurant wasn't as good as he'd thought.

'If the operation fails,' Tiverzin went on, 'and we've managed to get the agents out, it won't stop us losing our jobs . . . but at least we won't have to face a tribunal for

135

professional negligence.' She paused for emphasis. 'You see the necessity for precaution?'

Merkulov nodded and tipped back the last of his vodka. 'Even so, you're asking a lot, captain.'

'You mean, asking you to risk your career so that I can advance mine? Is that what you're talking about?'

Merkulov smiled with embarrassment at the forthright question. 'I'm glad you recognize the problem.'

'You stand to gain as well. Remember, my job will become available, and I'll be in a position to recommend a replacement.'

'With respect, captain, perhaps we don't all share your ambitions.'

Tiverzin's expression was inanimate. 'Perhaps we don't all buy our cars from illegal currency dealers.'

Merkulov's appetite vanished. The food in his mouth was almost impossible to swallow. He tried to smile – a vapid, instinctive response.

'Your methods of observation are enviable, captain.'

Tiverzin glared across the table. 'If you wish to indulge your bourgeois aspirations, comrade, may I suggest you act with a little more caution. On two separate occasions I've had to arrange special dispensations with the Second Directorate to avoid a departmental investigation.'

Merkulov said nothing. He wanted to wipe the sweat from his forehead, but he daren't lift his hand.

'How long have you been in the service? I'd have thought that by now you'd have learnt that Moscow doesn't only have eyes and ears, it has extra-sensory perception.'

Merkulov remained silent to the end.

'Kochev must only be told enough about the operational details to make him think he's being kept informed. Otherwise he'll smell which direction the trouble is in and run straight to Sofinsky. And remember – if Operation Lyosha fails, we go down with it.'

20

Out of the sky a Mirage F1 screeched across the airfield, its line of attack parallel with the centre of the runway. In the few seconds that its offensive lasted, the shadow of its squat wings jumped across the roofs of the grey-washed administrative buildings before it climbed on an almost perpendicular flight-path and was lost to sight in the desert haze.

Moments later, while the webbed strata of smoke still hung over the runway, an identical aircraft came in from the direction of the sea to continue the assault. Beyond the perimeter of the airfield, where the carcasses of an army tank and a lorry were burning, a geyser of fire erupted on the ground. From some unidentifiable target, a ball of oily smoke billowed upwards and the delayed thump of the explosion reverberated across the sunbaked plateau.

Scannell crimped his eyes and gazed at the aircraft as it veered skywards from the end of the runway, the trailing edges of its wings dragging behind them a curtain of heat. He watched with idle fascination as it became a twisting bird heading out over the Gulf, its afterburner, whose roar was still echoing in his ears, now a soundless orange glow.

That, then, was the French sales routine. During the afternoon there would be demonstrations by the Italians and the West Germans. More simulated missile attacks; more polite addresses from the military personnel. It was marketing presentation on a mega-scale. The number of noughts on the contracts showed they were dealing in the hardware of war.

Behind Scannell in the press stand, a corps of European

and American journalists were discussing the content of the stories they would file later in the day to their respective newsdesks. He had already let them know which deals he would be reporting. Such fixing of stories was a reciprocal arrangement often used by correspondents on overseas trips to make sure they didn't spend too much time trying to outsmart one another. The practice amused him; he had never been able to understand how democratic societies managed to maintain the illusion of a free press.

He went to the hospitality tent and asked for an iced cola. It was his intention, during the afternoon, to avoid the mêlée of the exhibition and seek out one or two of the foreign defence representatives whom, he felt, might make future contacts. It was one way of compensating for having to come on the trip, an intrusion on the work for his anti-nuclear feature. The arms demonstration, after all, wasn't in the international first division – just a jaunt to impress a bunch of nomads who wanted a few missiles to tuck under their beds, as Estabrook had put it.

As he turned to walk to a table, one of the members of the British commercial delegation approached from the other side of the tent.

'Mr Scannell? I'd like a word with you. Do you have a moment?'

Scannell recognized him; the man had sat two seats in front of him on the plane coming out to Dubai.

'Sure,' he said. 'About what?'

The businessman looked round at the crowded tables. 'Perhaps somewhere more private?'

Scannell eyed the man directly. Since his meeting with Whymark nearly a fortnight before, he'd been waiting for further contact. He wondered whether Whymark had chosen to use an intermediary. It would be understandable if he had, although the timing was unexpected.

'We'll go outside,' Scannell said.

They left the tent and mingled with the crowds of delegates

among the exhibition stands. The air was heavy with the odour of aviation fuel.

'What's the score?' Scannell asked.

The man hesitated. 'I thought we might . . . do a deal.'

'On what?'

'My name's Hennessy. I'm the deputy group marketing manager of DEM Gearing.'

Scannell knew the company. It was one of the smaller mechanical equipment manufacturers which supplied the British Defence Ministry, although he couldn't see what involvement Whymark would have had with it. Maybe his assumption had been wrong.

'What's so sensitive?'

'I've got a story to offer you.'

At once, Scannell's hopes were stifled by scepticism. It was impossible to count how many times people had approached him with unsolicited stories, of which a tiny number ever made it on to the agency's wires. Most were a waste of time.

'It involves one of our competitors, Somerville Stanley. They've got a Defence Ministry contract – to research and develop the transmission system for a new series of armoured vehicles.'

Scannell's excitement failed to rise. 'Why should that interest me?'

'Mr Scannell, I'm an accountant by profession. I've had certain information passed on to me proving that Somerville have been engaged in financial malpractices.'

There was an assertiveness about the man, an expectation of compliance that grated. None the less, something began to tweak at Scannell's professional instincts.

'These malpractices . . . Do they involve the Defence Ministry?'

'They do. '

'In that case, shouldn't you report it?'

The man's shrewd face showed no sign of the alarm that

Scannell was trying to induce to test the veracity of the claim.

'Yes, I believe I should,' the man said coolly. 'In fact, I did consider contacting the House of Commons public accounts committee at one stage. I know what goes on there, though. Someone would throw a security blanket over it. Nothing more would be heard.'

He was right, of course. That's exactly what would happen. Scannell took off his cotton jacket. Hooking his finger through the loop inside the collar, he carried it over his shoulder. The air was almost as clammy outside as it had been in the tent. As he walked, he was trying to make up his mind about the quality of the information. Forget the business niceties, he told himself. Press him. See how much he knows.

'What's the Somerville contract worth?' he asked.

'Almost five million. It's not huge – not by military standards – but we're talking about four or five per cent of the company's annual turnover.'

The answer was pat, but not so much that it raised suspicions about its source.

'The contract . . . it's non-competitive, I take it?'

'That's correct.'

Scannell anticipated what was about to come. Such contracts, arranged for security reasons outside normal public sector tendering arrangements, were a constant headache for the Members of Parliament who served on the Commons committee. The MPs were supposed to keep a watch on spending, but of the millions paid out each year by the Defence Ministry, it was impossible to tell how much was genuine expenditure and how much was a result of inflated contractors' bills. Tales of excess claims were rife, but without more rules on disclosure, there was no way of instituting checks.

'Have Somerville Stanley been overcharging?'

'They're making excess profits of at least four hundred

140

and fifty thousand on that contract alone . . . and that's a conservative figure.' As he spoke, the man's eyes had become furtive, the voice quieter, as though every person in the crowd was a potential eavesdropper.

'Presumably there'll be a ministerial post-contract review?' said Scannell.

'It's not as simple as that. We're talking about research and design work. It's easier to hide costs in that area than it is with straightforward manufacturing orders. They're breaking new ground . . . unproven technology. There are all manner of ways that the system can be abused.'

Scannell turned his head and shielded his eyes from the sun's haze. 'Such as?'

'Creative accounting . . . claims for equipment modification . . . personnel training . . .'

There was a pause. As they passed among the exhibition stands, Scannell weighed up the information. Whoever the man was speaking for, he'd been excellently briefed. If there was anything suspect about him, the only way to find out was to burrow under the skin. Scannell swivelled his head and confronted the man accusingly.

'How is it you know so much about Somerville Stanley's practices?'

The man gave a disarming smile. 'Mr Scannell, I'm surprised! You know, I really wouldn't have expected to hear that from a professional journalist. I'm sure you don't expect me to tell you. We have our sources, just as you do!'

'Have you got any documentary evidence?'

The man stopped and unzipped the briefcase he was carrying. He handed Scannell a sheaf of papers in a plastic folder.

'You'll find all you need in there.'

Scannell didn't bother to look inside. That could come later.

'I take it these are all copies?'

The man nodded. 'They can be authenticated.'

'I'll go through them when I get back to London. Where can I get in touch with you?'

'At DEM, but I'd honestly prefer it if we left it at this. If you're familiar with the activities of defence companies – as I'm sure you are – you really shouldn't have any difficulty seeing what's been going on. All the figures are there.'

They were walking towards the display area occupied by the British companies. As if following a natural course, the man turned to pass back through the part of the exhibition they had just left. For the first time, his tempered exterior showed signs of vulnerability.

'I think, perhaps, it would be wise for us not to be seen talking at any length.'

'Wise for who? You or me?'

The man ignored the question. 'You'll also see some entries in the documents related to commission payments.' He broke off while a truck passed along the dusty path. 'Has it crossed your mind, by any chance, why Somerville aren't represented on this trip?'

'No, I can't say it has. Should it have done?'

'They've got strong links with this part of the world. They don't need the sales promotion . . . Strictly private deals.'

Much as Scannell had tried to knock the story down, he had to admit that it had touched off a fuse in his imagination.

'You mentioned commissions. What's the relevance there?'

Once again, the man gave a crisp smile. 'You've got the documents, Mr Scannell. I suggest you look at their overheads on Middle East orders. You'll find there are two parallel sets of accounts. One set the auditors see, the other set they don't. It's a well-used device. The company has been paying commissions worth thirty per cent of the contract price.'

Scannell paused for a moment to absorb what the man was saying. At every point, the smell of a story was becoming stronger. If true, it was a good one. What he couldn't get out of his mind though, was the possibility that the approach was all part of some sophisticated set-up. Clearly there was no connection with Whymark, but to have two gratuitous offers of potentially strong material in so short a time seemed more than coincidental. The first thing he would do when he got back to London would be to check the man out with his company.

'You're saying they've got a slush fund?' he said, working to the heart of the man's allegations.

The man nodded. 'Financed by overcharging on British government work. A neat balancing act!'

Scannell stopped along the path. They were heading back in the direction of the runway. 'These figures . . . You realize that, if they're right, there could be a case of fraud?'

'I don't see any conditionality about it, Mr Scannell. There most certainly is.'

Scannell was silent for a moment. Across the other side of the airfield, a flight of four helicopters was about to take off. He had to raise his voice because of the noise.

'I take it you're not doing this out of a sense of public duty?'

The man's tough jaw became even more obtrusive. 'We're in a highly competitive business, Mr Scannell. When companies like Somerville are prepared to engage in illegal practices, one has to keep a step ahead to survive. I'll leave the documents with you.'

Scannell watched the man go, then, loosening his tie, he made his way back to the hospitality tent. He needed a drink. Whatever his doubts about the way in which the information had come to him, the documents in his hand contained a story he knew he would find difficult to resist.

The entryphone buzzed with an irritating persistence somewhere in Celia's submerged reality. She had fallen asleep reading a magazine while she waited for Richard to return home. There was an emptiness about her evenings while Scannell was away.

As she awoke, she straightened her clothes and hurried to pick up the receiver mounted by the door.

'Who is it?'

'Police.'

Celia was silent. A single fear entered her mind: Richard. She couldn't speak; her mouth was dry.

'Can we come up?'

Celia swallowed, and said shakily: 'What's it about?'

'Your son.' The voice at the other end of the entryphone was like an echo in a troubled dream.

'Has he been in an accident?'

The answer seemed a long time in coming. 'No. He's not hurt.'

She held the receiver vacantly. 'It's the ninth floor.'

When the officers came up, she was standing at the front door of the flat, looking out into the lift lobby.

'What's the matter?' she asked. 'What's he done?'

'Can we come in?'

Celia showed them into the hall and shut the door. The officers walked through to the living-room.

'Your son's been arrested with two other boys – taking and driving away a car.'

Celia took a packet of cigarettes from her bag. 'Where is he now?'

'He's answering some questions. If you'd like to come with us, you'll have to be there while he makes a statement.'

Celia fetched her coat from the bedroom and stubbed out her cigarette in an ashtray on the table.

'Will they . . . put him away?' she asked as they went down in the lift.

'Has he had any previous convictions?'

Celia shook her head. 'No.'

'He might be all right then. It depends who the magistrates are. He might get probation.'

Celia walked with the officers to their car. She was shaking with cold. One of them opened a door for her.

'You should kick his pants once in a while,' he said. 'That's what these kids need.'

In the police station, Richard was sitting in a back room where an officer was typing. Celia was shown through from the public waiting-room. Richard looked up, his expression defiant.

'Are you all right?' Celia asked him.

The boy nodded.

After making a statement he was released, and Celia took him home in a taxi. When they were inside the flat, she hung his jacket in a cupboard.

'Why did you do it?' she asked him.

Richard fetched a bowl of cereal from the kitchen, and ate it at the table as Celia plied him with questions. He ignored them all.

Household sat with Bill Webster, the news agency's chief executive, in the back of the Jaguar as it crawled with the lunchtime traffic along the Strand. As always, Webster held one of his big, half-smoked cigars in the crook of his fingers. He tapped impatiently on the leather seat.

'What about Scannell's big story? When will it be ready for syndication?'

Household turned. 'He's away at the moment. As far as I know, he's still building up a dossier. He's asking for more time.'

Webster frowned, his heavy eyes creasing into a scowl. 'It's been weeks since you told me about that. Shouldn't he have had the story by now? How long does he want, for Christ's sake?'

'I've given him another three weeks. It would be a mistake to squeeze him too tightly. It's a complicated assignment. He's got to have room to breathe.'

Webster grunted and his mouth pursed in an expression

of displeasure. 'Well you'd better tell him we can't wait forever, no matter how good the bloody thing is.'

The conversation petered out and Household focused his gaze on the busy street. Shopgirls rushing out to buy cosmetics in their lunch-hour; office-workers heading for sandwich bars. They were only a few feet away yet, metaphorically, they were a million miles from Webster's world, the cocooned luxury of the limousine.

'How quickly will it take to prepare the story for syndication once Scannell's got it?' Webster asked.

Household's moment of distraction ended and he turned from the window.

'The lawyers will need to spend some time going through it. We can't take the chance of him getting anything wrong.'

The radiophone buzzed, and Webster reached for the receiver. Cupping his hand over the mouthpiece, he said sharply to Household: 'You'd better make sure he doesn't – or I'll stitch his scrotum!'

Fifteen minutes later, the chauffeur dropped them outside the Defence Ministry building along Whitehall. As they stood on the pavement, Webster buttoned his jacket and looked at his watch. The luncheon appointment with Quigley had been fixed for one o'clock; it was now ten past.

'Why shouldn't we make the buggers wait for once?' He grinned, then leaned down to the driver's open window. 'We'll get a taxi back to the office. You'll never park here.'

As the car pulled away, he and Household walked to the entrance of the building and spoke to one of two security guards. The guard collected pre-arranged passes from a glass booth and went with them in a lift up to the fifth floor where an aide was waiting. The two visitors were shown through to Quigley's office.

'Good afternoon, gentlemen. I have to be at the House at two-thirty, so I suggest we start right away.'

Household, who had attended numerous government briefings during his time as a correspondent, was well acquainted with the trappings of ministerial privilege: the spacious room, the selected murals, the leather couch. It was the first time, though, that he'd been summoned for private talks. By the window, overlooking Whitehall, was a small dining-table laid for three. Quigley walked over to it and drew out a chair.

'Take a seat.'

As he spoke, there was a knock at the door and two catering staff came in with a food trolley. They served salad and cold meats.

'I specifically wanted to discuss your agency's policy regarding anti-nuclear coverage,' Quigley began when the trolley had been wheeled out. 'Some of our people are becoming . . . let's say, a little concerned.'

'About what?' said Webster.

Quigley waved his hand as though his words were readily disposable. 'Nothing to worry us unduly, but . . . I'm sure we can come to some satisfactory arrangement.' He gestured towards the food. 'Please . . . do help yourselves.'

As Webster reached for the plate of meats, he cast a sombre look across the table. Household felt his tension increase; Webster was never the most tactful of men, and he was unlikely to be intimidated by Quigley's position.

'Forgive me, Minister . . . you say concerned. Does that mean someone thinks the agency's stories are wrong? Or is it that they just don't like them being syndicated?'

Quigley gave a brittle smile. 'Actually, a little of both.'

Household resented the slight on the agency's reputation. Correctness in detail had been a hallmark of his editorship, and a tribute to this was the way in which newspapers would freely run stories straight from its wire service without further verification. As for the syndication policy, it was clear that Quigley had an axe to grind. Personally, Household would have politely received the criticism and ignored it. None the less, he felt that Webster would expect him to react.

'Our material is always double-checked,' he said defensively.

Quigley helped himself to a little food. The catering staff had left two bottles of wine, and Quigley poured three glasses.

'Don't misunderstand me,' he said. 'I'm not suggesting inaccuracies have occurred. It's the way things are presented . . . sometimes the perspective can become . . . distorted, so to speak.'

As the lunch progressed, he cited two or three examples of stories which he felt had placed an unfair emphasis on the government's nuclear commitments.

'Let's not mince words, shall we?' said Webster after listening for some minutes. 'Basically, you're implying that our coverage is biased. Perhaps you'd tell us what your justification is for saying that.'

Quigley smiled and rested his knife and fork on his plate. 'Let me just explain, gentlemen. I'm fully aware that not everybody supports the concept of an independent nuclear deterrent – and, naturally, they're entitled to that view.' He halted for a moment, as though choosing his words carefully. 'What I'm asking you to appreciate is that your organization is uniquely placed to influence large sections of the media. It has a responsibility to ensure that all views are properly represented. Indeed, one could say it had a public duty to do so.'

Household shifted awkwardly. When the luncheon invitation had come to his office four or five days earlier, he'd guessed that Quigley wanted to apply pressure, but he hadn't expected quite such a heavy hand. Although the Minister's language was couched in diplomatic courtesies, he was, for a government representative, being unusually candid.

'Whenever we run a critical story, we always give the other side the opportunity to reply,' Household said curtly. 'That accords with standard journalistic practice.'

'. . . And as an independent organization,' Webster added

pointedly, 'we have the right to determine our editorial policies free from external interference.'

Quigley took another small helping of food and sat back. Again, he smiled.

'Of course, gentlemen, and believe me, I'm the first person to champion the rights of free speech. On the other hand, we do have to make sure it doesn't conflict with the interests of national security.'

Webster looked intrigued as he listened to Quigley's words. As he faced the Minister, there was a look of an old, tenacious bulldog about him, heavy-necked and streetwise. Household reflected that, whatever the trappings, this man who had begun his career as an East London market trader would never shake off his background. In the stance was a threat of physical brutality; in the eyes, a mocking glint.

'Are you seriously suggesting that our stories are endangering the interests of the state?'

Quigley lifted his head slowly and met Webster's challenge. 'Put in those terms, there does seem to be that potential.'

Webster wiped his mouth with his napkin and let his hands fall to his lap. His expression was darkening.

'I don't understand, Mr Quigley. In what way?'

The politician, remaining unruffled, leaned earnestly on the table. 'To put it starkly, gentlemen, I think that one or two of your recent stories have bordered on propaganda. They could seriously undermine defence policy.'

Household felt his annoyance being drawn out, and he sat forward to counter what he saw as blatant government paranoia. However, Webster cut in before he had a chance to speak.

'Let's be clear what we're talking about, shall we? Are you concerned about genuine national interests, or the government's re-election prospects?'

Quigley attempted a laugh, but Household noted its false

149

ring. 'Re-election prospects?' His tone was light, as though self-questioning. 'I'm neither naïve enough nor, I hope, vain enough, to think I could materially influence that position.' He took a sip of wine, savouring it for a moment. 'You know, it may surprise you to hear this, but I don't believe it would be salutary for the country if I could. One of our greatest national achievements is an unfettered press.'

Webster laid down his knife and fork with a clatter. 'Look, Mr Quigley. You invited us here to talk about the agency's areas of coverage. If you're not happy about something, I'd appreciate it if you'd spell out exactly what you're asking us to do. Then we'll give you a clear answer.'

Still keeping up his imperturbable front, Quigley nodded. 'Of course. To be brief, I had hoped we might come to an understanding about the need for . . . a greater sense of public obligation. That, I would add, applies to the media at large.'

'Let's stick to our agency in particular, shall we?' said Webster. 'What applies to us?'

Quigley reflected. He looked first at Webster, then at Household.

'Perhaps one could say, I wouldn't like to see a situation arise . . . one, for instance, where D-Notices were constantly being issued. Or where reporters had to be excluded from departmental briefings and the like. I don't think that would be desirable for anyone.'

Household watched, almost as an outsider, as the confrontation developed between the two men. Quigley had now made his position perfectly plain: if the agency didn't toe the ministry line, it would incur heavy penalties. D-Notices didn't have to be complied with, but any editor or proprietor who ignored these official requests for reporting restraint was inviting a tough battle.

'You know very well that once we're blacklisted by one department, others are bound to do the same,' said Webster. 'Is that your idea of an unfettered press?'

Quigley gave the accusation a moment's thought before replying. 'One has to view the position realistically.'

'Realistically? You've already told us what the reality is . . .'

'Please, if I might just finish,' Quigley responded. 'Just as you enjoy the freedom to operate independently, so my department has a similar right. In other words, it reserves the option of withdrawing co-operation from irresponsible areas of the media.'

'How do you define that – *irresponsible*?'

'Basically, I would say, those it sees as abusing their privileges.' Quigley poured more wine into his guests' glasses. 'Incidentally, Mr Webster, I understand that your business interests are not confined to the media alone. Apparently you have other extensive holdings – in the manufacturing and high-technology industries, I believe.'

Webster looked as though he was filtering the words for hidden connotations. 'My companies have a policy of diversification, yes. That's well known.'

'Then perhaps you could explain a bewildering contradiction.' Quigley's voice had a hint of derision in it. 'From what I've been told, it seems that certain of them make generous donations to our party funds. Predominantly the high-technology companies, if I'm correct.'

Webster was about to answer him, but Quigley held up his hand and gave a short laugh.

'Don't get me wrong – not that we're not grateful! It just seems odd that, on the other hand, you have this news agency syndicating exposés – so-called exposés, anyway – all providing publicity ammunition for the political Opposition.'

Webster folded his napkin. 'I don't see any contradiction.' He seemed to find Quigley's touch of humour irksome. 'All of my companies operate autonomously. High technology is a growth area – and it's getting considerable government support. They happen to know which side their bread's buttered on. Does that answer your question, Minister?'

'And the exposés?'

'They're good for business. They boost the reputation of the agency. That's what news is all about.'

'It's as simple as that? A commercial stratagem?'

'Information's a product, like anything else,' Webster replied. 'If scandal sells, then I'll sell scandal. If anti-nuclear stories are the flavour of the month, then I'll sell those.' He sat back. 'From a business point of view, there's no difference.'

The lunch ended hurriedly, because Quigley was running behind schedule. As Household and Webster rode in a taxi back to the news agency's offices, they discussed the seriousness of the Minister's warning. Was it a posture, or would he really take steps to cut off the supply of official information?

'The bastard's bluffing,' Webster decided after consideration. 'D'you think they've got wind of Scannell's story?'

Household lifted a hand noncommittally. 'It's possible, but I doubt it. He's been playing it close to his chest. Even I don't know more than the bare bones.'

Webster nodded in agreement. 'That's what I'd have said. If they *had* known, they'd have tried to sweeten us. What Quigley said – it was all bullshit.'

Household kept his thoughts to himself. He wasn't unduly worried about the prospect of a fight with the Ministry. After all, it was in no politician's interest to sever a prime line of access to the Fleet Street papers. The critical question in Household's mind was why Quigley had taken the unusual step of issuing the warning. Certainly, the agency had syndicated material which couldn't have pleased him, but it was no more damaging to the government's electoral chances than other stories published by the campaigning newspapers. And, as far as he knew, no similar threats had been issued to them. There had to be a deeper cause for Quigley's concern, and Household was anxious to find out what it was.

21

From the steps of the court, Scannell and Celia flagged down a taxi. The case had gone better than either of them had expected. The solicitor they had engaged to act for Richard had read out a statement on Scannell's behalf which appeared to have been a key influence in the magistrates' decision to give a probationary sentence. As soon as the case had finished, Celia had sent Richard to school.

Back at the flat, Scannell helped her to prepare a hurried lunch. He could see that the court case had had a marked effect on her. Since his return from the Gulf, he'd found her untalkative, even withdrawn. He knew that she was secretly blaming herself for Richard's actions. Apart from trying to persuade her otherwise, he felt he could do little to help. Physically, she looked tired; run down. She picked listlessly at her food. Eventually she gave a sigh and pushed her dish away.

'Kids,' she said. 'Why do they do these crazy things?'

Scannell looked across the table. In Richard's case, he held his own opinions, most of which he was not inclined to voice.

'Perhaps you shouldn't give him such a free rein.'

Celia reacted starchily to his tone of mild rebuke. 'You talk to him then. You're the only person he listens to these days.'

Oddly, there was some truth in what she'd said. Over the last few weeks, the boy had started confiding in him – telling him things he certainly wouldn't tell his mother. It wasn't something that Scannell felt comfortable about. Indeed, when he'd first learned about the police charges, he'd been prepared to let him suffer the consequences, but that wouldn't have done anything to ease Celia's mind.

'Why not try to widen his interests?' he suggested.

Celia shrugged half-heartedly. 'You've been with him to the swimming-pool. And the chess games . . . he likes those.'

Scannell detected an element of jealousy, and he began to feel embarrassed. His efforts to get to know the boy hadn't, when it came to it, been anything more than smoothing his ground with Celia, although it was questionable whether he should have let himself be drawn in so deeply.

'What about outdoor sort of things? He's that age.'

Celia gave the matter some thought. 'He went fishing once with a friend. The boy's father took them. They camped for a weekend – in Wales somewhere.'

She seemed to be making a hint. Scannell knew that if he offered to do the same, it would only make it more difficult when the time came to break from them. He wondered what he could do to get out of it. In the end, he decided it would probably be less complicated to make the suggestion she was doubtless waiting for.

'Do you think he'd go with me?'

Celia's eyes brightened a little. 'I don't know. You could ask him.'

Scannell nodded, finishing his food. 'I'll see if I can get some free time . . . Easter perhaps.'

Celia cleared the table. Her silence showed him she was still turning over the events of the morning in her mind. When she sat down again, she seemed to become even more distracted. She brushed her hair back, as if trying to sweep away her anxieties.

'If I don't do something, he'll be out of my hands.'

'What about giving him an allowance? It might help him to feel independent. That's what they want, isn't it . . . kids that age?'

'And the money? Where does that come from?'

Scannell waited a moment before answering. He'd manoeuvred himself towards the easiest course of action.

'I don't know . . . there's my account, I suppose.'

Celia looked curiously troubled. She considered the proposition, then shook her head.

'No. That should be his father's responsibility. It wouldn't be fair on you.'

Scannell could tell the protest was false. There was something in her voice – a trace of self-pity – that annoyed him.

'I wouldn't have suggested it,' he answered shortly.

Celia again shook her head. 'No. He'd spend it like an idiot.'

'That's better than stealing it.'

The observation had come out with an incisive edge. The atmosphere in the room took on an uncomfortable stillness. Soon, Scannell stood up to leave. Celia followed him out to the hall. He went to open the door but, at the last moment, her hand tightened on his arm.

'Thanks, Tom.'

Scannell shrugged. 'It's okay. When things get a bit better . . .'

Celia looked up at him.

'Can't you stay longer?'

He moved closer to the door. 'It's work . . .'

As he turned away from her, he guessed she was wondering why he couldn't make excuses. Her face was blank, a little drained. He felt the pressure of her hand, and something inside him began to relax.

Scannell retained little sensitive material at his flat. Some documents he needed on hand; the others he placed in safe-deposit boxes. He kept two boxes, one at a branch of his bank, the other, in a different name, at the offices of a private security company at Cheapside in the City. The material at the bank was for regular reference, while the documents placed with the security company were mainly duplicates. Neither box was accessible to anyone else, except by means of an official warrant.

Among the recent additions to the boxes' contents were

155

documents that Whymark at the Ministry of Defence had passed to him indicating that a blacklist had been drawn up, on ministerial orders, of professional people working in the anti-nuclear field; people such as lawyers, journalists and college lecturers. Although Whymark had been unable to provide a copy of the blacklist itself, he had confirmed that Scannell's name was on it. Along with this material, Scannell had also deposited notes of his conversation with Whymark, who had told him about the existence of Unit Nine. This was the first Scannell had heard of an official dirty tricks department, and he'd resolved to find out more. After some pressing, Whymark had acknowledged that Malcolm Yardley – the name provided by Van Noort – had recently been transferred to the unit from Secretariat N-160. Slowly, things were beginning to gel.   Later in the week, following a further meeting with Whymark, Scannell copied and deposited two sets of additional Secretariat N-160 documents. After leaving the security company's offices, he returned to his flat and worked on an analytical feature which he'd promised the newsdesk for the next day. Like most correspondents, he preferred to write in-depth articles away from the interruptions of the office, away from the phone calls.

He hadn't been long at his desk, however, when the entryphone buzzed. It was an official from the Department of Health and Social Security who was making inquiries about sickness benefit payments. Scannell instructed the security desk to let the man come up to his flat.

'A letter was sent some weeks ago,' the man explained when Scannell opened the door. 'I'm sorry, but we don't appear to have received a reply.'

Scannell tried to think back. 'A letter?'

'Yes.'

'I didn't see one – at least, I don't think I did. Not from your department. What was it about?'

'You were off work after an accident – last November, I believe. Some minor inconsistencies came to light during the annual office audit. That's when the payments were apparently made – nothing to worry about.'

Scannell was mystified. He knew he hadn't received any benefits. The agency had paid his salary in full. That was its policy with all employees.

'Payments? I don't . . .'

The official smiled, and held up a folder of documents. 'I just need to ask you a few questions. May I come in? I know it's an imposition.'

Scannell asked for identification, and the man produced a card. It appeared genuine.

'I can't spare long,' Scannell told him. 'I've got a lot of work on.'

The man nodded as he stepped into the hall. 'I understand. It's just formalities.'

Scannell showed the man through to the living-room. The official sat on the sofa and placed his briefcase at his feet. He opened the folder and extracted several sheets of paper: typed memorandums and printed forms. Scannell stood by the window. He watched as the man took a pen from his pocket.

'So . . . I know it can be difficult to think back, but can you tell me exactly when the accident occurred?'

Scannell gave a date in November, and the man made a note.

'. . . And the period you were off work?'

'About three weeks.'

'Do you think you could be a little more precise?'

Scannell fetched his diary from the study. 'Here . . . two weeks and – let's see – four working days.'

The official checked through a set of departmental forms. He seemed concerned. 'I don't know . . . It does appear there's a discrepancy. Something odd over the amount of sickness benefit calculated.' The man took a leaflet from the folder. '. . . As defined under the provisions of the Social Security Act.'

Scannell was becoming impatient. He couldn't understand why the department should have sent someone to interview him personally.

'Everything's looked after by my company. They don't refer that sort of thing back to us.'

'Quite. But . . .'

'Why don't you see them about it? I'll let the office know you called. You can make an appointment with the personnel department.'

The official put away some of his papers. 'Of course. It's just that – well, we don't like to cause unnecessary embarrassment . . .'

Scannell's senses sharpened. 'Are you suggesting I've got something to be embarrassed about?'

The official gave an apologetic laugh and shook his head. 'Gracious, no – of course not.'

There was a short silence.

'Then what exactly *are* you trying to tell me?'

The official looked troubled. He produced another set of papers.

'I'm most awfully sorry, Mr Scannell. I really didn't want to bring this up. It's just something that came to light during our enquiries – at the Inland Revenue. I'm not sure . . . Is it possible, do you think, that there may have been one or two anomalies over your income tax? I realize this is all a little inopportune, but . . . well, I'm sure we can clear them up.'

Scannell's suspicions intensified. 'Enquiries?' He walked over to an armchair and sat down. 'Which department did you say you were from?'

The official hesitated and smiled deferentially. 'You do understand that I'm only bringing this up because I have to. It's head office – they don't like any loose ends. When it comes to tax evasion, whatever the scale . . .'

Scannell's eyes narrowed. 'When it comes to *what*?'

The man seemed to become a little flustered. 'I'm

dreadfully sorry. It's nonsense, I know. I only wish they wouldn't keep leaving things like this for us to clear up.'

'What do you mean – evasion?'

'It's silly. So small, comparatively. When it's a criminal offence, though . . .'

Scannell leaned forward and raised a finger. 'Listen, you'd better tell me what's going on. All my tax affairs are in order. They're handled by an accountant. If there's anything wrong, go and see him.'

The official frowned and fiddled with his pen. 'This is . . . As I'm sure you'll appreciate, everyone's responsible for their own tax returns. If there's been some mix-up by your accountant, I'm afraid it's up to you to sort out. Of course, some arrangement may still be possible. If it comes to a prosecution . . .'

There was a pause. Scannell's eyes suddenly lit up with vigour, and he faced the man accusingly. 'Look, I don't know who you are, but don't come here and start talking about prosecutions. Whatever mix-up there's been, you'd better check your own books first.'

'Naturally, I . . .'

Scannell stood up. 'I told you, I've got lots of work to do. So, if you don't mind . . .'

Shuffling his papers together, the official nodded again. 'Of course. I understand your feelings, Mr Scannell. These things are always sensitive.'

Scannell walked to the centre of the room, silently inviting the man to leave. 'Is there anything else?'

The man thought for a moment. 'There is just one other small thing . . .'

He searched in his briefcase for a further document.

'. . . Ah, here we are. It appears that earlier this week you acted as a character witness in a court case – a juvenile. The name of Richard Forde, I believe. Is that correct?'

There was no doubt now in Scannell's mind that which-ever branch of the Civil Service the official represented, it wasn't the Department of Health and Social Security.

'Just *what* do you want?' he demanded.

The man studied the sheet of paper, as though absorbing the information for the first time, then looked up. 'It's possible they might regard it as too insignificant a detail, but then . . . an adverse report from the probation officer? It might induce the authorities to reassess the arrangements for the boy.' He put the document away and clipped his briefcase shut. Smiling insipidly, he added: 'I simply point that out.'

As the man picked up his coat to leave, Scannell strode across to the hall doorway. He locked his eyes on him.

'Who sent you?'

'I beg your pardon?'

'I said, who sent you? Have you been told to put pressure on me?'

As he pulled on his coat imperturbably, the man held the cuffs of his jacket so the sleeves didn't ride up.

'I'm sorry, I don't understand. Pressure? Over what?'

'I don't know. My work?'

The man smiled again and picked up his briefcase from the sofa. He walked out to the hall. Reaching for the handle of the front door, he turned back.

'It's unfortunate, Mr Scannell, but you do seem to have got the wrong impression. I told you, I'm just trying to keep our books straight. It's as simple as that.'

After the man had gone, Scannell stood in the hall, more than usually aware of the flat's silence. Here it was: a door, a few thin walls – a vulnerable enclave in a hostile state. His adversaries, so long anonymous, were becoming bolder. They had started to identify themselves. Slowly, he knew, they were closing in.

22

At 11.10 precisely, as he did each evening, Hans-Heinrich Kepler closed the door of his study and went to the kitchen on the floor above. There he sat talking with his wife for ten or fifteen minutes while he drank a cup of coffee and a large brandy. It was a routine established over the years, and varied only when Kepler was lecturing late at the Hochschule.

Sometime between 11.30 and midnight they went to bed. His wife was a heavy sleeper; much heavier than he was. Hence his reason for taking the brandy before turning in. It was this general restlessness about him that would explain why, when a strange smell permeated the upper part of the house in the early hours of the morning, he was the first to wake.

It wasn't a noxious smell; more gently pungent, like that of scorched clothes. For a minute or two he lay in bed in a sort of half-sleep, trying to figure out what it could be. When it began to get stronger, he sat up and switched on the light. Everything in the room was normal. Indeed, now that the room was no longer in darkness, his senses were less concentrated and the smell seemed partially to fade. He sat propped against the pillow for a short while until his wife, who had been stirring since he folded back the blankets, rolled over and mumbled thickly: 'Go back to sleep.'

Kepler frowned, and took hold of her shoulder. 'Can you smell something?'

His wife lay still. He shook her irritably.

'I think something's burning.'

Alerted by a sharp chord in his voice, his wife lifted her head. She had lost most of her drowsiness.

'You'd better check downstairs.'

Kepler pulled himself out of bed and reached for his dressing-gown which was hanging over the back of a chair. Already a fear had pierced his mind as it had done many times in the past . . . What if there should ever be a fire? Years of work destroyed in minutes. It was a prospect of such incalculable consequence that he knew he wouldn't be able to get back to sleep until he'd satisfied himself that the house was safe.

'Look in the kitchen,' his wife said as he went to the door. 'I might've left a hotplate on.'

Out on the landing, Kepler stood perfectly still in the darkness. Definitely, something was wrong. There was a heavy, warm odour. He reached out for the light switch and looked down the stairwell. The light came on momentarily before the bulb flickered out. He was in darkness again, but what he'd seen in that split second had brought a tingling sensation to the palms of his hands. Thick skeins of smoke were crawling through the slats in the banisters. At that instant, his heart started to race.

'Liesel . . . get up!' he called out. '*Get up!*'

Going down, he took the stairs two and three at a time, stumbling as he went. On the second-floor landing, he tried another light switch, but it didn't work. He could tell from the difficulty he was already having in breathing that the smoke was thicker than it had been on the floor above, although there was still no sign of the fire itself. He thrust open the door of the bathroom to see whether there had been a wiring fault. The room was filling with smoke from somewhere, but there were no flames. As he came out again on to the landing, his eyes flashed upwards. His wife was hurrying down the stairs, still pulling on her dressing-gown.

'What's happened?' she called out. 'Where is it?'

'I don't know! Check the other rooms! Try the lights!'

His wife flung open the door to one of the spare bedrooms. Kepler heard a switch click, but no light came on. The next flight of stairs led down to the first floor and the kitchen. Perhaps that was where the fire was.

With one hand on the banister rail, he guided himself downwards. The heat quickly became fierce. Smoke was billowing up from below, thick and acrid. He struggled down, but he knew there was no chance of reaching the ground floor, either to get out of the house or to save his files. It was as the insurance company had said: as a pile of paper, the documents were worthless.

Now, through the smoke, he could see a layer of flame spreading like a huge puddle across the landing carpet. Already, the heat was searing the skin on his face. Soon his eyes felt as though they were gummed into their sockets. Irrationally, he tried to go further forward, pushing aside a piece of timber that had fallen across the stairway, but soon he found it almost impossible to breathe. Fear had drained him of oxygen. He began to choke. The fire was sucking the air from the stairwell, creating a gigantic vacuum.

'Hans . . . I can't see! *I can't see!*'

Kepler turned his face upwards. He could hear his wife, but he couldn't see her. Things were happening too fast now for him to think. The flames had already begun to lap around him. He pulled himself along the landing and up the stairs. As he reached the top, his wife staggered towards him, her eyes and nose streaming. Grabbing her, he tore the dressing-gown from her shoulders and flung it over her head. In the short time that they had been on the stairway, they had become enveloped in a lethal miasma. Kepler felt himself swaying, as though he were about to faint. He looked up to the top floor, but could barely see the way forward. Wherever the fire had started, it had taken hold with impossible ferocity. Flames had already started to crawl along the banister rail, blistering the varnish.

'Down . . . get down!' he yelled. 'On the floor . . . follow me!'

Draping his own dressing-gown over his head, he dropped

to his hands and knees. At that height, the smoke was thinner, and it was possible to take in traces of air. Even so, the heat was closing around them. He struggled to locate the stairway. At last, his hands touched the door of a cupboard next to it.

'Keep behind me . . . *behind me*!' he called to his wife. 'The bedroom . . . we've got to get out!'

Kepler was in the grip of a reality so unimaginable, so *un*real, that he was acting blindly, as if controlled by some remote and indifferent source. In the space of minutes, he had been detached from sleep and implanted in a psychotic pantomime. All transmission from thought to action was directed now towards one end: survival. He was past questioning whether that objective could be accomplished.

When they reached the bedroom, he helped his wife through the door and slammed it shut. Leaning against it, he fought for breath. At least there was some oxygen in the room. His wife was kneeling on the floor, her body heaving; he could see her by the light of a street lamp that was shining through the window. Her face was streaked with smoke and mucus. Kepler went over to her and tried to help her to her feet.

'Out,' she said breathlessly. 'How do we . . . get out?'

Kepler said nothing. He wiped her face on the sleeve of his dressing-gown. Suddenly her eyes widened.

'Your hair!' she cried.

Kepler lifted his hand to his head. His fingers contacted a bed of crinkly fibre that fell apart at his touch. Moments later, as he staggered to the window, he could sense himself losing control. The room, the darkness, the rush of the fire: his head spun as though a coil of film inside it had suddenly unravelled, splaying random images against his band of vision. Fear and instinct had fused now into a pervading energy that could take him through to new dimensions of depth and time, through to oblivion, through to death.

Ripping the curtains from their rail, he flung the window

open, and a blast of cold air swept into the room. He looked down into the street. The pavement was thirty or forty feet below. His wife crawled over to him and pulled herself up by the shelf.

'No!' she said. 'It's too high!'

Kepler turned. 'The sheets . . . Get the sheets!' He rushed across the room and started tearing at the bedclothes. 'Here – get the other end . . . Tie it to the blanket.'

His wife quickly knotted a sheet and blanket together. Kepler did the same. As they worked, the sound of the fire grew louder, like a hollow rushing from the foundations. In the rooms below, they could hear objects falling; the crack of timbers.

Then came a crash that shook the building's entire structure. Kepler stared at his wife, mesmerized.

'The floor . . . Hurry!'

Kepler didn't know which floor had collapsed. Right now, it hardly mattered. His wife knotted together the last sheet and blanket. In a minute or two, they had made a makeshift escape line that would reach a good way to the street below. Kepler gathered it together and hauled it over to the window. Desperately, he searched for an anchor-point. There was nothing. He picked up a chair and, with one of its legs, smashed the pane. Once he had knocked out the jagged remains of glass, he fed the rope round the wooden frame.

'Down!' he shouted to his wife. 'Now!'

From nearby houses, people had come out into the road. In the distance, Kepler could hear the sound of a vehicle's siren. His wife stared at him. Her cheeks and lips were bloodless.

'Go!' he yelled. 'There's no time!'

He pushed his wife on to the window-sill and tugged at the blanket-rope to make sure it was secure.

'Just hold tight . . . One hand . . . then the other!'

With her mouth grimly set, his wife lowered herself out of the window. For a few seconds, Kepler bore her weight as she took a grip on the rope. He clutched her shoulders. Her body was shaking. It struck him that she would be too frightened to hold on. As she eased away from his hands, he saw that her knuckles were tight. Her face was contorted like that of a victim on a battle frieze.

'Slowly!' he warned her. 'Slowly . . . Keep hold!'

In the street, now, the people and lights were a blur. The wail of the siren was closer. Kepler was confused.

'Keep going! Look at *me* . . . Don't look down!'

He glanced behind him at the room which had ingested heavy smoke from below. The heat was almost unbearable. Although there were no flames, the paint on the inside of the door had been scorched and was lifting like eggshell.

Suddenly, from the other side of the room came a tearing of wood, like the earlier crash, but louder. A huge hole had appeared in the floor. The bed had fallen lopsidedly into it and was jammed against the wall. Wreaths of flame sprouted around it. In moments the bed and the carpet around it were ablaze. Kepler turned to the window. Through it, he could feel air being drawn to the fire like a wind. He looked out.

'I'm coming down!'

He had no idea if his wife had reached the ground. All he was aware of in the seconds ahead was the scrape of his fingers on brickwork . . . the strained sinews under his arms . . . a rushing of blood in his ears and eyes . . . shouting . . . lights . . . an ugly scream . . .

At that moment, the rope jolted and he felt himself drift away from the side of the building as if he were free-falling. Somewhere in the night he heard a cry, then came a jarring thud. Leering over him was a distorted face, then another. Finally, there was a blend of light and dark . . .

23

Scannell had spent all day Saturday going through the Somerville Stanley source material, checking point against point, document against allegation. Even though it was due for syndication the following day, the suspicions he'd harboured about the story from the start were still with him. He didn't know why; he explained it to himself as journalistic instinct. Refuting this, though, was the documentary evidence – a wealth of it – and he tried to quash the doubts in his mind.

Then came the message.

He had just stepped out of the shower at his flat and was passing through from his bedroom to the living-room when he saw an envelope lying on the mat in the hall. There was no address on it, so it had obviously been delivered by hand, although he had no idea by whom. To get into the building, it was necessary to go past the security desk. Scannell looked out into the lift lobby, but no one was there. When he opened the envelope, he found a card. On it was typed a telephone number and an instruction for him to make a call at 9 P.M. from a public phone. The message was unsigned.

He looked at his watch: nearly 8.30. Hurriedly, he pulled on the first clothes that came to hand in his wardrobe. He was disturbed by the anonymous contact. He had no inkling who it could be. As he went out through the foyer, he inquired at the security desk if anyone had asked to come up to his flat. As he'd expected, there had been no callers.

Up by St Paul's there was a call-box: he would ring the number from there. Somebody was using the phone when he arrived, but the wait was only short. As he stepped into the box, he was aware of an uncomfortable tightness across his chest. He tried to let his muscles relax, but when he saw the reflection of his drawn face in the glass, it was clear that this was no momentary onset of disquiet. He picked up the receiver and dialled. After only a single ring, the phone at the other end was picked up.

'Yes.' It was a man's voice, evidently muffled to disguise its tone.

'This is Scannell. You asked me to call.'

There was a short pause, then the man said: 'You're working on a story . . . Somerville Stanley.' A moment later he added: 'Don't touch it. It's a plant.'

Scannell tensed further. 'Who's speaking?'

'I can't tell you that. All I can say is that it would be a bad rabbit to catch. All the documents have been fed to your contact. If your news agency goes ahead with syndication, it will be a grave error.'

'How did you find out . . .'

Scannell had barely begun to ask his question when the line went dead. He tried ringing the number again but there was no reply. He guessed it was a call-box.

Walking back to his flat, he felt shocked and perplexed. Who was it who could know about the story? He hadn't spoken about it outside the office, not even to Celia. And why should he accept the advice of an anonymous stranger?

Even as he posed the question, the answer was to the forefront of his mind. The warning had been preposterous except for one thing: the caller had said the story would be '*a bad rabbit to catch.*' The phrase wasn't meaningless, but its use was distinctly odd. It also happened that 'rabbit' was the anglicized version of the name Krolikov, his course tutor at Gaczyna. Only one source had that information – the KGB. And for them to take the risk of contacting an active field agent could only mean one thing: they could see him heading for disaster.

Suddenly the night had become cold. As he went along the walkway by the Museum of London he drew the lapels of his jacket round his neck. Often during his stay in the city he'd wondered if he had a *confrère* looking after his interests as all agents were supposed to have. Now he knew the answer. The call could have come from no one else.

The next morning Scannell went early to the office. As usual on a Sunday, there was only a skeleton staff on the newsdesk, operating with a small team of duty reporters. Specialist correspondents only came in if they had a pressing story to write, or if a major news story was expected to break. As Scannell approached the desk, Estabrook looked up in surprise. He had been ploughing through a pile of Sunday newspapers looking for stories which might need following up.

'Worried about your piece?' he said when Scannell pulled up a chair. 'Forget about it. It's all in the bag. I spoke to the lawyers last night. They've given it the all-clear.'

At first, Scannell said nothing. It was ironic that his relationship with Estabrook, who'd put his full weight behind the story, had never been better. Slowly, he looked up.

'Did they want any changes?'

Estabrook threw a crumpled newspaper, from which he'd cut several articles, into a large waste-bin behind his desk.

'A couple of amendments . . . nothing drastic. They just didn't want us to take any unnecessary risks.'

Scannell looked around at the two assistants on the desk; the copytaster sorting stories on the overnight Reuters tape; the trainee reporter working under Estabrook's guidance.

'Can we go to your office?' Scannell asked.

Estabrook looked puzzled. 'Why?'

As he spoke, he pushed the cuttings across the desk for the copytaster to attach to a clip. Scannell felt himself shrinking away from the task ahead. Estabrook was so unaware of what was to come, it was unnerving to watch him carrying out these routine newsdesk functions. With the main syndication deadlines hours away, it was the most relaxed time of the day.

Finally, Scannell pushed his chair back. 'It's about the story. We need to talk.'

Estabrook said nothing. He'd picked up another newspaper from the pile and was starting to flick through it. Scannell realized he had made himself sound too calm, too matter-of-fact. He hadn't put enough urgency into his voice.

'Something's cropped up,' he added.

Estabrook finished the story he was scanning, then folded the paper. As he lifted himself from his seat, he gave the copytaster a look of tedium.

'Mind the phones for me, would you? We'll only be a couple of minutes.'

Scannell followed him across the newsroom to the glass-panelled office that the departmental editors used when dictating confidential letters and conducting interviews. Inside was a desk heaped with oddments of paper. Scannell couldn't remember the last time it had been cleared. Because it was used by senior personnel, the cleaners who came in at night daren't touch it.

'What's the problem?' Estabrook said, walking over to the desk. He gave a disparaging smile. 'You're not getting cold feet, are you?'

Scannell closed the door, shutting out the background clatter of the machines in the wire-room. He sat down on one of the two spare chairs. He didn't answer at once.

'You'll have to take it off the newslist,' he said at last. 'We can't run it.'

For a moment, Estabrook appeared intrigued. 'Why? The scheduling's been arranged. When do you think we *ought* to run it?'

Scannell understood the reason for Estabrook's relatively calm protest. He had missed the point entirely.

'We can't run it at all. I've been sold a rotten one.'

Estabrook still maintained his dispassionate expression. It was as though he couldn't take in the significance of what

Scannell was saying. Then, slowly, twin points of anger were distilled in his eyes.

'Are you telling me that you've been working for nearly a fortnight on a story that only just now has fallen through?'

Scannell held his poise. 'I didn't know.'

For a second or two, Estabrook stared at him; just stared. As his disparate reactions came into focus, he shook his head with incredulity.

'After all the work the lawyers have done on it . . . all the documentation?'

Scannell was unable to respond. Estabrook's indignation became more open.

'Come off it, pal. The whole syndication schedule's been done round this piece.'

Scannell sat quietly. At last he said: 'Someone's tried to set me up. I don't know who.'

There was an extended silence. It seemed that Estabrook could find no words to match his rancour. In the end, he said bleakly: 'How did you find out?'

'A source.'

Again, Estabrook fell quiet. He fiddled with a box of matches on the desk, formulating a response. Then his face darkened further.

'No . . . Fuck it! You'll have to do better than that. I'm not going to pull it off the list . . . not just because you've got the squitters!'

'We haven't got any choice . . .'

'I've seen your source material. That's good enough for me. I'm going to speak to the lawyers again. If they say it's a fair business risk, then we're going to run it.'

'You can't. I told you . . . it's a plant.'

Estabrook had already reached for the phone. He picked up the receiver but, seeming to have second thoughts, held his finger on the cradle-button.

'How d'you know?' he demanded fiercely. 'Who's your source?'

'I can't tell you that.'

Estabrook gave a short laugh and banged the receiver down hard. 'Great!' He paused, then stood up. 'Listen . . . I've had enough of you prima donnas coming up with your insight pieces . . . your famous investigative features . . . stories that turn out to be so much horseshit! I tell you, unless you can give me a better explanation, then it runs – this afternoon, as planned. You can take your byline off it if you want. That's up to you.'

Scannell felt a crease of pain up the side of his neck. He became aware that throughout Estabrook's diatribe he'd been holding himself rigid – and with good reason. The threat was not light. Estabrook would see it through if he could. Somehow there had to be a way of convincing him.

'You've got to take my word for it. If we syndicate that story, we'll be the comedy kings of Fleet Street. My byline or not – everyone in the business will know who wrote it. I'll be totally discredited . . . so will the agency.'

Estabrook sat down again. The last element of Scannell's warning appeared to have brought him up short. He took a match from the box and began to chew the end.

'What makes you think someone's trying to discredit you? Why should they do that? Because of the anti-nuclear story?'

'Possibly. I don't know.'

Estabrook sat in further silence. 'Have you spoken to Household?'

'No. I wanted to talk to you first. If he knows you're prepared to drop it, he'll support the decision.'

Estabrook shook his head in a maimed expression of disbelief. He discarded the match in a waste-bin.

'Jesus,' he said finally, 'I hope he puts you against the fucking wall!'

24

From mid-morning, on the specially installed television monitors in his office, Fairweather had been watching the demonstrators gathering at Hyde Park. The police strength, he'd observed, was also building up. On the screen he could see their communications vans parked at strategic points in nearby streets.

He glanced out of the window. The spring sunshine of breakfast-time had given way to cloud in the past hour. As the early radio bulletins had forecast, the uncertain weather was general across the country. Not that that would do anything to curb the co-ordinated demonstrations. As always, the US bases and missile sites would be among the first targets. After that would come assaults on the UK's own naval and communications centres. Almost certainly, the protests, with a predicted 150,000 participants in London and 75,000 more at the other focal points, threatened to be the most vocal Easter denunciation yet of international nuclear weapons policies.

He stood up and straightened his jacket. It was time to go downstairs. The announcement he was about to make to the Unit Nine staff would, he was certain, be seen later as a watershed in the operation. It annoyed him, though, that it had taken so long to reach this point. The one compensating factor was the knowledge that, if Rodway had actually succeeded in his attempt to nail Scannell by planting the defence contracting story, the plan would have taken even longer to implement.

As arranged, Blom was waiting for him in Rodway's office. There was no need for a briefing; after weeks of carefully prepared meetings, both of them were perfectly aware of the

173

single matter on the agenda. Blom, who was carrying a clutch of papers, followed Fairweather into the conference room where the staff had been told to assemble. As the two men entered, there was an immediate hush. It was almost as if the staff knew what to expect. Fairweather and Blom drew out seats at the top of the table. A secretary brought them coffee.

'Sit down,' Fairweather told the gathering. After giving everyone time to find a seat, he went on: 'I know some of you have had to come in on your day off . . . Still, that's something we all have to live with. What's important is that everyone's here together.'

For some minutes he spoke of the unit's work, reminding the staff that their task was one of the most difficult of all security operations.

'That doesn't excuse the fact that the job isn't being done as well as it might be,' he added. 'It's no coincidence that I've chosen today to make an announcement. Out there –' he directed his gaze towards the window, 'the anti-nuclear campaigners are having a birthday party at our expense.'

As he was speaking, the members of staff cast glances across the table. His tone was, even for him, antagonistic and uncompromising; it was as though he wanted everybody in the unit to feel they were being personally criticized.

'I'm told efforts have been made to curb the movement's influence,' he went on. 'Whether that's true or not, it's still the single biggest internal subversive organization – and it's us who've got to deal with it.'

While Fairweather was speaking, Blom made one or two notes on a pad.

'I've decided to bring in some fresh minds at the top of the operational level,' Fairweather continued. 'Mr Rodway has agreed to take charge of another project. He'll be replaced by Mr Blom here. From today you'll report directly to him.'

Fairweather stopped talking briefly, giving the staff time to absorb the information. Then he concluded: 'I don't need to say that I expect you to give him full and immediate co-operation. We're going to turn this unit round and get some results.'

25

Scannell arrived at the quayside mooring and, from a foot-bridge further up the canal, waited for de Puydt to leave the houseboat. It was a cold April afternoon, the overcast sky a familiar monochrome. Beyond the next footbridge, a dredger was at work where old wooden piles were being uprooted to make way for a concrete quay. The construction crew were the only people along this quiet, backstreet canal, apart from occasional pedestrians coming along the brick path from the direction of the Prinsengracht.

Scannell focused his attention directly on the houseboat. It wasn't large – probably no more than two or three rooms – and, like Amsterdam's hundreds of other similar water-borne residences that clung to any spare canal wall, it looked as though it was held together solely by the caked layers of paint on its ramshackle boards.

For some days, Scannell had been monitoring de Puydt's comings and goings, relating them to schedules outlined in Van Noort's report. So far, the schedules had conformed exactly to what Scannell had seen. Van Noort, it appeared, had done a thorough job.

At 2.30, as Scannell had expected, de Puydt left the houseboat and walked off in the direction of the main canal. If he stuck to his routine, he would catch a tram into the city centre where he would deliver a batch of work to his agent. It appeared that he made a living as a freelance illustrator, mainly for small-circulation magazines.

Scannell stood by the metal railing, his eyes following de Puydt's progress along the quayside. When the Dutchman was out of sight behind an apartment building, Scannell moved down to the quay and stood less obtrusively by some flagstone steps that led up to the entrance of a narrow, gabled, building. He raised the zipper on his anorak to keep out the wind that came down between the houses. It would be best to give it half an hour before attempting to get on board the houseboat, he decided. That would give de Puydt time to walk to the tram-stop and, in the event of his having forgotten something, return home.

At three o'clock Scannell checked his watch. After making sure he wasn't being observed from the houses on the opposite quay, he climbed the three wooden steps that led up to the deck of the houseboat. At this point, there was no time for caution. He knew that the more he lingered on the deck, the more suspicious he would look to anyone walking past. In case de Puydt had left any visitors on board, he knocked at the main door. To his relief, no one answered. Nothing moved except the boat itself, which lifted gently in the water, stirred by his own weight. He gave the handle a quick turn, but the door was locked.

To look for an easier means of access, he went round to the other side of the deck. He didn't want to risk breaking in unless it was absolutely necessary. Round where the canal lapped against the low hull, he was uncomfortably in view of the high houses that overlooked the water. Hurriedly, he tried the handle of another door, glancing into the boat through a small, inset pane of glass. A rough push confirmed that this door, too, was locked.

Ultimately, he was forced to resort to methods he'd learnt in his training days. The front door was fitted with a conventional lock but, with the boat being as old as it was, the wooden frame was considerably out of alignment. He took one of several plastic credit cards from his wallet, inserted it into the gap and gave a sharp twist to the left. With only a gentle pull, the door swung open.

Stepping inside the houseboat, Scannell peered down a short stairwell. As a further precaution to make sure nobody was on board, he called out, but there was no answer. He closed the door behind him and went silently down the stairs. At the bottom, where a tiny gangway led to the main living-room, he stood still and listened. Apart from the dull chug of the dredger, whose rhythm he could feel through the floor timbers, there wasn't a sound.

Scannell looked at the three doors around him. First, he went into the main room. Surprisingly, it was equipped with modern stripped pine furnishings, although the place was in something of a mess. Clothes were strewn over the back of a settee, and books and papers were stacked on the windowshelves. He tried the other two doors, which opened on to a cramped bathroom and, a few steps along the gangway, a bedroom that appeared to double as a study. A portable typewriter stood on a table, and one wall was lined with bookshelves. Most of the space was taken up by a large drawing-board, which had an expensive-looking light attachment at the top.

A cursory search of the boat took Scannell from the cooking area of the living-room back through to the bedroom. He paid scant attention to the papers in the living-room, guessing that, if de Puydt did have something worth knowing about, he wouldn't have left it lying around so conspicuously. Instead, Scannell decided to concentrate his efforts in the bedroom. Starting with a set of envelope files above the table, he set to work.

It was a fruitless task. After half an hour of rummaging through old committee agendas and papers, frustration overcame his methodical approach. The next twenty minutes took him to the end of the bookshelves, but still he found nothing that would go any way towards exposing de Puydt.

A cupboard pushed against the side of the desk contained still more material. As Scannell turned his attention to a batch of clip-files, he realized that he was in danger of wasting the entire afternoon. Time was already pressing; if he stayed more than another forty minutes, he would risk still being on board when de Puydt returned. According to Van Noort's schedule, that would be at 4.45.

Scannell stopped to think. If de Puydt was working alone in the field, he had to have a safe storage place for confidential information. It was a basic operating principle. Another principle was that you should never choose a storage place in your own home, but this was a maxim that agents of any service were inclined to ignore. The simple fact was: your home was the one place where you could keep your eye on important documentation. He himself had been guilty of the practice on occasion.

Sitting on the bed, he tried to put himself in de Puydt's position. Where was the most likely place he would choose? Again, in pursuit of an answer, he went to the front of the houseboat and assessed each room in turn. The only conceivable place, in his mind, was the bathroom. It was somewhere he often favoured himself but, in de Puydt's case, there was a doubly good reason – one of inverse logic: the room was so tiny that there was, seemingly, nowhere to hide anything. There wasn't even a wall-cabinet: all the toiletries were lined up on a shelf above the basin.

The shelf.

Scannell examined it closely. It fitted neatly on to one of the painted plywood wall panels. He tapped the panel and those next to it. Together they made up a hollow bulkhead, but the one with the shelf fixture was, if anything, slightly duller in sound than the other two. Inspecting the fixture, he noticed a tiny gap running the length of the panel where it met a vertical baton. He pulled gently at the shelf and tried to prise the panel away with his fingers, but it didn't move.

By now, however, he was determined to see what was behind it. Working fast, he fetched a knife from a drawer in the cooking area. Before touching the panel further, he removed the toiletries one by one from the shelf and placed them in an identical pattern in the shower-tray. By doing this, he could be sure of putting them back correctly on the shelf before he came to leave.

Even using the knife, the panel proved difficult to work free without damaging the surrounding woodwork. He remembered seeing a screwdriver in a cupboard under the sink, and fetched that to take off the shelf.

The screws, in brass housings, were surprisingly free-moving, considering the bathroom's damp atmosphere. As he loosened the first one, he saw there was no trace of rust. He worked faster. Supporting the shelf with his left hand, he loosened the second and third screws. Soon he was able to lift the shelf away. Behind it, flush with the surface of the wall, was an inset catch, again of brass. Quelling a premature excitement, he hooked his finger into the ring of the catch and slowly eased the panel outwards. It opened on recessed hinges revealing the interior of a narrow cabinet divided by a shelf. Inside were two box files.

The moment he opened the first file, he knew he had found what he was looking for.

It was mid-afternoon when Celia was called in. As she walked with one of the departmental security escorts through the doors at the Great Marlborough Street offices, she knew she was going to have to do some fast thinking. It had been weeks now since her controllers had sent for her, and she'd begun to hope that they'd lost interest in the assignment. Consequently, she'd volunteered no information to either Greengross or Larsen. That, she was beginning to realize, had been a mistake.

Three of the controllers were sitting at a long table like a panel of assessors. Larsen was one of them – the only one she knew. He was to the left. It was the long-jawed, elderly one in the centre who spoke.

'Sit down, Mrs Forde.'

He opened a folder and didn't smile. Celia went to the

only chair. It was hard and wooden, like one from a doctor's waiting-room. It stood in front of the table.

'We want to ask you some questions – about Mr Scannell.'

The man, whom she presumed was the head of department, paused, as though expecting her to speak, but she remained silent.

'You've been seeing him frequently, I understand. What exactly have you got to tell us?'

The man's anaemic manner was disarming, and Celia was confused as to what she should say. She guessed that the conversation was being recorded. In a back room later, no doubt, they would dissect everything she said.

'You asked . . . I mean, I was asked to get to know him. That's what I've been doing.'

The head of department nodded. While Celia was speaking, he took off his glasses and began to wipe them meticulously with his handkerchief. He gave the appearance of only half listening, but she assumed this was just the discourteous habit of someone long accustomed to exercising authority. Then, suddenly, he put the glasses back on and looked up.

'The feedback – as you might have guessed – has been inadequate.'

Inside Celia, a spring began to wind up. She was unsure how to react. It was difficult to make out whether he was censuring her, or making a simple declaration of fact.

'I'm doing what I can,' she told him. 'He's not the most talkative man in the world.'

'Obviously you've spoken to him about his work?'

The head of department gave her a flat look. Everything about him, from his stiff cheekbones to his educated bearing, was intimidating. She noticed how Larsen was letting him carry the proceedings. Facing him directly, she was determined not to show how apprehensive she felt.

'I've stopped asking him. I didn't want to make him think I was digging for something.'

'Digging?'

'I . . . I ask him about things, but he doesn't ever spell anything out. He's talked about the pressure he's under . . .'

'What sort of pressure? Perhaps you'd explain.'

Celia shrugged. She was sitting with her hands tightly clasped in her lap, a posture she remembered having adopted in the interview with Larsen and Greengross. Sensing that it might reveal her inner qualms, she sat back in the chair and tried to look more relaxed. She made out to be considering the question.

'People getting on his back at work, I suppose. They want him to . . . to do things. He hasn't got the time.'

'What about the stories he writes? Does he ever talk about them?'

'Sometimes. It's a bit above my head.'

The questioning continued for some minutes. Everything that was put to her was in the same vein. What had Scannell told her? What had he mentioned about his work? She didn't know how to communicate that she was telling them the truth: he rarely said anything about his professional activities. Even if she had wanted to co-operate, all she could have given them was trivia.

The head of department – if, indeed, that was who he was – became demonstrably impatient.

'For heaven's sake, woman, you've been sleeping with him for weeks! He must have told you something!'

In the deepest niche of Celia's sensibilities, a flame of hatred suddenly ignited. It seemed she had assumed correctly at the start of the assignment that they viewed her as little more than a common prostitute, selling her favours for information. If they thought they would get anything out of her now, they were wildly mistaken.

'Why are you asking me all this? I've told you – whatever I do, I can't get anything out of him. Not that I know what I'm supposed to be doing,' she added cuttingly. 'Why don't you just take me off the assignment? I'll go back to my old job.'

A silence followed, during which the three men stared at her as though she had blasphemed against some religious doctrine. It was Larsen who eventually spoke.

'Let me remind you, Mrs Forde, that you have been re-graded.'

'De-grade me then. It's not as if I'm *earning* the extra money. There's nothing I can do.'

There was another uneasy silence. Then, for the first time, the man on the right of the table spoke.

'It happens, sometimes, that results are a long time coming. I think we all have to be prepared to exercise a little restraint.'

He seemed not only to be addressing Celia, but also his colleagues. She couldn't make out whether he was of superior rank to the other two. Certainly, he had no inhibitions about voicing his opinions.

'Tell us,' he added, looking openly at Celia, 'do you sympathize with the sort of things Mr Scannell writes about?'

Celia held back for a moment. 'I don't know. What things do you mean?'

'The anti-nuclear campaign . . . the peace movement. I wondered whether he might have brought the subject up.'

Celia thought back to the intermittent conversations she'd had with Scannell on the nature of his work, and was aware of her intellectual inadequacy. She found it difficult to express what she thought on such matters, and feared she would trip herself up.

'I don't know. How does anyone know what's best? It seems there's only a few politicians in the world who really know what's going on – and I doubt that sometimes.'

The controller considered her answer, but didn't seem to be satisfied.

'Let me put it this way . . . If you were sitting in Downing Street, say, or the White House, would you consider it desirable or rash to follow a policy of unilateral nuclear disarmament?'

Celia looked for the trap. What did he want her to say? As far as her reasoning on the matter went, if you were blown up, you were blown up. She gave the reply, though, that she thought they would be waiting for.

'That would depend what was happening in Moscow, I suppose.'

The controller nodded, but his expression didn't reveal how he interpreted the answer. After a short pause, he added: 'Would you be alarmed if you were told that Mr Scannell has . . . shall we say, subversive connections?'

This was the closest anyone in the department had yet come to disclosing the reasons for the operation against Scannell. Inside her, something shrank from hearing what was being said.

'You mean his contacts?' she asked.

The controller gestured sparingly. 'Whatever.'

Celia's trepidation was increasing. She didn't know what he was trying to tell her. Or was he just attempting to frighten her? Did they suspect the truth about her relationship with Scannell? They had used her to set a trap for him, and now she was falling into one herself.

'I imagine he sees people who give him information,' she said.

'Does he ever talk to you about these people?'

'No. Never.'

At least she was able to give a definitive reply on that one. She had no idea who his contacts were. The head of department, who seemed chafed by his colleague's more muted tone of questioning, again focused his eyes on her.

'Tell us, Mrs Forde – do you have any conception of the seriousness of your assignment?'

'Only what you've told me.'

The head of department gave her a piercing look, and she was forced to avoid his eyes.

'You may not realize it,' he continued, 'but Mr Scannell is playing a highly dangerous game. We need all the information we can get, so we can properly assess his position.'

The man on his right leaned forward and gave a brief smile. 'It could be, of course, that he's working totally legitimately. However, without that information, I'm afraid it could become a little difficult for us to guarantee his safety.'

Celia suffered a momentary bout of light-headedness. *His safety?* She had expected at last to be told something positive, so that she could decide for herself whether Scannell was concealing anything from her. But again she was being fed a concoction of warnings and enigmatic signals.

A few further summary questions were asked, then the head of department announced: 'I think that's all we need hear for today.' He looked directly at Celia. 'You can go now.'

Celia was shaken. It was such an abrupt conclusion to the interview that she felt she must have said something terribly wrong.

'Is that all?' she asked.

The head of department nodded. 'Think about what we've discussed. If you decide there's anything we should know, contact Mr Larsen's office.'

Hesitantly, Celia reached for her coat which she had folded over the back of the chair. The three controllers consulted quietly with one another as she walked from the room. Outside in the corridor, the security escort was waiting. He took her to the lift and down to the main lobby.

As she walked across Hanover Square in the afternoon sunshine, the head of department's parting words clung in her consciousness: *think about what we've discussed.*

What *had* they discussed? As far as she was concerned, the interview had been little short of an interrogation. She was still trying to weigh up the controllers' intentions in calling her in. Had they really wanted information, or were they trying to make her reassess what she thought about Scannell? Still echoing at the back of her mind was the warning about his safety. Why had the head of department said it? Were they trying to compel her into going further with the assignment than she'd ever intended? One thing alone was certain: they wouldn't be taking so much trouble over Scannell unless he had a high priority in the department's schedule. More than at any time in her life, she was at a loss to know what to do, or who to turn to.

Scannell stood in the bathroom of the houseboat and studied the box file's contents. Inside was an anonymous brown envelope, but the few sheets of paper it contained would give his story massive substantiation.

The documents, which bore a UK Ministry of Defence classification, amounted to a dossier of compromising material on leading members of CND and the European Anti-Nuclear Organization. It had clearly been collated from information supplied by inside sources. There was no time to assess it; that would have to be done later. One thing he could see at a glance, though, was that the dossier included details not only of the members' left-wing affiliations – a predictable line of attack – but areas of personal vulnerability which could provide fuel for a widescale defamation campaign.

Scannell wasn't surprised to find that members with homosexual tendencies had been singled out as potential blackmail targets, nor that information had been dug out on instances of juvenile crimes and drugs offences. These were classroom examples of easy victims – text-book cases. What did astonish him was the breadth of the data; everything from members' attendances at meetings where some publicly discredited individual happened also to have been seen, to courtesy visits to Communist countries. Nothing was regarded as insignificant; nothing too trivial. De Puydt had, it seemed, been working under instructions to co-ordinate every scrap of information that came to his attention. It was intelligence of a highly sophisticated order.

At the end of the dossier was a series of recommendations as to how smear tactics could best be used against the organizations. All the listed individuals were pinpointed as ripe for coercion.

Scannell stared at the report, wondering what action he should take. He glanced at his watch: almost 4.30. He was already into his safety margin. Spreading the sheets of paper on the floor, he took a Minox from his anorak pocket and swiftly photographed each sheet in turn. The hip-pocket camera was something he normally kept in his desk at the agency, but on trips abroad he packed it in his travel bag. As Van Noort had demonstrated, a single photograph could give a story dramatic credibility.

Scannell used the entire roll of film to make certain of having several good prints. From the bedroom, he selected a random document that he guessed de Puydt wouldn't miss from the files. This he needed for a comparison of typewriter faces – vital if it became necessary to submit evidence proving that the Dutchman was the author of the list of names.

As soon as he'd finished, he put the papers back in the brown envelope and set to work to leave the bathroom seemingly untouched. The time was coming dangerously close to making his continued presence on board seem reckless, but he had to make sure he left nothing out of place.

Two or three times he broke off to see if there was any sign of de Puydt returning. At one point, his attention was drawn to a figure walking towards the houseboat along the quay, but his experienced eye soon identified it as that of a workman. None the less, the initial shock made his hands tremble for minutes afterwards, lengthening the time it took to cover his traces.

Then, just as Scannell was closing the bathroom door, he felt the boat rock. For a second he thought it had been caused by his own movement but, as he stood still, he felt it again. Instantly, his skin tingled, and his breath seemed to catch. There was no mistake. Someone had come on board. The only time available for getting away or hiding was that which it would take de Puydt to insert his key in the lock and turn it.

Raising himself on tiptoe, Scannell was able to cast a glimpse through the window at the top of the stairwell. De Puydt had a woman with him. Her outline was visible behind a grubby net curtain. The signals that activated Scannell's reflexes became jumbled. De Puydt on his own would have been bad enough, but with another person as well . . .

Scannell evaluated a limited range of options. He knew that his only chance of getting out of the cabin was up the side stairwell, but if either de Puydt or the woman came round to the other door, that possibility would also be lost. There was a time, not so long ago, when he would have faced such a situation with calculated coolness. Perhaps, even, have tried to brazen it out. Now, though, his secondary survival systems were forced to come into play. All he knew was that he had to act – and quickly.

While the Dutchman was standing at the door, presumably searching for his keys, Scannell could hear him chatting casually to the woman. Neither of them could suspect his presence, he figured, or they would be moving with greater urgency. Treading gently across the hall, he lifted his right foot so it was on the first step of the side stairwell. If only he could get to the top, there was still a chance he could make it. By crouching low, he knew he couldn't be seen through any of the windows. As he climbed the steps, he steadied himself with his hands, careful to make no rapid movement.

In those few, crucial seconds, he acted purely mechanically. Just as he reached the top of the stairwell, he heard the main door open and the sudden loudness of the two voices. Only an angled, plywood bulkhead stood between him and certain detection. If he'd had the time, he might have questioned his judgement in coming on board at all, but the thought was only one of many turning in his mind.

As de Puydt and the woman came down the steps, Scannell swiftly turned the key in the lock. The door opened noiselessly, and he stepped out on to the deck. In the same instant, he closed the door and flattened himself against the cabin's outside wall. He held his breath and clenched his hands: they were moist with sweat. His pulse rate could have been measured in any one of a dozen points over his body.

With the most critical stage over, he waited. Waited for the rush of footsteps, the shouts of alarm. Waited, alternatively, for the slow tilt of the boat that would tell him that de Puydt – with greater reserves of calm than his own – was stealing up the stairway. Waited for the inching open of the door. That was the instant when his fist would crash into jawbone, when blind aggression would drive him to debilitate, to kill.

While his natural inclination was to get off the boat as quickly as possible, he knew that such action would almost certainly lead to his being spotted – either by de Puydt and the woman, or by someone on the quayside. That wouldn't matter if he could get away, but it could be disastrous if he were caught. To be questioned by the police, particularly in a country where he was travelling under a foreign passport, was a risk he was neither careless enough, nor desperate enough, to take.

As he stood motionless outside the door, his eyes darted from one window to another of the houses on the opposite side of the canal, all the time watching for faces. Further down the canal, just beyond the footbridge, a man in shirt-sleeves leaned out over a small balcony to water some red flowers in pots, but he was concentrating too much on his chore to be concerned with any activity on the boats.

When no sounds of alarm came from the cabin below, Scannell squatted on his haunches and worked his way to the stern of the boat. The nearest of the neighbouring

189

houseboats was about seven or eight metres away. Pausing only to make sure that the camera and documents were zipped tightly into the breast pocket of his anorak, he lowered himself into the water.

It was colder than he'd expected. Worse, he was immediately aware of the smell of engine oil and effluent. As his feet touched the bottom, they sank into treacly mud. The water rose almost to his chest. He wasn't unduly worried about soiling the papers and film, because the pocket had a waterproof plastic lining, but he knew that if he was in the water for any length of time, it could start penetrating the zipper.

He guessed the height of the canal wall. A metre, perhaps a little more, above the surface of the water. Too high to climb to the quay from his present position. During his earlier observations, though, he'd made a mental note of a tyre that was hanging from a rope beyond the neighbouring houseboat's mooring. That was where he would be able to pull himself up.

As he moved forward through the water, he hugged the canal wall. Although it took no more than two minutes to cross to the cover of the other houseboat, his problems weren't over. He couldn't follow the hull round, because of the danger of being seen. His only course was to squeeze between the boat and the canal wall. There was room, yes, but he would have to stay flattened against the brickwork. If, for some reason, the houseboat were to be forced those few inches closer to the bank – if, say, a motor-launch came down the canal at a critical moment – his head could be squashed like a piece of fruit.

There was no time for thoughts of melodrama. Moving behind the houseboat, he pressed his back to the wall. As he inched towards the stern, he helped himself along by gripping the cracks in the brickwork. When he was little more than halfway along, he became aware of somebody moving about on board. The houseboat bobbed ponderously, nudging his head against the bricks. Rather than wait for the movements to stop, he searched for another crack in the wall and edged himself forward. An arm's reach away was an iron ring cemented into the brickwork. It was about half a metre above the level of the water, but he gauged that with some effort he could grab it.

Roughly, his fingers scratched at the wall. He lifted himself up on his toes but, even as he reached out for the ring, he began to sink in the mud. The swaying of the houseboat was threatening to push him under the water. It was now or never. Lunging forward, he managed to curl his fingertips round the ring. His grip wasn't firm, but at least he had a hold. He brought his left hand up between his chest and the hull. Then he gave a gentle shove. The counterforce moved the boat slightly away from him, and he was able to fasten his fingers more firmly round the ring. With one strong pull, he was through to a wider gap.

Before hauling himself up to the quay, he paused to regain his breath. He also listened for anyone coming along the path. He could hear nothing. Nor was he visible from the houses opposite. With his left hand, he grabbed the rope that held the tyre. Then he brought a knee up to gain leverage against the rubber rim. With his free hand, he stretched up for the mooring rail that ran along the edge of the quay. Now he was able to haul himself out of the water.

As he rolled up on to the quayside, he glanced down at his clothes. His shoes and trousers were caked in a brown ooze. Somewhere he would have to make an excuse to a shopkeeper and buy replacements. Right now, though, the problem didn't worry him greatly. Picking himself up, he cast a fleeting glance back at de Puydt's houseboat and set off down the path at a steady run. He didn't think he'd been seen.

26

Tiverzin rode in the back of the black, chauffeur-driven Volga with Leonov, the assistant director of Active Measures. She recognized the prestige of being in the private company of a senior member of the directorate. At the same time, she was puzzled and a little daunted. He had invited her to lunch at his home. It was safer to talk there than in his office, he'd said.

They drove in from the directorate's offices round the orbital highway to the apartment block off Komsomol Avenue. It was an imposing address, although the block itself was plain and uninspiring. The driver parked outside a rear entrance and Leonov got out, his stout figure shuffling awkwardly on the pavement.

The overbearing façade of the building, as Tiverzin soon found out, belied its interior comforts. The entrance hall was thickly carpeted, and in one corner there was a reception desk like that of a hotel. A plain-clothes security guard came out of a side room to check Tiverzin's papers. Even though she was Leonov's guest, the formalities were followed to the letter. When the guard had satisfied himself that all was in order, Leonov nodded to him briefly and led Tiverzin over to a lift-bay.

As they rode up, Leonov lit a wretched-smelling cigarette, one of the *papirosi*, the type with a hollow cardboard holder, smoked by agricultural and factory workers. It was an indication of Leonov's coarse origins which, to Tiverzin's distaste, he made no attempt to disguise.

After the spaciousness of the entrance hall, Tiverzin was surprised to find that Leonov's apartment was scarcely bigger than her own. It had a second bedroom and a larger kitchen, but the decor was austere. Few pictures hung on the walls. The focal object was a framed, faded photograph standing on a sideboard. It showed a handsome young man with his arm round the shoulders of a girl in an open-necked blouse. It looked pre-war. Tiverzin had some difficulty recognizing the man as Leonov, but saw the similarity round the eyes and high cheekbones. The girl was also good-looking, with heavy Lithuanian features.

'My wife,' Leonov said, nodding in the direction of the photograph. He had come through from the kitchen with a bottle of wine. 'She died in 'fifty-six.'

Tiverzin said nothing, but lowered her eyes deferentially. She watched as Leonov opened the bottle; the label was French. Even the shops to which she was entitled to go didn't sell such select vintages – not at the prices normal people could afford. Leonov fetched two glasses from a cupboard.

'I'm having some lunch sent up,' he said. 'I have no time to prepare food.'

Again, Tiverzin answered with a nod. His apartment might not have been up to her expectations, but he certainly lived well.

After some preliminary enquiries about her work in the directorate, he asked her specifically about the progress of Operation Lyosha. As she'd suspected – and feared – this seemed to be the reason for the invitation.

'We're almost there,' she told him. 'Just one or two minor problems to sort out.'

Leonov lit another of his cigarettes. It was these, Tiverzin guessed, which gave the apartment a strong smell of staleness.

'From what I've heard, 10-10 is on a twenty-four-hour alert. Is that right?'

The statement was made in a casual, almost uninterested manner, but its impact was explosive. Tiverzin wondered where his information had come from. Surely not Sofinsky?

As far as she'd been able to find out, Sofinsky still believed 10-10 to be on a routine operating schedule. She sipped some wine to give herself time to formulate a reply.

'Yes,' she said finally, 'as a temporary measure.'

Leonov raised a heavy eyebrow. 'Perhaps you could tell me why the information hasn't been passed on to your superiors?'

Tiverzin's pulse quickened. Leonov had a way of looking at her that made her feel as if she were laying her heart out on the table ready for dissection. Just what, exactly, did he know? What was he after?

'I saw no immediate need,' she replied. 'The situation's being watched closely.'

'I'm glad to hear it.'

The conversation broke off when the doorbell rang and a woman brought in their lunch. Tiverzin didn't know whether it had come from a nearby restaurant or a special kitchen in the apartment block. At the moment, she had little desire to ask.

As the woman left, Leonov lifted the lid off a glass bowl. He gave an approving smile.

'There's one good thing you get the further you go up the ladder . . . fresh salad.'

It was the first light remark he'd made, and Tiverzin gave a nervous smile. Leonov served out some chicken pieces and potatoes.

For a minute or two, they ate in silence, then Leonov said: 'To be frank, captain, I'm a little troubled by the way you're doing things. Lyosha's a key operation. Everybody should be kept informed.'

The bluntness of the statement put Tiverzin further off balance. She started to wonder what more there was to come.

'Perhaps it was remiss of me, comrade colonel. I shall brief my staff on the need for a more efficient communications flow.'

Leonov nodded his approval. Tiverzin couldn't guess

whether he accepted the collective departmental blame, or whether he held her to be personally at fault. She decided, as they were on the subject, that she would try to find out his sources of information.

'Incidentally, comrade colonel, could you tell me if you've been receiving Line N reports?'

She tried to make the question sound like a passing thought.

Leonov gave her an enigmatic look. 'I receive many reports, captain.'

Later in the meal, Tiverzin broached the question from a different angle.

'You mentioned certain problems about Operation Lyosha. What have you heard exactly?'

Leonov washed his food down with a mouthful of wine. Patting his chest, and wincing with the pain of indigestion, he placed his glass on the table. Tiverzin felt that he was sizing her up, appraising her manner.

'You tell me,' he said obliquely.

Tiverzin hesitated. She didn't want to tell him more than he might already know, but at the same time she didn't want to be seen to be deliberately withholding information. Finally, she replied: 'We think Novost is about to be exposed.'

Leonov nodded solemnly, as though the disclosure were no surprise.

'Why didn't you tell your departmental head?'

'It's a crucial operation. I thought Kochev might recommend a shutdown. We can't let it fail. It's so near.'

'You think Kochev's losing his nerve?'

'I . . .'

Tiverzin checked herself. Whatever she might feel, she wasn't going to have words put in her mouth.

'If the operation is blown, we would have to bring 10-10 out. That could mean the end of Operation Aleksei.'

'What's so important about 10-10?' Leonov put to her.

'We've calculated that seven other agents in the British press and broadcasting services would possibly be at risk. That's almost half the operating force.'

Leonov took some more food. 'At least someone's doing their homework in your section.'

When Leonov had finished his meal, he fetched a fresh packet of cigarettes from the sideboard. Sitting back, he inhaled with a throaty rasp.

'One thing I've learnt in half a lifetime in the directorate, comrade, is that people function better in their work if they know what they're supposed to be doing. That's why I brought you back here today – to tell you what's going on.'

Tiverzin frowned. Whatever he was leading up to, it sounded serious.

'You might think the world starts and ends with Operation Lyosha,' he went on, 'but some of us have to take a broader view.'

'I realize that, but . . .'

'. . . Operation Aleksei is a major campaign. We're talking about France, West Germany, the Netherlands – the entire European Community, with varying degrees of penetration. You're a division, comrade captain, and sometimes divisions have to be sacrificed to save an army.'

Tiverzin felt the touch of a cold shadow. His meaning was plain.

'Are you saying we've got to shut Lyosha down?'

Leonov's face was set. 'No. I'm saying I want you to start making sure that proper schedules are filed on the day-to-day running of the operation. In the last two weeks, the head of the service has received independent reports from officers Kochev and Sofinsky. Both recommended that funds should be withdrawn. It's only because of my intervention that no such decision has been taken.'

Tiverzin was astounded. She couldn't understand why Leonov, who appeared to be threatening to abandon the operation, should have intervened to save it. Kochev had a powerful ally in Sofinsky, and for their combined recommendations to have been overruled, Leonov must have put up a determined resistance.

'Your intervention?' she queried.

Leonov leaned back. 'You youngsters –' he said, lifting his hand tiredly, 'to you every campaign has to be aggressive. Someone draws up a target, you send in a squad, you do your killing . . . and then you get out. It's an admirable military principle. Sometimes, though, wars need to be fought on the defensive. You have to study the mentality of your opponent . . . try to anticipate his intentions . . . pre-empt his attack.'

'Naturally we look at those things. It's just that time . . .'

'. . . Time is crucial to any operation, but that doesn't mean that things have to be rushed. Aleksei is long-term. For one thing, we have to convince our European neighbours that we don't want a war any more than they do. The United States is building up its nuclear weaponry on *their* soil. We've got to make them understand that it's Washington, not Moscow, who'll pull the trigger.'

For a moment, Tiverzin was silent. 'Where does that leave Lyosha?'

Leonov reached round to a nearby armchair where he'd put his briefcase. He took out a slim document in a transparent plastic folder.

'This is the report I've submitted to the Active Measures Committee. It recommends that you take over from Kochev if you can see the current operation through to its conclusion. I was the one who started Lyosha, and I'm not prepared to see it crippled this close to the end.'

Leonov broke off and poured more wine into both glasses. It was difficult for Tiverzin to take in what he'd said. Far from losing her job, which was what she'd half expected, here she was, being put in charge of the whole network – or as good as. Since the day she'd joined the directorate, her eyes had been set on a departmental controller's post. It hadn't mattered which one – any would have done. Any that would put her on the side of the desk giving the orders, rather than the side taking them. It had been a long haul, and she allowed herself a moment for silent congratulations on her staying power.

The moment, however, was short-lived. Leonov rested a hand on the table.

'Let me give you one word of warning, captain. If you think you can function with me like you've done with Kochev, then you'll be out before you get your feet under his desk. Do you understand that?'

Tiverzin felt adrift. Her eyes avoided Leonov's granite gaze.

'You're getting the job because you're the only one who knows enough about the operation to have a chance of success. The decision will be mine as to whether you abort Lyosha or go on. And remember, any mistake now could put Operation Aleksei in jeopardy.'

27

Scannell awoke refreshed. He'd slept for nine hours since his return the day before from Amsterdam, and as he lay in bed, indulging in a few minutes of meditation before his alarm was due to go off, he reflected that he could now start pulling the diverse threads of his story together. If all went well, he saw it being syndicated within three or four weeks. As to what would happen after that, he didn't like to speculate. Now that he knew his *confrère* was watching him, the recall order from Moscow was bound to come soon.

While in the shower, he contemplated the moves that would be necessary to finalize the story. With the inclusion of de Puydt's material, his dossier was now almost complete. He had to be able to convince the news agency's lawyers that he'd collated sufficient evidence to support the allegations in court – if it should come to having to defend a libel action. On that score, only two pieces of documentation remained to be acquired. First, there was Whymark's ministerial blacklist. Almost certainly, he would agree to hand this over, although additional pressure might need to be exerted. The man was already running scared; he would do anything for a pledge that would save him from further involvement. Second, and more important, was the file on the infiltration network that had been drawn up by Hermann. Following Hermann's death in custody, there had been an approach from a contact in the National Council for Civil Liberties who had suggested that a copy of the file might have passed into the hands of a trusted colleague. In the weeks since that information had filtered through, he'd exhausted every channel of communication to try to find out where the file had gone, but nothing had come to light. Now, if he really wanted to make sure his story would hold, he'd have to concentrate his efforts on tracing it. It was an area where he felt no certainty of success.

He ate a larger breakfast than normal, because he'd been too tired to prepare a meal the night before. On his way out of the apartment complex, he called at a newsagent for his morning papers. He would be in good time for the early editorial conference and, despite the difficulties over Hermann's file, felt in better spirits than he had done for some time.

That all changed when, in the back of a taxi, he opened the papers. The story hit him with the stealth of a premeditated attack. It was a disaster beyond comprehension: a page lead in the home news sections of both *The Times* and the *Guardian*.

Rapidly he read each version, but neither was materially different from the other. Their essence was that the Ministry of Defence had earmarked a site adjacent to the Fylingdales early warning station in North Yorkshire for development as a US medium-range nuclear command bunker. The story was attributed in each of the newspapers to the Aldwych News Agency.

Scannell was stunned. How could the agency have carried it without him knowing? And was it true? He was as close to Ministry of Defence sources as any journalist, yet he hadn't even heard a rumour. If it could be verified, then he could rightly be accused of gross ineptitude.

As soon as he arrived at work, he went to see Estabrook. He was outraged by the way the story had been syndicated behind his back, although his protest had to be muted. He faced Estabrook across the newsdesk.

'Where did it come from?' He dropped the newspapers in front of him.

Estabrook, who had just finished dictating the early news schedule to a secretary, ignored Scannell and called across to the copytaster: 'Let me know as soon as you see a confirmation statement.'

'Who got it?' Scannell demanded.

Estabrook looked up. 'Who got what, pal?'

'The story.'

Estabrook paused and glanced at the papers. 'Oh, that . . . Armitage is your boy. Good piece.'

Scannell's disbelief grew. Armitage was a young American reporter on the general desk. He had only been with the agency for a few months after a short spell on newspapers in Detroit. To be beaten to the story was bad enough, but when the reporter who'd got it was a relative novice, the humiliation was immeasurably heightened.

'When did it come in?'

Estabrook scribbled additional notes on the typed news schedule, then handed it to his secretary to be photocopied. Finally he turned his full attention to Scannell.

'He picked it up yesterday. Why?'

'Why wasn't I consulted?'

As Scannell had been speaking, Estabrook had stood up. His expression matched Scannell's for indignation.

'Because you weren't fucking well here!'

Scannell fell silent, as did the desk around him. There was nothing he could say. On previous occasions when Estabrook had accused him of professional laxity, he'd felt justified in putting up a defence. But this time there was no excuse. It was by far the biggest story he'd ever missed.

Estabrook, becoming tight-lipped, gathered together his papers and clipboard. His secretary returned with photocopies of the newslist, and he took them for distribution in the editorial conference.

'Are you sure the story's true?' asked Scannell, as he followed him along the corridor to the editor's office.

Without looking at him, Estabrook replied: 'We wouldn't have run it if it wasn't.'

'Was it a leak?'

'Armitage has got a copy of the blueprint. That'll show you all you need to know.'

'Did he have official confirmation?'

'He checked with his source.'

'Who was his source? Did he say?'

They reached the editor's door, where other section chiefs and senior correspondents were gathering. They had to wait for Household to finish a private meeting with the business editor.

'You wouldn't expect him to tell me that,' said Estabrook.

'I need to know where he got it from. The story's got a direct bearing on the one I'm working on. It could alert the other correspondents to areas I'm inquiring about. If there's any chance that it's untrue . . .'

Estabrook wheeled round. 'I told you, Armitage checked it out.'

Scannell thought he detected a note of uncertainty in Estabrook's voice, but tried not to attach too much significance to it. He'd seen the same thing countless times before: a sudden onset of doubt after a big story had been syndicated. It was understandable. There was always the chance that some awful mistake had been made which would require, at the very least, an embarrassing retraction. The news editor lived with those high-risk judgements, often based solely on his confidence in an individual reporter. It was an intuitive, unenviable job, and Scannell was obliged to admit that Estabrook performed it well.

As Scannell had expected, there were congratulations in the conference over Armitage's story. These were directed at the news editor, and Scannell stayed quiet. No one asked him why he'd missed the story, but he knew it must have been in everyone's mind.

After the conference, he went back to the newsroom with Estabrook. The look of concern was still on Scannell's face.

'Did Armitage try to contact the Ministry of Defence, do you know?'

202

Estabrook took his seat at the top of the newsdesk. 'He was trying till about ten last night.'

'Couldn't he get anyone?' Scannell spoke with bewilderment.

On a swivel table beside Estabrook's seat was a Reuters screen. Estabrook switched it on and surveyed the up-to-date run of foreign stories as he half listened to what Scannell was saying. After making brief notes on a pad, he looked up tiredly.

'There were some low-ranking press officers who he managed to get hold of at home. None of the others were available.'

Scannell looked dubious. 'That's odd. I've always managed to get hold of the chief press officer – or his deputy.'

'Armitage tried. He's got their home numbers. He couldn't get a reply.'

Scannell's scepticism was beginning to increase. Things were out of place; it had all been too easy. He remained standing by the newsdesk as Estabrook checked through the world currency prices on the monitor.

'Is it possible we've been misled?' Scannell suggested.

Estabrook twisted in his chair. 'Look, just get off my back, will you? First you miss the story – now you're trying to squirm out of it with some cheap gripe. Let Armitage take his credit, eh. He got it, and you didn't. It's as simple as that. Tough shit.'

Scannell waited a moment before turning and going back to his office. He sat at his desk and read Armitage's story again as it had appeared, re-edited, in each of the papers. He also studied the original story as it had gone out on the agency's wire service. The thought of his own incompetence appalled him – and yet he was certain there was something about the story that didn't ring true. It was too big for him to have missed. He would surely have heard something: a press officer becoming too voluble over lunch . . . a Civil

Service contact indulging in departmental manipulation and leaking the details of the story . . . a politician overstepping his brief at a press conference . . .

He went to the general desk to talk to Armitage. As Scannell had expected, the reporter was embarrassed to see him. Poaching on a senior correspondent's patch was an impolitic game to play. Armitage was fortunate that the story had come good – and that it had been so important. Otherwise he would have had some explaining to do.

Scannell stood beside the desk. 'Your story . . . Can I see the document you took it from?'

'Sure.'

Armitage, eager to appease, reached into a drawer. Scannell took the document without comment. It had an official Defence Ministry stamp at the top of the first page.

'I'll bring it back when I've had a look through.'

About three-quarters of an hour later, after he'd read the report from cover to cover, he came back to Armitage's desk.

'Did you know why I wasn't around yesterday?'

Armitage nodded. 'The newsdesk said you were in Amsterdam.'

'Why didn't you wait until I could be consulted? Didn't they tell you when I'd be back?'

'They said they didn't know.'

'I see.'

It was true that he'd not told the newsdesk a specific day when he'd be returning, but they must have known that he would only be away a day or two. Otherwise, he'd have had to have left a forwarding contact address. That was the way the system operated.

'Estabrook told me to write it,' the reporter added hastily.

Scannell nodded. A chain of events was starting to link together.

'Who was your source?'

Armitage glanced awkwardly in the direction of his

colleagues on the desk. They couldn't help but overhear the conversation as they worked at their stories.

'I was asked not to say.'

Scannell gave a disapproving glare. 'Oh? Who by – Estabrook?'

'No. The person who leaked the report.'

Scannell nodded. It was the answer he himself would have given. None the less, he wasn't prepared to let the reporter get away with it.

'Have you used the same source before?'

He knew that what he was asking amounted to a professional intrusion, but he wielded the seniority which demanded an answer.

'Yes . . . once,' Armitage replied. 'When I was covering for you.'

Scannell, who had been loosely turning the pages of the report during the conversation, glanced up. 'Is he reliable?'

A worried look came over the reporter's face. 'Yes . . . Why? Is something wrong?'

Scannell waited before answering. He knew he'd made Armitage start to doubt the soundness of his material. It was a technique which, ironically, he'd learned from Estabrook, who often made reporters stop and question their stories' authenticity before agreeing to run them. The method had saved the agency from any number of blunders, but on this occasion Scannell was using it to test the soundness of Estabrook's own actions.

Handing back the document, he said cryptically: 'I don't know.'

He returned to his room. His immediate task was to telephone the defence correspondents on those newspapers which had published the story. Despite the competitiveness among Fleet Street journalists, there existed a parallel camaraderie. It was, for instance, permissible to ask how a story had been viewed by the respective newsdesks, but not whether information was available for a follow-up.

After a quarter of an hour on the phone, he established what he'd expected. Namely, none of the correspondents had been able to get confirmation from the Ministry, which was why the story had been attributed to the news agency rather than being personally by-lined. It also explained why it had been placed in the home news sections of the papers rather than on the front or back pages. Given its importance, an 'outside' position was one it might normally have warranted. Although the attribution to the agency prevented the papers from claiming the story as their own – which would have accorded with standard practice – it safeguarded them, to some extent, if it was later found to have been wrong.

Scannell went in to see the editor. Household looked up from his desk. There was a reproachful air about him that overlaid his usual presence of calm.

'It was a bad one to miss.'

Scannell sat down. He was in no mood to appear contrite. 'We don't know if it's true yet.'

Household's brow knotted disapprovingly at the challenge. 'Estabrook took the decision that it was.'

Scannell let a hint of doubt show in his eyes. He paused, then reinforced his line of defence. 'Even if it is, I want to make an official complaint. It's about the way the story was handled. The newsdesk knew I wasn't going to be away for long. There was no urgency to run the story. They should've waited till I got back.'

Household turned critical eyes on him. 'Is this professional jealousy?'

Scannell was past caring about office niceties. Not only did he have a story at stake, but ultimately his freedom . . . his life. A wrong move now, a misguided action, and the whole edifice of plausibility that had taken him years to build up could come crashing down around him. It was an uncomfortable prospect.

'I don't know. Maybe.' His answer to Household's question was vaguely self-reproving, deliberately so. A sign

206

of fallibility might win some crucial support. 'The main thing is, I don't know what damage has been done to my feature.'

'Damage? How?'

'All my work might've been undermined. The whole of Fleet Street will be poring over Ministry of Defence policy now. You know what it'll be like – wolves at a carcass.'

'In that case, I suggest you bring your research to a speedy conclusion.'

Scannell's whole body was fused with frustration. Estabrook had certainly succeeded in bringing Household closer to his corner.

'I thought we'd decided we shouldn't rush with it. You said we'd wait till I'd got everything together – all the elements.'

Household's fingers moved slowly round his mouth: a habit he had when he was at his most troubled. 'I'm afraid the pressure's building up.'

'In what way? . . . From the directors?'

'Them, certainly. We're also getting open warnings from the Ministry. Webster and I had lunch there a week or two ago. They're making all sorts of threats.'

Scannell's eyes widened. Just how far had this thing reached?

'Threats?'

Household told him what Quigley had said. After hearing the details of the lunch meeting, Scannell knew for certain that the operation being mounted against him was far wider than he'd suspected. The immediate problem, though, if he was ever going to get the story out, was to win Household's full backing – and now. Suspicions had to be floated. It was the only way. From this point on, each day was going to bring a fresh series of hazards.

'Something's going on,' he said. 'I know it is.'

Household raised his head inquisitively.

'Going on?'

'They're trying to block me. I can feel it.'

Household shrugged indifferently. 'It's possible. Whether they are or not, we can't wait much longer for your story.'

Scannell gave a look of resignation that was also intended to carry a warning. 'If it's syndicated prematurely, it'll lose all its impact. You've got to give me more time. A couple of weeks – that's all I need. I'm almost there.'

While they were talking, the deputy editor came through from his office along the corridor. It was unusual for him to interrupt a private meeting, and Scannell guessed that what he had to say was important. He handed the editor a sheet of paper. It was a piece of tape taken from the Press Association wire.

'This has just been brought in to me. I thought you ought to see it.'

As Household read it, his expression clouded. Looking up at Scannell, he said: 'It looks as though you were right.'

Household handed the sheet of paper across the desk. It was an official statement from the Ministry of Defence denying the Fylingdales story. Scannell read the few lines of innocent-looking text, then raised his head slowly. He handed the paper back.

'Our story should never have run.'

An element of abstraction veiled Household's manner, as though he were trying to project forward in his mind the scenes of an unpredictable drama. Finally, he said: 'Check it out before we do anything.'

Scannell stood up to leave, but Household motioned for him to sit down again. 'No – do it here. I want to hear what they say.'

Scannell picked up one of the phones on Household's desk to ring the Ministry's chief press officer. It was a number he knew by heart. The call lasted less than a minute, after which Scannell replaced the receiver thoughtfully.

Household leaned forward, his impatience undisguised. 'Well?'

'The PA tape's right – they've denied it. The Secretary of State's due to make a full statement to the Commons this afternoon.'

Rueful, Household looked across to where the deputy editor was standing.

'It doesn't do a lot for our credibility, does it?'

The deputy editor shook his head despairingly and walked to the door.

'Do you want to leave it with me?' he offered. 'I'll get a couple of reporters working on a follow-up. We'll try to minimize the damage.'

Household nodded. 'It's all we can do.'

After leaving the editor's office, Scannell went to see Armitage. The reporter was grim-faced. A copy of the Press Association story was resting on the keyboard of his typewriter. There was a quietness on the desk – unnatural at that time of day. Scannell stood beside Armitage's chair.

'You've seen the denial statement?'

The reporter nodded. He said nothing.

'You'd better give me the name of the source.'

'I . . .'

Scannell glowered. 'You either give it to me, or to the editor. The choice is yours.'

The reporter shifted in his seat. Scannell gave him a few moments to come to a decision. At length, Armitage looked up.

'It was someone from the European Anti-Nuclear Organization . . . a researcher.'

'At head office?'

'Yes.'

'His name?'

The reporter hesitated, then replied: 'It was a woman. You know her, I think – Hazel Goddard.'

Scannell didn't stop to issue recriminations. They would come soon enough.

* * *

Household received the call from Webster on the internal hotline soon after Scannell had left the office. News, when it was bad, travelled fast. Webster asked him to come up to the directors' suite at 12.30. There was a strident note in the chief executive's voice which Household chose to ignore.

'I've already got a lunch engagement,' he explained.

'Then cancel it,' said Webster, and rang off.

At 12.25 Household put on his jacket and told his secretary to redirect any urgent calls to the deputy editor's office.

The sixth floor was a quiet sanctum compared with the bustle of the newsroom and the reporters' offices. Household went along to the directors' suite where he found Webster waiting for him. This fact alone was enough for him to expect the worst. Webster never normally waited to receive anyone. His heavy frame seemed enlarged as he stood looking out of the window.

A woman from the catering staff followed Household into the room and took his order for a drink. He asked for a tonic water with ice. As Webster turned to face him, he saw that his substantial hand was already clutching a scotch and soda. Webster wore a look of displeasure which had been a long time in its mould.

'I thought we'd better keep this private,' he said gruffly. 'It looks like we've got some sorting out to do.'

Household wasn't surprised by Webster's corrosive tone. Since the moment the Ministry of Defence denial had come through, he'd been subconsciously rehearsing a set stock of phrases. All of them now seemed somehow futile, so he said simply: 'Do you regard it as a question of resignation?'

Webster sat down at the dining-table, his bearish expression still fixed.

'On your part . . . no. But somebody's got bloody crazy judgement, I know that. How did it happen?'

Household explained the events surrounding the story.

'What about Estabrook? Was it his decision to run it?'

'It was mine, ultimately.'

Webster waved a hand. 'I don't want to hear any piss-pot martyrdom about responsibilities. I know how these things are delegated. What I *do* want to know is whether it was his decision to go for syndication.'

Household nodded. 'Obviously, as news editor, yes.'

'You told me he'd been giving Scannell a hard time. He was annoyed about him not generating enough news stories for the desk. Was this all part of some grand plan – a move to get back at him?'

Household appeared reluctant to answer. 'I imagine there was an element of opportunism, yes – but I'm sure there's no plan. The story came in late during the afternoon. Estabrook had little time to make an assessment.'

Food was served, and they were again left alone.

'Do you think we ought to stop Scannell's investigation?' Household suggested. 'Another mistake of yesterday's magnitude would do untold damage.'

Webster gave him a look that drilled to the bone. 'I said I didn't want your resignation. I'll have it, though, if you're thinking of caving in.'

Household's mouth was compressed. Webster clearly had a right to feel aggrieved.

'There's all the more reason now for Scannell to get his story – it's the quickest means we've got of hitting back. We've just got to make bloody sure he gets it right.'

Household found Webster's attitude characteristically belligerent. It was almost as though he refused to recognize that the agency had committed an error. More as though it had lost a round in its feud with the Ministry. Perhaps a reminder of the warnings about D-Notices and exclusion from press conferences would be in order.

'What about Quigley?' he said.

Webster cuffed the air in contempt. 'He can whistle up his arse! We're not a government wire service.'

In many ways Household admired Webster's stubborn approach. It was a stance that he, as editor, couldn't adopt:

too many people needed to be kept happy at the same time. But Webster, with his money and working-class Jewish upbringing, had survived with an abrasive confidence which an academic background would have smoothed away.

'Scannell's still got some way to go,' Household said. 'He hasn't even consulted the lawyers yet. I'll have to give him more time.'

'Then give it to him, for God's sake – but keep leaning on him.'

'I suspect I won't be the only one doing that.'

'Oh? What do you mean by that?'

'He said something odd was going on . . . that the Ministry was trying to block him.'

Webster gave a short laugh. 'Cheers,' he said, raising his glass. 'That means he's on the right track.'

Household kept his glass on the table. He was disinclined to view the threat so lightly.

'He's worked for me for some time. I know when a member of my staff is feeling the pressure.'

'That's what he's paid for, isn't it?'

'Not just deadline pressure. He seems preoccupied . . . on edge. I think they may have been trying to get at him.'

'Who's "they"?'

'I don't know. The Ministry of Defence? . . . The security service?'

'The security service? Where do they come into it? Has he said anything to you to suggest that's happening?'

'No. He's not the sort. He keeps his affairs to himself.'

Webster wiped his mouth with a napkin. 'Shit, he should be able to take it. We all get it in the neck in this business one way or another.'

Household hesitated. This last statement had brought up a subject in his mind that he'd been wanting to raise with Webster. Up to now, he hadn't had the opportunity to do so.

'Are you, by any chance, referring to your industrial interests?'

Webster looked up with surprise. There was a half-smile on his face.

'I don't know. Am I?'

'I was thinking about the stories in the Sunday press.'

Over recent weeks, two running stories involving Webster's non-media holdings had appeared in the business pages of the more enquiring newspapers. One had focused attention on a microchip company that had been refused planning permission for an extension to its plant in Wales. The other had disclosed the export licensing problems facing a computer software offshoot.

'The stories may not have been just coincidental,' Household suggested. 'It occurred to me that they might've been deliberately fed out . . . the Ministry's subtle way of getting at you.'

Webster shrugged indifferently. 'Could be. Don't worry – we'll get back at them, if that's what they've done. We can choose our time.'

He pushed his plate aside and lit a cigar. Meditatively, he drummed his fingers on his engraved cigar-case before putting it back in his pocket. Even now, it was difficult to see if he understood the seriousness of the situation.

'Just keep a fire going under Scannell,' he said. 'I want to get this Fylingdales thing behind us. There's too much going wrong at the moment.' He paused, then added: 'You know what? If those bastards at the Ministry start playing rough, they're going to give me the nettle.'

Household's answer came slowly. 'I'd be careful. That may be precisely their intention.'

It had been a bad day. Although, in the event, Scannell's own reputation had emerged untarnished from the fiasco over the report, the agency had been severely discredited. It would take a lot of hard work to re-establish its name for accurate reporting.

In the early evening, at the desk in his office, Scannell tried to work out how the story could have been planted. At lunchtime, he'd met Hazel Goddard from the anti-nuclear organization and had satisfied himself that she'd genuinely believed the Ministry of Defence document to have been authentic. According to what she'd told him, it had been leaked to her anonymously by post. Like the agency, she'd been taken in by the official stamp and reference numbers. During the afternoon, he'd checked it out further with the Ministry's press office, which had confirmed it as a clever fabrication. In the end, he'd had to put it aside and hope that, in the course of his other inquiries, he might get a stray lead.

All that was left now was to write a retraction. He fed a sheet of paper into his typewriter. When the draft was finished, he went through to the general reporting desk and showed it to Armitage. The reporter was in no position to raise any objection to its apologetic wording. Neither was Estabrook when the draft was placed in front of him for approval.

'I'm going home,' Scannell said. 'If the night-desk get any developments, they know where they can reach me.'

Half an hour later, arriving back at his flat, he planned to do some additional work on his feature. However, as he let himself in through the front door and pressed the light switch, the hallway remained in darkness.

At first he simply thought the light bulb had gone, but before he went to replace it, he checked the light in the kitchen. That didn't work either. He tried the others throughout the flat, as well as one or two appliances, but the electricity supply was dead. Although he was inexpert at household repairs, a quick inspection of the fuse-box confirmed that none of the fuses had blown.

He went down to Celia's – something he hadn't intended to do that evening. As soon as she opened the door, he saw that the lights in her flat were on. He went inside.

'I thought there might've been a power cut. My electricity's off.'

Celia gave him no welcoming smile.

'Nice of you to call,' she said, following him through from the hall.

Scannell turned. The sarcasm was not unexpected.

'Look, you know what it's like . . .'

'We haven't seen you for three days.'

'I told you – I had to go to Amsterdam.'

'You got back early enough yesterday. I saw your light on.'

Scannell hesitated. 'I know . . . I was tired.'

'You could've still come down, even if it was just to tell us you were home. You'd said you were going to.'

Scannell had known there would be a backlash over his decision to spend the previous evening in his own flat. Since the visit by the official purporting to be from the social services department, he'd been trying to distance himself from Celia. The threat against Richard had brought home to him the risk he was taking in prolonging the relationship. It was impossible to say how he felt about her. At one point, a month or two ago, he'd seriously thought that something longer-term might be possible, but he knew now that such a step was out of the question. His path had been laid out many years ago; the day, in fact, that his tutor in Leningrad had called him into his room and introduced him to a man from something called the Scientific and Cultural Institute.

'It was ten o'clock before we had our supper last night. Richard said we ought to wait for you.'

'You didn't have to.'

'That's not the point. You'd said you'd be coming down.'

He knew how Richard would be feeling. On the Easter camping trip they'd made to Norfolk, the boy had even asked him, in his confused way, why he didn't move in with him and his mother.

A little later in the evening, Celia went out to the kitchen to make coffee. As far as Scannell could see, it was as much to cure her restlessness as anything else. He turned to look

215

at the television. When Celia came back into the room, he absently studied her face. Over the past weeks, it had become severe and drawn. She looked older than he'd noticed before.

'Richard's gone to see one of his friends,' she said. 'God knows when he'll be back.'

As soon as they had finished their coffee, she went to the kitchen to wash up the cups and saucers. Scannell followed her out and looked for a tea-towel. On the draining-board were some dirty pans and dinner plates. Celia ran a bowl of water.

'I can manage all right, thank you,' she told him.

Ignoring what she'd said, he found a clean cloth in a drawer and started wiping the crockery. Between them they performed the chore in silence for some minutes, then Celia announced suddenly: 'I've been thinking . . . it might be better if Richard and I moved away.'

Her voice held a mixture of resignation and half-levelled threat. Scannell didn't know whether to take her seriously. Although it would help solve his own problems, he didn't want to drive her from her home. He put down the plate he was wiping and dried his hands on the cloth.

'Better? For who?'

'For all of us.'

Celia carried on washing up. There was a moodiness about her which Scannell found disturbing. He recalled fleetingly how she'd breezed into his flat those months ago when she'd first invited him to supper. It was that vitality, that openness, which had initially attracted him to her. This was a different woman he was looking at now: a woman who was tired and strained. Just as it had been at the school with Yelena, he wondered how much responsibility he bore for the change. Celia put a saucepan on the draining-board and he picked it up to wipe it.

'The pans need to drain,' she said tersely.

Scannell put the saucepan down and picked up a dinner plate. A further period of silence followed. He'd never felt comfortable carrying out these domestic tasks; he was always clumsy at them, and they seemed such a waste of time. Equally though, they were part of the permanence she'd wrought around him – the feeling, for the first time, that he was more than just a shell from which his own personality had long since been removed.

When they were coming to the end of the washing up, he started to put away the things he'd left on the worktop. Picking up a salad bowl, he opened a cupboard door and leaned forward to place the bowl on the upper shelf. Suddenly a crash came from behind. He wheeled round and saw Celia standing with her hands open. A china milk-jug had fallen to the floor and smashed. He didn't know whether it had slipped from the wet rubber gloves she was wearing, or whether she'd deliberately dropped it.

She turned towards him. There were tears in her eyes. She seemed to be shaking.

'Why can't you say something instead of just . . . just standing there!'

Scannell remained silent, holding the salad bowl. He watched as Celia raised her hands in exasperation.

'My God, this is insane . . .'

Scannell put the bowl down on the worktop. 'What do you want me to say?'

Celia shook her head. 'That's you exactly!'

'What? What's me?'

'If you can't *see* . . .'

She grabbed the tea-towel from his hands, threw it to the floor and marched out of the room. The door slammed behind her, drowning the words she hurled in her wake. A panel of glass at the top of the door fell in pieces and shattered on the floor. Through the jagged hole, Scannell saw her turn. She stared at him, surveying the destructive results of her outburst.

For a moment Scannell was locked in an emotional paralysis, unable to react. Whatever his response, he knew it would be inadequate or misjudged. He bent down and started collecting together the larger pieces of broken glass.

'We'll get someone in to mend it,' he said.

For a long time he stayed in the kitchen. He swept up the smaller pieces of glass, wrapping them in a paper bag. When he could find nothing more with which to busy himself, he went into the living-room. Celia was sitting on the sofa. Her head was resting on her hand, and she was staring down at the floor. She was still wearing her rubber gloves.

'I'm sorry,' he said.

She looked up, but didn't speak.

'We'll sort something out,' he said. 'Perhaps, if I didn't come down so much . . .'

'It's not that. I mean, it's everything . . . going on like this. You living upstairs . . . us down here. It's crazy.'

Scannell studied her as she fought her internal battle. For a mad second, he had an impulse to tell her of a plan that had been developing over days and weeks in his half-conscious thoughts – a plan that could take them all away from the whole masquerade. Then the moment passed, and he repressed the idea as a ridiculous fantasy.

'Were you serious?' he asked.

'What about?'

'Moving away.'

Slowly, Celia looked up. 'I don't know. I suppose it's crossed my mind.'

She stood up and walked towards the kitchen door. As she opened it, a little of the remaining glass loosened. She fetched a cup of water.

Later, they sat at the dining-table. Scannell took out two cigarettes. He lit one for her.

'You never say what you feel about me . . . about us,' she said. 'Do you *want* me to go?'

Scannell gestured emptily. This was the one chance he would have to tell her outright.

'It's up to you,' he said.

A button had come undone on her blouse, and she fumbled to do it up. The movement brought Scannell back to some kind of reality. Sooner or later, he knew he'd have to make the break. While she remained in his life, he was only an arm's length away from being caught.

28

The room was dark. Some hours before, it had been brilliantly lit, and three men had sat at the table questioning him. Then they'd shut the door and, from somewhere out in the passageway, turned off the lights.

Whymark had held out for longer than he would have thought possible. An inner stubbornness, which he was surprised to find he possessed, had reinforced his silence. Whatever questions they'd put to him, he'd refused to answer. Whatever threats they'd made, both to himself and his family, he'd resisted.

He didn't know how many days the sessions had lasted. Maybe four; maybe five. The hours were an endless corridor off which doors opened on to scenes of the past. He'd lost all track of time.

It had been nine o'clock in the evening when the two officers from the Ministry police had knocked at the door of his house. His wife had answered the call. The officers hadn't told her who they were.

Then had come the drive through the night. He'd guessed that the house they'd brought him to was one of the Protective Security section's interrogation centres. It was like a large country home set among sweeping lawns and cedar trees. He'd been led along a hedge-lined pathway. So unobtrusive, he'd reflected. So English.

They'd taken him downstairs. The room he was in was like a cell, but it didn't have a bed and there wasn't a lavatory. Up to the time of the first session, he'd been allowed to use a toilet along the corridor. Then they'd put an old tin bucket in the cell which nobody had bothered to empty. Finally, when they'd switched the lights out, they'd left him without even that.

Time had passed. He didn't know how many hours; probably fifteen or twenty. His watch had been taken away, along with his shoes and his jacket and tie, at the start of the second session. There had been six or seven further sessions since then.

Initially, he'd conditioned himself to the darkness, carrying out mental exercises to maintain his sense of reasoning. He'd heard of prisoners in Soviet psychiatric hospitals doing that. He'd also exercised by walking round the room, feeling his way by holding out his arm so his fingertips kept in contact with the walls. Then he'd started to lose his balance. After that, he'd given up the exercises and gone back to the chair.

At some point, the mental labours had also stopped. He'd started to become alternately excited and alarmed. He'd even gone backwards and forwards to the door and shouted for them to turn the lights on. No one had answered. For a time, he'd felt sure his interrogators were listening, then it had crossed his mind that they might have left him alone in the house; given up on him when they'd realized he wasn't going to co-operate. His wife would make inquiries, but she would be fobbed off with some invention about why he was being held incommunicado. That would be easy enough for them to do. He knew that from his time in the secretariat.

He sat down again. There was a period of restfulness, then he felt a desire to defecate. For a while, he managed to suppress it, but the pressure in his bowels and bladder gradually worsened. He began to sweat. Soon he couldn't think about anything else. Some time later, faced with a solitary option, he fumbled his way to a corner of the room and dropped his pants. The stench rose around him. He felt like a child doing it where he shouldn't. When he walked back to the chair, he noticed that his socks were wet.

In the end, the men came back. He'd been asleep. He

didn't know how long for. They opened the door before they switched on the lights and he stumbled to his feet in some irrational display of formality. There were four of them now. He thought he knew one of them. Two guards helped him out of the cell to another room across the passageway.

'Sit down.'

He felt for a chair.

'All we need to know is the name of your contact. Then you can go and get washed.'

Whymark looked down at himself. He wondered if he should be shocked. His shirt, which had been crisp and white when he'd been brought in for questioning, hung on him like a damp rag. It was smeared with excrement. He ran his fingers through his hair. It was clotted and wet.

'We're giving you the opportunity to explain privately what you've been doing. We're proposing to offer you immunity from prosecution. It could save your family from a lot of embarrassment.'

Whymark was confused. He'd expected to face a prison sentence.

'Will I be able to go home?' In contrast to what was going on inside his mind, his question was strangely coherent and reasonable.

Fairweather lifted his eyes. 'Naturally . . . As soon as you make a statement.'

Some time later, when they threatened to put him in the dark again, Whymark signed a piece of paper. He didn't know what it said.

29

In many ways, Scannell found Richard's attachment to him an irritant. It had almost turned him into a surrogate father, a role he was neither willing nor equipped to play. It had also imposed an extra burden on his conscience. This was particularly evident whenever he considered manufacturing a split with Celia, as he frequently did. His plans were always complicated by the knowledge that the boy's stability could be affected.

For this reason, Scannell had begun to discourage the familiarity that had been established between them. Sometimes, though, his involvement was unavoidable, such as when the boy sought advice over his typically adolescent problems or practical help with his school work. It was after a mathematics revision exercise one evening that Richard became frustrated with his progress. As he got up from the table, he pushed it away from him and the books scattered on the floor.

'What's the point?' he said. 'I'm going to fail anyway.'

The incident, inconsequential in itself, drew Celia's attention. Scannell had started to pick up the books when he glanced across the room to see her standing at the dining-room door.

'Leave them alone!' she snapped at him. 'He knew what he was doing. Let *him* pick them up.'

Scannell saw pure anger in her face.

'It doesn't matter,' he said quietly.

Richard glanced over to where his mother was standing, then he slouched out to the kitchen.

'I said, pick them up!' she shouted, storming after him.

Richard looked round obstinately. 'I'm getting something to eat – if that's all right!'

'No, it's not! You're picking up those things – now!'

Richard turned his back on her and swung the door shut behind him. Scannell could hear him opening the fridge.

'You come back here!' Celia rushed through to the kitchen. 'I don't care how old you are, while you're living here and eating my food, you do what I say.'

Scannell heard the fridge door slam. He went to the doorway.

'Go on,' Celia demanded. 'Pick up those books. Nothing gives you the right to behave like that.'

Richard shrugged, and went out to the living-room. Scannell was surprised to see that he'd admitted defeat so easily, but this soon turned out to be a mistaken impression. Richard walked straight out to the hall and took his coat from a peg. Celia dashed after him and tried to grab the coat.

'You're not going out till you do what I say!'

Richard stood staring at her. 'Just get out of my way, will you, woman!'

Scannell came through from the living-room. 'Celia . . .'

She twisted round. 'You stay out of it! You've done enough damage already!'

Scannell kept silent. Richard shoved his mother aside and opened the front door.

'I'll be back when I feel like it.'

Celia tried to restrain him, jamming her weight against the door, but he was far stronger and heavier than she. In the struggle, she stumbled backwards, and knocked over a lampstand. Scannell came across to help her pick it up, but she thrust him away.

'Just get off! Don't *touch* me!'

Scannell watched as she went back into the living-room and rummaged in her bag for cigarettes. She sank down in an armchair and stared at the wall. Scannell stood by the door, studying her face. Things had come full circle now. It seemed the two of them were on some inexorable collision course.

After a short while, Celia suddenly rose from the chair and marched out to the kitchen.

'It's no good,' she said as she went. 'I'll *have* to leave. I'll quit my job . . . it doesn't matter!'

Scannell maintained his silence. He fetched a bottle of brandy from a cupboard and poured two glasses.

'Why leave your job? What's that got to do with how Richard's behaving?'

Celia came to the living-room door. 'I'm his mother, aren't I? You wouldn't understand.'

She looked as though she was trying to come to terms with some deep-seated worry. Scannell gave way to a temptation to probe deeper.

'Is there something wrong . . . something the matter?'

Celia glared. 'Does something always have to be the matter?'

Scannell was unable to find a reply.

'Why does it always come back on me?' she protested, stepping into the room. 'What about you?'

It was as if she were trying to tell him something, coding her thoughts.

'You see –' she went on accusingly, 'the moment it's suggested that *you* might have something to do with the way I feel, you just clam up. That's what you do – all the time.'

'Celia, I don't want to argue . . .'

'Just stop needling me then.'

Scannell tried at intervals to talk to her, but finally she went to her bedroom.

It was about twenty minutes later that Scannell decided to go in and see what she was doing. He'd heard no sound from the room, and he was becoming concerned. He knew that she kept a bottle of sleeping-tablets in her bedside drawer.

Softly, he opened the door. 'Celia?'

225

The room was quiet, the curtains drawn. She was lying on the bed, fully clothed apart from her shoes.

'Celia, are you all right?'

She opened her eyes, but didn't move. He went over and stood by the bed. For a minute or two he stayed there, wondering how to snap her out of it. Then, saying nothing, he turned and left the room.

Towards the end of the evening he returned. She'd put on a nightgown and had pulled the quilt over herself. He leaned across the bed.

'Shall I stay tonight?'

'I want to go to sleep.' Her eyes remained closed.

'What about Richard?' he said. 'He's not home yet.'

'He'll come. You know what he's like.'

She said nothing as Scannell slipped off his shoes and sat on the bed beside her. He leaned back against the headboard.

After a minute or two, he said: 'Things are a mess, aren't they?'

Celia said nothing. Scannell sat in the darkness. This was the point he knew they'd been heading for since the evening they'd had the row.

'Maybe it's me who should move away,' he said.

He was surprised as Celia made a sudden movement. She'd turned towards him.

'Is that what you think's wrong?'

'What?'

'I don't know . . . That I don't want you around.'

He could only see the darker shadow of her face.

'Isn't it, then?'

She didn't answer. She just lay still. He could feel the cotton of her nightdress against the back of his hand, but resisted a desire to draw closer. A short while later, he reached on the floor for his shoes.

'Tom, don't . . .'

He sensed her hand behind him on the bedclothes.

'Don't go.'

He turned towards her. After all this time, he still couldn't make out what she really wanted from him.

'I'm sorry,' she said. 'I get screwed up sometimes, that's all.'

Again there was silence, although this time it wasn't so tense. He moved back against the headboard. As the minutes passed, his consciousness started to drift. Then Celia's voice cut through his random, half-formed thoughts.

'I'm not supposed to enjoy sleeping with you – you know that?'

It was as though she'd spoken in dream-language: nonsensical, and yet with a peculiar lucidity.

He became acutely awake. 'I don't get you.'

'When it's part of your job, it's not supposed to mean anything, is it?'

Scannell had sensed a tremulousness in her voice, and something inside him automatically recoiled.

'When what's part of your job?'

He sat still, perfectly still, against the pillows. Celia's eyes had been fixed on some indeterminable point in the darkness. Now she half faced him.

'Do I have to spell it out?'

A cold rod passed through Scannell's body. No, of course she didn't have to spell it out. It was totally clear why she'd been so edgy over the weekend – indeed, over the past few weeks. He'd watched her retreating into the enclosure of her deception, watching it work its slow torture inside her mind. He asked himself how long he'd known. Since the beginning? Possibly. But, until this moment, there had always been an element of doubt; always a chance that he might have been wrong. And that, in the end, is what he'd chosen to believe. There was no enigma, no special code. If he'd applied the principles of his training, he would have realized the language she was talking was as familiar to him as a classroom chant. He'd concealed the truth from himself because he'd been unable to do otherwise.

'I had to tell you,' she said. 'It's been driving me mad.'

Her voice was controlled now. He wondered about her seniority. Did she know who he really was, or had her controllers just put her on to him because of his work as a correspondent? Had she been told simply to carry out routine surveillance, or was there more to it than that? Could it be possible she'd been instructed to set a trap – and was this disclosure part of it?

As he reached for the cigarettes on the bedside table, he experienced a crawling sensation in his stomach, almost an excitement, a loosening, like earth breaking up in the rain. He tried to think how much he'd said to her. Had he, in all their time together, let anything slip? In the space of a minute he tried to summon up all their conversations of the last few months. Immediately his head became choked with confused memories.

'What do you want from me?' he asked.

Celia turned towards him. Her voice, when she spoke, was vague, distracted.

'Want? . . . Nothing . . . *I* don't want anything.'

'The people you work for then? What do they want?'

'Them? They told me to . . . to get to know you.'

'Because you happened to live here?'

Celia waited before answering, as though trying to draw together her thoughts. 'Yes . . . I suppose so. I didn't ask why – I knew they wouldn't tell me.' She turned towards him. 'Tom . . . I haven't said anything.'

This was the moment, the moment above all others, when he needed to appear calm. If she knew the depth of his anxiety, he'd be finished. Slowly, he pulled himself up on the bed.

'Said anything? . . . About what? What do they think I've done?'

Celia shook her head. 'I don't know.'

'Bloody hell, if this is what you get for just doing your job . . .'

228

'That's what I told them . . . that they had no right . . .'

Scannell's senses were sharper now. Her words played in his head. Had she, as it would appear, been speaking in his defence? Were her loyalties divided? And, if they were, could he turn her quandary to his advantage? For a start, if her controllers had gone to the trouble of setting her up as his 'shadow', they must at least have wired up her flat. Use her, he told himself. Try and steer her emotional turmoil in his favour.

She moved closer to him. 'Tom, I'm sorry.'

'What about the flat?' he said. 'Have they had it bugged?'

He felt her stiffen. As he'd hoped, the suggestion had frightened her.

'They wouldn't have done that, would they?'

'I don't know. It's possible.'

Celia's fingers tightened on his arm. 'Do you think they could have heard what I've told you?'

'We haven't been talking loudly.'

'What do you think they'd do to me if they found out?'

Scannell recognized her need for reassurance. He let his hand slip round her shoulder and she drew against him. He touched her hair, aware of its coarseness.

'You'll be all right. Christ, if they think I'm worth this sort of trouble, they must be a bunch of idiots!'

There was a short silence, then she said worriedly: 'Are you going to stay with me?'

Scannell turned his face towards her. 'I don't know . . . Do you want me to?'

'Yes, you know I do. When this all started, you were just someone who happened to live on the next floor up. Things are different now.'

Everything had begun to fit into a neat pattern for Scannell. The new car she'd recently acquired, the promotion, the change of office. He could see why the assignment had put her under such strain. It would have been a difficult job for a skilled field agent to undertake, but for someone who presumably had no training at all, it must have been a nightmare.

Now he had his own dilemma. Should he break with her immediately, or would that signal to her controllers that he'd found out about her? He guessed it would. No, subtler tactics were needed.

'Do you know who I work for?' he asked her.

She shook her head.

'There's a group called the European Anti-Nuclear Organization. I'm in charge of their publicity.'

There was a pause.

'Publicity? . . . Is there anything wrong with that?'

Her question had revealed a glimmer of optimism. Scannell gave himself time to consider it. He'd told her the name of the first organization that had sprung to mind. It was important to make sure the correct information would be fed back to her controllers.

'Let's just say, it wouldn't help my reputation as an independent journalist if people knew.'

'Yes, but why should they want me to watch you?'

'I don't know . . .'

He let his words taper off. He'd decided to volunteer nothing more unless she asked.

For a minute or two, neither of them spoke. Then Celia said: 'They told me you had subversive connections . . . Is that true?'

Scannell stretched his legs on top of the quilt. The darkness of the room seemed somehow analagous to his life: shadowy and unreal.

'I don't know . . . that depends on your point of view. Radical, perhaps. Not subversive. No one's trying to start a revolution.'

'What would happen if anyone found out about you – anyone at the news agency?'

'I guess I'd lose my job.'

Celia weighed up his answer. 'It's important, yes – I know

230

– but . . . does it matter that much? I mean, if it helped to put an end to . . . to all this?' She stopped to try to clarify what she was saying. 'There are other jobs, aren't there? Other things you could do.'

Her question remained unanswered. He eased her weight off his arm; it was becoming numb. It was as though she was seeking a way out – for both of them. He didn't know whether he sympathized with her predicament, or despised her for her narrow aspirations.

He closed his eyes. He could hear her regular breathing. Soon he was going to have to make some difficult decisions. In the meantime, it was essential to keep her controllers guessing. He hoped he'd given her enough to take back.

30

As the train pulled out through the suburbs of Paris, Scannell tried to settle down in the corner of the carriage for a night's sleep. Munich at 9.45 A.M., the information office had told him. It was going to be a long and uncomfortable haul.

By making a pillow of his jacket and resting it on the windowsill, he was able to stretch his legs across the seat. As soon as he closed his eyes, though, his thoughts returned, as they had done frequently during the last few days, to trying to work out who might have sent him the rail ticket – and, more importantly, why? It was anybody's guess. There'd been nothing else in the envelope. No letter, no contact number. Just the ticket and the seat reservation. A Berlin postmark. Sent to his home, too. A sign of discretion? The secretive approach had almost put him off making the journey, but in the end, his curiosity overcoming caution, he'd reasoned that as long as he kept himself in contact with other passengers, it would be difficult for anyone to move against him. Even so, the trip was a gamble; the stakes uncertain.

He slept badly. By early morning the train had crossed the West German border. Frontier officials had woken him and the three other passengers in the carriage to check their passports. Shortly after the train pulled out of Stuttgart, he picked up his travel bag and went to the lavatory to wash.

He'd stripped to the waist and had just soaped his face when there was a quiet knock on the door. He remained still. There was another knock, slightly louder. Quickly, he rinsed the soap from his face and tore off a paper towel. Natural wariness made him step out of the line of the door.

When you didn't know who was behind it, it was best not to take chances.

'Mr Scannell?'

He wiped his face and dropped the towel in a waste bin.

'Just a minute.' He reached for his shirt. 'Who is it?'

'I'll be in the restaurant car.'

The man outside the door had spoken in English with a pronounced, but cultured German accent. It wasn't a voice Scannell knew.

'What do you want?'

Scannell waited, but there was no answer. He started to button his shirt.

'Hello?' he called out.

No one spoke. Still keeping to one side of the door, Scannell let the water out of the basin. By now his body and brain were tuned for instant action. He listened for any sound outside in the corridor.

Hurriedly, he finished buttoning his shirt. He pulled on the sweater he'd been wearing and gathered together his toothbrush and soap in a polythene bag. His hand fastened on the strap of his travel bag, and he prepared to release the doorcatch. Then something made him stop. If the British security services had put a killer on his tail – a possibility that had entered his mind more than once during the journey – this was the prime opportunity to carry the job out. Most of the passengers were still trying to sleep. The passport officials had paid their visit. And here he was, trapped in a closet with nothing to protect himself but his own hands.

In the end, he hit on a simple ploy. He began banging on the door. If there was anyone outside, the commotion would be certain to drive them away. Eventually, he heard a woman's voice. She was speaking in German, asking him if he was all right.

'The door's stuck!' he called out in English, and shook the handle ferociously.

As he didn't want the woman rushing off to fetch a guard,

he soon pulled the door open. The woman stared at him as he came out. He muttered something to her about the shortcomings of the railway network, then went off to find the restaurant car.

The man was seated at a table towards the front of the car. Scannell had no trouble guessing that he was the person who'd spoken to him. The only other people in there were two teenage girls with backpacks and an elderly couple who showed no interest in him when he looked their way. The man, on the other hand, who was wearing a dark business suit, held his gaze, then gave a low nod. Scannell went up to his table.

'Do you mind if I join you?'

'Not at all. I've ordered rolls and coffee – is that all right?'

'Fine . . . thanks.'

Scannell sat down. The man's courtesy pleased him; he began to feel safe. That in itself sounded a note of alarm, and he prepared his lines of defence.

'Was it you who sent the ticket?'

'Yes . . . in a manner of speaking. I made the arrangements on someone's behalf. I'm a lawyer.'

'A lawyer?'

'I have a practice in Bonn. I believe you know one of my clients . . . Herr Kepler.'

So that was it. Scannell wondered why it hadn't dawned on him before, but Kepler was the last person he would have expected to get in touch with him. What's more, the lawyer was hardly the type to be associated with a radical group. He was Establishment, from his tightly knotted tie to his black brogue shoes.

'How is Herr Kepler?'

'You heard about the fire at his home?'

Scannell nodded.

'I'm afraid he was seriously injured,' the lawyer said. 'His back . . . it was broken.'

'The fire – was it arson?'

234

The lawyer's eyes showed a glint of suspicion. 'I believe you might be better placed than me to speculate on that, Mr Scannell.'

Scannell wondered what the thrust of the remark was, and took it to be a confirmation of his own suspicions about security service involvement. Little more was said until the waiter had brought the breakfast. Scannell was hungry after his sleepless night, particularly now that he appeared to be under no immediate threat. He took a tub of meat paste from the plate. As he was eating, the lawyer reached for his briefcase on the seat next to him. From it, he took a brown foolscap envelope stuffed with documents, and laid it on the table.

'You're to have this . . . my client's instructions.'

Without a word, Scannell took the envelope and peered inside. He drew the sheets of paper out, and ran his eyes over them. It was only after some moments that he realized what he was looking at. He found it difficult to contain his surprise.

'Where did these come from?'

'You recognize the material?'

Certainly he recognized it. The first sheet was undoubtedly the list of names he was to have been given by Hermann on the night of the accident.

'You knew Hermann?' he asked the lawyer.

The man nodded. 'I knew *of* him. He passed the documents on to my client shortly before his arrest.'

Scannell was astonished at just how cautious Kepler had been. He must have had the documentation at the time he was helping him search through his files, but he'd said nothing.

'Why has Kepler given them to me? Can I use them – I mean, for publication – or are there conditions attached?'

'Herr Kepler mentioned no conditions . . . only that he shouldn't be identified as the source.'

As they finished breakfast, the train began to slow down.

It was approaching the city of Ulm. The lawyer zipped up his briefcase and rose from his seat.

'If you'll excuse me, Mr Scannell, I'll be leaving you here. My client made one request . . . that you shouldn't try to contact him. He doesn't want to be involved.'

'Okay,' Scannell agreed, 'but if any problems crop up . . .'

'I'm afraid he's in a highly fragile state, both physically and mentally. You see – his wife died in the fire.'

Soon after the lawyer had gone, Scannell went back to his carriage. He decided he would stay on the train through to Munich and use the time to study the documentation.

At a glance, the papers, coupled with the information from de Puydt's files, would prove beyond doubt that DI5 had been operating a network that penetrated to the heart of the anti-nuclear movement. As Hermann had promised, there was a complete list of names of infiltrators at both regional and national levels. One of them was of particular interest. Scannell stared at it in disbelief: *Hazel Goddard*.

He would never have suspected. But when he thought back to the way in which she'd been involved in the leaking of the Fylingdales story, it all fell into place. Her contact, according to the documentation, was Malcolm Yardley. It seemed that Goddard had been using a line of communication that led directly back to Unit Nine.

31

Celia had been summoned from her desk by one of the departmental attachés who had accompanied her in an official car up Whitehall and across the West End. With this sort of treatment laid on, she was even more wound up than she had been the last time she'd been called in to see her controllers. The fêting continued when, instead of being taken to the interview room at Great Marlborough Street as she'd expected, she was shown up to a plush suite on the top floor. Larsen was there, along with the head of department. However, the other man on the previous panel – the one who'd tried to put her at her ease – had been replaced by a woman. Celia had never seen her before. She was perched at one end of a leather chesterfield, and Larsen was at the other. Between them was a small stack of files. The head of department invited Celia to sit in one of two linen-covered armchairs which stood on either side of an antique coffee-table. It was only the view over the Soho roof-tops that broke the illusion of being in the morning-room of a country cottage.

'Tea?' the head of department offered. He picked up a china pot from a tray.

Celia shook her head. 'No . . . No thank you.'

The thought of trying casually to drink a cup of tea in the company of these three was enough to make her deposit the whole lot in her lap.

'You're sure?' the head of department asked.

'Yes. I . . . I've just had something, before I came. Thank you.'

The head of department poured tea for Larsen and the woman. For himself, he half filled a glass from a carafe of

237

water on a side cabinet. As he sat down in the armchair opposite Celia, he took a small tablet-box from the pocket of his grey waistcoat.

'Excuse me . . . doctor's orders.' He swallowed a pill with a sip of water. 'Yes, now . . . We were wondering whether there was anything, possibly, that you wanted to tell us . . . Anything that might be on your mind.'

Celia had been dreading this moment, dreading it ever since the evening when she'd told Scannell about the nature of her work. She faced the head of department directly, suspicious of his polite, rather condescending tone. She remembered only too well how caustic he'd been the last time he'd spoken to her.

'No,' came her delayed answer. 'I don't think so.'

The head of department stroked the loose skin under his chin with a thumb and finger. He said nothing. His eyes seemed to draw her guilt to the surface. It was as though he knew the truth.

'I see. Nothing that you feel uncertain about – that you might wish to report?'

Celia's eyes flickered in the direction of Larsen and the woman. Neither of their faces gave anything away. Larsen, as always, appeared humourless and cold, the ultimate bureaucrat. As for the woman, she was the type who would always present a professional face. Dressed like a public relations executive, she was probably one of the psychologists from the personnel vetting section.

Celia's eyes came back to the head of department. 'I don't know what I'm supposed to be doing.'

The head of department looked mildly irritated. 'I thought it was made clear to you at our last meeting.'

Celia took time phrasing her reply. There was too much at stake to risk being brash.

'Why are you so interested in him?' she asked.

'Interested?'

'Yes. Why was I asked to do this job?'

After a short silence, the head of department answered: 'You were ideally placed. I'm certain you must have discussed this with Mr Larsen.'

So saying, he turned towards Larsen, who nodded diffidently.

A series of routine questions followed. Celia had been asked most of them before, except that far more details were demanded this time. No matter how hard she tried to sound convincing, she sensed that she was appearing evasive. All the time, one thought played in her mind, and there came a point when she could hold back no longer.

'You think he's working for someone, don't you?'

The moment the words had left her lips, a gulf seemed to open in front of her. She stared at the head of department, wondering what his reaction would be. To her astonishment, after a second's thought, he smiled.

'Working for someone?' His elderly brow wrinkled. 'For whom?'

Celia shrugged self-consciously. 'I don't know. One of the Communist countries?'

'That's very interesting. What makes you say that?'

'All the pressure you're putting on him.'

'Pressure?'

'The problems with his credit cards . . . the summons for not paying his electricity bill . . . his phone going wrong . . .'

'I'm sorry, I don't understand. Perhaps you'd explain.'

Celia started to run through a series of problems that had recently beset Scannell, starting when his electricity supply had been disconnected. Then, when she saw the look of disbelief on the head of department's face, her monologue tapered off. She shook her head.

'It doesn't matter.'

The head of department sat forward and clasped his hands. 'Don't you think you're being a little over-imaginative, Mrs Forde? Those things happen to all of us from time to time.'

'Not *all* the time though – and not all at once!'

The head of department looked as if he were about to respond, then he changed the subject. 'Tell me, has he ever spoken to you about his connections with the anti-nuclear movement?'

'He might've done. I can't remember. We talk about lots of things.'

'Such as . . . ?'

'Work . . . who's paying what bills . . . Just normal sorts of things.'

The head of department considered what she'd said. He seemed disturbed.

'. . . And yet, in all this mass of trivia, you can't recall whether he's mentioned his connections with the anti-nuclear movement?'

Celia declined to answer.

'I know it can be difficult to remember things sometimes, but I do feel I should remind you about the nature of your assignment.'

A band of metal seemed to clamp Celia's head. 'I can't. I mean, he'll lose his job if . . .'

'Yes?'

There was a protracted lull. Over on the chesterfield, the woman was toying with a gold bracelet whose safety chain made a light scratching sound against the clasp.

'If what, Mrs Forde?' said the head of department. 'If you *say* anything?'

Celia still wouldn't let herself be drawn.

'What exactly has he told you to make you believe that?'

Celia lowered her eyes.

'*What*, Mrs Forde?'

The calls on her conscience were driving her into a tunnel that was rushing with noise. Whatever she felt about Scannell, these people were her employers, and this was the security service of her country. The panic built up like a rip tide.

'You must tell us what you know, Mrs Forde. It's most important.'

She continued looking downwards to avoid the head of department's accusing stare. All the time she was trying to straighten out in her mind what she really felt about Scannell. There was never an answer, never an absolute conclusion. Then, from some pocket of inner will, she found a fresh resistance to this mental barrage, and a plan began to formulate. If she told them the truth, it was just possible they might leave him alone.

'. . . He's got some . . . contacts.'

'Perhaps you'd speak up, would you? I'm afraid it's a little difficult to hear what you're saying.'

Raising her head slowly, Celia said once more: 'He's told me about his contacts.'

'Oh? What sort of contacts?'

She shook her head. '. . . I don't know.'

'I see. He's told you about them, but you don't know who they are.' The head of department's tone was distinctly predatory now, more like it had been in the interview room. 'Well?' he demanded.

Celia sat for a long time. Despite repeated demands to tell them what she knew, she continued to baulk.

'You'll tell his agency,' she said.

At this, the head of department eased himself stiffly to his feet. With one hand in his pocket, he walked slowly across the room, then back to his chair. He stood behind it, leaning on his outspread arms.

'I'm quite prepared to put up with your little guessing games, Mrs Forde, but you have to understand that we're dealing in matters that go . . . well, some way beyond this room.'

He stared at her. This was a more familiar face she was seeing.

'I should add that what we do with our information is our business. And what *you* do with *your* information is our business as well. Let me just warn you that if you withhold anything that concerns the department, the consequences could be most serious.'

A silence fell on the room. Larsen and the woman both studied Celia attentively. Celia knew she was trapped. She had to go ahead.

'He's involved in something . . . I don't know . . .'

'Yes, we *are* listening.'

'Something called the European Anti-Nuclear Organization.'

'I see. When you say involved . . .'

'He's . . . he's in charge of their publicity.'

'For how long has he done that, do you know?'

'No. A long time, I think . . .'

Her voice trailed off.

'And he believes his position would be at risk if his employers were notified?'

'Yes.'

'A justifiable concern.'

Celia waited until the head of department had sat back in his armchair, then said: 'I want to make a formal request to be taken off the assignment.'

'I think that would be a little rash at this stage.'

'I want to resign then. I'll leave the department altogether.'

'It would be nice, I know, if life were as simple as that. Unfortunately, there are times when our good offices are required in ways which may not be immediately apparent.'

Celia closed her eyes and held her head still. Her plan, such as it was, could hardly be said to be working. These people wanted Scannell, and they were determined to get him. She felt the helplessness of someone facing a firing squad, except that the bullets were words, and the ropes that bound her were her own confused loyalties.

She was aware of somebody approaching her chair. She opened her eyes. It was the woman. She was holding a glass and the carafe of water.

'Would you like a drink, Mrs Forde?'

Celia nodded. The woman poured some water and handed it to her. Celia took a sip, then placed the glass on the table. The woman went back to her seat.

'I'd like you to tell us a little more about your personal relationship with Mr Scannell,' the head of department continued.

Celia straightened her collar. 'There's nothing to tell.'

'No? Well then, perhaps you'd tell us what your feelings are towards him?'

'Feelings?'

'Yes. I mean, would you say, for instance, that you were . . . in love with him?'

It was such an extraordinary question to be asked in a professional context that Celia could only shrug.

'Possibly,' she said. 'I don't know.'

'And what about his feelings towards you?'

'You'd better ask him.'

'All in due course. For the time being, we'd like to hear your own, your *personal* views.'

'He's not the sort of man who shows his feelings.'

'From what you've told us, it would seem he has a strong bond with your son. Does that concern you?'

'What's that supposed to mean?'

'Only what I say.'

'I was divorced when my son was seven years old. He doesn't see much of his father. Tom . . . Mr Scannell, has given him a lot of time and attention. I'm grateful for that.'

The head of department nodded. 'Of course.'

He'd taken a leather-bound jotter from his jacket pocket and was making brief notes.

'Has Mr Scannell said much to you about the time he spent in Australia?'

'Only that he started work there – as a reporter.'

'His last job was what? Do you know?'

'I think he said he worked in Sydney.'

'That's right. The *Morning Post*, I believe. And have you any idea where he went after that?'

'As far as I know, he came over here – to England.'

'Has he ever mentioned, at all, about any trips he might have made on the way?'

'No. I can't remember anything . . . not specifically.'

The head of department paused, then asked cryptically: 'His accent – would you say it was noticeably Australian?'

Celia thought. It was something she'd asked herself several times since she'd learned a little about his background.

'Not really,' she replied.

'Isn't that a little unusual, wouldn't you say, for someone like that? Someone who spent a good deal of his formative years in another country?'

Celia took another sip of water. 'I don't see what you're getting at.'

There was a break in the questioning as the head of department poured more tea for Larsen and the woman. As he sat back, he said: 'Tell us, what do you know about his medical history?'

Celia was muddled, her thoughts shambling along a dark path. Somewhere on the way was a hidden tripwire, she could sense it, but she couldn't guess where it was strung.

'Has he had any operations at all, do you know?'

'. . . No. I don't think so.'

'No operation scars?'

'I haven't looked.'

'But you sleep with him.'

Celia sat upright. 'I don't pore over his body.'

The head of department seemed not to notice her indignation. Eyeing her squarely, he said: 'Has he, for example, been . . . circumcised?'

The question was phrased so matter-of-factly, so ingenuously, that Celia half disbelieved what she'd heard.

'I beg your pardon?'

The question was repeated. Celia stared in astonishment.

'I don't believe this . . . This is crazy.'

'I know the question may sound a little impertinent, but I can assure you that every detail has its relevance in an assignment of this nature. Perhaps you'd be good enough to answer.'

Celia folded her arms. 'As it happens, no, he hasn't! Perhaps you'd like to know what colour underpants he wears!'

'I don't think that will be necessary.'

Celia sat in controlled silence.

'We are a little concerned about your expectations following the completion of this assignment,' the head of department went on. 'You realize, of course, that it's shortly due to be terminated.'

'No one's said anything, no – not to me.'

'The major ground has been covered, so you'll be able to be relieved from your field duties.'

'When?'

'Oh, a week or two at the most. Your salary arrangements and grading level will remain as previously discussed.'

'Will I be going back to my old job?'

'I suggest we leave that for another time. Someone from personnel will be in touch with you.'

Celia looked hard at this vindictive coterie. She wondered how they had been recruited, and how they had risen to their positions. Did they share her sense of bafflement, of painful ignorance over the workings of this invisible department? Or were they a party to its secrets? Had they, as would seem to be the case, known the answers before they'd asked their questions?

'What will happen to me and . . . ?'

She stopped.

'Yes?'

'Nothing.'

'To you and Mr Scannell?'

She nodded weakly.

'Actually, we feel it might be advisable if you were to move out of your present flat. It might help to make the transition period easier.'

'I haven't thought about . . .'

'. . . The department will make sure you suffer no financial shortfall. Indeed, it may be possible to arrange an advantageous mortgage facility.'

'I don't want to move.'

'No? Why's that? Because of your situation . . . your relationship with Mr Scannell?'

Celia remained silent. The head of department was about to add something when Larsen leaned across and spoke to him quietly. Afterwards, Larsen selected a green envelope file from the pile on the chesterfield and passed it across the table. The head of department drew out a photograph and a smaller, red file. He offered them to Celia.

'Perhaps you'd care to see these.'

Hesitantly, she extended her hand. She studied the photograph. It showed Scannell meeting two men. The background was dark and out of focus.

'If you look in the red file you'll see some more photographs.'

With nervous fingers, Celia opened the file. She didn't know what to expect. The file contained about half-a-dozen loose-leaf pages, each showing a number of passport-size photographs of men and women.

'Do you recognize any of them?'

Celia flipped conscientiously through the pages. She stopped when she came to the fourth.

'This man here is in the other picture.'

'Quite. His name is Igor Zarkich. He's a senior representative here in London of Aeroflot, the Soviet airline.'

Celia stared at the photograph of Scannell. It was him with the man called Zarkich: there was no question about it. Suddenly, her body temperature seemed to have dropped.

'Who's the other man?' she asked quietly.

'His name's Vladimir Androsov. We haven't got a separate picture of him. He was in the country for a short while earlier this year . . . a member of an agricultural delegation.'

Celia scrutinized the photograph of the three men.

'It could have been doctored,' she said unconvincingly.

The head of department craned his neck to look at the photograph. 'Yes, I imagine it would be technically possible to achieve,' he agreed, 'but why?'

Celia laid the file and the photograph on the table. She was utterly deflated.

'I don't know. To turn me against him?'

As the head of department listened to her answer, he gave a slow shake of his head, as though he found her train of reasoning painful to follow.

'To turn you against him,' he repeated abstractedly. 'Now, why should we wish to do that? All we want to find out about him is the truth. If he's got nothing to hide, then it's pointless us wasting our time.'

Celia hesitated. 'Does that mean you *do* suspect him of working for someone – another country?'

The head of department addressed her severely. 'Let's just say we think it's best that you should be fully aware of the position you're in.'

Celia looked again at the photographs. The evidence couldn't have been clearer. Her thoughts were so torn that she didn't know who to believe.

32

Fairweather and Blom walked down Rochester Row to one of the flats which the department kept available for senior members of staff. It was a taxi ride from Unit Nine's offices. Fairweather had suggested it would be a suitable place for a meeting where they could talk without interruption or formal constraints.

Walking on the inside of the pavement, Blom glanced at Fairweather with curiosity. There was a determination about the jutting jaw. Something had happened, and Blom had a shrewd idea what it was.

The house was Georgian, with a wrought-iron balcony and a large lacquered door. A housekeeper let them in. The flat, which had two bedrooms, was on the first floor. It had been used recently: Blom could smell cigar smoke through the clinical odours of toilet cleansers and furniture polish. Its tall front windows overlooked the main road.

Fairweather showed him through to a small drawing-room and, after hanging his coat over the back of a chair, went directly to a drinks cabinet. He poured two scotches.

'Ice? Soda?'

Blom shook his head. 'Just as it is.'

They sat in a pair of Edwardian armchairs whose elegance belied their discomfort. Fairweather pulled out a footstool and loosened his tie. Picking up his drink from a table, he sat back, his feet up.

'It seems that Special Branch have been getting some help from ASIO.'

Blom nodded. He understood the reference. For some weeks, according to his independent sources, the Australian Security Intelligence Organization had been providing both manpower assistance and file access to two Special Branch officers who had been sent out to investigate Scannell's background.

He sipped his drink. 'That was also the information I received.'

'So I understand.'

Fairweather's voice held ill-concealed resentment. This was no surprise to Blom. He'd already pinpointed the cause of the other man's irritation.

Blom settled back in his chair. 'I was going to pass it on as soon as we'd run our own checks. I didn't want any more impetuousness – there was enough of that under Rodway.'

There was an uncomfortable silence while Fairweather stared at the fire burning in the grate. Blom knew that the veiled accusation of Fairweather's indirect responsibility for Unit Nine's past lack of success had struck its target.

Eventually, Fairweather lifted his eyes. 'You know they've established that Scannell's an imposter.'

Blom wondered whether to pretend he was shocked, but decided against it. Fairweather clearly knew that he'd been receiving parallel reports. There wasn't much he could say about it. If the unit was going to operate effectively, the communications link had to be direct.

'Special Branch sent me a telex. It came late last night. Do you know if it's been confirmed?'

Fairweather shifted his outstretched legs and turned his head. 'You seem to know as much as anyone. You tell me.'

'I don't know. That's why I asked. Have you had any details about what they've found?'

Fairweather absently raised his glass and watched with innocent fascination the light patterns from the fire shining through the whisky. After a few moments, he lowered the glass.

'ASIO opened up their list of unidentified dead. It took a lot of searching, so I'm told. They ran extensive computer checks.' Pausing, he added: 'Ever heard of the Simpson Desert?'

Blom shook his head.

'Part of it's in South Australia. There was a body found there eleven years ago. It was barely more than a skeleton. A man in his late twenties.'

'Scannell?'

'It raised questions. Death was thought to have occurred at least two years before the body was found. There were no vehicles abandoned in the vicinity, so nobody knew how it had got there. That alone was enough to give rise to suspicions of foul play.'

'Are they proven?'

'The general reckoning was that it had been dropped from a light aircraft. The case was coded on ASIO's lists – basically as a matter of routine. The police made some inquiries around the time the body was discovered. They drew a blank, though, early on.'

Blom gave an enquiring look. 'I take it there was no documentation on the body?'

'There was no body on the body!' Fairweather paused again as though debating whether he should have made the lighthearted remark. 'It was only through checking against dental records that his identity was established. Even then, confirmation was difficult. The face and skull had been badly damaged.'

'That's all they've got – dental records?'

'No. There's a further record in a Melbourne hospital . . . He had a circumcision operation when he was thirteen. We know for a fact that the man we've got under surveillance at the Barbican hasn't been circumcised.'

Fairweather smiled whimsically as he spoke, and Blom made a face of jaunty surprise.

'I won't ask how you got that information.'

Fairweather smiled again. 'We have our ways.' He got up and poured more drinks. 'The problem,' he said, handing a glass to Blom, 'is that while we know who he *isn't*, we don't know who he *is*.'

Blom raised his eyes. 'A sleeper?'

'Almost certainly . . . And I'd guess KGB. They're the only ones who could afford to go to those sorts of lengths. I mean, what are we talking about? One man's fake identity. If someone was killed simply so an agent could step into his shoes, then they had to have a serious assignment for him.'

Blom gave a slow nod. 'When's he being brought in?'

Fairweather opened his hands uncertainly. 'Special Branch are waiting for our instructions. I haven't decided what's best to do. What do you think?'

'Perhaps it would be wise to leave it a little longer. If you step up the surveillance on him, there might be a chance of finding out who his contacts are. If he's part of a big ring, we might be able to crack it all in one go.'

Fairweather nodded. 'I was working along those lines.'

The conversation continued late into the evening. Fairweather was planning to sleep at the flat, but Blom declined an invitation to stay as his guest.

'My wife,' he said, when he'd finished his fourth scotch, 'doesn't appreciate me staying away unless she's had good notice.'

As he went to the door, Fairweather handed him his coat. Fleetingly, Blom wondered if this man with whom his own reputation was becoming inextricably linked would be the next departmental casualty. It had taken too long to get this far. Despite the facts that had come to light, the shadow of ineptitude which had cast itself over Unit Nine was proving difficult to shake off.

Blom went down the stairs. The hallway was noticeably more chilly than the flat.

33

Celia sat at her desk and tried to concentrate on her work, but it was impossible. Every cash-form she checked, every document she typed, appeared as meaningless characters on paper. She was making errors on almost every line.

Two days before, she'd had the interview with the three controllers. Since then, not a minute had passed without her thoughts returning to the photograph of Scannell with the two Soviet agents. It was as though its image had been grafted on to her retina.

She still found it difficult to believe, but the evidence was overwhelming. Only heads of department or higher ranks had access to F22s, or 'red files'. She knew that; everybody in the department knew it. The possibility that the file had been deliberately interfered with was unthinkable. A form had to be signed in triplicate before any file could be released from the archives, and a senior signature was required. Any tampering with the contents would be noticed immediately. She was sure that no one above the level of departmental head would be so interested in Scannell as to condone such questionable practices.

At four o'clock in the afternoon, when she'd completed less than half her work schedule, she collected her coat and went home. An hour before, she'd telephoned Scannell's office and asked him to meet her at a swimming-pool in a City health club, of which they were both members.

The moment of truth, she'd decided, had arrived.

When she came out of the changing rooms, she saw that Scannell was already sitting by the poolside. He was on a low bench, a towel draped over his shoulder. There were only a few other people there. The office workers would be another hour yet. Scannell stood up as she walked round the pool towards him.

'What made you want to come here?' he asked.

She folded her towel and hung it over a rail. 'I just fancied it.'

Scannell dropped his towel over the same rail and dived in. Surfacing, he was about to swim back to the side, when Celia, who had dived in straight after him, held him back.

'I had to ask you to come here. It's the only place I could think of. I wanted to make sure they wouldn't be able to listen to us talking.'

Scannell doused his face and swept his hair back. 'Act normally,' he said, glancing round, 'just in case any of these people are friends of yours.'

For a few minutes they swam and dived until they ended up near the centre of the pool again.

'What's the matter?' Scannell asked her.

Celia told him about the further meeting she'd had with her controllers.

'What did they want?' he asked suspiciously.

'They want me and Richard to move.'

Scannell swilled his hands in the water. 'Are you going to?'

'I don't know.'

'Did they ask any more about me?'

Celia studied his eyes. 'Yes. That was what the meeting was all about.'

Scannell hesitated. 'What did you tell them?'

For a moment, Celia didn't answer. She watched his reflection moving on the water. Then she said: 'I was under pressure.'

Scannell's eyes widened in accusation. 'You didn't tell them about the organization . . . my work?'

Celia looked at him closely. 'I'm frightened, Tom. I don't know what it's all about. I've got them telling me one thing, and you telling me something else. I don't know who to believe.'

When she had come to the pool, her intention had been simply to tell Scannell about the suggestion that she should move home. She hadn't wanted to give him any finer details of the meeting, and had hoped he wouldn't ask. When he persisted, she was plagued with guilt. Her attempts to bring herself closer to him only seemed to erect more barriers.

After further questions from him, she said finally: 'They think you're working for someone else . . . another country.'

Scannell stared at her. 'What?'

'Are you?' she asked earnestly.

He held his penetrating gaze. 'What do you want me to say? Of course I'm not!'

'They showed me a photograph.'

She watched for signs of deception, vestiges of guilt. The movement of his eyes, the pattern of his expression.

'A photograph?' he said. 'What of?'

'You – and two men. One of them worked for Aeroflot. The other one was a member of a Soviet delegation.'

A silence followed. So now it had arrived: the supreme test for which he had been conditioned.

Turning in the pool, he said: 'This is ridiculous . . . insane. I mean, what sort of photograph? It must have been a fake . . . doctored.'

Celia wiped water from her face. 'You haven't answered my question.'

'I've told you, I'm a journalist trying to do my work – and it's not being made easy for me!'

'Why did you meet the men?'

'Meet? Celia, what is this? I told you, I didn't meet anyone – at least, not to my knowledge.'

'I saw it. It wasn't a fake, Tom . . . It couldn't have been. You were looking right into the man's eyes.'

'For God's sake, they've got sophisticated equipment. They wouldn't have shown you some crude montage.'

Celia shook her head. 'I don't know any more. I don't know who's lying and who's not.'

Scannell reached for her wrist in the water. He gripped it tightly.

'Jesus Christ, Celia, don't you see? They're trying to turn you against me . . . getting at you . . . all the time. They're just a bunch of frustrated spies!'

He suddenly realized he was raising his voice, and glanced round anxiously.

After a few minutes he swam with her to the side of the pool. No one was nearby. She would ask him now; try to find out if her department had some elaborate plan to discredit him. That was what he seemed to be implying.

'Tom, do you think they're trying to do something to you?'

'Like what?'

'I don't know . . . anything. What about your job? Are they trying to make you lose it . . . undermining you?'

Scannell lifted a hand and wearily brushed the water. 'God knows. I suppose . . . Bloody hell, how should I know? You've told them all they need!'

There was a long silence. Scannell gripped the side-rail while Celia let her hands float idly.

At last, she said: 'I'm sorry, Tom. I didn't know what to tell them. I thought the truth might – I don't know – that it might at least show them what they were doing.'

'It doesn't matter. They can do what they like. I haven't done anything wrong . . . not illegal.'

They said nothing as they walked to the changing rooms. Just before they went through the separate doors, Celia stopped him.

'I'll make them think I believe them,' she said resolutely. 'I'll find out what they're trying to do to you.'

As she walked through to the lockers, she realized she would never know whether to believe him. Now, however, belief hardly mattered. It was, as she had come to realize, a question of loyalty. And, in the end, she'd decided to give hers to Scannell.

34

Scannell paid off the cab driver who dropped him outside the elegantly refurbished town house in a quiet square in Highbury. Through the branches of the trees in the front garden, he could see a light in a drawing-room window. Standing on the pavement, he gave himself a few moments to overcome a slight breathlessness which he put down to natural apprehension. He looked at his watch: he was fifteen minutes early. He decided to walk round the square to kill time. While it wouldn't be courteous to be late, he didn't want to appear ingratiatingly keen.

The dinner invitation from Household had intrigued Scannell. His relationship with the editor had always been strictly professional; they had barely met socially, apart from at occasional staff functions. The invitation had been all the more surprising because it had only come the previous afternoon. Indeed, Scannell had wondered if another guest had dropped out at the last minute, and he'd been brought in simply to make up the numbers at the table.

The cab drove off and Scannell walked away from the house. A short distance behind him in the street a car engine misfired, and he turned his head sharply. His heart gave a jump. That was how he was now: permanently wound up, his nerves as tight as coiled steel. Ever since Celia had admitted her role to him, he'd known that the time he had left in London could be counted in days. It was inconceivable that his controllers weren't aware that she was on the DI5 payroll. Even so, it was strange that he'd received no instruction as to what countermeasures he should take. Did they intend to recall him, or would they want him to see the story through? Undoubtedly they would have him under surveillance – his unknown *confrère* would be watching from somewhere – but it was possible they didn't appreciate the story's explosive potential. If this were the case, the order for his recall could come at any time. The thought of having to leave his home at perhaps twenty-four hours' notice sent him cold; but that was how it would be. He'd always known that. Yet despite his dread at receiving the instruction, he couldn't make a move without it. It was too risky to try to get out of the country through normal channels. He would be detained before he could show his passport at an airport gate.

Apart from his own precarious position, his other deep concern was for Celia. Somehow she didn't seem to realize the trap she'd set for herself in making her disclosures to him. This supported her contention that she was only low-grade personnel, but it meant that her department would regard her as all the more dispensable. When it came to matters of national interest, the life of a middle-aged clerical officer was hardly a paramount consideration.

Beyond the square, the car engine misfired again. This time Scannell didn't turn. His mind was fixed on a problem which had to be resolved – and quickly. There had been a time when, if faced with such a crisis, he would already have made moves to contact the embassy. This would have broken a key operational rule, but the transgression would certainly have been overlooked in the circumstances.

So why hadn't he made contact? Why was he continuing to leave himself so dangerously exposed?

For some days, he'd been trying to work out what he really felt about Celia, and how long he could continue lying to her. Now that she had made her confession, he saw his own deception as a double betrayal. At one point, in an irrational moment, he'd considered asking her to help him acquire political asylum. Aside, though, from the likelihood that he would simply be inviting a long jail sentence, betrayal of his country was not a price he was yet willing to pay –

not even for her. Repeatedly, he'd asked himself how much he meant to her, and she to him. The truth was, he didn't know.

Or did he?

As he turned the corner of the square and headed back towards the house, he pushed his hands deep into his coat pockets. His fingers were clenched. He knew the answer — of course he did — but he wasn't admitting it, not when it could place both their lives in jeopardy.

He walked up the flagstone path and, standing on the doorstep, pushed the button. The door was opened by Household's wife. She had met Scannell once before when Webster had taken over a country hotel for a weekend editorial strategy conference, but she seemed to have difficulty placing his face. He stood on the threshold and waited to be invited in. She offered her hand for him to shake and the gesture seemed odd; too manly, somehow. Then he remembered she was a barrister by profession, which probably explained her businesslike air.

As he might have guessed, Household's home spoke of taste and middle-class prosperity. Scannell couldn't help reflecting on how unsurprising such a lifestyle now seemed to him. Did he despise it because of its exclusiveness, or admire its decency? He didn't know. Each viewpoint always had its other side. That was something his instructors had never properly taught him. He guessed that his counterparts among Celia's colleagues had experienced the same narrow training. Little consideration was given to the morality of the opposing side's argument, nor how an agent should reconcile his private observations with his loyalties to his home state.

Household's wife showed Scannell into the drawing-room. She had the same cultured presence and stand-offishness as her husband, but lacked his underlying warmth. She poured drinks and began a stilted conversation.

Scannell was relieved when Household came down the

stairs. He was buttoning the cuffs of his shirt and his tie was undone round his collar. He held out his hand to Scannell.

'Sorry to keep you waiting. I got held up at the office.'

His wife glared at him stonily. 'You might have finished dressing before you came down.'

Household looked in a mirror over the fireplace while he knotted his tie. His wife fixed him a drink and placed it on the mantelpiece.

'I'll see if the girls have got the supper ready.'

Scannell wondered for a moment if they kept servants, then he remembered from a conversation with a senior section editor who had been previously to the house that there were two teenage daughters in the family.

Household told Scannell to take a seat. Awkwardly, they made conversation about peripheral aspects of the investigative feature. Perhaps it was Scannell's imagination, but it seemed that something was preying on Household's mind. Once or twice, Scannell found he had to repeat himself.

Throughout the meal, he struggled for things to say. It surprised him that he had turned out to be the sole guest. The reason for inviting him was still a mystery.

Almost as soon as they had finished eating, Household's wife excused herself from the table.

Glancing at Scannell, she said: 'I'm starting a fresh case tomorrow. There's a lot of preparatory work I have to do.'

Scannell nodded and rose slightly from his chair. The evening was making him increasingly unsettled.

One of the girls went out to the kitchen to make coffee.

'Why don't we go back in the other room?' Household suggested. 'It's more comfortable.'

Again, in the drawing-room after Household had poured brandies, there was a further period of strained conversation. The girl brought in a tray of coffee, but she immediately left them alone. After Household had picked up his cup, he suddenly sat forward as though he had rallied himself to broach a delicate subject.

259

'I suppose you're wondering why I invited you here like this – out of the blue.'

Scannell couldn't find an appropriate answer.

'I've spoken to Webster,' Household added. 'He says we can't run your story.'

Scannell was conscious of a massive silence that seemed to expand inside his head. It was a moment or two before he could speak.

'Why?' he said. 'Why now?'

'He believes it's potentially too damaging for the government.'

Scannell was hardly listening. Household's words were falling like echoes in an empty room.

'I know what you're thinking,' Household continued, 'and I agree. Webster's not capable of making a decision on ethical or political grounds . . . only commercial. In those terms, it's indefensible. It would generate substantial syndication revenue.'

Scannell looked up. 'Are you suggesting there's another reason?'

Household's expression gave way to an inner gravity.

'It's possible. That's why I asked you to come here. I didn't want to discuss the situation in my office, for obvious reasons. Given the nature of your story – and the time you've spent working on it – I think it's only fair to tell you that I've been making extensive inquiries into Webster's business dealings.' He paused and looked at Scannell. 'You'll appreciate that what I'm telling you is strictly between ourselves.'

Scannell nodded. Thoughts were turning in his head like tickets in a lottery can. It was impossible to tell which one would ultimately be retrieved.

Household hesitated, then, studying Scannell's face for a reaction, went on: 'It's conceivable that Webster is operating as an agent for the Eastern bloc.'

Scannell stared. He took a sip of brandy to appear controlled.

'That's some charge. Have you got evidence?'

'The ownership of his companies is highly complex. As you know, they all operate under the umbrella of Exos International. Apart from the seventy-three per cent Exos holding in our agency, it also has extensive interests in two high technology groups – GGL Semiconductors and GGL Business Software International.'

Scannell lit a cigarette to give himself time to respond. He dropped the dead match in an ashtray and looked up questioningly.

'All the activities are detailed in the annual accounts,' he said. 'They've always met with the auditors' approval.'

'As far as company law requirements go, it's true what you say – the group's affairs are in perfect order. But the further back you trace the chain of control, the more difficult it becomes to identify the true owner.'

Scannell's mind had begun to career, desperately trying to keep ahead of Household's revelations. He felt like a beleaguered analyst who, every time he is about to conclude a calculation, has it thrown into confusion by the introduction of fresh data.

'Who owns Exos International?' he asked.

'The ultimate holding company is a private concern, Exos International Investments. It's registered in the Isle of Man. Any company there can operate under a cloak of total secrecy.'

'What about the directors? Do you know who they are?'

'They're faceless. The company's just a nameplate. The directors are Swiss nominees . . . bankers and lawyers. They simply act as trustees. It's impossible to find out who the real owners are – the beneficial shareholders.'

Scannell sat back. He was calming slightly, which helped his head to clear. This was his only chance to get information potentially more significant than any that had ever passed through his hands.

'What about profits?'

'Ultimately they go back to the holding company. The subsidiaries can be fed with capital whose source can't be identified. They can be kept afloat indefinitely – whatever the commercial exigencies.'

Scannell waited. Warning sounds were growing louder. If he said the wrong thing, if his tone was at variance with what Household might expect, he would deal himself a suicidal blow.

'Exos has got overseas interests, hasn't it? Where do they fit in?'

Household's brow knotted. 'There are companies in the US and France . . . and in West Germany, I believe. They all come under the central control of the Manx operation.'

For perhaps half a minute the only sound in the room was the ticking of an antique carriage clock on the mantelpiece.

At last, Scannell asked: 'What makes you think he's a Communist agent? If the companies are some sort of front, he might be working for our own security service, mightn't he?'

Household nodded. 'It's possible – but unlikely. I've also been looking into his personal background. His family are Jewish . . . East European origin. They emigrated to this country from Magdeburg. That was just before the Second World War. Their name was anglicized. Webster was actually born Wilhelm Weber. He still has relatives alive in East Germany and Poland.'

For Scannell, it was one shock after another. An astonishing collage was beginning to unfold before him.

'How certain are you about all this? I mean, that he's involved in espionage activities?'

'I don't have any proof – not as such. But does one always have to have conclusive evidence before one acts? Let's say, I feel certain enough to alert the authorities. They should at least check him out.'

Over a period of a few minutes, Scannell's position had been laid chillingly bare. Rather than working alone, as he'd always thought, he was only a part of a diverse network which Webster was controlling. That would explain Webster's reluctance to run the story: it was so potentially harmful to the British government's interests that DI5 would rip the network apart. The truth was, as Scannell now saw it, that he had done his job too well.

His confusion whirled. Who were the other agents in the network? Did he know them? Did any of them work for the agency? Did they *all* work for it? Should he alert Webster over what Household had told him?

All his assumptions had been fragmented. There were other questions too. How much, for instance, did the British security service really know? Should he break his primary instruction and contact the Soviet embassy? Should he silence Household before he had a chance to alert the authorities? How great was his own personal danger? And was Celia still working against him? Would the KGB kill her?

For a moment, Scannell quelled his feelings of desperation with the thought that if Household, using standard sources of information, had been able to find out so much about Webster, the security services must surely have the same intelligence to hand. They would have vetted him and given him clearance, or he wouldn't have been permitted to build up his organization.

This train of logic soon collapsed, however, when Scannell reasoned that there must be many self-made men in the country with East European origins, so DI5 wouldn't necessarily suspect an espionage connection. However, if Household were given the opportunity to present his evidence to them, they would put Webster under a microscope. His sources of funding would be bound to trigger wider investigations.

Aware of the break in the conversation, Scannell asked for more coffee. Household reached for the pot on the tray.

'Do you want me to make some more enquiries about Webster?' Scannell asked. 'It might be easier for me than for you. I could make it seem as though it was part of my story – pressure from the Ministry.'

Household shook his head. 'No. Just get your story prepared on the schedule we've agreed. It's a matter of genuine public interest. I think it should run.'

'You'll go against Webster's instructions?'

Household pondered. 'I don't know. I've got a week to consider it.'

When Scannell left later that evening, he walked back to his flat rather than take a taxi. It was quite a distance, all along Upper Street, Islington, and past the Angel, but he needed the air. As well as that, he needed time to think, to concentrate. He wondered how he could have been so blind for so long. Because of his lack of foresight, an entire network was threatened. It was an emergency of the gravest order. After some consideration, he reached the disturbing conclusion that his objective must be to ensure that Household shouldn't be allowed to alert DI5. An operational execution, quick and clean. But that would mean having to get out of the country – a move he'd already ruled out as too hazardous – and, in turn, leaving Celia.

The more he thought about it, the more outrageous the idea seemed. The fact that he could even dwell on such a cold-blooded act haunted his conscience. He could, of course, alert the embassy . . . Let their operatives carry out the task. But that would only keep his hands clean, it wouldn't exonerate him of moral responsibility. His ultimate allegiance was being put to the test, and he knew he lacked the killer instinct the situation demanded.

As he went across the walkway to his apartment block, his mind was made up. Gradually, thoughts about what action he should take against Household had been supplanted by another plan, and his remaining hours as a free citizen had to be spent making sure it was failsafe. If it wasn't, the consequences would be too dire to contemplate.

35

Tiverzin parked her car in its regular place at the directorate. Before she got out, she studied her face in the rearview mirror and applied a little more make-up. She looked haggard, which was understandable, since she could count on her fingers the number of hours' sleep she'd had in the past week. Dark shadows under her eyes; lines of tension round her mouth; taut muscles in her neck and cheeks. There were some things, like anxiety, that make-up couldn't hide.

On her way to work she'd reflected on the recent developments in Operation Lyosha. It hadn't been so long ago when, returning from her holidays, she'd expected to have seen its successful completion. Right now she would have been in an unassailable position to take over the running of Aleksei. But things hadn't turned out as she'd expected, and now she would be fortunate to keep even her present job.

If her fears had accompanied her to work, she had even more cause to be alarmed when, an hour later, a call came through from Leonov's office. Her presence was required immediately. No explanation was given.

Riding in the lift to the fifth floor, she hoped Kochev would be at the meeting; even Sofinsky. Much as she mistrusted their motives in recently approving a further three-month funding for Lyosha, at least their attendance would signify a straightforward policy discussion.

As it was, Leonov was alone, a squat figure in the heavy chair behind his desk. His gaze didn't waver as she entered the office. A solitary file was in front of him. The signs were bleak.

'Sit down, captain.'

Leonov's voice was curt. It had none of the warmth that

he'd shown at their private luncheon together those weeks before, and he'd pointedly omitted addressing her as 'comrade'. At the time of the luncheon, he'd all but given her Kochev's job. That prospect was dead now. She was in deep trouble, and she knew it.

Leonov's tired eyes studied her closely, and she noticed how old he seemed. Her mind flashed back to the photograph of the handsome young couple that she'd seen on the sideboard at his apartment. It occurred to her, as it had done at the time, that he'd invited her there because of some unspoken sexual intent. Maybe, if she'd given him stronger signals, he'd have made his intentions clearer. Such a move might have solved much of her present problem, but the opportunity had been irrevocably lost.

Leonov folded his hands on the desk. 'Last night I received a Line N report. A request has been made to bring out 10-10.'

Tiverzin felt a finger of ice curl through her insides. She couldn't comprehend what had happened. For three days she'd been instructing Merkulov to block all Line N traffic. All communications had been answered personally from her office. Nothing had been referred to a higher authority. Of course, she'd known that the tactic wouldn't work for long, but if it had enabled Novost to complete his story, then she would have had ammunition enough when the recriminations began. Now Merkulov had failed her. Somehow, despite all she'd done to shield him from investigation, he'd allowed a report to get through.

Facing Leonov, she positioned herself firmly in her seat. 'I'm sorry, comrade colonel. I don't understand.'

'I've authorized an emergency evacuation. They're bringing him out tonight.'

Tiverzin curbed her natural instinct to protest. This was worse, far worse, than she'd expected.

'What did the report say?' she ventured cautiously.

'It originated from the surveillance cell . . . the one that's been watching Novost. Last night he had supper at his editor's home – a highly unusual occurrence. It's believed that the editor has been making discreet inquiries into 10-10's business and personal affairs.'

Tiverzin blinked slowly. '. . . I don't understand. The cell . . . they should've been watching. The inquiries – how long have they been going on?'

'For a number of weeks, it seems. We've had to assume that this information was communicated to Novost.'

A knot of rage tightened in Tiverzin's chest. All along she'd argued with Kochev that 10-10's choice of editor was an unacceptable risk. While the news agency had needed to install an authentic front-man, even among Fleet Street's sharp-minded executives there were any number of less questioning individuals – ones who wouldn't have been such a danger to admit to the fold. It seemed that 10-10 had viewed the man as someone who could be manipulated, interpreting his self-effacing nature as weakness . . . an impression which events had shown to be fatally mistaken.

'You're certain that's what's happened – that the editor knows?'

Leonov's jaw hung slightly open as he breathed heavily, struggling to suck a little oxygen into his coked lungs.

'Senior Line N personnel believe that 10-10 is about to be uncovered. They're our people on the spot . . . They should know, if anyone does. That's why I've authorized the escape route.'

Tiverzin listened passively to Leonov's declamation. It was all she'd feared. If 10-10 was being brought out, nothing was left of the operation. An emergency shutdown would be the next step.

'There are other causes for concern about Novost,' Leonov went on. 'As you undoubtedly know, the DI5 woman has confessed her role to him.'

'Yes, but it's still not known if . . .'

'That worried the surveillance cell,' Leonov interrupted

her, 'but they were prepared to maintain the watch on him. They'd decided to take no action . . . not till they were sure of his intentions. There was still a chance – a small one, certainly – that he was playing along with her . . . using her as a line of information to her controllers.'

Leonov reached with effort across the desk for his cigarettes.

'Unfortunately, captain, things have changed. Over the last week or so it has become increasingly clear that their relationship is in dangerous territory. The *confrère* has reported severe problems. It is now believed that Novost is considering a defection.'

Tiverzin tried to look surprised, but it was difficult. She could pretend, of course, that it was something sudden, something that had been brought on by the shock of the accident or his feelings towards the woman, but that would simply be self-deception. Inside, she knew that the signs had been there much longer than that. For – what? – two years, maybe three – maybe as long as she'd been running Lyosha – there had been the observed bouts of depression, the erratic use of prostitutes, the increasingly frequent trips to Geneva. Certainly, he'd always had bona fide meetings to cover – at the United Nations agencies, or the interminable arms negotiations – but only a fool, a stupid fool like herself, would have had any doubt that he'd been packing money away into some secret account. The trouble was, all agents did it. If it wasn't Switzerland, it was the Cayman Islands, or some obscure South American backwater. It was an accepted perk of the job, a safety net, which was why she'd never been totally sure if he was wavering. Not only that, but he'd been *the* key agent, on whom her own success had so heavily depended. In recent months, perhaps, the warning signals had been clearer. If there hadn't been the need for him to conclude his story, she would have ordered his return the moment she'd known about the woman's admission. Still, that was in the past. Now there was the future – a permafrost, dark and eternal – that she had to face up to.

Leonov looked up from his desk. 'Can you tell me, captain, why the seriousness of the situation was not brought to our attention?'

Tiverzin hesitated.

Leonov stared. 'Yes?'

'We were so near.'

Tiverzin's reply was almost inaudible. Leonov had to lean forward to hear her.

'So near? Did you know what the woman had told Novost?'

Tiverzin nodded mutely.

Leonov sat back. 'This would all be bad enough, but I understand you have also been covering up for misdemeanours among your senior staff.'

All remaining feeling emptied from Tiverzin's body. So that was it. They'd got at Merkulov. She asked herself how they'd found out, then she remembered her own words to her operations controller: *Moscow not only has eyes and ears, it has extra-sensory perception.* In hell's name, why hadn't she seen it coming?

Leonov lifted himself to his feet and shambled to the window. For some moments he stared out at the surrounding woodland, then he turned.

'You understand, of course, what it means?'

Tiverzin said nothing. There was nothing to say.

'You'll have to face a tribunal. In the meantime, you'll be suspended from duty without pay.'

Tiverzin hardly heard the words. Her eyes focused vacantly on the old man.

'What about Novost? What will happen to him?'

Leonov came back over to the desk and lowered his stiff carcass back into his seat. He clasped his hands and thought. There was a weary fatality in his expression.

'There's only one thing that can happen. We can't risk a defection . . . not now. He's got to be stopped.'

36

Scannell arrived home from work after spending the afternoon drafting the outline of his story. It was a story he knew he would never write.

He'd seen the surveillance team outside the apartment block that morning. Four men and two women. A round-the-clock watch; from the embassy, he presumed. They weren't DI5, or they'd have been more circumspect. No, these people bore the hallmarks of the KGB. Their intention would be to let him know he was under scrutiny; to instil panic; to frighten him into making errors.

He gave no signs of alarm, even though their strategy was supremely effective. They were increasing his edginess by the hour. Even so, he had two advantages. First, as non-residents, they couldn't step inside the block without being challenged by the porter on the security desk – a degree of exposure they would never risk. Second, he knew they would be expecting to keep up the pressure for at least two or three days.

Scannell planned to act much sooner than that.

During the afternoon he'd collected from his safe-deposit boxes all the documents relating to his story. As soon as he was inside his flat, he compiled a single set. It constituted an impressive dossier. The rest of the papers he burned in the kitchen sink, washing away the charred remnants.

Soon afterwards, there was a knock at the door. He stood still and listened. His nerve-ends bristled. Had the people outside come for him? Surely they weren't moving in for the kill already?

There was another knock.

'Tom, it's me.'

He was relieved to hear Celia's voice. He went to the door and let her in, afterwards securing the lock and hooking the safety-chain across to the jamb. She followed him through to the kitchen, self-consciously smelling the air.

'What's been burning?'

'Toast,' he replied quickly, and held up his hand to stop her speaking. 'I thought we'd go out to dinner – or the theatre.'

Celia looked puzzled. 'What?'

'I've had a busy day. I thought it'd be nice to go out.'

Celia looked at him strangely, then moved closer. 'Is something the matter?'

He looked at her, frowning, and stepped away. 'Coffee?'

She nodded. 'Yes.' Her reply was uncertain.

Scannell waited, then opened and shut the cupboard doors. He didn't look inside.

'I've run out,' he announced. 'We'll have to go down to yours.'

Placing a finger against his lips, he picked up the set of documents and slipped them into his briefcase. Hurriedly, he ushered Celia out to the lobby. As they were walking to one of the lifts, he whispered: 'They might've been listening in.'

Celia looked alarmed. 'What's happened?'

'We've got to talk. We'll go out . . . Somewhere where they can't hear us.'

The first place that came to his mind was an Oxford Street jazz club he'd once visited. It was one venue where, although they might be followed, they wouldn't be overheard.

It was half-past eight when they arrived at the club. A support band was playing. Scannell led Celia over to a small table close to the bar, then queued for drinks. When he came back, Celia said with concern: 'Tom, what's going on?'

There was a searching tone in her voice which cut deep into his ethic of allegiance. He knew that the time had come.

He couldn't hold back any longer. In so many ways, his hand had been forced.

'I've got to get away . . . tonight.'

Celia stared uncomprehendingly.

'They know,' Scannell added.

Still Celia said nothing. She just looked at him with growing suspicion. He reached for his drink.

'I have my bosses too.'

He watched her eyes, trying to guess what was going through her mind. It was possible her affection would turn to hostility when she learned the truth, but sooner or later it would have had to have come out.

With unintentional formality, he said: 'Celia, I lied to you.'

Sitting forward, his arms on the table, he waited for a reaction, but she remained rigid. Scannell continued talking, mainly because he couldn't bear the lack of response.

'You asked me who I was working for. Your department was right. My real name is Sergei Lyudin. I've been stationed here for nearly eleven years.'

The revelation unfolded itself so easily that he was surprised how such a simple act could have caused him so much agonizing. It was as though he'd spoken as a character in a tableau, with words supplied by some secondary source.

'Moscow have blocked my story. That means a call has gone out to bring me in.'

Celia's eyes were fixed on him. Not a muscle in her face moved.

'You'd better not tell me any more.'

Her voice, sharp and clipped, seemed to belong to somebody else; somebody he didn't know.

He sipped his drink, setting the glass down slowly. After a long silence, he said: 'We're in trouble.'

Celia's eyes flickered. 'We?'

'Yes. My controllers don't know how much I've told you. You may be at risk.'

Again, he tried to read her thoughts, and noted the controlled terror that showed behind her eyes.

'I'll talk to my head of department. I'll ask for protection.'

'There's Richard as well,' Scannell said ominously. 'There are many ways.'

The noise of music and chatter intruded on their conversation. Celia was toying anxiously with the stem of her glass. Suddenly, Scannell was deeply afraid. He knew that Celia didn't understand his position. He was both hurt and annoyed. He'd expected more from her. Perhaps, if he explained about his assignment, she would realize the commitment he was making.

'I want you to know everything – so you can decide what to do.'

As he spoke, he found the act of disclosure to be an intense purgative. The feeling was strange, almost beyond confessional; his exterior was being stripped away like paintwork, uncovering a personality he hardly recognized as his own. It was the cruellest of ironies that, at the same time as this self-emergence, this opening-up, he should be fighting for survival.

Soon after the band had started playing again, Celia looked up. Scannell had spelled out his full role, as well outlining – as far as he could – the scope of the operation in which he was involved.

'So the photograph . . . it wasn't a fake.'

Scannell shrugged. 'I don't know where they got that from. I haven't met anyone. I've always worked alone . . . strictly alone.'

Celia was all fear now. The dim lighting masked the greyness of her face. He hated to see her like it. He wanted to hold her, to cut away the ugliness that engulfed their lives, but he knew that comfort and reassurance would have to wait. Otherwise their relationship would end with one, or both of them, kneeling in a cellar with a cold barrel at the neck.

'What do we do?' she asked.

Scannell reached for the cigarettes. 'Do you want us to stay together?'

'. . . I don't know.'

'I had to lie to you. There was so much at stake. It's taken me until now to know what to do.'

Celia's hand trembled as she lifted her glass. 'And all that time you watched me going crazy.'

Scannell stared at her. He was struck, for the first time, by the extent of his own selfishness. What had he done to her? Hadn't he seen? It was always someone else who had to suffer the consequences. His burden of blame was heavier than he could ever have imagined.

'I spent eight years at a place called Gaczyna. It's a training school. They teach you how to forget to feel.'

Celia smiled bitterly. 'They do a good job.'

There was another long break in their conversation. They looked at one another across the table. They had reached a point of emotional stalemate. In the end, it was Celia who gave way.

'Can't you go and see someone?'

Scannell frowned. 'Who?'

'I don't know. The Home Office? They might be able to do something.'

'I can imagine what.'

The scared look came back into Celia's eyes. 'Would they put you in prison?'

'They might. Or deport me – if they didn't want the publicity of a trial.'

'Would they try to . . .'

Celia stopped short before asking the question.

'. . . Try to kill me?' he concluded for her. 'They might. My controllers might too, if I don't go back to Moscow. They wouldn't want the risk of your department getting hold of me. Nor the Americans.'

Celia stared into the darkness beyond the low stage. People

274

were at a counter buying food. Others were dancing. She was hit by a fierce jealousy. Why should other people's lives be so normal, so uncomplicated?

She turned to him. 'Could we stay together, even if we wanted to?'

'It might be the only way. I need time . . .'

A little later, he fetched more drinks. After he had sat down again, Celia leaned forward. The look she gave was earnest and inquiring.

'Didn't you know what I was doing until I told you?'

Scannell thought. It was a question he'd asked himself dozens of times since the evening of her admission, but even now he had no clear answer.

'Possibly. I suppose half of me didn't want to go back. I've been away too long.'

'You carried on using me. How could you have done that?'

Scannell shrugged and opened his upturned hand. It was a remote, unsatisfactory gesture. He was unable to explain how he could never have made a reciprocal confession, not on impulse. He was too professional for that.

After a time, he said simply: 'I'm sorry.'

A little later, when he started to lift his glass, she laid her hand on his arm.

'Tom, are you scared?'

He nodded. 'Yes . . . of course.'

For the next half-hour, Scannell revealed still more about himself: his training; his period at Leningrad University; his memories of his mother, who, he'd learned some years before, had died while he'd been stationed abroad. He spoke briefly, too, about his sister and her children, although he doubted they would recognize him now. He didn't mention Yelena; somehow there didn't seem much point. She, like his sister, was probably struggling in some teaching job, trying to see her family at the weekends.

'Loneliness never bothered me . . . not till I knew I

was going to have to go back. That's when I realized that everything was here – everyone I knew. What would I go back to? I can't go barging into other people's lives. You and Richard are more . . .'

He broke off.

'What?' asked Celia quietly.

Scannell suddenly felt embarrassed. 'More my family, I suppose . . . more than anyone else.'

All the time he'd been talking, he'd noticed how Celia was studying him, as though unsure whether she was hearing further fabrications. Even now, he wondered if he was going to lose her.

When he had finished, she said with a note of challenge: 'What are you asking for?'

Scannell tapped his cigarette against the side of the ashtray. 'Nothing. Just you . . . and for these –' he waved his hand helplessly, 'these people to get out of my life.'

Celia pressed her fingertips against her forehead. Scannell saw the distress and knew he was only adding to her troubles.

'It's my problem,' he said.

Celia lifted her hand away from her face. 'You expect me to just . . . leave you? Now? After what you've told me?'

'I don't know. It might be better.'

For several minutes they stopped talking. The music from the band was loud, but Scannell was aware of it only as a distant, monotonous medley. All the time, Celia was vacillating. At last, she made a decision.

'I'll come with you . . . if you want me to. There must be someone we can find who can help us.'

Scannell made no expression. These were the words he had craved to hear. Even as she spoke, though, the weight of responsibility became crushing. If she was going to come away with him, she had to understand the seriousness of the position.

'There'll be no going back.'

'Do you think I don't see that?'

Finally, he stood up.

'We'd better be going. We haven't got much time.'

It was gone 10.30 when they arrived back at the Barbican. One of the surveillance team was standing at the far end of the walkway. Scannell saw him step back into the shadows cast by the balconies of the flats above.

'Quickly.'

Scannell glanced round and grasped Celia's arm. They took the lift to her flat and found Richard in the kitchen preparing a meal for himself. Celia removed the pan from the cooker and took him out to the lift lobby, which was the one place she felt free to speak. Richard protested.

'Hold on – I haven't eaten anything since lunchtime!'

'You can get something later.'

He looked unsure of himself, and his anger increased. 'What's up, for Christ's sake?'

'We're going away. I'll tell you about it, but not right now. We haven't got time.'

'You mean we're leaving the flat? . . . *Tonight?*'

'Yes. Just for the time being.'

Richard's astonishment seemed to act as a brake for his thoughts. He gave his mother an indignant frown. 'Why all the whispering?'

Celia glanced towards the door. 'Someone might be listening. Tom's in a lot of trouble – over one of his stories. Some people are after him. We need to see what we can do to help. Don't talk about what I've said . . . not when we're inside the flat. Just get changed.'

Richard's eyes narrowed vindictively. 'Who's after him?'

'It doesn't matter.'

'What did he write?'

'I said I'd tell you, but not now.'

They went back inside the flat. Celia packed two bags, while Richard dressed in jeans and a jumper.

Scannell, meanwhile, had gone up to his own flat. He

also put on a pair of jeans, together with a sweatshirt and windcheater. He transferred the dossier from his briefcase to a holdall, then stuffed a change of clothes and a toilet bag on top. Leaving the lights on to make it seem he was still at home, he went back down to Celia's. She and Richard were almost ready.

They locked up the flat and stepped out into the lobby. Scannell pressed the button for the lift. He chewed his lip impatiently as they waited.

'As soon as they know we've left the flats, they'll have a man on every exit. We've got to move – fast.'

Instead of leaving the block by the main entrance, which Scannell knew would be under heavy surveillance, they continued down to the lower basement level. Bags of rubbish were heaped for collection in the service area. Scannell stepped quickly across to a black steel door marked *Maintenance Engineer*. He glanced round to make sure that Celia and Richard were behind him.

'Quick. Through here.' He took a key from his pocket.

Celia looked at him accusingly. 'Where did you get that?'

Scannell slipped the key into the lock and gave it a sharp twist.

'I used to know one of the women in the estate management office. Her keys got left in my flat one night . . .'

Celia said nothing, but her disapproving glare showed what she thought of his methods. She and Richard followed him through into a concrete chamber littered with workmen's debris. Quietly, he clicked the door shut. His eyes flashed round to meet Celia's and Richard's.

'This way. Mind your heads.'

During the next couple of minutes, Scannell led them along a labyrinth of dimly-lit service tunnels. The low ceilings were strung with pipes, and the walls carried legions of heavy-duty cable. No matter how quietly the three of them tried to run, they were chased by the echoes of their own footsteps.

Briefly, they stopped to catch their breath.

Celia clung to the strut of a soil-pipe. 'Do you know where we're going?'

Scannell frowned. 'Sort of. I came down here once. It was a while ago though.' He wiped his forehead, and pushed his fingers back through his hair. 'The best way out is just up ahead.'

He cast his eyes along the tunnel's narrowing perspective. Ever since the first few weeks after he'd moved into the complex, he'd known most of the conceivable escape routes from both the building and the estate itself. At regular intervals, he'd also undertaken checks to make sure no alterations had been made.

'Come on.'

He touched Celia's arm, and moved forward. He was walking softly now, his rubber-soled trainers padding along the concrete floor. As he approached a branch in the tunnel, he signalled for the other two to stay close.

'We get out here,' he whispered. 'No noise.'

Already he could feel the night's mild air against his face. Soon he was peering through a steel-barred gate that sealed the way out to a narrow stairwell. Gently, he pushed against the gate. As he'd expected, it was locked, although he knew from his past inspection that the maintenance key should open it. After inserting the key, he turned it slowly, clenching his teeth. To his relief, it revolved freely.

He eased the gate open a fraction so he could see to the top of the stairwell. He made no movement, no sound. For more than a minute he stood listening, gradually becoming conscious of his exaggerated heartbeat. When he felt certain that no one was up above, he opened the gate another touch. At that moment, an iron claw seemed to grip his chest. By the entrance to the stairwell, he'd seen a shadow move. There was no doubt. Instantly, he drew back. Eyes closed, he pinned himself to the wall. His breath came in shallow draughts.

As his eyes opened, he stared at Celia. With a backward movement of his head, he signalled to her that the exit was being watched. After another few moments, he reached out to pull back the gate. The action was carried out with the delicacy of someone testing the speed of a guillotine blade, his senses primed to retract in an instant. Silently, he inched the gate towards him, praying that the hinges wouldn't squeak. It was crucial that he should lock it, otherwise it would give the surveillance team open entry to the tunnel system. So far, he'd presumed that they didn't have a key.

Again, he closed his eyes as he felt the lock about to bite home. It gave only a soft click as it sprang into place, but it was enough to send a shock-wave through his central system. He turned to Celia and pointed feverishly back down the tunnel.

'Back . . . The way we came.'

He glanced behind constantly as they retraced their footsteps through the warren, but it seemed their luck had held out. They hadn't been seen.

Up in the basement lobby of the apartment block, he watched through the three sets of glass doors that separated the building from the adjacent underground car park. As residents, they could get out, but no one without an official pass-key could get in. The greatest danger would be in trying to find a way out to any of the surrounding streets.

'Okay. Let's go.'

They stepped swiftly through the doors and out into the car park. As they started to run towards a nearby ramp which went up to the street, Richard pointed out the figure of a woman standing close to the entrance. Scannell steered Celia close to the car park wall.

They emerged at one of the complex's central gardens. Scannell trained his eyes on the distant walkways, and listened for anyone who might have followed them from the apartment block. As far as he could tell, all was clear. He motioned ahead.

'Along by the lake.'

When they came to the corner of the wall where the path met the waterside, he knew they were approaching the point of greatest danger. The rectangular expanse of water stretched across to a wide piazza.

'Keep close in,' Scannell instructed. 'Don't try to take it too fast – and careful with the gates.'

The path ran behind a series of pillars that supported an adjacent building. Richard was just about to start out along the path, when Celia clawed him back. At the same time, she snatched at Scannell's windcheater and pointed across the lake. Immediately, Scannell's head shot up. Celia's sights were fixed on the corner of the building opposite. Scannell had failed to see two men standing by the wall of a suspended walkway. They were probably less than fifty metres away.

'Back!'

In an instant, Scannell had drawn Celia and Richard down the path and against the wall where they were hidden from view.

'Wait here.'

He crept forward alongside the wall, using the additional cover of shrubbery. The men seemed relatively relaxed, and one offered the other a cigarette. If they were part of the surveillance team, they clearly regarded themselves as an outer flank, unlikely to be troubled. After a few minutes' observation, he returned to Celia and Richard.

'It's the only way. We'll go one at a time.'

As Richard started out along the path, Scannell kept his eyes anchored on the men. Celia followed close behind Richard, who got through the first gate without a problem. The two of them crept from pillar to pillar, until they reached the end.

All the time, the tension was building up inside Scannell. When he came to make the crossing himself, he resisted the temptation to glance back across the lake. He fastened his eyes straight ahead and walked casually, with one hand in his windcheater pocket, so that if he was spotted he could be mistaken for any resident. He held his breath, expecting at any moment to hear a challenge shouted from the walkway.

Despite his fears, and against his expectations, he reached the safety of the pillars at the end of the path. Now there was just a last short stretch to the corner of a building where he'd told Celia and Richard to wait. Again, he walked purposefully, but without hurrying.

When he rounded the corner, he looked across at the men. One of them had made a half-turn in the direction of the lake, but he appeared to have seen nothing. Scannell swung his holdall over his shoulder.

'Come on. We'll get out at the far end and find a taxi.'

Just as he turned to press on, an inbuilt caution made him cast a final glance over his shoulder. To his alarm, he saw that one of the men was speaking into a handset. His colleague was gazing out over the lake. Scannell held Celia and Richard perfectly still.

'Shit! They must've seen me!'

Grabbing Celia's bag, he broke into a fast run, plunging down into another car park under an apartment block. He was heading for a little-used exit gate that he'd remembered on the eastern side of the complex. Again, though, he was brought up sharply. Even as he approached the gate, he could see a man leaning against a wall outside.

'Down here. There's another way out . . . further on.'

Running hard now, they passed through more doors and up a tiled stairway. A further connecting passage took them through to a car park at the estate's northern end. Here, at street level, Scannell stopped to observe the roadway through a large ventilation grille set in the brickwork.

Still breathless, he turned to Celia. 'I can't see anyone. There's an exit . . . at the end.'

They crouched low and moved cautiously forward until they came close to the ramp that would take them out to the street. To Scannell's consternation, there was no attendant in the booth. Without the security check, anyone could get into that area of the complex without being challenged.

He stood still, again listening for any sound. To give him cover while he peered across at the nearby buildings, he hugged a brick wall. Not far away was the public entrance to the arts centre, but that had now closed for the night. As far as he could tell, there wasn't a soul on the pavement outside.

In the darkness he crossed the ramp, half stooping, until he was able to use the bulk provided by a parked delivery van to gain a wider view of the street. He was about to signal the all-clear to Celia and Richard, when suddenly a man in a zip-up leather jacket ran out from a sidestreet and down towards the exit. Scannell shrank back.

Crossing directly in front of the van, the man took up a position on the pavement no more than three or four metres away from the corner of the wall behind which Celia and Richard were pinned.

Scannell's spine set like a stave. Why now? Of all times, why now? If they'd just been a few seconds earlier . . .

Scannell watched the exit. The man began to pace slowly up and down. He appeared to be intensely keyed up, turning his head at every sound, switching his gaze to every movement in the darkness. As the seconds ticked away, Scannell knew the surveillance team would by now be combing the complex. All the time, the net would be tightening.

Looking through the van's windows, he assessed the man's physical characteristics. Stocky, but muscular rather than fat. The face: an expression of determination and toughness. It would be like taking on a Kremlin bodyguard.

The only element Scannell had in his favour was surprise. He had to give himself time to think, but his head spun like a lunatic's. He had only one option. The man had to be rushed from behind, and the strike had to be instant – and deadly.

Careful not to kick any stray stones, he began to circle the van. When he reached the front, he got down on his hands and knees and surveyed his quarry from beneath the wheel-arch. Still the man was standing at the same spot, his attention focused on the buildings down the street. Scannell unclipped the strap of his hold-all. Move decisively, he told himself. Remember, there would be only one chance.

It came quicker than he'd anticipated. Down towards another apartment block, a man and a woman crossed a junction. They briefly caught the surveillance agent's eye and, as he moved a couple of steps in their direction to take a sharper look, Scannell knew he couldn't delay.

Skirting round the back of the van, he stepped out from behind it and started edging across the ramp. The man was still watching the street. Scannell willed him not to look round. If he should do so now, the tables would be immediately turned. Almost certainly, the man would be armed. At this distance, even with a handgun, Scannell knew he was an impossible target to miss. His life could end with the scuff of a shoe.

As he came up behind the peering figure, he straightened to give himself maximum purchase on the ground. Blood rushed through his ears and eyes and brain. Only an arm's length to go, only a split-second before the final pitch.

Raising the strap of the hold-all, which was stretched like a heavy thong between his hands, Scannell sprang forward and brought it over the man's head, at the same time snapping it back sharply and crossing his arms. The effect was startling. Instantly, the man let out a choking cry and his body arched backwards, bringing Scannell forcefully to the ground. Somehow Scannell managed to hang on to the ends of the strap, twisting and jerking it, throwing the whole weight of his body behind the single-minded action. His intention had been to pull the man off balance, then deal a knockout blow, but already the stakes had been raised.

Hands thrashed in the darkness and two fingers searched to gouge at Scannell's eyes. He also felt a thunderous pain in his groin as a knee rose with the resolution of a piston. The face that flashed beneath him in the glow of a streetlight was distorted into a killer's snarl.

As he stared at the face, Scannell's bodyframe stiffened with hostility; he had become an animal of prey. His hands were shaking with strain, squeezing away the life that threatened him. Still the man's fingers searched for his eyes and, as they moved down his face, tried to rip at his mouth. Scannell heaved back, dragging the man's head and shoulders forward. His hands tightened still more. Behind him he could feel the man's knees ramming his shoulder-blades, his feet grappling to get a hold on his head.

The man bucked and twisted. Scannell strained forward until he could smell warm, sour breath. The eyes that stared up at him were bulging and glazed.

Die, Scannell's mind screamed. *Die, you bastard!*

For several seconds the legs kept crashing into his back. Then, after the man's body formed an arc in a final spasm of self-preservation, his strength began to slip away. Scannell kept his grip on the strap, even now drawing it tighter.

Moments later, the man gave an involuntary moan, and his arms slid to the ground. His frame had become limp, and an opened tract released a flood of urine. Scannell recoiled as he felt the hot wetness against his clothes, a peculiarly repugnant verification that the job had been done. He sank on to the man's chest, rasping for breath.

Almost at once, Richard stepped out from the cover of the wall and ran forward to pull Scannell away. He helped him to his feet.

'You all right?'

Scannell nodded. Slowly, he began to gather his senses. He looked round at Celia, who had also ventured out from behind the wall. She didn't speak.

Suddenly, in the distance, inside the complex, came a

shout. Scannell's eyes were instantly alert. He pulled himself away from the wall.

'We've got to move him! They'll find him!'

Gripping the man's shoulders, he started to drag him across the ramp. Richard helped to push the body beneath the van. As soon as it was out of sight, Scannell went back to where Celia was standing and snatched up his holdall. She was staring, as if mesmerized, at the patch of urine on the concrete where the man had been lying. Scannell took hold of her arm.

'Come on . . . We've got to go.'

They stepped out to the street. One or two cars passed, but there were no pedestrians. Scannell started walking fast. Celia and Richard strove to keep up with him, hurrying through the narrow market lanes until they came out near Old Street station.

'We'll travel apart,' Scannell said. 'You two get a taxi to Heathrow. Book in at the Post House Hotel. Use another name.'

Celia looked at him in deep confusion. 'Heathrow?'

'People pass through all the time. They won't remember you.'

'What about you?'

Scannell strove to think where he could meet up with them. 'I'll get a sleeper to Scotland. I'll meet you in the buffet bar at Norwich station – between seven and nine o'clock tomorrow evening. If I'm not there by then, go home. You'll know they've found me.'

A look of desperation came to Celia's face. 'I won't be able to pay for the hotel. I haven't got enough money.'

From his pocket, Scannell pulled out an envelope. It was full of notes. He gave her a sheaf and she regarded him dubiously.

'When did you get this? Where from?'

'This afternoon . . . I drew everything out of my account.'

Celia stuffed the money blindly into a side-pocket of her handbag. Meanwhile, Scannell turned to Richard.

'There's a caravan site – near the place we camped. Head for there. Do whatever your mother says.'

Scannell moved towards Celia. Briefly, he held her shoulders. He kissed her forehead.

'We'll be okay,' he whispered.

Moments later, he stood across the road in a doorway while Celia and Richard waited for a taxi. Two or three passed, but they were already hired. Then, in the distance coming along from Finsbury Square, Scannell glimpsed a yellow light. He pointed it out to Richard, who hailed the cab vigorously. It swung into the kerb.

As it pulled away, Scannell caught Celia's eye. She was looking out of the side window, brushing back a loose strand of hair. She looked afraid and disoriented.

Scannell stood motionless. An unfathomable guilt gripped him so he could neither think nor move.

37

Fairweather ran the towel over his face, wiping away the induced heavy sweat. On the opposite bench in the sauna, Blom gritted his teeth against the heat. He was watching Fairweather with curiosity. For once, the man's air of self-assurance was lacking. He wasn't in complete control of the operation, and he didn't like it. The signs of disquiet were evident in the firm set mouth and the lean eyes.

Fairweather wiped his shoulders and adjusted another towel on which he was sitting. Leaning forward, he breathed deeply, as though trying to filter a trace of coolness from the dry, baked air. It was another unproductive exercise. Earlier that morning, back at the office, the impression had been the same. He was engaged in an endless search for something that eluded him. Sinking back against the pine boards, he looked up at the ceiling and closed his eyes.

'Four days. Where is he? Where the *fuck* is he?'

Blom kept his thoughts to himself. The problem of Scannell's whereabouts was as disturbing for him as it was for the section chief, but there was nothing that could be said which would resolve it. A general alert had gone out to all police forces and the Customs and Excise department. Apart from feeding a story to the media – and publicity was the last thing the service wanted – there was nothing more to be done.

Fairweather shook his head, and ran his hands down his arms.

'Every airport's been checked. Every seaport . . . Every ferry line. He must be somewhere.' Fairweather draped his spare towel over his knees. 'What about the Americans? Have *they* said anything?'

Blom shook his head. 'No. We've kept them out of it since the Kepler fire.' With a trace of a smile, he added: 'They got their fingers burned.'

Fairweather's face remained serious. 'I take it you're in contact with their liaison man at Grosvenor Square, though?'

'Daily. They want him as badly as we do.'

Secretly, Blom knew why Fairweather was giving the matter so much personal attention. It was the Rodway syndrome: failure was beginning to stalk him. If Scannell wasn't found soon, it would become increasingly difficult for him to justify his position.

Raising his eyes, Fairweather said: 'Do you think the KGB have taken him back?'

'It's possible. They must have emergency routes . . . ones we don't know about.'

Fairweather considered the point, then shook his head adamantly. 'No. He's still in this country. I know he is, damn it! They must've instructed him to go to ground. They're keeping him out of the way until they decide they can risk getting him back to Moscow. If they got caught trying to take him out now . . . Jesus, there'd be a diplomatic bloodbath.'

The two men had been in the sauna for almost three-quarters of an hour. Blom's thoughts started to drift as tiredness overcame him. He had no sympathy for his colleague. All Fairweather was concerned about was his personal reputation and the damage that might be done to his own promotion prospects by Scannell's disappearance. As for himself, Blom saw deeper motivations, like duty and good citizenship.

'I've been called in to see the MoD,' said Fairweather. 'I want a report from your unit. An up-to-the-minute account of all inquiries.'

'When by?'

'The meeting's on Friday. I need it on my desk tomorrow afternoon. I might want some changes made.'

'It'll have to be brief . . . The timescale's too tight.'

Fairweather brushed back his hair. 'As long as I've got something to present. We need to be seen to be working, even if we're not getting results.' He paused, then asked: 'What about Webster? Have we found out anything more there?'

'No. Nobody knows anything.'

On hearing the question, Blom had felt a further layer of heat creep under his skin. The unit had been working day and night to find out what had happened to the man. One day he'd been at his desk in his office; the next he'd vanished. No notes; no sign of abduction. The word had gone round the department that he, like Scannell, had been a KGB sleeper, but the case had yet to be proven. Everyone was still asking questions. Sooner, rather than later, some sort of truth would emerge. The press were already making tentative inquiries.

Fairweather stood up and wrapped the towel round his waist. He moved to a corner seat.

'Bugger it, this is too hot for me.'

Blom looked up and smiled dryly. 'In here, or at the department?'

Fairweather returned the smile. 'Both.'

He seemed to welcome the release of tension. When he next spoke, he sounded more composed.

'It was interesting – what the agency's editor had to say. I take it you heard the tapes?'

'I read the transcript.'

'If we can find out more about the ownership of Webster's companies, then we might get somewhere. There must be a link between him and Scannell. The problem is – only Scannell can tell us what it is. That's why we've got to find him.'

'Special Branch are working on it.'

'Have they got any leads?'

Blom had hoped that Fairweather wouldn't draw him into

detailed areas of the inquiry, but now that the subject had been raised, it needed to be addressed fully.

'There's a possibility he may have gone to Norfolk.'

Fairweather frowned. 'Norfolk? Why the hell would he go there?'

'Countryside . . . resorts . . . caravan sites. They're being checked out.'

'Has a lead been confirmed?'

Blom shook his head. 'No. A man fitting his description was seen at a railway station in Norwich the evening after Scannell left his flat. It's a possibility, no more.'

'I want to be told the moment the Special Branch find out.'

The two men endured a further few minutes in the sauna, then Fairweather lifted himself from the bench.

'I've had enough. This seat's baking my balls off!'

Blom followed him through to the changing rooms. After showering, they dressed in an open area by the lockers, rather than in the private cubicles.

Standing up to tuck in his shirt, Blom said: 'It was a mistake to let him get away.'

Fairweather recognized the criticism and reacted sharply. 'Special Branch men were on twenty-four-hour surveillance. Short of arresting him, there was nothing else they could've done. The KGB were crawling round the apartment block.'

Blom kept his silence. He knew that if Rodway had been allowed to operate without interference from the beginning, Scannell would have been brought in for interrogation weeks ago. Everybody, from the F Branch chiefs down, had under-estimated the skills of the former unit head. As it was, Rodway had lost his credibility after Scannell's accident. It had been a big mistake, for which the department had paid a higher price than anyone could possibly realize.

38

Scannell kept a silent vigil on the Place Corbeau. For two days after taking the room he scarcely stepped outside the door. When he did, it was to use the bathroom on the landing down a half-flight of stairs.

It had been Celia's idea that he should come to Brussels. Defection was now his only option, but first he had to strike a bargain to make sure that DI5 wouldn't simply hand him over to the KGB. One lifeline was a press contact in the European Commission and, after three days at the caravan site in Norfolk, he'd decided to take the risk. Using one of two false passports which had come from his safe-deposit boxes, he had crossed the Channel by ferry from Folkestone. That had been the easy part; far easier than he'd expected. Now, holed up in his room, he faced the toughest assignment of his career.

Sitting in the shadow of the dusty curtains, his attention switched constantly from the tiled rooftops to the shop doorways; from the parked cars to the streets that led into the square. Soon he was able to tell from a brief observation the pedestrians who were resident in the square and those who were just passing through. He also kept his eye on the newsagent's shop on the opposite side of the square. He had hidden his dossier near the shop in case his room should be searched if he went out.

He slept only in snatches. Through the long hours of the night he watched through partially drawn curtains as the lights in the neighbouring houses were switched off one by one. Being close to the centre of the city, the two cafés and the restaurant in the square stayed open until the early hours. Then came the chilly wait until dawn.

All he'd had to eat during the two days was a tin of meat and a stick of bread that he'd brought with him to the house. The room had no cooking facilities, just an electric kettle. Each hour, on the hour, he drank a cup of weak, black coffee. He had only bought a small jar, and daren't risk leaving the house until he was sure it wasn't under surveillance. The scheduled activity of making the coffee helped to keep him alert, while the warmth in his stomach staved off hunger. His staple diet was cigarettes.

On the morning of the third day, he decided that the house was safe. For the time being, at least, he'd found a hiding-place. It was nightfall, though, before he ventured out, crossing the square to a café called Lubka's. He ordered a meal, selecting a table by the window so he could keep the house in view. The time had come for him to make a move.

Three unmarked Special Branch cars travelled through the night into the East Anglian countryside. Blom was in the front passenger seat of the first car.

As they approached the coastal village of Newport, he said: 'Slow down. Just sidelights now.'

The cars drew up at the entrance to a caravan park. Eleven plain-clothes officers got out. Blom issued hurried instructions.

'Two of you stay here by the gate. The rest of you – no noise.'

The officers split into two groups. Those with Blom spread out among the caravans and silently made their way across the site. The other group ran down the shingle side path.

Within two minutes, a grey and green caravan by the site's rear entrance was surrounded. All the men, with the exception of Blom, were armed.

The caravan's lights were on. Behind the curtains a figure could be seen sitting in the bay window. The blurred light of a television set was also visible.

Blom, accompanied by two of the officers, stepped

forward. As he knocked on the door, the officers positioned themselves either side of it. They crouched, their guns trained at head height.

Blom knocked again, then stepped back into the shadows. Apart from the indistinct voices on the television, no sound came from the caravan. Blom motioned to one of the officers, who reached forward and banged twice.

'Open up,' Blom called out. 'It's the police!'

A slight movement came from inside the caravan. A curtain at a side window was lifted, then it dropped back.

'Open the door!'

The two officers braced themselves as a key was turned in the lock. Slowly the door swung open.

'Put your arms straight out in front of you and come out!'

Richard appeared in the doorway. Looking frightened, he stepped down on to the grass.

'Lie down – on your face!'

The two officers kept their guns on the doorway.

'Now the woman,' Blom called out.

The boy lifted his head to speak. 'Mum's over at the washroom.'

'Is Scannell in there?'

'No.'

'Where is he?'

'I don't know.'

Blom signalled for two more officers to come forward. They crept up to the bay window and waited. When Blom nodded, they smashed the main pane of glass with their gun butts, then ducked below the front of the caravan.

Around the site, faces were appearing at other windows. Lights came on in caravans where the occupants had gone to bed. Several doors were opened.

'Everybody stay inside,' Blom warned.

Suddenly, Celia came down the cinder track that led from the washroom. She was carrying a towel and toilet bag.

When she saw the men around the caravan she stopped on the spot, then made as if to run.

'We've got the boy here!' Blom called out.

Celia hung back. After a moment's hesitation, she turned. 'What have you done to him?'

'Nothing. He's all right. Where's Scannell?'

Slowly, Celia started walking back towards the caravan. 'He's not here. He's gone away.'

'If he is inside, you'd better tell him to come out. He could get hurt.'

'I told you, he's not here.'

Blom ordered the broken glass to be removed from the smashed window. The curtains were gingerly drawn back.

'Come on out, Scannell!' shouted Blom.

When no reply came, one of the officers by the door warily looked into the caravan. He turned.

'No one's in there.'

Richard was pulled to his feet and the caravan was searched.

'Okay,' said Blom finally, 'let's take them away.'

That night Scannell slept for three hours. It was a fitful sleep, but the stretch was longer than any he'd had since his arrival in the city. He lay on the bed in his clothes, always expecting the knock on the door which would spell the end of his freedom, and perhaps his life.

Before dawn, he was awake, watching at the window, but it was hours before he dared step outside. At nine o'clock he washed and shaved, then went round the corner for breakfast. After leaving the backstreet café, he took the Metro to Schuman station. He was familiar with that area of the city from trips he'd made to cover meetings on EEC defence policy.

It was a short walk across to the offices of the European Commission at the Palais Berlaymont. His press card was a sufficient stamp of officialdom to allow him up to the suite occupied by the chief press attaché, a man named Colin Jensen. Scannell had given his own name at the reception desk. He was out in the open now, trusting his fate to a bureaucratic machinery whose technicians could sign his reprieve or hand him over to his executioner.

The press attaché's secretary showed Scannell through to the main office. Jensen stood up to greet him, extending his hand. He'd changed little since he'd worked with Scannell on the staff of a London newspaper some years previously.

'Tom, good to see you. What brings you over here?'

Scannell was reassured by Jensen's congeniality.

'Have you got a few minutes? It's important that I talk to you.'

Jensen seemed to catch the note of urgency in Scannell's voice and agreed to interrupt his schedule. The two men sat at a low table by the window of the large office which overlooked the Rue de la Loi. Scannell couldn't hide his nervousness, and Jensen seemed genuinely concerned.

'Tell me, is something wrong?'

Ever since Scannell had taken the decision to come to Brussels, he'd wondered how his words would sound when he came to make the testimony of his lifetime. Now that the moment had arrived, he hesitated, almost changing his mind. It still wasn't too late. He could concoct some plausible story to explain why he'd presented himself at the office. Then he remembered Celia and Richard. Their lives depended on his action too. Almost against his will, he began to speak.

'I'm going to tell you something that will put you in an impossible position, but you're my only chance of survival. I've come to ask you for help.'

Jensen listened in disbelief as Scannell outlined the nature of his KGB role. He shook his head. 'I don't know what to say.'

Scannell looked up. 'Basically, unless you can do something to help me, you're talking to a dead man.'

'What is it you're asking me to do?'

'I need to be able to negotiate. I'm prepared to give myself up to the British authorities . . . tell them all that I've just told you. I haven't got any affiliations now with the KGB. I know what they can do to people. They'll do the same to me.'

'Why should the British authorities believe you?'

Scannell looked across the table, his hands in his lap. 'I don't expect they will, but what have I got to lose? I told you – I'm bargaining to stay alive.'

The cars had arrived sometime after midnight at the Special Branch operations office in Tothill Street. Richard had been given a bed for the night, while Celia was taken to an upstairs interview room. There she was left alone with Blom. He asked for coffee to be sent in and put a packet of cigarettes on the table with the invitation for Celia to help herself. The questioning began shortly after one o'clock.

'It's quite a situation you've got yourself in,' he observed.

Celia said nothing.

'What made you go off like that? Did you think we wouldn't find you?'

'No. We knew you'd come.'

'What then?'

Blom studied her across the table. Her hair was limp and her face lined. He remembered a photograph of her that Rodway had shown him when she'd first been assigned to the job. The intervening months had taken their toll. Clearly, she was close to being broken, but he didn't want to act too fast. More would be revealed with gradual pressure than by sudden demands for information. Experience had taught him that.

'I asked you why you went away with Scannell.'

'What choice did we have?'

'You could have come to us – or asked to speak to your superiors.'

'That wouldn't have helped Tom, would it?'

Blom looked at her disapprovingly. 'What makes you say that?'

'Because it's true. Anything might've happened.'

'Meaning what?'

Celia shrugged. 'You would have deported him . . . or worse.'

'We might be professional, but we're not heartless. You were in an understandable predicament.'

Celia let her hands rest loosely on the table. Blom could see she wasn't convinced. He poured more coffee as they talked. It took him more than half an hour before he worked round to asking her of Scannell's whereabouts.

'I don't know,' she said flatly.

'You mean he just went off without a word? Nothing about when he'd see you again?'

'That's right.'

'What, a woman he'd taken into hiding and whose life he'd devastated? That sounds like the action of a man who doesn't care very much.'

'If that's what you think, then think it.'

'Could it be that he didn't want you around any more?'

'Could be.'

Blom admired her fidelity. It had become a challenge for him to wear it down, but her resistance was stronger, far stronger than he'd expected. By three o'clock he still hadn't received an answer to his crucial question. His manner had already become more aggressive. The time had come to be positively threatening.

'You'll never see Scannell again, you know that.'

'I thought you said you weren't heartless.'

Blom ignored the response. 'He'll be imprisoned. Then, in four or five years' time, when his name's been forgotten, he'll be quietly swapped with someone we want to get back from the Soviet Union.'

'At least he'll be safe there.'

Blom smiled. 'I think he might disagree with you on that.

Besides, without protection from us, the KGB won't let you and your son stay around for long enough to see.'

The blade had gone in. There was a short silence until the pain registered.

'That's up to us,' Celia said defiantly.

Blom unclipped his cufflinks and rolled up his shirtsleeves. He'd been carefully choosing the time when he should adopt his main tactic. Slowly, he started to walk across the room as if in thought, then he turned back.

'Of course, you do want to keep your son?'

Celia remained calm, but Blom detected a glint of panic in her eyes. He could feel her wriggling like a fly on a pin, but he resisted the temptation to crush her. This insect's legs would be pulled off one by one.

'He's been something of a wild lad in the past, hasn't he? The stolen car, for instance. I gather he's on probation. I don't think we'd have much trouble transferring him to a special centre.'

Celia flared. 'You couldn't do that. Not without a court order.'

'True. I'll have the papers prepared when the day staff come on after breakfast.'

Celia started to rise from her chair. 'You bastard. I'll . . .'

Blom's eyes flashed. 'What? Make things worse for yourself? I can have the boy taken away just like that.' He snapped his fingers. 'And then we'll send you back home to your cosy little flat and you can wait for your KGB friends to come and visit. I'm sure there's lots they'd like you to tell them.'

Celia closed her eyes, as if trying to erase Blom's words.

'They're highly skilled workers, the KGB,' he went on. 'I've seen what they do to people who conceal information.'

Celia sank back in her chair.

'It's either you or them,' she said wearily. 'What's the difference?'

Blom's expression darkened. 'Basically, the difference between life and death.'

He stood up again and walked to the window, stretching his back. A patch of his shirt was stained with sweat.

'All I want to know is where Scannell's gone. Then we'll send you away to a hotel in the country for a week or two so you and your boy can pick up the pieces. After that, the choice is yours. A new identity . . . whatever you like. You can stay in this country, or go abroad. We'll make sure you're safe.'

He came across the room and leaned on the table in front of her.

'You see, we can be very accommodating.'

Celia stared at the floor. Blom sat back in his chair, giving her time to contemplate his offer. He had no need to press her any further; he knew he'd won.

Her voice was quiet when she spoke. 'Would you be prepared to guarantee he'd be all right if . . .'

Blom waited. 'If what?'

'. . . If I told you where he was.'

'It's not my place to guarantee anything. However, I do know there are arrangements that could be made. I believe he's carrying a dossier of highly contentious information. No doubt appreciation would be shown for its safe return.'

Celia studied Blom's face, searching for a sign that he was lying, but his eyes gave nothing away. Somewhere, far in the night, Scannell was relying on her judgement. She was the only person he'd ever confided in, and now she was about to break that trust. Would Blom try to have him killed, or seek to save him? She was gambling with her lover's life.

At last, she made her decision. It was instinctive, based only on hope. When she spoke, her words were almost inaudible.

'He's gone to Brussels.'

Blom nodded slowly. 'I see. Where's he staying?'

'I don't know. He went there to see someone he knew. Someone who he thought might be able to help him.'

'Who?'

'I don't know his name. Tom didn't say.'

Blom fought the temptation to physically wring more information out of the woman. He was so near, yet so far. One slip, one premature step, and it would all be lost. He took a deep, silent breath.

'This man that Scannell went to see . . . do you know what he does for a living?'

Celia took a cigarette from the packet, which was slowly emptying. 'He was someone Tom used to know in London.'

'A journalist?'

'I'm not sure. He might've been.'

'On a newspaper?'

'No. Not any more. I think he's some sort of a press officer.'

'If he's in Brussels, is he connected with the EEC?'

Again, Celia fell silent.

Blom leaned forward. 'If you know, you must tell me.'

Celia lowered her eyes. For Blom, it was answer enough.

'There are a lot of organizations serving the EEC in Brussels,' he said. 'Do you know which one he works for?'

He tried to put a trace of gentleness in his voice. He willed her to speak.

'Well?' he asked. 'Did Tom say?'

'What will you do to him when you find him?'

Blom looked at her forthrightly. 'Let's cross one bridge at a time, shall we? All we can do is try to get this thing sorted out in the best way for everybody.'

Celia stared at him. He said nothing. There was no doubt in his mind that she knew more than she'd told him. He could see she was wrestling with her conscience. Then she shook her head disconsolately, as though realizing her options had run out.

'The man's name is Colin Jensen.'

'I see . . .'

'He's a press attaché with the European Commission.'

Blom eased himself back from the table. Some moments later, he started to roll down his shirtsleeves.

'I expect you're tired. If you like, you can have a room here to get some sleep and freshen up. Someone will be along later in the morning. You can talk then about where you and your son would like to go.'

Scannell and Jensen sat at a pavement table outside a brass-erie near the Boulevard Anspach. At Jensen's suggestion, they had taken a taxi downtown, where he had arranged for them to meet a woman called Susan Chambers, a British member of the European Parliament in Strasbourg. She was also a member of the Parliament's committee on external economic relations, Jensen had explained. Like other committees of the Parliament, it met in Brussels, which was where Chambers spent much of her time. Jensen had telephoned her before leaving his office. While he hadn't disclosed the nature of his request to see her, he had expressed urgency.

After he and Scannell had been talking for a few minutes, Jensen stood up.

Scannell shifted in his seat. 'Where are you going?'

Jensen grinned. 'Don't worry. I'm only taking a leak. Look, you can see the door from here.'

He went into the restaurant. When he came out of the lavatory he went up to the barman. Scannell, who had been watching him through the window, rose to his feet, suspecting that Jensen might be sounding an alert. Then Scannell saw the barman reach for a packet of cigarettes. Jensen came out to the terrace.

'I was only buying these.'

Unwrapping the cigarettes, he offered one to Scannell. It shook between Scannell's lips as he accepted a light.

'Say, you're in a bad way.'

'I can't stay sitting out here much longer.'

'It's all right. She said she'd be here as soon as she could make it. I know her quite well. If anyone can help you, she will.'

Daylight had begun to break when Blom left the office. It was almost four o'clock in the morning. He walked round the corner to a side-street hotel called the Ventnor, off Petty France, where Special Branch kept three private rooms. Collecting a key from the night porter, he went up to a room on the second floor. He took off his tie and jacket and selected a beer from the refrigerator, then flopped in an armchair. Although he was exhausted, he decided against sleep. Before leaving the office, he'd checked the times of flights to Brussels. The earliest, by British Airways, was at 8.05. To get to the airport, he would have to leave the hotel soon after six.

As he drank his beer, his mind was on the Forde woman. It had always intrigued him how people relinquished their secrets so readily. She'd had no need to, apart from the threats. He would have been able to carry them out, certainly, but the procedure wouldn't have been easy, not as easy as he'd made out. Memorandums would have come from Curzon Street forbidding him to let the woman go into open court.

At six o'clock he walked back to Tothill Street and instructed a driver to take him to Heathrow.

The flight left on schedule, and arrived at Brussels National at ten o'clock local time. Blom had arranged for special customs clearance. From the airport, he took a taxi to the offices of Bastin and Massinger, agricultural equipment importers, on the Avenue Louise. Although the offices were across the city from Nato headquarters, the two buildings were linked by direct, private telephone and telex lines. While the books of Bastin and Massinger showed it was a flourishing business enterprise, its main function was as a front company for Nato's Central European intelligence operations.

Blom presented himself to the acting controller of the office and handed over an introductory letter from F Branch's Night Control. Within half an hour of his arrival he had been allocated temporary office space and the services of two duty field agents.

Shortly after 11.30, he spoke on the telephone to Jensen's secretary. Yes, he was told, the press attaché had been contacted by a man named Scannell. They had left the office about a quarter of an hour before. No, Jensen hadn't said where they were going.

'Is there anywhere you can think of?' asked Blom urgently. 'Anywhere that Mr Jensen takes people to when he's got an informal appointment? A restaurant? A club? Coffee house?'

The secretary named four or five possible places.

Putting the phone down, Blom turned to the agents who had been detailed to work with him. 'Listen, can we get a car?'

One of the agents nodded. 'There's an office pool.'

His colleague immediately put through a call to the administration and supply department.

Blom picked up the sheet of paper on which he'd noted the addresses provided by Jensen's secretary.

'We haven't got much time,' he said. 'I've got to find this man before he talks.'

39

Scannell heard the police car before he saw it. At first, he thought it must be on its way to an accident or break-in, then he realized it was coming towards the brasserie, weaving skilfully through the traffic.

He sat transfixed at the table, mystified as to how they had discovered where he was. A glance at Jensen provided the answer. The press attaché must have told the barman to make an emergency call.

'Bastard,' Scannell hissed, as he jumped to his feet.

Only one way was open for him to go: down the street away from the police car. But even before he could start to run, a green Peugeot had swung round the far corner. It, too, was heading for the brasserie. He was caught; a beast in a trap.

He looked up and down the street, desperately seeking a way of escape. The Peugeot was already pulling across the road, and the police car was screeching to a halt by the kerb. He stared at the Peugeot and at once felt his blood drain. At the rear window was a face he recognized. It was a man who had been at a press conference given by the Ministry of Defence following the Fylingdales story. It could be no coincidence that he was here now. A name flashed across Scannell's brain; a name that appeared in his dossier as the new head of Unit Nine. The man he'd been introduced to was Blom.

In the moment that Scannell stood inert, Jensen leapt up and tried to grab him. The table crashed across the pavement, and Scannell lashed out blindly. Somewhere in the blur he saw his fist strike flesh, and Jensen buckled.

Scannell glanced at the press attaché's sprawled figure,

fleetingly amazed that one punch could have felled the man. Immediately he saw that it hadn't. Blood was pumping from Jensen's temple where it had been drilled by a bullet.

Scannell's reflexes swung him round. He glimpsed a figure in a camelhair coat and leather gloves. It was Blom who had fired. The bullet had missed its real target, which Scannell knew was himself. The Peugeot had braked to a halt at an angle across the road, its doors flung open. The street's traffic was suddenly in chaos.

Scannell rushed across the terrace, overturning tables and chairs. Instant wreckage. Gaczyna; first-year exercises.

Pulling open the door of the brasserie, he performed the same drill inside. The tables had been neatly laid with red chequered cloths and arranged along one wall ready for lunchtime service. Between them and the bar was a narrow aisle. Ignoring the manager and the solitary waiter, who had taken refuge behind the bar, Scannell tipped up each table as he came to it. None of the customers moved as they were confronted by a crazed man tearing their meals from under them. He threw chairs into his trail of destruction, making it impossible for anyone to pass through without first clearing a path.

Running through the kitchen, he came out to a small, square courtyard.

Then he stopped dead.

At every stage, it seemed, a fresh trap was sprung. The walls of the yard were at least two metres high. At the far end was a gate, but it was bolted, and dustbins had been pushed against it. There was no time to shift them.

He sensed his last seconds of freedom being wasted in a whirl of confusion. Walls. Blom. Dustbins. Blood. Police. Sky. His head spun; his pulses thundered.

Breathe deeply, and think. *Assess.*

Rusty railings ran along the top of one wall. They would give way if he tried to climb over them. He turned to the wall opposite, which trailed a discoloured vine. Dragging forward one of the dustbins, he jumped on to it and grabbed a clump of the vine. His hands tore against the bricks, scattering loose mortar, but he managed to pull himself up. From inside the brasserie he could hear people shouting. Without looking round, he dropped into a cobbled alley on the other side of the wall.

In the next half-hour he ran through a maze of further alleys and sidestreets. He had only the vaguest idea where he was, aware simply that the area formed the old artisans' quarter known as Les Marolles.

Eventually he came out on the Rue de la Régence, where he quickly mingled with the pedestrians. Although he felt more at ease now, he was constantly looking over his shoulder, ready to retreat into a doorway if he thought he was being followed. He also kept a lookout for the green Peugeot that haunted him at every street corner.

Using buses and the Metro, he criss-crossed the city, going miles out of his way before heading back to the Place Corbeau. At no time did he see anyone he suspected of following him, but the shock of having been confronted by the man from the Ministry of Defence had told him it would be rash to underestimate his pursuers' doggedness.

Blom. Who was he? The camelhair coat and the accent tailored to match. Scannell had only spent a few minutes talking to him at the press conference, but his face had stuck in his mind. Perhaps it was the way the man's eyes had studied him, taking an intense interest in everything he'd said. It was clear now: Blom had to be DI5. The forces had been lining up, even then.

It was after two o'clock when Scannell arrived back at the square. Rather than going straight to his room, he took a window seat in Lubka's so that he could watch the house. He ordered coffee and Pernod. The alcohol was partly to congratulate himself for his escape, but mostly to calm his nerves.

At the back of his mind was the thought that an innocent

press attaché would now be going out to lunch before starting on his afternoon's work if, earlier in the day, he hadn't had a visit from an old acquaintance seeking help.

Later, back in his room, Scannell felt a profound sense of relief. The four walls with their bland paper had become his sanctuary in a world gone mad. To occupy himself while he considered his next move, he tidied up, though there was little mess. From time to time he glanced out of the window to check the street below.

There was no change.

After a while, he lay on the bed and loosened his shirt. With his confidence temporarily bolstered at having shaken off the police and Blom, he succumbed to the luxury of sleep.

On waking, he had the impression that something was different. He lay still and stared at the door. It was closed, but not locked, in case he needed to leave hurriedly. The key was on the sideboard where he'd left it. He looked at his watch: twenty to five. He'd been asleep for nearly an hour.

Silently he raised himself to his feet, listening to the sounds in the square and on the stairway. Nothing seemed out of the ordinary. He went to the window, careful to stay behind the curtains. His eyes, which had become familiar with every rooftop, every resident's car, every recessed doorway, slowly scanned the intimate world framed before him.

Even before it came to his attention, he was aware of the blue Datsun parked outside the lampshade seller's a few doors along from Lubka's. Two men were in the front seats. It was possible that they were ordinary citizens, but a deeper instinct told him otherwise. He edged away from the window as one inescapable fact lodged in his mind: KGB surveillance teams always worked in pairs. So they had traced him to Brussels, too.

A wave of anger rose inside him: anger that they had intruded on his private territory. Here, for a short time, he'd seen himself simply as a human being in a room, but they had transformed him back to a creature in a bolt-hole, hunted and morose.

After his fury had abated, he lay back on the bed and tried to decide what he should do. He glanced at the briefcase on the chair, realizing now that it had been a grave mistake to leave his dossier across the square. To retrieve it, he would have to walk right past the Datsun, and that would be tantamount to a walk to the death cell.

He sat up and smoothed his hair. Something had to be done. If they had chronicled his movements this far, it was only a matter of time before they would locate the room. Somehow he had to distract them so he could reach the dossier. There had to be a way. *Think.*

He went back to the window. The car was still parked in the same place. His attention moved round the square as he silently contemplated how long it would take him to run to one of the sidestreets.

Then something caught his eye that numbed all thought of escape. A man was sitting on the wooden bench by the glass telephone booth in the centre of the square. Scannell didn't know whether he had missed him when he'd looked before, or whether the man had arrived in the last few minutes. It didn't matter anyway. The camelhair coat and the leather gloves were unmistakable. But there was no sign of the green Peugeot. Blom had come to finish the job alone.

At first, it appeared that he was keeping perfectly still; unnaturally so. But after Scannell had watched him for a short while, he saw that his gaze was moving steadily from house to house. Every window of every apartment. Blom was willing him to show his face.

Scannell let the curtain slip down and stood back from the window. Knowing that he was cornered, his thoughts started to race in cross-currents. He had to get out of the building. Door-to-door enquiries would soon begin. If Blom didn't make the first move, the KGB men would.

Scannell considered his options. Capitulation. Negotiation. Escape.

Escape . . . it wasn't really a consideration. Blom or the KGB would soon be on his tail. If they could find him here, they could find him anywhere. As he'd told himself when he'd decided to come to Brussels, the running was over. Negotiation was his only chance. Perhaps now was the time to follow Celia's advice and put his trust in someone. But was Blom the right person?

Scannell was surprised that, when he finally made his decision, he was so quick to act. It was as though it was what he'd been wanting all along.

Blom had stood up, and was walking ruminatively across the square away from the house. Scannell took a notebook from his briefcase and tore out a sheet of paper. He scribbled down his telephone number, folded the sheet and wrote Blom's name on it. Then he went down the stairs and lifted a sash window that opened on to a yard at the back. Earlier, on his way up to his room, he'd seen two boys mending a bicycle. They were still there. The bicycle, now apparently repaired, was standing against the wall. Scannell called the boys over.

'I want you to do a job for me.' He took a 500-franc note from his pocket. 'I'll give you this.'

The older of the boys squinted up at him suspiciously. 'What d'you want us to do?'

'There's a seat out in the square next to the phone booth. I want you to go past it and leave the note on the seat.'

'Just that? That's all?'

Scannell nodded. 'Don't stop. Just put the note on the seat. If anyone calls out to you, ride away. Got it?'

The boy glanced again at the note. 'Five hundred? You sure?'

Scannell calculated that the money was equivalent to about

six or seven pounds. He could see that, for a boy of ten or eleven, it might seem unduly extravagant.

'For the two of you – to share. Just do what I've told you.'

The boy pocketed the money and went over to the bike. Scannell returned to his room and watched as the two youngsters rode unsteadily towards the central pedestrian area. The older boy was standing up and pedalling, while his friend balanced on the saddle. They bumped up the kerb.

Blom was over the far side of the square, his attention drawn to a courtyard through a large green door.

As the boys cycled past the seat, the one on the saddle leaned out with the note. The bike scarcely slowed. They rode out of the square behind a row of parked cars.

Scannell kept a constant watch on Blom now. There was a good chance he would return to the seat, as it was the focal point of the square. It was simply a question of waiting.

As Scannell had expected, Blom eventually walked back across the pedestrian area, stopping briefly to look at the troughs of flowers. For a minute or two, he stood surveying the square, then he sat down on the bench. At first, he seemed not to see the note. Then, with furtive curiosity, he reached out and picked it up. Scannell saw him lift his head, casting his eyes again around the windows of the grubby buildings. He seemed to be considering whether he was being set up. As Blom's gaze came round towards the house, Scannell shrank back. He'd expected no sudden reaction, not from a man who operated with such calculation and perseverance. Blom was staring at the note, as though still wondering what to make of it.

Suddenly, Scannell's entire body began to sweat as he experienced a feeling of utter rashness. In giving Blom his number, he'd all but disclosed his whereabouts. It had been the only way, though. Unlike public phones in the UK, these in Brussels couldn't take incoming calls. Short of marching out to face Blom direct, it was his sole means of bargaining. He was now resigned to a course of action that would give him a tactical advantage only for as long as he was able to call the other man's bluff.

Slowly, Blom rose to his feet and went to the phone booth. Scannell observed carefully to make sure that he only dialled once. He was relieved that no attempt was made to trace the origin of the number via the operator. Blom clearly knew that he was being watched, and he was clever enough not to make the mistake of panicking his quarry.

Almost immediately, the phone on the sideboard rang. Keeping away from the window, Scannell reached for the receiver.

'Yes.'

'Is that Scannell?'

'It is.'

'What do you want?' Blom's voice was controlled.

Scannell peered across the square. 'To talk.'

'What about?'

'A deal.'

Blom seemed to hold back, then said: 'Where can I meet you?'

'I don't want to meet you . . . not yet. I can see you from where I am. That's good enough.'

Scannell observed as Blom again glanced reflexively at the houses around him.

'You won't see me,' Scannell said.

Another short pause followed, then Blom asked: 'What sort of deal do you want?'

'I've got a dossier.'

'On what?'

'Unit Nine.'

'I don't understand.'

Scannell became angry. 'Don't play with me, Blom. I know who you are.'

There was another break, then Blom said: 'Tell me what you know about Unit Nine.'

'It's all in the dossier.'

'What is?'

'Evidence proving that the British government has run a dirty tricks campaign to undermine the anti-nuclear movement . . . And showing how some of the movement's top members have been framed – by you.'

'By me?'

'By DI5. I know that's who you work for.'

Ignoring Scannell's last statement, Blom said solemnly: 'You realize that these are serious allegations?'

'Serious enough to cause an election defeat for the government?'

'Is that what you want?'

'It's the truth.'

'From someone whose life has been a total fabrication?'

Scannell faltered as he considered Blom's words. He wasn't quite sure of their implication.

'I can prove how Unit Nine worked in conjunction with Secretariat N-160, and how Hermann was arrested on false charges.'

'Is there anything else in the dossier?'

'Names.'

'Of whom?'

'Infiltrators into the European Anti-Nuclear Organization, and what positions they hold. A top source inside the Defence Ministry . . . Liaison officials working for Secretariat N-160 . . .'

'Can I see the dossier?'

'It's possible.'

'Is that your deal?'

'Part of it . . . maybe.'

'And the rest?'

Scannell waited before answering. It disturbed him that, while talking to Blom, he'd failed to keep a watch on the other parts of the square. He was relieved to see that the Datsun and its two occupants hadn't moved, but there was always the possibility that Blom might have an agent posted out of sight who might try to trace the phone call.

'I'm an agent for the Soviet Union,' he said, resuming the conversation. 'I've been stationed in London as a feeder to influence the movement.'

A long silence came from Blom's end of the phone.

'Are you still there?' asked Scannell.

'Yes, I'm here.'

'If my dossier gets into the hands of the press, the operation will have succeeded. The Soviet Union will, in effect, have destroyed the British government. The Americans will be forced to close their bases . . . the North Atlantic alliance will crack.'

'And all the work of one man . . . Or are there others working with you?'

Scannell barely heard Blom's question. He had recoiled at the thought of the picture he'd painted. He no longer knew who he was fighting for. Perhaps no one; just himself. By helping the peace movement, he'd been backing the right side, but for the wrong reasons.

'You haven't answered me,' came Blom's voice. 'Are others operating with you?'

Scannell stared at the phone booth and brought his mind back into focus.

'Yes . . . some.'

'Can you give me any more details?'

'When you agree to the deal.'

'Let's be specific, shall we? What are your terms?'

'Immunity from prosecution – a guarantee signed by the Home Secretary. That'll have to be placed in the hands of lawyers, together with a copy of the dossier.'

Scannell edged back into the shadows of the room as he saw Blom once again scan the square like a predator determined to recapture a lost scent.

'If anything happens to me, the lawyers will have the authority to release the details of the guarantee and the dossier to the press. I also want protection from the KGB for Celia Forde and her son – and new identities for all of us. Passports, birth certificates . . . National Insurance numbers.'

'They're heavy conditions.'

'Not considering the alternative.'

'Which is . . . ?'

'I send the dossier straight to the press.'

'The government doesn't like blackmail.'

'Negotiation,' Scannell corrected Blom. 'We see it from two different standpoints. As well as the dossier, I'm prepared to supply any information you require on the KGB training system.'

'Before I make any commitment, I must see the dossier.'

'Have you got the authority to negotiate?'

'I've got the authority to present your case.'

Scannell looked again across the square to where the Datsun was parked. It was still worrying him.

'I want the KGB men out of the way first.'

'You're talking about the men in the blue car?'

'Yes. They mustn't be around.'

'I can have them arrested within ten minutes. Would that satisfy you?'

'How do I know that once I've given you the dossier you won't have me killed?'

'That's a chance you'll have to take. Obviously you appreciate the value of your information.'

'I also have a separate copy of the dossier. If I'm not back in London by the end of this week, I've left instructions for it to be sent to the newspapers.'

Scannell wondered if Blom could detect that he was lying.

'How do I know you haven't already sent it?' said Blom.

'We both have chances to take. Ring me back when the KGB men have gone. And don't try to trace an address from the number. If you do that, I promise you, you'll never see the dossier.'

The police took nineteen minutes to arrive; Scannell timed them. They came in two cars, and numbered seven officers, all in plain clothes. The men in the Datsun, taken off guard, were arrested without a struggle. Passers-by looked on as the men were hustled away. All the time, Blom remained in the phone booth.

When the police cars had gone, Scannell lit a cigarette and waited for Blom to call. He watched as Blom dialled, and picked up the receiver after a single ring.

'I'm impressed.'

'We won't be able to detain them. They'll be released under diplomatic immunity.'

For perhaps half a minute neither man spoke. Only one matter needed to be discussed. Both waited for the other to raise it.

Finally, Blom said: 'The dossier.'

Scannell wiped away a line of sweat on his upper lip. At this critical moment he was seized by a decade of suppressed fear. Could he go through with it? Did he have any choice? It was a gamble of unimaginable risk. The breathlessness that he'd experienced in London returned, and the room swam.

'The dossier,' he heard Blom say again.

There was a sinister note in the man's voice, Scannell was sure of it. Was Blom tricking him? Was there someone else the dossier could be handed over to? Was it too late to contact anyone? Susan Chambers maybe? Jensen had said she might be able to help.

'I'll give you ten seconds to tell me where the dossier is, or I'll put the phone down. Then I'll come and find you.'

Blom's threat had a bleak inevitability.

Scannell stared out of the window. He burned with a desire to kill the man. The knife in the sideboard drawer . . . a sudden rush across the square . . .

'Your time's up,' said Blom. 'I'm putting the phone down.'

'No,' cut in Scannell. 'I'll tell you where it is.'

He paused, concentrating on the silence from Blom's end, then went on: 'The newsagent's shop across the square. Outside, on the pavement, there's a litter basket. Under it there's a loose paving-stone. That's where the dossier is. Ring me back as soon as you've got it.'

Scannell clamped the receiver back on its cradle. He watched impassively as Blom crossed the square. Again Scannell contemplated escape, but without the dossier he had no prospect of buying his defection. No, his only chance of being reunited with Celia was through Blom.

The retrieval of the dossier took a matter of minutes. Scannell looked on as Blom returned to the phone booth.

'I want some time,' Scannell said. 'I want the signed guarantee before I go back to Britain.'

'I can't just leave you here,' replied Blom. 'The information you've got is too important. Anything might happen to you.'

'I won't go anywhere. I've got nowhere to go.'

Scannell waited for Blom to answer, but there was silence.

'Blom?' he said. 'Are you there?'

The silence continued, then Blom said quietly: 'It's all over, Sergei.'

Scannell was taken off balance. It was so long since he'd heard the name spoken that he hardly related it to himself.

'You know,' he stated emptily.

'We've been friends for a long time, you and I, but you weren't aware of it.'

Scannell was now totally thrown. Blom's sudden change of tone . . . the familiarity . . . he couldn't understand.

'What do you mean?'

'No *confrère* should ever reveal himself to his agents, but I feel I owe you the honour. You did a good job, Sergei, but

317

in the end you did it too well. I thought you were so strong that you couldn't fail me. I was wrong.'

As Scannell listened, he felt a sharp current surge through his body.

'I never imagined . . .'

'No, you were never meant to. Did you realize that you almost ruined the network? An escape line had to be opened so we could take Webster out. I shielded you all through your story. They'd have arrested you months ago if I hadn't delayed them.'

Blom was standing still now.

'You may not understand,' he said, 'but a *confrère*'s job is the most frustrating one in the world. You want to help your agent get there, but you can't. You can only protect.'

'I was working on my own,' Scannell declared. 'No one protected me.'

'You escaped from that houseboat. You'd taken a reckless chance. Three Interpol officers had their promotion prospects put back a year because they arrived too late to arrest you.'

'And you fixed it?'

'That was my job. When we had to open enquiries in Australia, I thought you'd never last. It was fortunate that the Moscow directorate had done a clean sweep. You owe them a lot.'

'The British sent someone out there – to Australia?'

'Two senior Special Branch officers . . . in March. I tried to stop them by overloading the expense estimates. It was a gamble . . . for a time it was ruled out. They weren't that strong on you then. The problem was Unit Nine, a man called Rodway. He was sharp; sharper than I'd have liked.'

'Is that who you're working for – Unit Nine?'

'A holding brief. I managed to get Rodway removed. If he'd seen the preliminary results, he'd have stepped up the inquiries. But I couldn't hold out indefinitely. I hoped

Moscow would call you back, but they miscalculated. That was what nearly destroyed it for us . . . for everyone.'

Scannell closed his eyes and tried to gather his senses. He remembered the anonymous telephone warning over the Somerville Stanley story: the oblique reference to his former course tutor, Krolikov. The warning could only have come from Blom. He would have been one of Krolikov's contemporaries.

Scannell questioned how freely he had been allowed to operate. Had any action he'd taken over the past months – the past years – been self-motivated, or was he simply programmed from Moscow? He opened his eyes and leaned over the table to gain a clear view of the square. Blom was gazing from the phone booth, but not in the direction of the house. If he hadn't traced the address, there was still, perhaps, the chance of making an escape.

'Who were the men in the car with you this morning?' Scannell asked. 'Were they KGB as well?'

'No, they were Nato staff. I had to use them to help find you in a hurry. I couldn't risk having you talk.'

'You shot Jensen deliberately?'

'I had to. I didn't know how much you'd told him.'

'How did you find me here?'

'Your friends in the Datsun. They got a lead on you when you left the brasserie. They followed you back here.'

'KGB?'

'Embassy.'

'You'll have to report my arrest. The police who took those men in will want to know why they were called.'

There was another moment of silence.

'The police were from the embassy too,' Blom said quietly.

Scannell nodded. Nothing surprised him now.

'Have you spoken to Celia?' he asked.

'She and her son were picked up last night.'

'I didn't tell her anything. You can let them go.'

'That's not up to me.'

319

Scannell said nothing for a long time. When he finally spoke, it was with hollow resignation.

'Why didn't you take me when I was in London? You let her condemn herself by going away with me.'

'I couldn't risk it. We hadn't had the instruction from Moscow.'

'Is it too late for me to do anything? If you're my *confrère*, surely you can pull strings.'

'I'm sorry, Sergei. I never wanted it to come to this. You held out far longer than anyone could reasonably be expected to. But then the demands on an agent in the field aren't reasonable. You have to have your soul cut out. Your problem was that it grew back.'

Scannell noticed that while he'd been listening to Blom, the blue Datsun had reappeared in the square. It parked next to the telephone booth. Only one man was in it.

'What do you intend to do with me?' Scannell asked.

As he put the question, he turned his head. He had heard the handle click behind him, and the door to the room swung open. A man stood on the landing. In his hand was a gun.

Scannell glanced down into the square. Blom, still holding the receiver, was now looking up at the window.

'They want you back, Sergei,' he answered. 'You're going home.'